SEE D[...]
AND [...]

Lindsey Davis has written over twenty historical novels, beginning with *The Course of Honour*. Her bestselling mystery series features laid-back First Century detective Marcus Didius Falco and his partner Helena Justina, plus friends, relations, pets and bitter enemy the Chief Spy.

After an English degree at Oxford University Lindsey joined the Civil Service, but became a professional author in 1989. Her books are translated into many languages and have been dramatized on BBC Radio 4. Her many prizes include the Premio Colosseo, awarded by the Mayor of Rome 'for enhancing the image of Rome', the Sherlock award for Falco as Best Comic Detective and the Crimewriters' Association Cartier Diamond Dagger for lifetime achievement. She was born in Birmingham but now lives in Greenwich, London.

SEE DELPHI AND DIE

LINDSEY DAVIS

arrow books

Reissued by Arrow Books 2013

1 3 5 7 9 10 8 6 4 2

First published in Great Britain in 2005 by Century

Arrow Books
Random House, 20 Vauxhall Bridge Road,
London SW1V 2SA

www.randomhouse.co.uk

Addresses for companies within The Random House Group Limited can be found at:
www.randomhouse.co.uk/offices.htm

The Random House Group Limited Reg. No. 954009

A CIP catalogue record for this book
is available from the British Library

ISBN 9780099515241

The Random House Group Limited supports the Forest Stewardship Council®
(FSC®), the leading international forest-certification organisation. Our books carrying
the FSC label are printed on FSC®-certified paper. FSC is the only forest-certification
scheme supported by the leading environmental organisations, including Greenpeace.
Our paper procurement policy can be found at:
www.randomhouse.co.uk/environment

Typeset by SX Composing DTP, Rayleigh, Essex
Printed and bound in Great Britain by Clays Ltd, St Ives plc

For Elys,
Who tried to teach me Latin,
and gamely tried again with Greek,
But who above all introduced me to archaeology

PRINCIPAL CHARACTERS

In Rome

Julia Justa	a mother, with anxieties
D. Camillus Verus	the senator, who leaves her to it
Caesius Secundus	a father seeking answers
Marcella Caesia	a daughter seeking excitement (deceased)
Tullia Longina	a mother-in-law, seeking a quiet life (thwarted)
Claudius Laeta	an imperial official, seeking promotion
Polystratus	a travel salesman, looking for fools

On the 'Tracks and Temples Tour' with Seven Sights Travel

Valeria Ventidia	a blissful bride (deceased)
The Sertorius family	father, devoted mother, two charming children
Cleonymus and Cleonyma	moneyed folk in search of adventure
Amaranthus and Minucia	a sporting man and his home-sick woman
Indus	trying not to be found by someone
Volcasius	avoided by everyone
Marinus	an unscrupulous widower, seeking funds
Helvia	a resourceful widow, seeking companionship
Turcianus Opimus	not long for this world

Travelling independently

M. Didius Falco	an informer
Helena Justina	his wife, partner, assistant, and travel guide

Albia	a Briton, aspiring to Roman culture
Young Glaucus	son of Glaucus, an aspiring athlete
Gaius and Cornelius	Falco's nephews, generally looking for trouble
Nux	his dog, generally right in it

In Olympia

Barzanes	an interesting site guide
Milo of Dodona	a strong man on a mission
Lacheses	an interfering priest
Megiste	a very well organised towns-woman
Myron	a flautist
A palaestra superintendent	a thug

In Corinth

The governor	away on duty (*never* in Corinth)
Aquillius Macer	a quaestor, learning on the job
Phineus	a really excellent tour guide
Philomela	a culture-loving nightingale (or swallow)

In Delphi

Tullius Statianus	a distraught bridegroom, seeking the truth
Lampon	a poet who knows too much

In Athens

A. Camillus Aelianus	a dedicated scholar
Minas of Karystos	teaching Aulus everything he knows

Travelling elsewhere

Marcella Naevia	Caesia's aunt and travel companion

PART ONE

ROME

He decided upon a tour of Greece, to see those things which, through their fame and reputation, had been magnified by hearsay . . .

He travelled across Thessaly to Delphi, the celebrated oracle. Then he went to the Temple of Zeus Trophonius and saw the mouth of the cave which those who consult the oracle enter . . .

Then to Athens, also renowned for its hoary antiquity, but still with many sights to see . . .

He proceeded to Corinth. The city was then a splendid one . . . The Acropolis set on an immense height, girdled with walls and flowing with springs . . .

After that Epidaurus, celebrated for the splendid temple to Asclepius . . .

Then to Olympia. Here he saw many sights, but what touched him profoundly was the Zeus — he felt he beheld the god in person.

Livy, on Aemilius Paulus taking recreation in 167 BC

Roman Province of Achaea

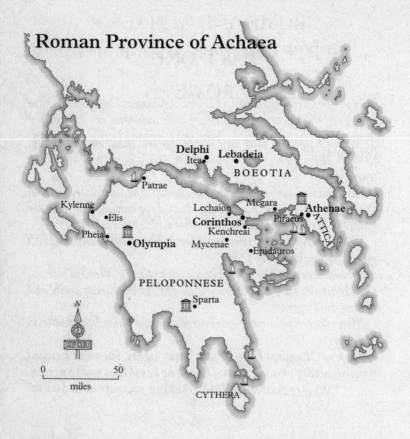

Delphi Lebadeia
Itea
BOEOTIA
Patrae
Kylenne   Lechaion   Megara   Athenae
Elis   Corinthos   Piraeus   ATTICA
Pheia   Kenchreai
Olympia   Mycenae
Epidauros

PELOPONNESE
Sparta

N

SPQR

0   50
miles

CYTHERA

NOTE: Due to the difficulty of reproducing them on a small scale, site plans have not been provided. Plans of ancient Olympia, Corinth, Delphi and Athens are readily available in guidebooks and websites, should readers feel these would add to their enjoyment of the story.

ROME AND ACHAEA:
SEPTEMBER–OCTOBER AD 76

Three years after the 213th Olympic Games; one year before the 214th [Note: this numbering assumes that the Neronian Games of AD 67 are omitted, after being declared illegitimate]

I

'Marcus, you must help me!'

I am a private informer, a simple man. I was stunned by this dramatic plea. My silk-clad, scented mother-in-law rarely needed anything from me. Suddenly the noble Julia Justa sounded like one of my clients.

All I wanted that evening was a better dinner than I could expect at home, where – not for the first time – I had made a bad mistake in buying a cook. Julia Justa had already enjoyed herself that night reviewing my dismal record in acquiring household slaves. In return for the dinner I would also have to put up with barbed comments about the failings of Helena and me as parents. Helena would retaliate, while her father and I grinned behind our hands until both women rounded on us, after which the slaves would carry in dessert and we would all fall on the quinces and figs . . .

Family life. I knew where I stood with that. It was better than the old days, when I worked alone from a two-room doss where even the gecko had sneered at me. There, the women who had sought me out were two ranks and many degrees of politeness below my mother-in-law. Their pleas were dismal and they needed help for filthy reasons. What they offered in return went far beyond the grudging thanks I would expect here, though it rarely involved money.

'I am, of course, at your disposal, dear Julia.'

The senator grinned. 'Not too busy at the moment?'

'Surprisingly quiet,' I told him. 'I'm waiting for the normal rash of divorces when couples come back to Rome after the holidays.'

'Cynic, Marcus! What is the matter, mother?' Helena sized up a platter of fruit; she was looking for a piece to give

1

to our elder daughter. Favonia, our youngest, was happy to spend half an hour sucking a single grape but little Julia, left to herself, would take a bite out of every peach and pear, then surreptitiously put each one back on the dish.

'Everything is the matter!' Julia Justa posed in a refined manner, yet several rows of pendant gold beads quivered among the fragrant folds of sage green silk on her bosom. Beside her on the couch, the senator moved away slightly, afraid that she might bruise him with an angry elbow.

Helena now shot her father a brief glance as if she thought he was trouble-making. I enjoyed watching the interplay. Like most families, the Camilli had established myths about themselves: that the senator was constantly harassed and that his wife was allowed no influence at home, for example. The legend that their three children were a constant trial held most truth, although both Helena and her younger brother Justinus had settled down, with partners and offspring. Not that I made a reassuring husband.

It was the elder son, Julia Justa's favourite, who had caused her current anguish. 'I am devastated, Marcus! I thought Aulus was doing something sensible at last.'

At twenty-seven, Aulus Camillus Aelianus was still a happy bachelor who had lost interest in entering the Senate. He was feckless and rootless. He spent too much; he drank; he stayed out late; he probably womanised, though he had managed to keep that quiet. Worst of all, he sometimes worked for me. Being an informer was a rough trade for a senator's son; well Hades, it was rough for me, and I was slum-born. The Camilli were struggling socially; a scandal would finish them.

'He *agreed* to go to Athens!' his mother raved, while the rest of us listened. To everyone's surprise, attending university had been his own choice – the only hope of it working. 'It was a solution. We sent him so he could study, to develop his mind, to mature –'

'You cannot have heard from him already?' It was only a few weeks since we waved off Aulus on a ship for Greece. That was in August. His mother had fretted that it would be months before he bothered to write home; his father had joked that that would be as soon as the letters of credit ran out, when Aulus scribbled the traditional plea of 'Safely arrived – Send more cash immediately!' The senator had warned him that there was no more cash; still, Aulus knew he was his mother's pet. He would write to Julia and she would work on Decimus.

Now we learned that Aulus had let himself be sidetracked and, oddly for an intelligent fellow, he had owned up to his mama. 'Marcus, the damn ship stopped at Olympia. Of course I don't mind Aulus visiting the sanctuary of Zeus, but he's up to something else entirely –'

'So what is the big draw? Apart from sun, sport, and avoiding serious study?'

'Don't tease me, Marcus.'

I tried to remember whether they had held Olympic Games this year. Nero famously altered the centuries-old timing, so the mad emperor could compete in events during his tour of Greece. Unforgettable and embarrassing: a catalogue of pretending to be a herald, giving dreary recitals, and expecting to win everything, whether he was any good or not.

I fancied the date had now been altered back. By my rapid calculation the next Games would be next August. 'Relax, Julia. Aulus can't be wasting time as a spectator.'

Julia Justa shuddered. 'No; it's worse. Apparently he met a group of people and one of them had been horribly killed.'

'Oh?' I managed to keep my voice neutral, though Helena looked up from mopping juice from Favonia's white tunic.

'Well, Marcus,' Julia Justa said darkly, as if this was clearly my fault. 'It is just the kind of situation you taught him to get excited about.' I tried to look innocent. 'Aulus is suspicious because it is very well known that another young girl from Rome vanished at the last Olympic Games. And *she* was eventually found murdered too.'

'Aulus is trying to help these people?'

'It's not for him to involve himself –' I saw it all now. My task was to take over and steer young Aulus back on his way

3

to university. The noble Julia was so eager to have him with his nose in a law scroll, she was ready to sell her jewellery. 'I will pay your fare to Greece, Marcus. But you must agree to go and sort this out!'

II

Taking orders from a subordinate is bad enough. Following up some lousy lead he has only bothered to pass on via his mother must be the billygoat's armpit. Even so, I did ask to read the letter.

Later, safely back at home, Helena Justina poked me in the ribs. 'Own up. You are fascinated.'

'Mildly curious.'

'Why did my ridiculous brother alert Mama?'

'Too lazy to write separately to us. He wants to know what the father has to say – the father of the first dead girl.'

'Had you heard about that?'

'Vaguely. It's the Caesius case.'

'So you are going to see the father? Can I come too?'

'No.'

Helena came with me.

We knew in advance the interview would be sensitive.

This was the situation: at the Olympic Games three years ago a young girl, travelling with a group of sightseers from Rome, went missing. Her distraught father tried to investigate; in fact, he had been doing so non-stop – far too long to nag on about it, the hard-hearted Roman public thought. He went out there and doggedly searched until he found the girl's remains. He tried to discover the circumstances of her death, then was soon making well-publicised claims that his child had been murdered. He had been agitating for answers ever since.

Finding the girl's body annoyed the authorities; they had failed to investigate properly in the first place, so they resisted reopening the enquiry. Knowing the daughter was dead took Caesius no further. Eventually he ran out of time, money, and energy; he was forced to return home, case unproven. Still obsessed, he had managed to rake up some interest among the Forum gossips, which was why I had heard of him. Most people dismissed him as a man crazed by grief, an embarrassment. I had felt some sympathy. I knew how I would react if one of my girls ever went missing.

We went early to his house. It was a warm, clear Rome morning, on the way to a very hot noon. The hint of haze above the Capitol, as we rounded it into the Forum, would soon become a flagrant dazzle, too bright to look up at the new Temple of Jupiter with its golden roof and stinging white marble. Over the far end of the Forum hung a cloud of dust from the huge building site of the Flavian Amphitheatre; no longer just the biggest hole in the world, its walls were slowly rising in a fabulous travertine ellipse and at this hour it was the busiest area of activity. Everywhere else there were fewer crowds than usual. Anyone who could afford to leave town was away. Bored senators and bloated ex-slaves with multimillion businesses had been at the coast, in the hills, or by the lakes for a couple of months; they would not return until the lawcourts and schools reopened later in September. Even then, sensible ones would find excuses to delay.

We kept to the shade as we crossed at the north end and made our way towards the Via Lata district.

I had written a letter of introduction and received a short note back that I might call. I guessed Caesius would view me as a ghoul or a shyster. I could handle that. I had had enough practice.

Caesius Secundus was a widower, long-standing; the daughter who disappeared had been his only child. He lived in a faded town house off the Via Lata, just before it turns into the Via Flaminia. A cutler hired part of his ground floor for a workshop and selling space. The part where Caesius lived looked and sounded half empty; we were admitted not by a porter but by an all-purpose slave in a kitchen apron, who showed us to a reception room then went back to his stockpot.

Despite my fears of rebuff, Caesius saw us at once. He was tall and must have once been quite heavily built; now his white tunic hung slackly from a stringy neck and bony shoulders. The man had lost weight without yet noticing that he needed new outfits. Time had frozen for him, the day he heard his daughter had disappeared. Perhaps now he was back in Rome, in his own household, he would be reminded of mealtimes and other normal routines. More likely he would resist being cared for.

'I know why you have come.' He was direct, rushing into the business too fast, despite his worn look.

'I am Didius Falco. Let me introduce my wife, Helena Justina –' Stately and pleasant, she lent us respectability. With the fine carriage and elegant robes of a well-bred matron, Helena always distracted attention from my rough manners. I managed to conceal the fact that her presence physically distracted me.

'You want to talk about my daughter – Let me first show her to you.'

We were astonished, but Caesius merely led us to a cool internal colonnade beside a small courtyard. On a Corinthian pedestal stood a half-statue of a young woman: white marble, good quality; a portrait bust with the subject turned slightly to one side, gazing downwards demurely. Her face had been given just enough character to seem taken from life, though the newness of the work suggested the commission was post-mortem.

'This is all I have now.'

'Her name was Marcella Caesia?' Helena asked, studying the statue thoughtfully.

'Yes. She would have been twenty-one.' The father stared at the bust just a little too long. A chair stood close by. He probably brooded here for long hours. For the rest of his life, time would be measured by how old his lost child should have been, had she lived.

He led us back to the original sparsely furnished room.

7

Caesius insisted that Helena took a comfortable basket chair with its own footstool, perhaps once his wife's. Arranging her skirts, she glanced at me. I took out a note-tablet and prepared to lead the questioning, though Helena and I would share it; one of us would talk while the other observed.

'I warn you now!' Caesius blurted out. 'I have been targeted by many frauds who made me great promises, then did nothing.'

I said quietly: 'Caesius, here's the deal. I am an informer, mainly in Rome. I have taken assignments overseas, but only for the Emperor.' Mentioning Vespasian might impress him, unless he had supported Vespasian's opponents in the imperial contest – or if he was a strong republican.

He had no time for politics. 'I can't pay you, Falco.'

'I have not asked for money.' Well, not yet. 'I know you have an intriguing story.'

'How does my story profit you? Do you have a commission?'

This was hard work. If there was trouble in a foreign province, Vespasian might agree to send me, though he would not welcome the expense. This girl's death was a private matter – unless Caesius was some old crony of the Emperor's who could call in favours; he would have done it by now if he could, and not exhausted himself for three fruitless years on a solo effort. 'I offer nothing; I promise nothing. Caesius, a colleague asked me to check facts. Your story may help other people – ' Caesius stared at me. 'So – if you want to tell me what happened to your daughter, on that basis, then please do.'

He made a slight hand gesture: appeasement. 'I have been hounded by monsters making false offers of help. Now I trust no one.'

'You have to decide if I'm different – but no doubt the confidence tricksters said that too.'

'Thank you for your honesty.'

Despite his claim to trust no one, Caesius was still open to hope. With a wrench, he let us win him round. He took a breath. Clearly he had told the story many times before: 'My poor wife died twenty years ago. My daughter Caesia was the only one of our children to survive infancy. My background is in textile importation; we lived comfortably, Caesia was educated and – in my opinion, which of course is biased – she grew up sweet, talented, and worthy.'

'She looks it, in her portrait.' After my rude start, Helena was being the sympathetic partner.

'Thank you.'

I watched Helena, doubting if she had meant the routine praise. We had daughters. We loved them, but were under no illusions. I won't say I regarded girls as hell-raisers – but I was braced for future confrontations.

'So why was Caesia in Greece?' Helena asked.

The father flushed a little, but he told us honestly, 'There had been trouble over a young man –'

'You disapproved?' It was the obvious reason for a father to mention 'trouble'.

'I did, but it came to nothing anyway. Then Caesia's aunt, Marcella Naevia, decided to travel, and offered to take her niece. It seemed a gift from the gods. I readily agreed.'

'And your daughter?' Helena had been a spirited young girl; her first thought was that Caesia might have been difficult about being packed off abroad.

'She was thrilled. Caesia had an open, enquiring mind; she was not at all afraid of travelling; she was delighted to be given access to Greek art and culture. I had always encouraged her to visit libraries and galleries.' A look in Helena's fine brown eyes told me she knew I was thinking the young girl would be more delighted with Greek muleteers, all muscles and mischief, like classical gods.

My turn again: 'So how was the trip arranged?' I sounded dour. I already knew the answer: it was our link with the more recently murdered woman. Caesia's aunt travelled with a party; she had hired specialist tour guides.

This was a fad of our time. We had safe roads, free passage on the seas, a common currency throughout the Empire, and tracts of fascinating conquered territory. Inevitably, our citizens became tourists. All Romans – all those who could afford it – believed in a life of leisure. Some rich idlers set off from Italy for five years at a time. As these culture-cravers crowded into the ancient places of the world, toting their guidebooks, histories, shopping lists, and itineraries, a travel industry had evolved to cash in.

I had heard leisure travel was sordid. Still, people speak badly of all successful businesses. The public even despises informers, I am told.

'Everything began competently,' Caesius conceded. 'Organisers called Seven Sights Travel arranged the trip. They emphasised that it would be cheaper, safer, and much more convenient if a group went together.'

'But it was not safer for Caesia! So what happened?' I demanded.

Again the father steadied his breath. 'I was *told*,' he stressed, 'that while they stayed at Olympia, she disappeared. After extensive searching – that was how they described it anyway – the rest of the group continued on their way.' His voice was cold. 'Like me, you may find that surprising.'

'Who informed you?'

'One of the Seven Sights staff came to my house here.'

'Name?'

'Polystratus.' I wrote it down. 'He was sympathetic, told a good story, said Caesia had suddenly left the party, no one knew why. I was too shocked to interrogate him closely; in any case, he was just a messenger. He seemed to be saying Caesia had caused them inconvenience, by flighty behaviour. Apparently the other travellers just woke up one morning, when they were preparing to embark for their next venue, and she was not to be found.' Caesius became indignant. 'It was almost as if Seven Sights were claiming financial compensation for the delay.'

'Have they softened up now?'

'Given that she is dead –'

'Now they are frightened that *you* may sue *them*!'

Caesius looked blank. He had not thought of it. His one

motivation was finding the truth, to help him in his grief. 'The tour had a travelling manager called Phineus. Falco, it took me some time to find out that Phineus had left the group when Caesia disappeared; he returned at once to Rome. I find his behaviour deeply suspicious.' Now we were getting to his angry theories.

'Let me identify suspects for myself, please,' I instructed. 'Was there any information from the girl's aunt?'

'She stayed in Olympia until there seemed nothing else she could do. Then she abandoned the tour and returned home. She was devastated when I finally discovered my daughter's fate.'

'Can you put us in touch with the lady?'

'Unfortunately no. She is abroad again.' My eyebrows shot up. 'She enjoys travel. I believe she has gone to Alexandria.' Well, that's the trouble with holidays; every time you take one, you need another to recover. Still, it was three years since her niece died; Marcella Naevia was entitled to resume her life. People must have said Caesius should do the same; he looked tetchy.

While I noted down the aunt's movements, Helena took over. 'So, Caesius. You were so dissatisfied with the official version of events, you went out to Olympia to see for yourself?'

'At first I wasted a lot of time. I assumed the authorities would investigate and send me word.'

'No news came?'

'Silence. So it was almost a year later that I travelled there myself. I owed it to my child to discover what had happened to her.'

'Of course. Especially if you have doubts.'

'I have *no* doubt!' Caesius burst out. 'Someone killed her! Then somebody – the killer, the tour arrangers, some other tour member, or the local people – covered up the crime. They all hoped to forget the incident. But I shall never let them forget!'

'You went to Greece,' I intervened, calming him. 'You spent a long time haranguing the authorities in Olympia. In the end, you yourself discovered human remains outside the town, with evidence that confirmed it was your daughter?'

'The jewellery she wore every day.'

'Where was the body?'

'On a hillside. The Hill of Cronus, which overlooks the sanctuary of Zeus.' Now Caesius was struggling to sound reasonable, so I would believe him. 'The locals claimed she must have wandered off, maybe on some romantic whim to watch the sunset – or sunrise – or listen for the gods in the night. When they were being most offensive, they said she was meeting a lover.'

'You don't believe that.' I passed no judgement on his belief in his daughter. Other people would give us the unbiased view of Caesia.

'This is a very hard question,' Helena enquired gently, 'but could you deduce anything from your daughter's body –'

'No.'

We waited. The father remained silent.

'She had been exposed on a hillside.' I kept it neutral. 'There was no sign of how she died?'

Caesius forced himself to relive his grim discovery. 'She had been there a year when I found her. I made myself look for signs of a struggle. I wanted to know what had happened to her, remember. But all I found were bones, some scattered by animals. If she had been harmed, I could no longer tell how. That was the problem,' he raged. 'That was why the authorities were able to maintain that Caesia had died naturally.'

'Clothing?' I asked.

'It looked as if she was . . . clothed.' Her father stared at me, seeking reassurance that this was not a sex crime. The second-hand evidence was insufficient to judge.

Helena then asked quietly, 'You gave her a funeral?'

The father's voice was clipped. 'I want to send her to the gods, but I must find answers first. I gathered her up, intending to hold a ceremony, there in Olympia. Then I decided against it. I had a lead coffin made for her and brought her home.'

'Oh!' Helena had not been expecting the reply. 'Where is she now?'

'She is here,' answered Caesius matter-of-factly. Helena and I glanced involuntarily around the reception room. Caesius did not elucidate; elsewhere in his house there must be the coffin with the three–year–old relics. A macabre chill settled on this previously domestic salon. 'She is waiting for a chance to tell somebody something of importance.'

Me. Dear gods, that was going to be my role.

'So . . .' Chilled, I ran slowly through the remainder of the story. 'Even your sad discovery on the hillside failed to persuade the locals to take the matter seriously. Then you nagged at the governor's staff in the capital at Corinth; they stonewalled like true diplomats. You even tracked down the travel group and demanded answers. Eventually you ran out of resources and were forced to return home?'

'I would have stayed there. But I had upset the governor with my constant appeals.' Caesius now looked abashed. 'I was ordered to leave Greece.'

'Oh joy!' I gave him a wry smile. 'I love being invited to participate in an enquiry where the administration has just blacklisted my client!'

'Do you have a client?' Helena asked me, though her glance told me she had guessed the answer.

'Not at this stage,' I responded, without blinking.

'What exactly brought you here?' Caesius asked narrowly.

'A possible development. Another young woman has recently died in bad circumstances at Olympia. My assistant, Camillus Aelianus, was asked to make enquiries –' That was pushing it. He was just nosy. 'I am interviewing you because your daughter's fate may be linked to the new death; I want to make a neutral reassessment.'

'I asked all the right questions in Greece!' Obsessed by his own plight, Caesius was showing just how desperate he was. He had hardly taken in what I said about the latest death. He just wanted to believe he had done everything for his

13

daughter. 'You think that if the questions are asked by a different person, there may be different answers?'

In fact I thought that by now everybody under suspicion would have thoroughly honed their stories. The dice were thunderously loaded against me. This was a cold case, where the nagging father might be quite wrong in his wild theories. Even if there really had been crimes, the first perpetrators had had three years to destroy any evidence and the second ones knew all the questions I would ask.

It was hopeless. Just like most of the dud investigations I accepted.

Belatedly, Caesius was taking in the fact that another girl had been killed and another family was suffering. 'I must see them –'

'Please don't!' I urged. 'Please let me handle it.'

I could see he would not heed me. Caesius Secundus was fired by the hope that a new killing – if that was really what had happened – would provide more clues, more mistakes or muddled stories, and maybe a new chance.

III

The coffin of Marcella Caesia stood in a dark side room. Its lid was painstakingly forced open with a crowbar. The surly slave who forced the curled lead edges apart plainly reckoned I was yet another callous fraud preying on his master.

Do not expect me to dwell on the contents. The dead girl had been bleached and sun-baked for a twelvemonth on the mountainside and animals had got to her. There were a lot of loose bones, a little shredded clothing. Collecting the relics must have been difficult. The coffin had been on a sea voyage since. If you have ever seen a corpse in that condition, you know how it was. If you never have, be grateful.

'How was the body lying, Caesius? Could you tell?'

'I don't know. I thought she had been left on her back. That was merely my feeling. Everything was widely scattered.'

'Any indication that she had been buried? Could you see a shallow grave?'

'No.'

Under the fierce gaze of Caesius Secundus, I endured the experience, walking around to view the coffin from every angle. I saw nothing helpful. Out of decency, I gave it time, then shook my head. I tried to find reverence; I probably failed. Then I left Caesius raising his arms in prayer, while his daughter's remains were resealed by the purse-lipped slave, hammering over the lead lip of the coffin lid as best he could.

It had one result for me. Mere curiosity changed to a much harder mood.

*

15

In that angry frame of mind, I addressed the new case, the second young Roman girl dead in Olympia. I set about investigating her in Rome.

Aulus had written a few facts. This victim was called Valeria Ventidia. At nineteen, she had married Tullius Statianus, a decent young man from a well-to-do family, their middle son. The Tullius family were supporting an older son for election to the Senate. They had not intended anything similar for Statianus, so perhaps as a compromise his parents gave the bride and groom a wedding gift of a long tour abroad.

I was unable to trace Valeria's own relations. So far, there was no Forum gossip about this case. I only tracked down the Tullii because of the other son, who was standing for election; a clerk in the Curia grudgingly let himself be bribed to scribble an address. By the time I turned up there, Caesius Secundus had ignored my plea, tracked down this family, and preceded me to confront the groom's parents.

It did not help. He imagined that grief gave him an entry, and that if there was something unnatural in the bride's death, her new in-laws would share his indignation. I could have told him this was unlikely. But I had been an informer for nearly two decades, and I knew people stink. Bereavement does not improve anybody's morals. It just gives them more excuses to slam doors in the faces of more ethical people. People like Caesius Secundus. People like me.

The Tullii lived on the Argiletum. This hectic thoroughfare leading north from the Curia passed itself off as a prime address; however, it had a bad reputation for riots and rip-offs, and the private houses there must be frequently bothered by street brawls and bad language. That told us the family either had over-grandiose ideas, or old money that was running out. Either way, they were bluffing about their importance.

The groom's mother was called Tullia, Tullia Longina. Since she shared her husband's family name, it must be a marriage between cousins, probably for money reasons. She

16

agreed to see us, though reluctantly. To knock on the door of a private house, unannounced, always puts you on the wrong foot. I could shoulder my way into most places, but a Roman matron, mother of three children, by tradition expects less crudity. Upset her, and a slab-like slave would soon evict us.

'My husband is attending to business –' Tullia Longina was eyeing us up more critically than Caesius had done. I looked slightly less suave than a gladiator. At least Helena, clad in clean white with gold glinting at her throat, seemed reassuring. Once again, I had taken her with me. I was in a raw mood and needed her restrained back-up.

'We could return at a more convenient time,' Helena offered, not meaning it.

We noticed the woman's guarded look. 'Better to speak to me. Tullius is annoyed already – A man called Caesius has been here; are you anything to do with him?'

We tutted and looked grieved by his interference. 'So you know what happened to his daughter?' Helena asked, trying to win the woman's friendship.

'Yes, but my husband says, what has it to do with us?' Mistake, Tullia. Helena hated women who sheltered behind their husbands. 'Valeria's – accident – is very unfortunate, and a tragedy for my poor son, but we feel, what is the purpose of dwelling on what happened?'

'Maybe so you can console your son?' My voice was hard. I was remembering the dank contents of the lead coffin at the Caesius house.

Tullia still failed to spot our rudeness. Again, her wary expression came and was quickly supplanted. 'Well, life must go on . . .'

'And is your son still abroad?' Helena had recovered herself.

'Yes.'

'You must just want him home.'

'I do! But, I confess I am dreading it. Who knows what state he will be in . . .' Next minute the mother was telling us that his condition was amazingly stable. 'He has decided to

17

continue his journey, so he will have time to come to terms –'

'Did that not surprise you?' *I* thought it astonishing, and I let her see it.

'No, he wrote us a long letter to explain. He said the other people on the trip are comforting him. He will stay among his new friends. Otherwise, he would have to make his way back to Rome, entirely alone, whilst in such trouble and unhappiness –'

Unconvinced, I cut across this: 'So what does he say about the death?'

Once more, the mother looked anxious. She was intelligent enough to know we could find out the facts some other way, so she coughed: 'Valeria was found one morning, outside the lodging house, lying dead.' Already despising Statianus, I wondered what kind of newly-wed husband spent a whole night separated from his bride, not raising the alarm. One who had had a fight with her, perhaps?

'Was there any thought of who might have done such a thing?' Helena took over before I lost my temper.

'Apparently not.' The mother of Statianus seemed a little too tight-lipped.

'No doubt the local authorities investigated thoroughly?'

'A woman in the party summoned a magistrate. Created a fuss.' Tullia seemed to think this responsible move was over-officious; then she told us why: 'Statianus found the investigation very difficult; the magistrate was set against him. A story began that my son must have had something to do with what had happened to Valeria – that maybe they had quarrelled – either that she had lost interest in him, or that his behaviour towards her drove her away . . .'

The mother had said too much and knew it. Helena commented, 'You can see how a breach might happen with a new married couple, youngsters who had known one another only slightly beforehand, under the stress of travelling –'

I sneaked in a question: 'Was it an arranged marriage?' All marriages are arranged by someone, even ours, in which we two had simply decided to live together. 'Did the couple know one another? Were they childhood friends?'

'No. They had met several times in adulthood; they were content to be partners.'

'How long ago was the wedding?'

'Only four months . . .' Tullia Longina wiped away an invisible tear. At least this time she made the effort.

'Valeria was nineteen. And your son?' I pressed on.

'Five years older.'

'So who arranged things for Valeria? Had she family?'

'A guardian. Her parents are both dead.'

'She is an heiress?'

'Well, she has – had – a little money, but to be honest, it was something of a move downhill for us.' So the careful Tullii had got away with putting in a small marriage portion. Money, therefore, seemed an unlikely motive for killing Valeria.

I asked for, and to my surprise was given, details of Valeria's guardian. Not much hope there; he was an elderly great-uncle, who lived away in Sicily. He had not even attended the wedding. Fixing up Valeria must have been a duty call.

'They were not close,' Tullia told us. 'I believe they had not even met since Valeria was a very small child. Nonetheless, I am sure her great-uncle is heartbroken.'

'Your son less so?' I queried coolly.

'No!' Tullia Longina exclaimed. 'Even the magistrate could see in the end that he is innocent. The whole party were exonerated and allowed to go on their way.'

'What happened to Valeria's corpse?' I asked.

'A funeral was held at Olympia.'

'Cremation?'

'Of course,' said Tullia, looking surprised. Thank the gods. That saved me sniffing at another set of bones.

Helena moved slightly, to break the tension. 'What was your reaction when Caesius Secundus came and told you something similar had happened to *his* daughter?'

'Oh the circumstances are *quite* different!' On the limited

19

information we had, I could not see that. Caesius had no idea how his daughter died. Either the Tullii knew more than they were saying about Valeria, or they were determined to say she had suffered an 'accident' even though Aulus had written that in Olympia there was no dispute that she was murdered. The Tullii were definitely brushing Valeria's death aside – just as Caesius thought everyone had done to his own daughter. Still, their son had survived; his two brothers were flourishing; the Tullii wanted to get on with their lives.

'Is there any chance that we could see the letter Statianus wrote?' Helena then requested.

'Oh no. No, no. I no longer even have it.'

'Not a family for keepsakes?' Helena barely hid her sarcasm.

'Well, I have mementoes of all my sons when they were little – their first tiny sandals, baby cups they drank their broth from – but no. We do not keep letters about tragedies.' Tullia's face clouded. 'They are gone,' she said, almost pleading with us. 'I understand the other father's grief. We are all very sorry, both for him and for ourselves; of course we are. Valeria was a lovely girl –' Did she really think that, or was she merely being courteous? 'But now she is gone and we all need to settle down again.'

Perhaps she was right. After this interview, Helena and I decided there was no point pursuing the Tullii. I thought we had probably heard the husband's views in his wife's last statement. *She is gone, and we all need to settle down again.* Two months after a death this was not particularly callous, not from parents-in-law who appeared to have barely known the girl.

'Did *anybody* know Valeria?' Helena wondered to me. 'Know her properly?'

I thought Statianus was an enigma too. However bland the excuses, I still thought it incredible that he should lose his recent bride, yet continue his travels among a bunch of strangers as if nothing had happened.

'The trip to Greece was to celebrate the marriage,' Helena

agreed. 'So if the marriage had ended, what was the point in continuing?'

'It was paid for?'

'*My* parents would demand their money back!' She grimaced, then added brutally, 'Or Papa would quickly fix up a new match, then re-run the tour with wife number two.'

I joined in the satire. 'Right from Rome, or from the spot where the first bride perished?'

'Oh from Olympia. No need to make the bridegroom relive sights he had already enjoyed!'

I grinned. 'People think *me* crude!'

'Realistic,' Helena countered. 'This trip must have cost the Tullii a very great deal, Marcus.'

I nodded. She was right. Tomorrow I would seek out and interview the agents who had fixed up the expensive package.

IV

I wore the toga I had inherited from my brother. I wanted to look prosperous, yet overheated and stressed. I piled on some flashy jewellery that I keep for when I act as a crass new man: a torque-shaped armband and big ring with a red stone carved with a man in a Greek helmet. Both came from a stall in the Saepta Julia that specialised in kitting out idiots. Polished up, the gold almost looked real – though not as real as my own straight gold band that told the world I really was a new entrant to the middle class. Vespasian had conned me into taking equestrian rank – so I was *really* gullible.

Beside the ancient Forum of the Romans lies the modern Forum of Julius; next is the Forum of Augustus; after that you run into the infamous area once called the Subura. Julius Caesar supposedly lived there, when he was not bedding the teenaged Cleopatra or dividing Gaul into parts. The legendary Julius had louche taste. If he lived in the Subura, trust me, he was lucky to survive to the Ides of March.

This dangerous dump was now recategorised as the Alta Semita, the High Lanes district, though little had changed. Even I, in my single days, drew the line at an apartment in the High Lanes. You only die once; you may as well live a little first.

The Seven Sights travel bureau was here – well within reach of the Argiletum where the Tullii lived and the Via Lata home of Caesius. It occupied a one-room lock-up in a dark alley, off a low street where I passed a knife fight being ignored by some small boys having a cockfight near to a dead beggar. I could see why locals would want a getaway. When I stepped across the threshold, I looked nervous and it was not acting. The male occupant ignored me as I glanced along faded wall-maps of Achaea and Egypt, pausing at the sketch of a miserable Trojan horse.

'Poor gee. Looks like he's caught the Strangles from his stablemate. Or has he just got woodworm?'

'Planning a trip, sir?' The bored salesman retaliated for this bad joke by showing me a set of mainly missing teeth. I tried not to stare at the gaping rictus. 'You've come to the right place. We'll make everything run smoothly.'

'How much would it cost?'

Keener, the salesman approached. He was a swarthy, paunchy fraudster, with a short curly beard and lashings of hair oil. He wore a mid-calf tunic in vomit yellow, straining across his belly. 'How long have you got, and where do you want to go?' I won't say this man was avoiding my gaze, but he was watching an invisible fly that he had dreamed up to the left of my ear.

'Greece, maybe. Wife wants to visit her brother. I'm scared of the price.'

The agent applied a sympathetic pucker of the lips. With practised ease, he hid the fact that fleecing scared voyagers was the sole reason Seven Sights existed. 'It need not be exorbitant!'

'Give me some idea.'

'Difficult, sir. Once you take off, you're bound to get hooked. I wouldn't want you to be locked into a package if you hankered for a little add-on – suppose you had gasped at the Colossus of Rhodes, then heard of some up-country village that made fabulous cheeses –' I thought the Colossus had been snapped off at the knees in an earthquake; still, I love cheese. I brightened. That made *him* brighten. 'Now with our mix-and-match infinite journey plan, sir, anything is possible – right up to the moment you decide to come home so you can boast to all your friends. Tell you what, legate, how about I mooch along to your house and talk you through it?'

I looked nervous. I *was* nervous. 'Well, we're just thinking about it –'

'Absolutely fine. No obligation. I'm Polystratus, by the way. They call me the Seven Sights facilitator.'

23

'Falco.'

'Excellent. Falco, let me drop by with a few maps and itineraries, spread them out in the comfort of your own home, then you can choose at leisure. Make sure the wife is in; she'll just love what we have on offer.'

'Oh she's mad to spend some money,' I confirmed gloomily. While he hid his glee, the appointment was made for that same night. Seven Sights never let a victim cool.

Our current address was a tall town house on the Tiber Embankment in the shadow of the Aventine Hill. It had previously belonged to my father, Didius Geminus the notorious auctioneer; we still had a couple of rooms furnished with grand, unsaleable furniture, which Pa kept 'forgetting' to remove. One of these salons was ideal for making Polystratus think us wealthier than we were. He tottered in with an armful of scrolls, which he dropped on a low marble table. Helena encouraged him to relax on a metal couch which still possessed uneven cushions; smiley lion's head finials showed off what looked like real gilding.

Polystratus gazed around admiringly at Pa's special brand of décor. This was one of the rooms that periodically flooded. At least the blotched frescos might stop the facilitator adding noughts to his estimate. Millionaires would have had new paint.

I introduced myself as Procurator of the Sacred Geese of Juno. Untrue, since I had been 'let go' by the tight-pursed Emperor. My post had been made redundant; nonetheless, I still sometimes went up to the compound and endured a peck or two for old times' sake. I could not bear to think of the Sacred Geese and the Augurs' Chickens suffering neglect. Besides, we were used to the free eggs.

Helena Justina was giving her jewellery a good workout this week; tonight she had on a rather fine amber necklace, plus ridiculous gold ear-rings like chandeliers which she may have borrowed from a circus artiste we knew. She scrutinised Polystratus slyly, while I perfected our winsome tourist act.

He had late-luncher's breath, but had covered it up

24

especially for us by sucking a lavender pastille; it slid in and out through that wide gap in his teeth. Perhaps he had hoped I had a wife he could flirt with. Tonight he had changed from the ghastly yellow outfit I saw him in this morning; he had smartened up for the occasion and was now in quite a respectable long tunic, dried-blood red with an embroidered hem. I reckoned he bought it as a cast-off from some touring theatre company. It looked like something a king would wear in a very boring tragedy.

'Put yourself in my hands, madam!' cried Polystratus saucily. Already Helena disliked him and he seemed none too keen on her either, since she looked ready to stop me signing any expensive contracts. I could see him struggling to get the feel of our relationship. For fun, we had changed places in the game now; I was pretending to be travel-crazy, while Helena played the sourpuss. This did not fit what I had said at the bureau, so Polystratus clearly felt caught out.

'I rather like the sound of the infinite journey plan,' I pleaded with Helena. 'Go as we please, not tie ourselves down, wander wherever the fancy takes us –'

'Excellent!' Polystratus beamed, eager to let me do the work for him. 'May I ask what you do in life, Falco?' He was testing my collateral. How wise. If only I had some to test. 'Are you in trade? Import–export? Maybe favoured by a legacy?' His eyes wandered around the room, still seeking evidence of money. There was a highly polished silver display-stand that must seem good for an excursion to a few Arcadian temples. The back was caved-in, although from where he sat he would not see the defect.

'Marcus is a poet!' Helena quipped wickedly.

'No profits in it –' I smirked. All businessmen say that.

Polystratus was still taken with the silver stand. Family habit kicked in. I wondered if I could sell it to him. Still, Pa would haggle about sharing the commission . . .

Helena noticed my daydream and aimed a kick at my shin. 'I really must go and see my little brother, Polystratus; that's all. It's my wild husband who is interested in tailor-made trips. Last I heard, he was hankering for Egypt.'

'A classic romantic!' the facilitator chortled. 'We do a nice little Spring Excursion to the Pyramids of Giza. Alexandria is a hot draw. Gaze at the Pharos. Borrow a scroll from the Library, a scroll that may once have rested at the bedside of Cleopatra while she made love to Antony . . .'

Helena, who collected information, shook her head at me. 'Did you know that Augustus went to pay tribute at Alexander the Great's tomb; he covered the corpse with flowers – and inadvertently broke off a bit of Alexander's nose?'

'What a lady!' Polystratus thought women with a sense of humour should be locked in the pantry – however, he knew that was out of the question if the cash in our bank chests had come as her dowry.

'She's a treasure!' I meant it. It unnerved him. He dealt in cliché wives. 'Tell us about these tailor-mades of yours,' I insisted, still the stubborn husband who was yearning for adventure. 'It has to be Greece, for her brother –'

'No problem with that,' Polystratus assured me. 'We can do you a spectacular Pythons and Phidias circular itinerary –'

'I really want to go next summer, to catch the Olympic Games.' I glanced at Helena, implying she had refused permission.

'Oh bad luck! Our Tracks and Temples tour is there at the moment.' For the first time I wondered why, if the Games were not until next year. Still, Olympia has an age-old religious sanctuary, its statue of Zeus one of the Seven Wonders of the World. 'Funnily enough,' Polystratus confided, 'I had a letter back about that group only today; they are having a wonderful time. Absolutely thrilled with it, all of them.' That would be all except the late Valeria Ventidia, and possibly her bridegroom. Polystratus could have no idea we knew about the murder.

'So how do your arrangements work?' Helena enquired. 'Do you have someone who escorts people, to find good accommodation and organise the transport?'

'Exactly! For our Greek adventures, that's Phineus. Our best guide. A legend in the trade, ask anyone. He does all the legwork, while you are out enjoying yourselves.' And if a client disappeared, I knew from Caesius, this Phineus legged it back to Rome.

Helena was frowning nervously. 'So if anything went badly wrong –'

'Not on our trips!' snapped Polystratus.

'What if there was a terrible accident and someone died on the journey?'

Polystratus slurped through his missing teeth. I wondered just how many bar-room brawls a man had to partake in to wreak such dental havoc. 'It can happen.' Changing his tactics, he lowered his voice. 'In the *rare* eventuality of a tragic accident, we do have expertise in repatriation, both for the living and the not so fortunate.'

'So consoling! You hear such stories,' Helena murmured meekly.

'Believe me,' Polystratus confirmed, 'I know of companies who behave quite shamefully. Some old gent swallows a grape pip and chokes, then the sobbing widow finds herself abandoned with no money and no donkey, hundreds of miles from anywhere – I can't even tell you the appalling things that happen – but we,' he pronounced, 'have been organising happy travel for two decades. Why, the Emperor Nero wanted to see Greece on one of our journeys, but unluckily for him, it was booked out. We always say that when he slit his throat with a razor it was out of disappointment that we had no room for him!'

I gave the agent a sickly smile. 'I met Nero's barber. He does a superb shave. Xanthus. What a character. Now he's working for a retired rebel chieftain in Germany . . . He was heartbroken that Nero committed suicide using one of his best razors.'

Polystratus did not know how to take that. He thought I was poking fun. 'Nobody who goes with us ever has any trouble, I can promise you.'

The Nero line was his official joke. Unluckily for Polystratus, we already knew that his promise of freedom from trouble was a lie.

V

We put off Polystratus by saying we would think about his Acropolis Adventure, definitely, really soon. I even managed to persuade him to sneak me a copy of the route of Tracks and Temples, implying I would hide it under my mattress then book myself a boy's sporting escapade next year.

That would have been one way to investigate Olympia. Seven Sights Travel were the link between the two young women's deaths: Caesia and Valeria had both travelled with this pushy team. So we could have sat back until the next Olympics, travelled with Seven Sights ourselves, and just waited to see which female tourist had an adventure too many . . .

Falco and Associates were not so irresponsible. Anyway, I was being sent to Greece – assuming I went – this year, to nudge Aulus on his way to Athens. The noble Julia Justa wanted her baby signed up with a rhetorician *now*! If I failed to arrange it, in a year's time I was likely to find myself divorced.

Why stick with one sponsor, when you can fix up two? I took myself to the Palatine. I was fobbed off with an excuse I knew of old: that the Emperor was visiting his Sabine estate. In any case, Vespasian would quite likely pooh-pooh the Olympus trip but afflict me with some ghastly political mission in the foggy north (like the one where he lumbered me with the imperial barber, Xanthus).

Instead, I set about persuading one of the palace bureau chiefs, Claudius Laeta, that the double death could lead to a crisis in public confidence: Caesius was still denouncing a cover-up; Valeria Ventidia had been sister-in-law to a

28

senatorial candidate; any moment now, these shocking murders would feature in the *Daily Gazette* . . . Laeta knew I had contacts at the *Gazette*.

'Women are being preyed on?' The slimy swine sounded too keen on that idea.

'Unmarried girls and young brides,' I specified. 'High potential for public revulsion.'

'Officially, our position is that we wish senatorials would stay in Italy.'

'Well, they won't do it, Laeta. So are respectable families to be unprotected, while travelling in a Roman province?'

'Your high-mindedness stinks, Falco!'

To get rid of me, Laeta agreed to fund one week at Olympia investigating, plus travel to Corinth so I could report to the governor (the worst aspect of the job, since he would hate having a palace intermediary poking about his province unasked).

I had no intention of using Seven Sights. I assembled my own travel group. First, while most people were wondering who I would take with me, I made sure I left the right ones behind. I did not tell my father I was going, even though he had business contacts in Greece. They were dubious. The Greek art trade is notorious. Leaving him behind saved more trouble than anything.

With more regret, I also declined Helena's younger brother, Quintus. I liked him as a travelling companion; he was organised, easygoing, and spoke very good Greek. But his young Baetican wife, who had just given him a son, was vexed with him; blatant pressure from the rest of the Camillus family persuaded me – and Quintus – that his domestic ties came first. (In the event, this was to rebound badly. For once, the problem would not be my fault.)

Helena took a tricky decision about our own children; here, I was blamed. Helena said that our trip last year to Britain with Julia and Favonia had been a strain for them and for us; they needed a more settled routine; since we planned to be in Greece for only a few weeks, this time our children would be left with their grandmother (her mother). Among

Roman officials it was standard practice for infants to remain in Italy while their father served abroad.

I let Helena explain these arrangements to my own mother. Luckily Ma was feeling her age and she recognised that a senator's house, full of spare rooms and doting slaves, was a good place for two lively toddlers. She did point out that most travelling officials left their wives at home, especially if they were good mothers. Helena deflected Ma; I only found out afterwards she did it by saying that she and I needed more time alone if we were to produce our next baby . . . Ma did not know that the bundle of dried sausages she gave us (since it is well known that you starve abroad) were nestling in a luggage pack between other items for every eventuality: sunhats, snowboots – and a soapstone pot of alum anti-conception wax.

Yes, Helena Justina was coming with me. Why ask?

And of course the next question was: what about Nux? I begged my mother to babysit my dog. Already put out, Ma told me where to stuff that bright idea. Nux came with us. Now I was damned as the man who happily abandoned his children – yet refused to part from a smelly mongrel.

Albia, our foster-daughter, wanted a jaunt. Many people asked us why, if we were leaving our children, we took their nursemaid. The straight answer was, Albia was not the nursemaid. The other answer was, we had intended her to stay behind.

Albia hailed from Britain – one of the casualties of the Great Rebellion. We believed that her parents were Romans, massacred by the rampaging tribes. The war orphan had been living on the streets when Helena found her. Giving a feral scavenger a home with us was madness – yet it was one small reparation for the British tragedy. Conscience. Even informers have it. I had seen Londinium, after the tribes burned everything, and I would never forget.

'So what am I doing with you?' Albia demanded dramatically. She was dressed like a Roman girl, yet as we sat on our roof terrace, her crossed arms and hunched shoulders were those of a barbarian waif who had been cruelly made captive – in fact, the classic pose of any teenager thwarted by adults. 'You never told me I was merely to look after your children, saving you the price of a slave!'

'Because that was never true.' I was not having my daughters brought up by slaves, for one thing.

It would be reassuring for Julia and Favonia to have Albia rush to comfort them as they screamed in their cribs. But Helena knew she was being tested. Albia was adept at throwing the sympathy dice; she always knew she could make us scared that our goodwill gesture would go bad. 'You were offered a place as part of our *familia*, Albia. Anyway, we believe you were freeborn, a Roman citizen.'

'So you are teaching me about Roman life?' This was leading to a classic adolescent demand for everything money could buy.

'We never promised you *Greek* life!' Chortling, I was no help; still, the game was lost. 'Helena, she's right; no Roman girl would miss the chance of being a thorough nuisance on a foreign trip.'

'Does this have your approval, Marcus Didius?' Helena glowered.

'Don't play the submissive wife with me! Sweetheart, it seems our work is done with Albia. She is the complete Roman woman – wheedling, devious, and brutal when she wants something.'

'Such humour!' mocked Albia, flouncing off in triumph – another trick she had learned since she lived with us.

'You have to be consistent,' Helena grumpily conceded.

'Let her come. We are investigating female victims: I'm taking Albia as bait.' When women were goading me, I could be heartless.

'Oh grow up, Marcus!'

I also kidnapped two of my nephews: Gaius and Cornelius. Gaius had been on expeditions with us before and his mother, my useless sister Galla, had no chance of stopping him when he saw an escape from his horrible home life. His cousin Cornelius was the only other one I could prise from

31

his parents; my sister Allia would never have agreed, but her useless husband Verontius thought it was a great idea – purely on the grounds that it would upset Allia. Gaius was lean, cocky and aggressive, while Cornelius was his fat, silent, sweet-natured foil. I wanted them to sit on our baggage and look tough, if we ever had to leave it somewhere.

The final member of our party was Young Glaucus. In taking him, I was repaying favours. Glaucus senior was my personal trainer at the gym I attended. He himself would have enjoyed this trip, but he put a lot into his business and could not get away. His son, who was offered to me as a bodyguard and athletics adviser, was around eighteen: quiet, pleasant, intelligent, well-mannered, and respectful of his father. Too good to be true? – he was hankering to take part in the classical Games. Glaucus had been teaching him sports since he could only toddle. My role was to give the young athlete a prior visit to Olympia to decide if he was really serious about competing. Too bad there would be no contests there now.

Jupiter knows who his mother was; the older Glaucus used to get a winsome look when he spoke of her. She must have come from somewhere in North Africa, and been endowed with extraordinary looks. The son was striking. On top of that he was a massive specimen.

'He's really going to make us unobtrusive!' Helena chaffed.

'Planned distraction. While people are staring at golden boy, they won't think twice about us.'

Albia (sixteen, and ready for emotional disaster) was already staring hard at him. So far, Young Glaucus acted the dedicated athlete, fettling his fine body while unconscious of his handsome face. Albia seemed set to enlighten him.

This was the select party with whom I set off, anxious to be on the move before autumn arrived. (And before Pa gave me a hideous list of Greek vases to import for him.) Time was against us. After October, the seas would be closed. Getting to Greece was still feasible, though coming home might pose problems.

Never mind that. We put ourselves in the mood of leisure tourists. We felt like gods, wandering about the continents on the lookout for wine, women, adventure, and arguments . . .

But our purpose was grave. And since I had chosen to drag us down the toe of Italy to take ship at Rhegium, opposite Sicily, we were exhausted, tetchy, and much poorer before we even left the land. Most of the others recovered on the voyage. I get seasick. Helena had brought ginger root. It never works on me.

By the time we sailed, both Helena and I had realised that leaving the children was a huge mistake. She buried her head in a scroll, looking persecuted. When I was not throwing up, I put it out of my mind by exercising on the deck with Young Glaucus. That made me seem even more of a heartless bastard.

Adventures began immediately. The weather was already uncertain. Our ship's captain was having some private breakdown so had locked himself in the only cabin, where he remained out of sight; the bos'n kept schmoozing Helena, and the helmsman was half-blind. Halfway across, we hit a lightning storm that threatened to sink us – or force us off course, which was worse. Being dragged to some rocky Greek island peopled by goats, fishermen, abandoned maidens, love poets, and sponge-divers would have made our journey a complete waste of time. Traders take the risk because they have to; I was starting to feel tense. We had far too much luggage – yet nothing good enough to buy off any islanders who made their living 'salvaging' shipwrecks.

We reached land eventually, at a port called Kyllene up in the Gulf of Corinth, which would serve our purpose. Instead of being on the west coast, a mere ten or fifteen miles from Olympia, we now had more than ten miles to travel south to Elis, at which point we could take the Processional Way over the uplands – another fifteen miles. (That's fifteen miles according to the locals, so we knew in advance it would be twenty or more.) By the time we tumbled off the boat to search for lodgings, travel had lost any glamour and I just wanted to go home again. An aspect the tour guides always forget to mention.

It gave us some idea how unsettled each of the Seven Sights Travel groups might be when they landed at their first new province.

PART TWO

OLYMPIA

There are lots of truly wonderful things you can see and hear about in Greece, but there is a unique divinity of disposition about the games at Olympia . . .

Pausanias, *Guide to Greece*

VI

First stop Olympia.

Wrong. First stop Tarentum. Second Kyllene. Third Elis. Fourth Letrinoi. *Fifth* stop Olympia.

From Rhegium we had sailed around the foot of Italy and north again: the wrong direction, though apparently this was the way Greek settlers in Southern Italy always sailed to the Games. Then, after an unbudgeted-for stay in Tarentum, we endured another long haul down towards Greece, and met the storm.

The winds dumped us at Kyllene, a typical tiny seaport, where because of the weather they had run out of fish and run out of patience, though they still knew how to double-charge for rooms. I was calm. I take my duties as the lead male in a party seriously: these duties are, to rebuff lechers, to outmanoeuvre purse thieves, to wander off at unexpected moments, and when everyone else is at breaking point to exclaim very brightly, *'Well, isn't this fun?'*

Luckily we had brought maps; the locals seemed to know nothing about their district. They all pretended they never went to Olympia themselves. We travelled inland to Elis, an ancient town which had grabbed the right to host and organise the Games. From Elis (which acquired this right by fighting for it), heralds with olive wreaths to signal universal peace are dispatched throughout the Greek world, to proclaim a truce in any current wars and to invite everyone to attend the festival. Competing athletes are made to spend a month in training at Elis (spending money, I thought cynically) before processing to Olympia.

We knew Aulus had landed further down the coast of the Peloponnesus and gone up to Olympia by river. The

Alphaios is navigable; after all, this was the mighty river Hercules diverted to wash out the Augean stables. Helena had looked at the map, and for us she chose the traditional road route. It was centuries old and apparently had not been visited by a maintenance team since it was hacked from the rock. Taking the Processional Way also brought us into close contact with Greek donkeys, a subject on which our diaries would elaborate at full-scroll length – had we any energy left to write them.

It took us two days from Elis. We had to stop a night in Letrinoi. Spectators and competitors at the Games do this, but they bring tents. We were stuck with cramped accommodation in the village. We went to bed late and we started out early.

At Letrinoi the Processional Way picked up the spur from the coast at Pheia, another visitors' route, though its condition did not improve. In some places the Greek road-makers had dug out double ruts to guide chariot wheels. One way. We were several times forced off the road by carts whose wheels were stuck in these ruts. The few passing-places were occupied either by pilgrims heading back to Elis and Pheia, who had seized them as picnic spots, or by boot-faced locals grazing mangy goats.

Once or twice, it was our turn to grab the picnic spots. We spread out a simple woollen rug and squashed on it together, turning our rapt gaze to the sunny, pine-clad hills over which we were slowly climbing. Then we all stood up, and tried moving the rug in the hope of a sandier base with fewer pointed stones. As the water gourd went round, we dropped rancid sheep's cheese down our tunics, and argued over the olives. As usual, Helena had been charged with topographical research, so she kept up a commentary to instil us with awe for the revered religious site we were about to invade.

'Olympia is the main sanctuary of Zeus, whom we call Jupiter. It is holy and remote –' I let out a guffaw. This area was remote all right. 'And was old even before the great temple was built. This is a sanctuary of Gaia, the Earth

38

Mother, who gave birth to Zeus – I don't want any of you trying any fertility rites, incidentally – and we shall see the Hill of Cronus, who was the father of Zeus. Hercules came here on his Twelfth Labour. The statue of Zeus in his Temple was created by Pheidias, whom we call Phidias, and is one of the Seven Wonders of the World. As you all know . . .' She tailed off, having lost her audience. I, for one, was nodding in the sunlight.

Gaius and Cornelius were wrestling each other. It struck me that Cornelius was one of those large chubby lads who is constantly taken for older than his real age; he might be only about eleven, which meant I must look out for him. Gaius must be sixteen now, tattooed and rat-like in appearance, though he had a sweet streak, buried beneath his desire to look like a barbarian mercenary. Both these rascals had a wild black mass of Didius curls; my fear was that strangers would think they were my sons.

'Is Young Glaucus going to compete in the Games?' Cornelius asked me. He did not ask Young Glaucus, because Young Glaucus never said much. At the moment he was carrying out an exercise where he crouched on all fours, slowly raising and holding his opposite arms and legs; it would have been straightforward, had he not been supporting one of our larger baggage packs on his huge shoulders at the time. As his sinews flexed and trembled, I felt myself wince.

'Yes, Cornelius. He is sizing up the situation, ready for next year. Mind you, I promised his father I'll bring him safely home again, with no fancy notions.'

'Isn't that what you told *my* father?'

'No. Verontius said I could swap you for a nice little Athenian handmaiden.' Verontius had indeed told me that. Thinking I might do it, Cornelius looked worried.

'You have to be a Greek,' put in Gaius. 'To compete at the Games.'

'Not any more!' scoffed Cornelius. 'Romans rule the world!'

'We rule with a benign sceptre, tolerating local customs.'

39

As their uncle, it was my duty to teach them politics. The Greeks no longer held a monopoly on democratic thought and I kept my ears peeled at the baths; I had heard the modern theories. The lads stared at me, thinking I had gone soft.

Our tolerance of foreigners was soon tested. We were joined by a couple of downhill joggers who looked enviously at our patch of sitting space. We edged up and offered four inches of ground. In the spirit of Olympic idealism (and hoping to share their flagon), we made friends. They were sports fans from Germania: a couple of big, flabby, fair-haired River Rhenus wine merchants. I recognised the pointed hoods they wore, on capes with triangular front flaps. We discussed northern places. Then I joked, 'So what made you get the date wrong?'

'Ah that Nero! He mixed us up.'

The year before he died, the Emperor Nero had visited Greece on a grand tour. Wanting to appear at all the traditional Games (and clearly oblivious to the Greeks-only rule), he had made the organisers bring forward the Olympic Games by two years, just so he could compete. He then outraged Greek sensibilities by 'winning' first prize in the chariot race even though he fell out and never finished. Since then, the judges Nero bribed had had to pay the money back and the Games had been reassigned to their ancient four-year cycle – but people were now thoroughly confused.

As younger men, the Germans had been here in that famous imperial year of farce; they confirmed what we had heard: attending the Games could be a nightmare.

'Thousands of people crammed into a temporary village that simply cannot hold them. The heat was unbearable. No water, no public baths, no latrines, no accommodation available – The noise; the crush; the dust; the smoke; the long hours and the queues –'

'We had to sleep under a blanket tied to bushes last time. The permanent lodging houses are always taken by the rich athletics sponsors and the chariot-horse owners, who of course are even richer.'

'So what did you do this year?'

'We brought a decent German tent!'

'But found there were no sports?'

'Oh we just enjoyed the magical atmosphere of the sanctuary, and promised ourselves we will come back next year.'

'It's quite a trip for you.'

'The Games are that special.' Their eyes glazed, though that could have been the wine. 'The remote sylvan place, the atmosphere of devotion, the spectacle – the victory feasts . . .'

We asked if they had heard about a Roman girl being murdered this year. They looked intrigued, but said no. Then one of Germans solemnly pointed out: 'It is no place for a girl. Women are traditionally barred from the site during the Games.'

'Except virgins – so that's a rarity!' They both burst out laughing with full-bodied Rhineland humour.

We smiled politely but felt prim. Well, we were Romans talking to foreigners from one of our provinces. They were jolly lads, but it was our duty to civilise them. Not that I could see them submitting to the process.

Our awkwardness could only get worse. We were now in the cradle of democracy, which we had seized for ourselves a couple of centuries ago. Nowhere in the Empire did Romans feel so out of place as in Greece. Imposing democracy on a country that in fact already possessed it raised a few questions. Bludgeoning the originators of the world's great ideas (and blatantly stealing the ideas) did not make us proud. We were bound to spend a lot of time being lofty, during this trip. It was our only defence.

I could see that Seven Sights Travel might well bring their tours here in years when no Games were being held, in order to avoid the horrendous conditions we had just heard described. And if women were still barred from attending the stadium and hippodrome, it would be tedious for female travellers in Olympic years. Now Romans were in charge of this province, the men-only rule could have been abolished – but I knew that Rome tended to leave the Greeks to their own devices. The Emperors wanted their own great festivals, held in Rome, to enhance their prestige. It was not in their interests to modernise the old Hellenic ceremonies. They paid lip-service to history, but they liked to see rival attractions die out.

We could overlook the fact that one of our own rulers had devalued the judging. I wondered what the imperial attitude would be if Olympia acquired a violent reputation. Would Vespasian, the champion of family values, take it upon himself to have the place cleaned up?

Probably not. It would be a Greek problem. And if the victims were Romans, they would be seen here as bringing harm upon themselves. We would get the old excuses: outsiders failed to appreciate local customs; they were trouble makers who asked for it; rather than being pitied, the dead women ought to be blamed.

VII

Final stop: Olympia.

Every seasoned traveller will tell you: always reach your day's destination while it is still light. Listen to this advice.

For instance, when approaching a settlement that lies between two substantial rivers, both prone to flooding, you will avoid the boggy ground. The surrounding hills will not loom dark and menacing; the pine trees will waft delicate odours, not creak above you threateningly. You will be able to tell whether you are at a cowshed or a foodshop, and if a foodshop, it will be obvious that the owners have made their pile and shut up until the next festival, hence they have stacked the chairs on all the tables – so you will not make a fool of yourself demanding food from two sinister men without an oil lamp who would not have authority to sell you dinner even if there was any.

If you arrive by daylight, as you head further up the street, or what passes for a street, you won't be left wondering what disgusting mess you have just stepped in. As you stumble uphill and downhill, trying to find the sanctuary, members of your party will not irritate all Hades out of you with endless arguments about whether the two men really had a love tryst at the dark bar. Nor will you offend your companions by yelling at them to damned well keep together and stop wittering.

Next: when you reach the welcome light of a luxurious two-storey hotel, you will not feel so relieved to find civilisation that you announce you will take the best room in the house – even though the leering porter exclaims what an excellent choice; it is the lovely corner room with dual-aspect views – a room which turns out to be thirty-five feet square, and blows your entire week's budget.

After which, you may notice that this enormous building seems entirely empty so you could have haggled over the price – then you could have stuffed all the rest of your group at the far end of the hall and got some peace by yourself.

By this time, your wish to exclude others from your presence includes your wife, who will insist on asking why you are so proud you cannot simply go back to the leering porter and tell the bloody man that you have made a mistake and now want a cheaper room.

She is wasting her breath. You are so exhausted you are face down, fast asleep.

This is the best ploy, since you know from experience that – freed from the rules of paternalism – your dear wife will now quietly return to the leering porter herself and fix up the right accommodation. Probably at a discount.

If she still loves you, she will come back and get you.

If her name is Helena Justina, she may even wake you up in time to share with your companions some of your mother's spiced Roman sausage, now unpacked from among your spare tunics, along with a stoneware bottle of passable Greek wine which Helena Justina, the delight of your heart, has persuaded the porter to give to her as a welcome-to-Olympia present.

VIII

Dawn brought sunlight and harmony to the broad, wooded valley. A cockerel woke us early, then went on crowing all day long. We rose from our beds like good tourists, hungry for breakfast and history. Tourists revive fast. Once I had cleaned off yesterday evening's cattle dung from my boots, we were ready for the next long day of stress.

We were staying at the Leonidaion, courtesy of one Leonidas of Naxos, who had cannily provided his descendants with an income by building this enormous old hostel for visiting VIPs. The four-square monster had a quiet central courtyard with shrubs, water features, and a few chairs, where the night-watchman, who doubled as the day porter at present, told us with relish that he did not provide breakfast out of season. Luckily the boys came back from a walk, bearing pastries; we spread ourselves in one of the outer colonnades and while we were eating, the porter gave in to the chance to make a quick drachma, and reported that his sister would make us evening meals. We thanked him, and made him accountable for our luggage. Helena asked if he had seen anything of her brother Aulus, but he said not. We went out to play.

Like our German friends, the porter had regaled us with stories of how, if the Games had been in progress, all the peaceful area around our hostel would have been over-whelmed. For weeks, Olympia became a vast festival camp. Outside the sporting and sacred areas sprawled tented sites; after they were cleared of their crowded marquees when the Games ended, the ground would be covered with a hot mulch of trash and human squalor. According to the porter, it rivalled the mounds of slurry from the cattle of King Augeus which Hercules had sluiced away in myth.

There was no natural water source, and no latrines had ever been provided until we Romans came. Except in the Altis, as they called the walled-in sacred area, a reek of human waste would hang everywhere. The flies which famously torture spectators would hover in drugged clouds above the litter.

The locals tidied up every four years for the next Games. Maybe we were too fastidious, but a year in advance, the place still seemed a mess. Even my dog balked at nosing among the old mattresses, gnawed bones from roasted meat, and broken amphorae. Nux adored everything the streets of Rome offer to a hound with disgusting standards; here she took one breath then slunk to heel, shocked. I patted her and tied her on a leash. The last thing we wanted abroad was a dog with a diseased digestive tract; we might need her to bark for assistance when the people were laid low. As they were bound to be.

Walking north from our hostel, we found greater decorum. Nervous about the anti-women rules, Helena and Albia had prepared a story about visiting the Temple of Hera, where women must be allowed since there were running races for girls. In fact nobody ever turned them back. The place was devoted to the male body, however. Wherever we went, we marched in the shade of statues, hundreds of them, some given as thank-offerings for good fortune in war by cities, but mostly dedicated by the victors themselves as the lasting memorial to their prowess. It was no place for prudes. Nude men on tall plinths were showing off their stone assets everywhere we looked.

We spent a morning sightseeing: Young Glaucus led us instinctively to the gymnasium. He was ecstatic. Though he was itching to try out the sports facilities, he came with us into the sacred area.

Within the walled enclosure, we were overlooked by the dramatic tree-covered Hill of Cronus, where Marcella Caesia's corpse had been found by her father. Closest to the gymnasium stood the Prytaneion, a building where fabulous feasting occurred to celebrate victories. Near to this was the gaily painted Temple of Hera, the oldest temple on site. It had three long aisles, each full of astounding statuary, including a fabulous Hermes with the young Dionysus. Glaucus gazed reverently at the gold and ivory table, which during the Games would be carried out to the judges' enclosure; on it would be placed simple wreaths of wild olive, the only prizes awarded here. Of course Olympic winners would be received back home with mass adulation, a pension in vast vats of olive oil, seaside villas, and lifetime permission to bore the populace with sporting stories . . . Glaucus was already dreaming.

In outside spaces stood many altars, some with smoke from that morning's sacrifices wreathing up into the air. One was phenomenal: the Great Altar of Zeus. Upon an ancient stone base reared a curious rectangular mound, maybe twenty feet tall when we saw it. During every set of Games a hundred oxen were slaughtered for Zeus, a gift from the people of Elis who ran the festival. Over the centuries, the ash of past sacrifices had been mixed with water from the River Alphaios; it set in a hard paste that was added to the mound. Steps had been carved out, leading to the top of the altar, where the god's choice cuts were burned.

As we approached the stadium, we saw a line of forbidding statues of Zeus, called the Zanes, erected to damn for ever athletes who had cheated: their names and crimes were inscribed on the bases. Beyond them lay a long colonnade, used for the contests for heralds; it had a sevenfold echo which Albia and the lads tested to the full. At this corner of the enclosure an arch marked the competitors' tunnel to the running track. The bronze trellis gates were closed, but we found a way to clamber into the stadium after a steep climb up and over the spectators' stand.

Young Glaucus inspected the curious starting blocks. 'You curl the toes of your front foot in these grooves and wait for the signal. There's a trip-rope system to deter false starts. If a runner takes off too soon, before the judges loosen it, he'll knock the rope down. He is made to withdraw, and the judges flog him like a slave. There are not,' stated Glaucus, 'many false starts!'

The hippodrome lay alongside the stadium. There Glaucus explained the starting gates, where up to forty chariots could be held in wedge formation that gave the outer pairs an equal chance with those at the centre. We imagined them bursting forth to the roar of forty thousand spectators, who stood on carefully designed elliptical banks. Everyone had a good view down the course – though we noticed with smirks that it was much smaller than the Circus Maximus.

Coming out, we wasted time trying in vain to get into an enormous villa Nero had built for himself by the hippodrome gates; the authorities had locked it up and hoped it would fall down. Glaucus went back to the gymnasium to practise. The rest of us sauntered through the main sanctuary, reaching the famous Temple of Zeus. This did contain one of the Seven Wonders of the World, so it was no surprise that although we had barely seen ten people so far, at this point we came face to face with an official guide.

'You speak Greek – oh you speak Latin?' He changed swiftly to Latin, though we had not said a word. 'Where are you folks from? Croton? Rome? My brother lives at Tarentum.' Oh no. 'Xenophon's fish bar; do you know his place?'

Our guide was named Barzanes. Should you go to Olympia, try to be snaffled by a different one.

'First I will show you the workshop of Phidias.'

We had seen it for ourselves already. That did not stop him.

As we stood for the second time in the enormous workshop being regaled with facts, Helena was the only one of us prepared to be civil to the guide. He was tall, with a small head set on lop-sided shoulders, one wider than the other. He wore a long belted robe like a charioteer, and carried a stave with which he gesticulated enthusiastically.

Yes, it was miraculous to find ourselves standing in the

48

very place where one of the world's greatest artists had produced his masterpiece. To prove it, we were shown surviving moulds, faulty casts, and minuscule bits of marble, gold sheet and ivory. Funnily enough, they were for sale; this charade for the public must have been going on for five hundred years. At Barzanes' voice, souvenir-sellers had popped out of nowhere. We were even offered a blackened cup that said I BELONG TO PHIDIAS. It was an exorbitant price but I bought it, even though the sculptor's name was spelled the Roman way. It was the only way to escape. I would give it to my father as a souvenir. It did not matter if the cup was a fake; so was my father.

We hustled Barzanes back to the Temple of Zeus. In fairness, our guide knew a whole whack of statistics: 'The temple was financed by the Elians and took ten years to build; it has thirty-four columns, topped with plain square pediments; above the columns you will see a painted frieze of innumerable mouldings in deep hues of red, blue, and gold –' He was unstoppable. 'The roof is of Athenian Pentelic marble, drained in rainstorms through over one hundred marble waterspouts in the form of lions' heads. Twenty-one gilded shields which you see now, but which were unknown to the ancients, have been placed here by the Roman general Mummius after he sacked Corinth –'

Oh dear. We tried looking innocent, but felt like bastard conquerors.

'Here on the west pediment is the battle between the Centaurs and Lapiths at the wedding of Pirithous –'

'This has two morals,' I said to Gaius and Cornelius. 'Do not invite barbarians to your wedding and – since the Centaurs got drunk and went after the women – do not serve too much wine.'

Barzanes kept going strong: 'On the east pediment, as the athletes approach to make their dedication to the god, they look up and see the chariot race between Pelops and Oenomaus for the hand of Hippodameia. King Oenomaus killed unsuccessful suitors, and nailed their heads above his palace gate.'

'Seems fair,' I said. 'Speaking as a father.'

'There are two stories –' Greece never seemed to have one myth where a guide could relate two. 'Either Pelops bribed the King's charioteer to replace Pelops' axle pins with wax ones, or Poseidon gave Pelops a matchless winged chariot and caused Oenomaus to be pitched out and killed –'

'Is this myth intended to encourage competitors to use tricks and to cheat?' asked Helena drily.

'The true message is that they should use their best endeavours – cunning brains as well as bodily strength.'

'And winning is all,' Helena growled.

'There are no second prizes at the Games,' Barzanes acknowledged.

'You are accepting my scepticism very generously.'

'I have acted as a guide for Roman ladies before.'

Helena and I exchanged a glance, wondering if he had been employed by Seven Sights.

Unlike many temples, visitors were allowed to enter the interior. Of course that did not mean they could enter for free. We gave Barzanes a sum he suggested, to bribe the priests. We then coughed up an extra fee to acquire 'special' permission for Albia and the lads to climb some spiral stairs to the upper floor to view the statue at close quarters. Finally we gave Barzanes himself a large tip for his facts and figures. He stayed behind on the temple steps in the hope of more people to hijack.

I wanted to interrogate him about the murders, but no mission was going to stop me seeing one of the Seven Wonders of the World, especially with Helena. Informers are street-level muckers, trading in grime, but I had a soul. Personally, I found it necessary for the job.

IX

We all paused to accustom our eyes to the lamplit gloom, after the noonday glare outside. Then we simply gasped with awe. It seemed only fair. The great Phidias had intended that we should.

There were other statues; the temple interior was an art gallery. They were wasted. All we could do was to stare up at Zeus, utterly smitten. From fourteen yards high, his head skimming the rafters, he seemed to be gazing down on us. At the steps of his throne stretched a glimmering pool, a rectangle of olive oil in which the Father of the Gods was blearily reflected. Its moisture helped preserve the ivory of the chryselephantine colossus, though temple priests also burnished it with more oil daily. We were aware of their presence. Moving about discreetly, they tended their charge, supposedly all descendants in an unbroken line from the craftsmen who had worked for Phidias.

I had heard about this statue all my life. I could not now remember how and where I first read of it or was told of it. I had known what it would look like: the massive seated god, bearded and crowned with olive branches, his robe of gold adorned with creatures and flowers, his sceptre topped with the gold eagle, the winged figure of Victory in his right hand, the ebony and ivory throne adorned with precious stones and vibrant painting.

So many things in life are disappointing. But sometimes life confounds you: a promised Wonder of the World lives up to your hopes.

Helena and I stood for a long time, hand in hand. I felt the warmth of her bare arm alongside mine, the faint tickle on

51

the top of my foot from the hem of her long gown. Helena was as cynical as me, but she knew how to give herself up fully to the enjoyment of great things. Her thrill became part of my own.

Eventually she dropped her head briefly against my shoulder, then told the excited youngsters that they could climb up to the higher level. Left alone, Helena and I turned a little towards each other and remained there together for a few more moments.

At length we walked quietly outside to the dazzling sunlight in the sanctuary, still hand in hand.

X

We paused on the steps until our breathing returned to normal. Our skin felt clammy with the mingled effects of incense and fine olive oil droplets.

Barzanes had failed to find another group. Although we had already tipped him, he hovered near us. He must have seen hundreds of awestruck spectators returning from their visit. He watched us approvingly.

Helena went off quietly to see the temple priests. We had had no sighting of her brother Aulus and if he was still here, we needed to track him down. If he had travelled away from Olympia, he would have left a message at the main temple, to be picked up by anyone who came after him. Aulus had his own assured style; he must have been certain I would rush out to Greece in response to his letter home.

Aulus would have given the priests money, but I made sure Helena could pay them another gratuity. It would be expected. Best to keep in with them. Zeus was indifferent to mortal men, but priests were easily slighted and in a sanctum like this they wielded enormous power.

I moved down the steps and joined our guide again.

'Did you enjoy your visit?' he asked.

'We are stunned!'

'Do you believe in the gods?' Barzanes now seemed more subdued. It was an odd thing to ask so abruptly.

'Enough to have cursed them, many times.' I recognised that he was trying to throw me off balance; I had met it before in my work. His attitude had changed; I wondered why. 'I believe in human endeavour. I am impressed by the statue of Phidias as a great feat of craftsmanship, devotion, and imagination . . . I believe,' I said softly, 'that most

53

mysteries have a logical explanation; all you have to do is find it.'

I left him to work out what mysteries I meant.

I gazed around the Altis, where the ancient temples, tombs, and treasuries were bathed in light beneath a monochrome blue sky of deep intensity. The cockerel who woke us this morning was still crowing in the distance. Somewhere nearer, a bullock bellowed, hoarse with anxiety. 'We did the tour. Now let's you and I talk about my mission, Barzanes.'

'Your mission, Falco?'

It was Falco now. Among my group I had been 'Uncle Marcus' or 'Marcus Didius'. So while we had been inside the temple, someone had told the guide my third name. Olympia seemed deserted, but I had been noted. Somebody had known in advance that I was coming. Presumably, too, rumour had whistled around on sweet little wings to proclaim why.

Maybe a god had betrayed me; I doubted it.

'I am trying to imagine how it can be.' To begin with, my voice was quiet but heavy. 'Travellers come here, just like us. Like us, they must all be overwhelmed by their experience. This is a place where humankind is at its finest – nobility of body, allied to nobility of spirit.' Barzanes was about to interrupt me, but he held back. 'Athletes and spectators assemble here as a religious rite. To honour their gods. To dedicate themselves to high ideals. Offerings are left in the olive groves. Oaths are sworn. Training, courage, and skill are applauded. Guides exalt that spirit to the travellers . . .' My voice hardened. I had a message to send to the establishment here. 'And then – let's imagine it, Barzanes – somebody in this holy place shows his barbaric nature. A young bride, barely two months married, is murdered and dumped. Tell me, Barzanes, are such things understandable? Are they common? Do the gods in Olympia accept this cruel behaviour – or are they outraged?'

Barzanes lifted his uneven shoulders. He remained silent, but he had dallied to speak to me and there must be a purpose. Perhaps it had been decided by the priests that this issue should be cleared up at last.

I knew better than to hope for it.

'The group in question was brought by an outfit called Seven Sights Travel. Regulars on the circuit. A fellow called Phineus leads them.'

At last Barzanes nodded and spoke up: 'Everyone knows Phineus.' I gazed at him but could not detect his opinion of the man.

'They must have been shown around the site,' I said. 'It would have been part of their deal, because this year they certainly were not here for the Games. Phineus must have booked a local site guide. Was it you, Barzanes?'

Barzanes came up with the kind of weak excuse I had heard in so many cases: 'The guide who took that tour is no longer here.'

I scoffed. 'Run away?'

Barzanes looked shocked. 'He has finished for the season and returned to his village.'

'I guess that will be a very remote village, very many miles away . . . So did he talk about this group, at the end of the day, when you guides were sitting together gossiping? If not, did he comment on them, after the girl was dead?'

Barzanes smiled gently.

Helena Justina came out from the temple, carrying a scroll. After a quick glance at what was going on, she positioned herself within earshot, while pretending to engross herself in the letter.

I was not giving up. 'Tell me what happened, Barzanes.'

'Pilgrims come here constantly. Exercises, sacrifices, prayers, consultation of oracles – even out of season we hold recitations by orators and poets. So tours of the Altis are regularly provided.'

'But any guide would remember a tour where someone who took part was later brutally murdered. How many were there in the Seven Sights group?'

Barzanes decided to co-operate. 'Between ten and fifteen. There was the usual mix: mostly persons of some age, with a few young ones – adolescents who kept wandering off. One woman kept asking silly questions and a man in the party gave her answers, wrongly.'

'Sounds typical!' I smiled.

Barzanes acknowledged it. 'Unfortunately so. Afterwards, the guide could not even remember the bride and her husband. They had made no impression.'

'So they were just listening quietly, subdued by the unfamiliarity of travel . . . Or had they worn themselves out in the marriage bed?' I grinned. Barzanes gazed at the footpath.

'They were sleeping in tents, Marcus!' Helena broke in. 'Barzanes, would a group like the Seven Sights not stay at the Leonidaion?'

'If no persons of rank were in occupation, it would be allowed. But only if they paid. Otherwise their organiser would bring tents, or hire them. Much cheaper. Phineus would know how to do it. If the intention is to visit many festivals, he will carry his own equipment in the baggage train.'

I wondered if the newly-weds had understood this limitation when they booked in. I could imagine the toothless agent in Rome, Polystratus, 'forgetting' to mention that the tourists would be camping. 'Barzanes, those good people wanted to be enthralled by your special site. Olympia owes them respect for their tragedy. So what happened to them?'

The guide shifted his feet. 'Among hundreds of people travelling around Greece, there will always be deaths, Falco.'

'We are not talking about heart attacks caused by sunstroke or over-eating at feasts.'

'Valeria was battered to death, Marcus.' Helena's voice was cold. Aulus must have supplied this information; it did not match the bland details we had heard from the mother-in-law back in Rome. 'Juno, Aulus says she was killed with a weight.'

'A *weight*?'

'A long-jumper's hand weight.' Young Glaucus would have to tell us more about these implements.

'Her head was smashed with it.' Barzanes knew that all right.

I scratched my chin, thinking. What had happened to Valeria Ventidia – a ferocious attack, not far from her companions, with the body left in open view – bore little resemblance to what had apparently happened to Marcella Caesia three years earlier – unexplained disappearance, then discovery only much later, in a remote spot. The foundation for our visit was that these two women's deaths were linked. Not that discrepancies would stop me investigating both.

'Barzanes, we were told the girl's body was discovered "outside the lodging house". But if the party were camping, that doesn't fit. I cannot believe she was beaten to death in public, within a few feet of her companions. They would have heard the disturbance.'

Unused to speculating on crimes, the guide looked vague.

'She wasn't killed near the tent. Her husband discovered her, Marcus.' Helena was still skimming through her letter. 'He found her dead at the palaestra, then he carried the corpse back to the camp. Witnesses saw tears streaming down his face. He was hysterical and wouldn't leave her. He had to be separated from the corpse almost by force. But the big issue in the investigation was whether Statianus seemed like a distraught husband or a deranged killer.'

'The magistrate released him,' I reminded her. 'Though release is not always exoneration.'

The story was taking a dark tone. I began to see why Aulus had been intrigued when he met the group. And I wondered whether Tullia Longina, the mother-in-law in Rome, had told us the truth as she knew it, or toned it down. Nobody who knew these details could call Valeria's death an 'accident'. Was Tullia Longina minimising the horror to seem more respectable, or had Statianus lied in his letter to his mother? I did not necessarily condemn him for that. Any boy has to fib to his ma from time to time.

'Most people decided there was no proof – but the husband must be guilty,' Barzanes commented.

'Easy option.' My voice grated. 'Best for everybody here that the foreigners brought their own killer – and then took him away with them. The establishment can forget all about it.'

'You're being rude,' Helena reproved me softly.

'It was sacrilege!' raged Barzanes. Which told us for sure just how the sanctum priests viewed it – and why they wanted a cover-up.

Unfortunately we were then interrupted. Our youngsters came pelting out through the temple porch behind us. They had glowing faces, still enthralled by the Statue of Zeus.

'We saw the god's face right up close!' Gaius was bursting with excitement. 'The statue is made from enormous sheets of gold and ivory – it's hollow with a huge support of wooden beams inside –'

'Full of rats and mice!' squealed Albia. 'We saw mice running about in the shadows!'

'Nero tried to steal the statue –' Gaius, the natural leader of this little group, had found another guide and grilled him. 'But the god let out a huge burst of raucous laughter so the workmen fled!' Like me, Gaius avoided spiritual explanations. He lowered his voice tactfully: 'It may have been the supports shifting, after the workmen disturbed them.'

I looked around. In the turmoil of their arrival, the tour guide Barzanes had made good his escape. I reckoned if I tried to find him another day, he would be missing from the site.

Cornelius had a brisk attitude to wonders. '*Io*, Uncle Marcus! This is a grand place here – so where will you be taking us to next?'

XI

'I am increasingly impressed by my brother!' Back at the hostel, Helena studied his letter more carefully.

'In good Roman homes,' I pointed out to Albia, 'nobody reads correspondence on their dining couch. Helena Justina was brought up in senatorial style. She knows the evening meal is reserved for elegant conversation.'

Helena ignored us. Her father read the *Daily Gazette* over breakfast; otherwise, in the Camillus household meals were a chance for family rows. So it had been in my own family. We, however, never read on our couches because we could not afford couches; nor did we own scrolls. The only time anybody ever sent us a letter, it was the one from the Fifteenth Legion that said my brother had been killed in Judaea.

'Aulus has changed,' said Helena. 'Now that he is a scholar, suddenly his letters are full of fine detail.'

'Has he gone on to Athens like a good boy?' Never mind fine detail. I wanted to establish whether I was off the hook with his mother.

'Afraid not, darling. He has joined the sightseeing tour.'

'Oh wicked Aulus!' Nux looked up, recognising the growl I used for reprimanding her. As usual she wagged her tail at it.

'He has given us a list of the people in the group, with his comments on them,' Helena went on. 'A map of where their tent was, showing how it related to the palaestra. And a heading for notes on the case – but no notes.'

'Tantalising!'

'He says, *sorry, no time* – with *actually, no bloody ideas!* scribbled afterwards, using a different pen nib.'

'That's the old Aulus. Slapdash and unapologetic.' All the same, I would have liked to have him here, to insult him to his face. We were a long way from home. Evenings, by starlight, are when you yearn for the familiar: places, things, and people. Even a rather brusque brother-in-law.

'He seems to have equipped himself with a very nice traveller's writing-set,' Helena mused, inspecting the handwriting. 'How useful for his studies – if he ever starts.'

'Unless his inkpots have stupendous seals, the ink will dry out while he's travelling. If he's very unlucky, it will leak over all his white tunics.'

Any minute now, Helena and I would move from missing Aulus to missing our children. To sidetrack that, Helena showed me the list of participants in the travel group Aulus had drawn up for us:

Phineus: organiser; brilliant or appalling, depends who you ask

Indus: Seems to be disgraced (Crime? Financial? Politics?)

Marinus: Widower, looking for new partner; amiable cove

Helvia: widow, well-meaning = fairly stupid

Cleonymus and **Cleonyma**: come into money (freedmen?) (awful!)

Turcianus Opimus: 'Last chance to see the world before I die'

Ti Sertorius Niger and mousy wifey: ghastly parents; him *very* rude

Tiberius and **Tiberia**: horrendous children, dragged by parents

Amaranthus and **Minucia**: Couple; running away? (adultery?) (fun folk)

Volcasius: no personality = no one wants to sit with him

Statianus and **Valeria**: Newly-weds (one dainty and dead/one dumb and dazed)

'Rude, but lucid!' I grinned.

We all agreed they sounded dire, though Helena's conscience made her suggest that Volcasius, with whom nobody wanted to sit, was perhaps only shy. The rest of us guffawed. I pictured this Volcasius: bony legs, always in a very large hat; a man who ignored local customs, offended guides and hoteliers, had no sense of danger when boulders were falling down rain-sodden mountainsides, always last to assemble when the group were moving on – yet, sadly, never quite left behind.

'Smelly,' Gaius contributed; he was probably correct.

'Like you are, Gaius!' muttered Cornelius.

Every group of people thrown together by accident contains one creep; we had all met them. I pointed out how fortunate my companions were that I had assembled our party on scientific lines, omitting anti-social loners in large hats. They guffawed again.

'A man like that could be the killer,' Helena said.

I disagreed. 'More likely he himself would be murdered by someone he had driven crazy with his odd behaviour.'

As Helena stacked our foodbowls neatly, she asked, 'I wonder where they have all trotted off to? That's one thing Aulus doesn't say.'

'Sparta.' I knew this from the Tracks and Temples tour itinerary I had pinched from Polystratus. I went to fetch it from my baggage pack, to double-check. One thing was certain: my personal group was *not* going to Sparta. Helena and I had a pact. She hated the Spartan attitude to women. I loathed their treatment of their inferiors, the Helots: con-quered, enslaved, maltreated, and hunted down by night as sport by belligerent Spartan youths.

I had brought other lists among my note-tablets. One was a roll-call of the tour Marcella Caesia took three years ago, the names given to me in Rome by her father. I lined up his research against our new list, but apart from Phineus there were no matches.

'So the mystery is solved: we want Phineus!' declaimed Albia.

Informers are more cautious; most of us have made mistakes over naming suspects too fast. I explained that Phineus would be crazy to be so obvious, that it now looked as if the two dead women had met dissimilar fates, probably at the hands of different killers – and that accusing Phineus was too easy.

'Simplicity is good!' Albia argued. She waved her wrists and posed her head elegantly, as if she were modelling Roman fashions under Helena's tutelage.

'If you accuse an entrepreneur unwisely, it's a very simple lawsuit for defamation.'

'Then you could defend us in court, Marcus Didius.'

'I only chase achievable compensation; I won't go bankrupt! I could just as easily mess up my life by becoming a trapeze artiste. Danger, thrills, and –'

'Going up in life,' capped Gaius.

'See more of the world,' joined in Cornelius, catching on fast.

'In all its ups and downs!' I quipped. Helena shot us a look implying none of us had reached formal manhood.

After we stopped giggling, I explained that we had to find solid evidence, using mundane investigation techniques. All the young people lost interest. This would be how it felt to run an educational leisure tour, with reluctant adolescents hating the culture. Bored young people might start plotting mischief – though not, I thought, actual murder.

Albia was annoyed that I had dismissed her theory, but she did support me next morning when I went to reconnoitre the spot where the Seven Sights tour had camped. Helena wanted to come, but was unwell; Greek food had struck her down. After breakfast Albia and I walked quickly south-wards from the Leonidaion along the embankment formed by the great retaining wall of the River Kladeos. The Kladeos was a hesitant trickle, wandering among bulrushes, though no doubt in flood it became dramatic.

Jumping fleas pinged around our feet. The air was thick with vicious insects.

'This is nothing, Albia. Imagine this place during the Games, when a hundred oxen are slaughtered at one sitting. Don't even try to calculate the quantities of blood involved. Plus hide, bones, horns, entrails, scraps of uncooked or uneaten meat. While the smoke is soaring up to the gods on Mount Olympus, down here the flies are in their own heaven.'

Albia picked her way cautiously. 'I can see why those two Germans we met said they always prayed it would not rain. The ground would become very muddy.'

'Mud and worse!'

We found where the camp had been. Aulus had drawn a clear plan. He was a strong, rough draughtsman, using thick stubby lines, but what he meant was clear enough. We could just about discern pale grass, about the footage of two ten-man army tents. We even found tent-peg holes and trampled hollows where they had had a couple of doorways. For a wide area around, three-year-old detritus disfigured the riverbank, left behind by the spectators at the last Games. But where the Seven Sights people camped, there was absolutely no rubbish.

'The travel company are *such* tidy people, Falco!' Albia had learned informing irony. 'They have been so careful to remove any clues.'

I planted myself in what would have been the outside approach to the Seven Sights tent, feet apart and thumbs in my belt. It was my favourite belt and this was a useful stance for thinking. The belt had stretched in two places to accommodate my thumbs. 'I doubt if there were many clues, Albia. And I don't credit the Seven Sights party with immaculate housekeeping.'

'Then who did it?'

'Barzanes said the girl had been killed somewhere else and the corpse was just carried here afterwards. Forensically, you might search a crime scene. But here, cleaning up so thoroughly gains nothing.'

'Forensically,' Albia repeated, learning the new word. 'Why then, Marcus Didius?'

'The place was regarded as polluted. Murder ruins the good name of the sanctuary, and maybe brings bad luck as well. So they eliminated all trace of everyone who stayed here with Valeria.'

'The priests?' Albia's grey eyes widened. 'Do you think the *priests* killed Valeria?' There was heavy derision in my foster-daughter's tone. She had learned on the streets of Londinium to distrust all authorities. I cannot say that attitude had been discouraged by Helena and me.

'Albia, I believe anything of priests!'

We stood in silence, feeling the sunshine and listening to birdsong. Beneath our feet the grass, starved of nourishment while it was covered by tents, was already greening, the blades standing up again stalwartly. Leafy hills surrounded us, thickly covered with olives, plane trees, larches, and even palm trees, above a thick undergrowth of vines and flowering shrubs. The conical Hill of Cronus dominated, waiting for me to tackle other secrets.

With its bright skies, tumbling rivers, sacred groves, and its ancient attributions, this remote spot hummed with fertility and folklore. At any moment I expected some lithe god to hail us and ask if we knew any virgins who might consent to be ravished in the interests of mythology.

'Albia, Valeria Ventidia was not much older than you are. If you had been with that party visiting Olympia, how would you feel about it?'

'Older than we *think* I am!' Albia could never miss an opportunity to remind herself how little she knew of her origins. She had no birthday. We could not say for sure whether she was fifteen, sixteen, or seventeen. 'Aulus made the people sound bad. I would not have liked it.'

'Say you are Valeria and you feel that way. Would you duck out of any organised events?'

'What could she do? Staying in the tent alone might be a bad idea. If some man knew Valeria was there by herself . . .'

'True. While the male tourists studied sporty things, Valeria and the other women of the party would have been taken around together sometimes.'

'She might not have liked those women.'

'When you travel in an escorted group, you have to live with your companions, Albia, whoever they are. How do you think the women occupied themselves? There are poets and musicians to listen to.'

Albia pulled a face. 'You could look around, like we all did yesterday. Valeria could go out by herself – but that might be a worry.'

'Men might make personal overtures?'

'You know they would do, Marcus Didius.'

True again. A young woman would be an immediate target. Men hanging around a sanctuary alone would be odd types by definition. Groups could be even more threatening. We did not know whether Valeria Ventidia was pretty, but she was nineteen. Wearing a wedding ring would not help.

'If she was spotted alone, she would be thought to be waiting for men's attention. Of course,' murmured Albia slyly, 'Valeria might have liked that.'

'Albia, I am shocked! Valeria was a bride.'

'She married because she was told to.'

'And Aulus says her husband was a dumbcluck!'

Albia giggled. 'Why stay chaste for a man like that?'

Perhaps because in a sanctuary like this, word would soon get around if you did not.

XII

Feeling my responsibilities more than usual, I escorted Albia safely back to the Leonidaion, where I told her to check up on Helena. I had arranged to meet Young Glaucus. There was a lavish new Roman clubhouse, donated by the Emperor Nero after his visit ten years ago, but since Nero's death it had remained unfinished. So I walked on to the old palaestra, into which Glaucus had wormed his way yesterday. As I went, the workshop of Phidias and the shrine of the Unknown Hero were on the right; to the left stood a bath house and an enormous outdoor swimming pool. A door porter refused me admittance to the sports facilities, so I waited until somebody else distracted him, then slipped past. There was no way Claudius Laeta and the Palatine auditors would pay a subscription to join this élite exercise club. My official expenses hardly covered a bread roll a day.

The indoor sports facilities at Olympia were as grandiose as you would expect. Yesterday we had spent most time admiring the gymnasium; that sumptuous facility had a mighty triple-arched gateway, leading to a vast interior where running could be practised on a full-size double track, safe from rain or excessive heat. It was so large that in its central area discus and javelin practice could occur even while races took place on the perimeter.

Attached to the gym was the palaestra – more intimate, yet still impressive. It had four grand colonnades, each housing rooms with specialist functions, around a huge central workout space that was open to the skies. In one preparatory room athletes oiled themselves or were oiled by their trainers – or their boyfriends. Another contained bunkers of fine dust which was slathered all over them on top of the oil. It came in different colours. After practice, the dust and oil and sweat would all be scraped off. Because there were splendid full-scale baths elsewhere in the complex, washing facilities here were basic – a clinical strigil-and-splash room and an echoing cold bath.

The main courtyard was used for contact sports. During the Games this area would be jam-packed, but it was quieter off-season. Upright wrestling was carried out on a level sanded area, called the *skamma*, also sometimes used by the long-jumpers, which could lead to arguments. Ground wrestling, with competitors flailing on the floor, took place in a crude mudbath where the sand had been watered to the consistency of sticky beeswax – a sure draw for exhibition-ists. Both types of wrestling were considered refined in comparison with boxing, where – with the aid of spiteful arm-protectors with great hard leather knuckle-ridges – opponents might have their faces mashed so badly that none of their friends recognised them. It was in boxing, the ancient sport of beauteous, golden-haired Apollo, that a savage fight occurred where a man going down from a great blow to the head somehow retaliated by jabbing his oppo-nent so hard he tore out his entrails with his bare fingers.

Even boxing paled beside the vicious no-holds-barred Greek killer of a sport they called pankration. Pankration fighters used a mixture of boxing and wrestling, plus any blow they liked. Only biting and eye-gouging were against the rules. Breaking the rules was much admired, however. So was the breaking of ankles, arms, heels, fingers and anything else that would snap.

Being peopled by brutes who gloried in these hard sports, the palaestra had its own atmosphere, one I did not like. It had its own smell too, as all sports halls will. Yesterday Glaucus and I had agreed not to bring Helena, Albia, and my young nephews in here – even if it had been possible. Today I stared at the occupants, but this was definitely not my kind of hole. Back home, Glaucus senior's gym at the rear of the Temple of Castor was just as exclusive, yet it had an air of civilisation – not to mention a peaceful library and a man on the steps selling hot pastries. Nobody came here to read. It was just a fighting pit for bullies. Glaucus had somehow talked his way in, on the strength of his size and visible prowess, but in an official year of the Games neither Young Glaucus nor I would have got anywhere near the inside.

I wondered whether Phineus ever managed to infiltrate the men on his tours. I bet he did. I bet that was why they all thought he was good.

Working around the open court I had to sidestep around several slobs looking for a quarrel. I had outsider written all over me. I only hoped my name and mission had not been passed on to these bruisers, as it had been passed yesterday to the guides in the sanctuary.

Glaucus liked the long jump. He had told me where to find him at practice today – a long room off the southern colonnade, which had side benches for spectators, though it was possible to look in from the corridor too. A musician was playing double pipes which he had tied to his brow with headbands in a curious traditional way. He was meant to assist the athletes with their concentration and rhythm. The fluting sounds were an odd contrast to the mood of aggression elsewhere. I almost expected to discover a roomful of dancing girls.

No chance of that. I could not imagine what I considered normal sex ever happening here. Two centuries of Roman rule had not changed the atmosphere in any Greek palaestra. The erotic charge was automatic. A palaestra was where young men congregated and older men openly came to gape at their beauty and strength, hoping for more. Even I was being sized up. At thirty-five, scarred and sneering, I was safe from old goats wanting to ask my father for permission to sponsor, seduce, and smooch me. Just as well. Pa would probably bellow with laughter, extract a big bribe, and hand me straight over.

It was a relief to sidle into the sanded practice room.

'Falco! You all right?' Glaucus looked nervous. He was supposed to be my bodyguard. I could see him regretting that he had told me just to turn up.

'Don't worry; I can handle those idiots.' He believed it. His father trained me. 'You watch yourself, Glaucus!' Glaucus shrugged, unfazed. He was good-looking enough to be a target, but seemed utterly unaware of it.

Before he joined me on the spectators' bench, he finished his next jump. No run-up; the skill is in the standing start. I watched, as he prepared himself on a take-off board. The musician went into a strong rhythmic beat. Glaucus fixed his mind on the jump. In each hand he was holding a weight. He swung them back, then swept his arms forwards, using the weights to propel himself. He was good. He flew across the sand, straightened his legs, and flexed, making a clean landing. I applauded. So did a couple of sleek young bystanders, attracted by this handsome dark-skinned stranger. I waved them away. I didn't care if they thought Glaucus and I were lovers, so long as they slunk off and left us to talk privately.

Weights were hanging on the walls – lead and iron varieties, in pairs, mostly boat-shaped at the bottom, with top handles to grip. These were familiar to me. My father sold a popular range of fake Greek vases and amphorae, which he claimed had been prizes at the Panathenaic Games; his discus and javelin throwers were most popular but there was one version which showed a long-jump competition. Pa's artist was quite adept at red-figure Greeks, bearded, with pointed noses, slightly hooked shoulders, and outstretched legs as they completed throws or leaps. Many an over-confident connoisseur had been bamboozled into buying.

Glaucus saw me inspecting the displayed weights, and shook his head. Opening his left palm, he showed me one he had been using. It was a different design. This was made of stone, a simple double-ended cylindrical shape, like a small dumb-bell, with fingers carved into the body to grip. 'These are what we moderns use, Falco! Those old things are just hung up as a historical memento.' He passed me the modern weight; my hand dropped. It must have weighed five or six Roman pounds. 'About twice as much as the old kind. And you can get some even heavier.'

'Is this your own?'

'Oh yes. I use the ones I'm used to.'

'I know jumping is difficult – but don't these make life even harder?'

Glaucus smiled. 'Practice, Falco!'

'Do they really help propel you further?'

'Oh yes. They add several extra feet to a jump.'

'They certainly turn *you* into a sandflea!' I applauded him, grinning. Then I became serious. 'I wonder which type was used on Valeria?'

Glaucus was ahead of me. He signalled to the musician, who stopped piping. He was a pallid wisp, malnourished and insignificant, who had been improvising while we talked; his tuneless drivel told us he was the off-season act. 'Falco, I'd like you to meet Myron.' The musician started a bow, then lost confidence. 'Myron, tell Falco what you told me.'

'About the woman who was killed?'

'Valeria Ventidia, a Roman visitor. Was she known around here in the practice rooms? Had she been hanging about the athletes?' I asked.

'No. It's not allowed.'

'Was the palaestra busy at that time?'

'It's very quiet this year. Just a few stragglers and people who turn up on spec.'

'So tell me about the murder. You heard how it happened? Did the weight used in the murder belong to someone in particular?'

'No, it was taken from the wall here. It was found in the porch afterwards, covered with blood and strands of the girl's hair.'

'Tell him about the weight, Myron,' Glaucus urged.

'It was very old, historic, very unusual. Formed in the shape of a wild boar.'

'Any chance I could see it?' I would have liked to examine it, even after all this time, but Myron said the bloodstained weight and its partner had been taken away.

'Where was the young woman found? In the porch too?'

'The slaves who come at first light to clean and to rake the sand found her lying in the *skamma*.'

70

'She was killed *inside* the palaestra?'

'It seems so.'

'Was there any evidence at the scene? If she was battered, there would have been blood –'

Both Glaucus and the piper laughed. 'Falco, the *skamma* is the practice ground for boxing and pankration!' Glaucus was shaking his head at my gaffe.

'There is blood in the *skamma* sand every day.' The piper had to emphasise the point. 'Who knows whose blood it is?' He chortled, showing the casual heartlessness that might have been encountered by Caesia's father and Valeria's husband when they appealed for help.

'So, what's the story? What do people think?' I demanded. 'Look, if a museum-piece weight was used, it may have been taken down from the wall display to show to the girl. There are plenty of the new ones lying around –'

'To *show* her?' Glaucus was clearly an innocent.

'I imagine,' I told him, feeling old, 'it is a well-worn chat line in athletics circles. Approach an attractive young lady, who looks easily impressed. Try out the enticing ploy: *Come to the palaestra and see my jumping weights.*'

'Ah!' Glaucus had rallied, though he coloured. 'Well, I suppose that's better than: *Look at my big discus, little girl!*'

XIII

I asked the piper to introduce me to the palaestra super-intendent. Glaucus removed himself, in case he was detected as an interloper in their high-grade club. He took himself off to the gymnasium for a spot of javelin practice.

Myron performed the introduction I had requested.

The palaestra chief lived in a small office that smelt like a cupboard full of very old loincloths. He was a six-foot monster, whose neck was wider than his head; he could only have started life as a boxer. He still wore a leather skullcap as his daily headgear. From the state of his face, he was not particularly successful and had suffered at the hands of rivals. He had two cauliflower ears and a broken nose, with one eye permanently closed. When Myron saw me adding up the damage, the musician whispered, 'You should see his opponents!' Then he slid off somewhere else fast.

I spoke to the superintendent very politely, in his own language. 'Sorry to bother you. My name is Marcus Didius Falco. I have come from Rome to look into what happened to Valeria Ventidia, the young woman who was murdered here.'

'Stupid little bitch!' His voice was less powerful than his stature suggested. His attitude lived up to expectations.

'I know it's a nuisance.' I kept my voice level. It was certainly possible she had behaved stupidly. 'Can you tell me the background?'

Suspicion slowly worked its way into his one eye. 'You working for the family?'

'Worse than that, I'm afraid. I'm looking for a story to stop the family petitioning the Emperor – if a good story exists. I gather that a fuss was made here at the time and now

72

the stink has wafted all the way back to Rome. I am supposed to find out whether we can blame the girl, or better still of course, blame her husband.'

'Blame *her*!' he snorted.

'You know that for sure?'

'Nobody knows anything for sure. My people found her cluttering up the *skamma*. I had her thrown out into the porch. I don't allow women – alive or dead!'

I quashed an indignant retort. 'Someone must have brought her in behind your back?'

'If it was up to me, I would bar women for a twenty-mile radius.'

'Plenty of people feel the same way?' If his attitude was common among competitors and male spectators, it could make life very uncomfortable for women visitors.

'We ought to go back to the old days – women were hurled from the Typaean cliffs!'

'Bit drastic?'

'Not drastic enough.'

'And now?'

'They get refused entry to the events. But the silly whores come wandering all over the place. If I catch the bastard who sneaked one in here, I'll break every bone in his body.' He meant it.

As for the woman, if this tyrant had caught her in his precious palaestra, would he go as far as killing her? I reckoned if he had done, he would be boasting more.

'I take it your palaestra stays open after normal hours?'

'We never lock up. The porter knocks off but we leave out a few lamps, in case competitors are desperate for a last practice.'

'Why should anyone be desperate this year?'

'What's your point, Falco?'

'No Games, no competitors. No competition, no need for late-night practice. The aficionados aren't coming till next year. I bet this place was deserted. Anyone could slip in a girlfriend and hope for his fun undisturbed.'

The superintendent glowered. His bad eye watered.

'Athletes who come here are dedicated. They practise full time.'

'You can't have it all ways. If athletes were in here, I want to know who they were, and I'll question them . . .' The superintendent was not going to tell me. I guessed they weren't around that night, so I left it. 'Had the woman been bothering your members, all doe-eyed?'

'I'd like to see her try! My members have only one thing on their minds.'

'Really?'

'You haven't got the first idea. Dedication. They go in front of the statue of Zeus Horkios to swear they have been in training for ten months. That's just the start. The judges have to confirm that accredited contenders have practised, at Elis or here, for a whole month, under Olympic supervision. They are got in shape by coaches and doctors, they have diet and exercise regimens laid down for every minute of the day – bugger it, they even have their sleep regulated.'

There was no mileage in restating that this was not an Olympic year; I went along with him. 'So the last thing those boys want is some skirt messing with their brains?'

The superintendent was still giving me the 'looks can kill' glare he had developed for the start of his fights, when each man paces around trying to make his opponent concede from sheer terror. 'Let me tell you – they tie a tight piece of string around their prick and even if they have any energy to spare for screwing, they can't get it up!'

I winced. Anyone who has ever entered a gymnasium has heard that story. Nobody I ever knew had really seen it done. Even so, I knew the slang: '"Putting the dog on the lead"?'

'Get you!' The superintendent had a punch-drunk brain. There was so little undamaged sweetbread in his skull, only one idea could feature. 'The brazen bride must have been meeting a lover, but it was not one of my members. Some bastard outsider slipped her in after hours, then she played him up and he cracked her one –'

'Several, as I heard. Can I see the weight that killed her?'

'It's not here.' I did not believe him. I bet he had snaffled it to gloat over. However, he was too big to argue with. 'She deserved a bashing,' he reckoned.

Helena Justina would protest that no woman 'deserves' murder. Until I knew just how Valeria was lured here, I would reserve judgement. If she flaunted herself, she was stupid. 'Tell me about afterwards, then. Wasn't there a magistrate dabbling with the investigation?'

'Aquillius. From Corinth. Thank the gods he's taken himself back there.'

'On the governor's staff?'

'Bloody quaestor.' Some youngster in his first ever senatorial post, then. In fact, not even ensconced in the Senate; just serving in a minor finance post in order to show he was fit for election. Bound to know nothing. Bound to have messed up. Bound to get uppity if I ever told him so.

'Anybody here on the site I ought to report to?' I asked. 'Don't want to step on toes. Who took the most interest here?'

'Lacheses. In the Altis. At the Priests' House.'

'Chief priest?'

'Zeus, no! Chief priest has better things to worry about.'

I thanked him, though it hurt to do so, and he swore at me again. I got out of there, with cold sweat running down my back.

I went to see the priest. This was about as useful as scratching a gnat-bite with a feather. Still, it had to be done.

The Priests' House was on the north side of the Altis, in the shadow of the Hill of Cronus, near the Prytaneion where victory feats took place. It was not the main administrative centre for the Games, but it contained council rooms where meetings could be held. Presumably the shrine attendants could use it as a secular drop-in when they were off duty. I was so secular I was kept in the porch. It took nearly an hour for Lacheses to deign to appear.

He was lean and louche. Few priests are as venerable as you imagine; this one was about thirty – some winner in the social lottery who could as easily have ended up with a tax-farming concession instead of a religious post. He wore a long tuft of beard, twirled up at the end, and he really thought he looked good with it.

I had told him, in Latin, that I represented Vespasian. He replied in Greek. 'I am here to help.' He had a special slimy tone for dismissing intruders who came asking awkward questions: 'The death of the young woman was deeply regrettable. Everybody grieved for her. Please transmit our assurances to the Emperor: it was properly investigated at the time. A senior official from Corinth concluded there was no evidence to bring charges. Nothing more could be done. Nothing more can be said.' He said it anyway. 'We would prefer that the sanctity of this holy place should now be allowed to resume undisturbed.'

'So would I.' I had given up and agreed to use Greek. There was grit in my throat. 'I mean, *I* would prefer that young females from Rome should stop dropping dead at your sanctuary.'

He gave me the chin-up look with his tufty beard again, as if he were an Olympic judge on one of Pa's red-figure vases. If he had had a judge's long stick in his hand, he would have jabbed me with it.

'Are you responsible, Lacheses, for clearing the site where the party had pitched camp?' He looked indignant; I just managed to restrain myself from grabbing him by the priestly robes and squeezing his windpipe until he wet himself. 'Settle down. I realise the ground had been polluted.' I bet nobody had ever said the far more polluted palaestra porch and *skamma* needed to be kept out of bounds to members until they had been sprinkled with holy water and an olive branch. Nothing would interfere with sport. 'Were any clues found at the campsite?'

'Nothing significant.'

'What was learned about the young woman?'

'She had quarrelled with her husband.'

It was the first I had heard of it, though I was not surprised. 'That's definite?'

'Several of her companions had heard them. He did not deny it.'

'What were they fighting about?'

The priest looked astonished. 'I have no idea.'

'Nice respect for the confidences of the marriage bed! Don't you think it might be relevant? Might this quarrel not explain why, if he did kill her, the husband was moved to do it?'

'Nobody is accusing the husband,' the priest assured me suddenly. He had smelt the danger of a libel or mal-administration charge. 'Everything was investigated. Nothing pointed to any particular suspect. There are people coming and going all the time at Olympia. It was obvious that the killer was probably a stranger, and that in the mêlée after the death was discovered, he must have slipped away.'

'Visitors to the shrine were allowed to disperse?'

'Oh we could not possibly –'

'Forget it! No one expects you to corral your pilgrims, just for one little dead Roman girl. Are you expecting this happy killer back on your patch next Olympics?'

'That is in the hands of the gods.'

I lost my temper. 'Unfortunately we live in modern times. I am starting to think, Lacheses, that my role will be calling the gods to account. You have just under a year before your sanctuary is flooded with people – my advice is, use that time to catch this man!'

The priest raised his eyebrows, appalled at my attitude. 'Have you finished, Falco?'

'No. What about the *other* girl? What about Marcella Caesia, whose father found her bones on the Hill of Cronus, a year after she had disappeared?'

He sighed. 'Another regrettable incident –'

'And how was that investigated?'

'Before my time, I fear.'

'Fear is the right emotion,' I warned him. 'These deaths are about to fly right in your face, like evils whizzing out of Pandora's jar.' I resorted to fable for my own satisfaction; like my anger, it was lost on Lacheses. 'If I find out that *anybody* in this retreat or the overblown sports hall attached to it had a hand in Marcella Caesia's death or that of Valeria Ventidia, holy retribution will be spreading like plague here – and anyone who has fobbed me off will be the first to answer!'

I sensed that the priest was about to call for guards, so I spun around and left.

Was it not Hope that remained in the jar after Pandora meddled? Not that I had much hope in this case.

XIV

The harassing morning had brought me one advance: I now knew first hand why Caesius Secundus felt he was given the run-around. I could see why he became frustrated and obsessed. I could even understand why the Tullius family had limply given up and got on with their lives. Bitterness and anger rose in my mouth like bile.

I strode across the Altis, heading for the south-east corner where at the back of Nero's half-finished villa there was an exit through the boundary wall. Halfway there I passed a decrepit wooden pillar. In its slight shade I came across my group: the tall, white-clad figure of Helena Justina; Albia, slightly shorter and livelier; chunky Cornelius; Gaius, scowling as usual as he plotted revenge on society for imagined slights. I did my duty and snarled a greeting.

'Marcus, my darling! We have been having a tourist morning. We fixed up a special "Pelops" circuit for ourselves.'

I was in no mood for happy tourism, and said so. Helena still looked pale, and moved sluggishly. 'I thought you were back at the room, doubled up,' I accused her.

She pulled a face. 'Too much oil in the doorman's sister's oregano and lamb hotpot, maybe. Now look – My brother's letter said Valeria and the other women were taken on a circuit of Pelops memorabilia, the day Valeria died.'

I groaned at the thought, but I gave in. Helena made everyone sit on the ground in a circle, in the shade of a couple of palm trees.

'This is the last pillar from the Palace of Oenomaus.' She pointed to the misshapen wooden shard where I had found them. 'You will be disappointed to notice that none of the suitors' severed heads has lasted.' Even the pillar had hardly lasted. It was silvered and rotting away. It reminded me of a balcony when I lived in Fountain Court; I had prodded the wood, and my fist went right through the supporting beam.

'At least its poor condition has saved it from having "Titus was here" carved all over it by visiting Romans.' Gaius and Cornelius immediately sauntered over to the pillar, in case after all there was a sound spot they could desecrate.

Pulling me round to face to the west, Helena directed my attention to a walled enclosure. 'Cornelius, come back here and tell Uncle Marcus what we learned about that ancient monument.'

Cornelius looked scared. My sister Allia was an easygoing lump who never quizzed him on lessons. He had been to school. Ma paid for it. She had wasted her money; Cornelius could hardly write his name. Still, Helena had been ramming facts into him. 'It's the burial mound of Pelops,' Cornelius recited. 'It is called the Pelopion.'

'Good boy! The mound must be a tomb only, Marcus, for we have seen the bronze chest that contains his mighty bones. All except what, Gaius?'

Gaius smirked at Cornelius, knowing he had got the easy question. 'Shoulder blade! Gigantic. Made of ivory.'

'Correct. Albia, how did that come about?'

Albia grimaced. 'This story is disgusting. You will like it, Marcus Didius.'

'Oh thanks!'

'Pelops is the son of Tantalus, who was a son of Zeus, though not a god, only a king. Tantalus invited all the gods from Mount Olympus to a party on a mountain top –'

'He wanted to test if the gods were really all-knowing,' Helena helped out.

'Everyone brought food for a lucky-dip picnic. The gods put nectar and ambrosia in their hampers. Tantalus served up a stew, to see if they would realise what they were eating.'

'What was it? The doorman's sister's oregano hotpot?' I asked.

'Ugh. Worse. Tantalus had killed and cooked up his own

son, Pelops! The gods *did* notice – but not before Demeter the Harvest Queen had eaten her way all through a shoulder bone.'

'She was grieving for her daughter, and rather absent-minded.' A faraway look came over Helena, and I knew she was thinking of Julia and Favonia. 'Then?'

'Then Rhea chucked all the bones back in the pot, gave it a big stir, and reassembled little Pelops, giving him a new shoulder made of ivory.'

'Which you have *seen*? Don't you believe it!' I scoffed. They glowered at me, wanting to believe the myth.

'Tantalus was horribly punished!' Cornelius had become keen on divine retribution. 'He must stay in Hades for ever, staring at a plate of food and a cup of drink, which he can never reach.'

'That wouldn't suit you, Cornelius.'

'No, but Pelops was better than ever after he was mended, and went out into the world to be a hero.'

'So that was when he came to Olympia and cheated in the chariot race?'

'No choice, Marcus.' Helena was smiling. 'Oenomaus was challenging his daughter's suitors using a set of magic, unbeatable steeds.'

'Unfair! But Pelops had his own magic horses, didn't he? Given to him by Poseidon?'

'Perhaps. In a different version, Hippodameia was as keen on Pelops as he was on her. She was desperate not to see his handsome head skewered above the lintel. So she went to her father's charioteer, Myrtilos, and persuaded him to sabotage Oenomaus' chariot by putting in a wax cotter-pin, making a wheel fall off. Now Myrtilos, rightly or wrongly, thought he had agreed to spike the chariot in order to sleep with Hippodameia himself. After the race he tried to claim his reward. Pelops and Myrtilos fought; Pelops drowned Myrtilos in the sea, but as he finally went under, Myrtilos called down a curse on all the descendants of Pelops and Hippodameia. They had, of course, two bonny sons, Atreus and Thyestes.'

81

I wagged a finger. 'I sense a bout of Homer coming on!'

'There is more to your Uncle Marcus than a tough nature and a cheeky grin,' Helena told the boys. 'He comes scowling along, fresh from haranguing witnesses, then suddenly he demonstrates how much he reads. So your turn, Marcus.'

'I'm grown up. I don't have to recite lessons.' The boys looked impressed by my rebellion.

Helena sighed. 'Spoilsport. It's a second helping of human stew, I'm afraid. Atreus and Thyestes quarrelled incessantly over their inheritance. Finally Atreus cut up all of his brother's children – except one – and served them at a feast where Thyestes was the guest of honour. Thyestes failed to spot the family's signature dish and he ate up heartily. The only survivor was called Aegisthus.'

Helena was flagging so I relented: 'The famous son of Atreus is King Agamemnon. His nagging wife is Clytemnestra. In his absence at the Trojan War, she becomes the lover of moody cousin Aegisthus. Aegisthus is getting revenge for the new stew incident; Clytemnestra is getting her lust satisfied. On his return from the Trojan War, these lovers murder Agamemnon, whose son and daughter then murder them, providing material for many tragedians.'

'The moral is: only eat salad. If a travel group are going on to see Troy,' said Helena, 'Olympia makes an appropriate starting point.'

'Yes, the Seven Sights group don't just get sport; they are on a drama-rich route. After a detour to Sparta, their next stop is Mycenae, Agamemnon's palace. Then Aulis, whence the Greek ships departed, and on to Troy – Troy is rubbish nowadays, I have heard, just touts and tacky souvenir stalls. So tell me, Helena, is that why you were fascinated with Pelops?' I asked.

'Well, he represents heroic mortal man. He seems to have had a bad conscience; there are a host of memorials he set up – Myrtilos, Oenomaus, the previous suitors –'

'Big of him. I'm damned if I'd honour your old lovers!'

'Didius Falco, you are an informer; you don't have a conscience.' Untrue. Helena knew that very well.

'The whole Peloponnese is named after Pelops!' chirped Cornelius. He had taken to showing off.

Gaius stretched out full length on his back. 'This place is stuffed with relics. As well as his shoulder bone we saw his ceremonial dagger with a gold pommel, in the Treasury of Sikyon –'

'And Hippodameia's couch,' said Albia. 'And her shrine.'

'Girls' stuff!' I mocked. 'Now look. I am glad you are all having a good time as sightseers, but we came to Greece on a case.'

'I *am* pursuing the case,' Helena growled. 'Imagine it. The men on the tour had become obsessed with all the bloody sports – boxing, wrestling, and ghastly pankration. The women were sick of the men coming home, prattling about violence and blood. They fixed up a Pelops tour as a distraction. Later that evening, Valeria went to her death – so I am trying to deduce what was in her mind that day.'

'Get anywhere with this theory?'

'I am wondering,' she carried on regardless, 'did the courtship of Hippodameia hold a special resonance for Valeria? If she had found she was unhappy with her own new husband, was she affected by the story of a spirited young woman who gained herself a man who really wanted her? Perhaps it made Valeria restless.'

I gazed at my girl thoughtfully. Helena herself had had an arranged marriage, to a weak man who failed her. She stuck it out miserably for a few years, then divorced him. I knew Helena remembered how depressed she had been, both in her marriage and after it fell through.

'Sweetheart, are you suggesting that Valeria Ventidia was afraid she had committed herself to second-best for ever, so became reckless of her own safety? She wanted to ditch Statianus and find herself an old-style hero?'

'No, I just suspect that while the women were trailing around the Altis hearing about Pelops, poor little Valeria accidentally caught her killer's eye.'

'So this brute offered her a ride in his racing chariot?' I suggested with a leer. Then more seriously, 'No, because whoever he was, I'm certain he drew her to the palaestra with sportsman's gossip about long jumps.'

'Couldn't afford a chariot,' Gaius intoned, with envy. 'Uncle Marcus, you have to own *millions* to race chariots. So much, it is the owners and not the drivers who receive the crowns for winning.'

'Right. Not a charioteer then.'

Helena pressed on. 'Another question: *who* took the women on the tour? None of the guides will own up.'

'Still, you managed to find the various relics by yourself.'

Gaius rolled on to his stomach as he and Cornelius chorused, *'Helena is clever!'*

'Well, why are the guides so sneery? Pelops is the founder of the Games.'

'Or it's Hercules!' Helena told me. 'Anyway, the cult adherents want to keep this site as primarily dedicated to Zeus. Pelops is relegated, a mere symbol of human endeavour. The gods rule this grove.'

'And Zeus is top god . . . Well, I'd say the women's Pelops excursion has no bearing on what happened to Valeria.'

Cornelius was looking anxious. 'At least she wasn't chopped up and eaten in a stew!' It was a shock to discover that I had a nephew who was sensitive. 'Uncle Marcus, is it safe here? I won't end up in a pot being eaten, will I?'

'You take care. Even Zeus himself had a narrow escape,' Helena teased him. 'Cronus, his father, who used to be king of the heavens, had been warned that a son of his would depose him. Every time a child was born, he ate it. After she bore Zeus, his mother had to hide the baby, disguised as a stone, hung between heaven and earth where Cronus would not find him and gobble him up.'

Cornelius covered his ears and ran off, squealing.

That grisly tale brought my attention back to the Hill of Cronus, where Marcella Caesia had died, with her body laid out under the stars, until her stubborn father came at last and found her. A Roman parent, more caring of his daughter than the average mythical Greek.

Gloomily I wondered what was happening to Julia Junilla

84

and Sosia Favonia back in Rome. My mother-in-law kept a quiet house. I was fairly sure the noble Julia would not issue any challenge to the gods at a pot-luck picnic. Her cook would be spoiling my daughters with treats – our worst problem would be bringing them back to normality when we returned home.

XV

We were running out of options.

We were low on food too. Helena had told the doorman we would skip having meals from his sister. She had put together a scratch supper with purchases from site vendors. There was bread, and some vine leaf parcels, with the remains of our Roman sausage.

'I need to have meat!' Young Glaucus complained, ranting that Milo of Croton, the most famous Olympic athlete of all time, had eaten twenty pounds of meat and twenty pounds of bread a day, washed down with eighteen pints of wine. 'Milo trained by carrying a calf on his shoulders. As it grew day by day and week by week into a full-size ox, the effect was like cumulative weight training. In the end, he ate the whole ox in a single sitting.'

'We are not lugging a bull calf around with us, Glaucus, even if you volunteer to carry him. Anyway, Milo of Croton was a wrestler. Anyone can tell from your pretty face that you are not.'

'Pentathlon,' Glaucus disabused me. 'Discus, javelin, long jump, foot race – and wrestling.'

'So how come your beautiful physiognomy has never been ruined?'

'It's three out of five. First athlete to win three events, wins overall. Remaining trials are cancelled. I try to come through in the early bouts, so I won't have to wrestle.' He gave a slow grin. 'Or when the opponent looks like a crusher or a gouger, I always concede.'

'But *secretly*,' demanded Gaius, 'are you a crack crusher yourself?'

'Not really,' said Glaucus.

Then he went out to hang around the many shrines in the Altis, hoping for a sacrifice in process. Even when the hundred oxen were slaughtered at the Games, only the legs, tails and guts were carried up the steps on the Altar of Zeus. The body steaks were used to feed the crowd.

Before he left, Glaucus said, 'Falco, the killer of Valeria is probably an athlete, yes? Assume he chose a sport he knew: only a pentathlete would use the jumping weights. Long-jumping only happens in the pentathlon.'

'Thanks, Glaucus. I agree he is most likely an athlete – is now, or has been in the past. A pentathlete would fit neatly, but life isn't like that. I think he could be anyone familiar with the palaestra – boxer, wrestler, even a pankration fighter. It's depressing. I don't fancy trying to interrogate every hardened Olympic champion, in case one of them kills girls.'

'All the current champions will have gone on the circuit,' Glaucus reminded me.

'How many Games on the circuit, Glaucus?'

He grinned. 'Well, the big four are the Pan-Hellenics: Olympia, Delphi, Nemea and the Isthmus, which don't happen every year. The Panathenaic in Athens is annual. Add in all the other cities – well, you are looking at about fifty, Falco.'

Oh, easy then!

Helena Justina slept peacefully that night. I remembered how last night, when she kept creeping out to be ill after the oregano hotpot, I had woken once to an unexpectedly empty bed. I sat up in alarm, my heart pounding. At that moment I knew all too well how Tullius Statianus must have felt – assuming he did have some feelings for Valeria – alone in his campbed, when she never came home.

The vine leaf parcels went through me like a rat down a drain. It was my turn to be groaning and drenched in sweat all night. My turn too, as I lay tossing and waiting for the next agonising onslaught, to wonder why anybody ever wanted to travel.

87

I was not the only one awake. The sound of crying drew me
to the boys' room. By moonlight through an open shutter, I
saw a piteous spectacle. Cornelius was sobbing his heart out,
overwhelmed by homesickness. He had never even left
Rome before, and had had no real concept of how long we
would be travelling. I sat on the bed to console him, and next
thing I was trapped there by the hefty, tear-stained eleven-
year-old, who had fallen fast asleep.

I dragged my arm from under him and straightened him
out so he wouldn't fall off the narrow mattress if he flailed
around. I covered him up with a thin blanket for comfort,
then tortured myself again with sentimental thoughts of
Julia and Favonia back in Rome. Who was tending *my* little
ones, if they cried in the night?

Settle down, Falco. They were safe. They had four old
slave nursemaids who had looked after their mother once,
their noble grandma, their doting grandpa, and if all else
failed each of my materially spoiled darlings would be
tucked up in bed with a whole row of dolls and miniature
animals.

Somewhere in the Altis an owl hooted. My stomach
emitted a lugubrious glug. I sat still, using the time before
my next bout of suffering to think. Diarrhoea can be the
informer's friend.

I could see the dim shapes of Gaius (snoring) and Glaucus
(breathing the slow measure of the fit) in two other narrow
beds. Had the Leonidaion been more crowded, perhaps all of
us would have had to share a room. We had made our
resources stretch to two rooms. Seeking economy, Helena
and I had Albia in with us, which rather inhibited marital
affection. We put up with that – or found ways around it. All
our accommodation was on an upper storey, or I might have
closed the shutter even in the boys' room to keep out thieves
and amorous gods disguised as silver moonbeams.

Now I started wondering about sleeping arrangements
among the Seven Sights Travel group, at least when they
were not camping. According to the list Aulus left us, the

group contained a family of four; well, they might bunk up together. Then there were three couples, of whom one was the newly-weds and another seemed to be eloping adulterers; both of those pairs would presumably be anxious for privacy. Completing the group were four – no, five – single people: one female and four male, including Volcasius, the weird one, with whom nobody would ever want to share. Some would have brought slaves, whom the snobbish Aulus had not bothered to list. It could mean that when they stayed at an inn, Phineus had to find them nine rooms, not to mention whatever he wanted for himself, their drivers, and any run-arounds (who must exist, though Aulus had not listed them either).

That meant, either Phineus routed them on main roads, where there might be good, Roman-style mansios – official or semi-official travel lodges with high standards of accommodation and stabling – or else this misfit party of wealthy innocents would find themselves lumped together in all sorts of combinations. On the boat over, they would have been lucky to find even one cabin. Arriving at Olympia, to be faced with just a couple of large tents for the whole group, must have been their first big, bad experience on this trip. For some of them, a serious shock. And they had then been forced to stay camped out on the riverbank for weeks, while Valeria's death was investigated.

By the time they returned to their itinerary these people, who had been strangers to start with, would have known each other very well indeed.

I needed to find them and study them myself. But, as dawn broke and my guts settled down at last, I went out to do one more piece of sleuthing at Olympia. Cornelius stirred, so I woke him and took him with me, as a treat. It turned out to be a bigger adventure than either of us expected.

XVI

It was barely light. All over the Empire slaves were rousing themselves, or being roused by short-tempered overseers. The most unlucky were stumbling grey-faced to hard labour in the mines, to do appalling, filthy work that would slowly kill them. The fortunate merely had to lay out a clean toga or tidy fine scrolls in a beautiful library. By far the majority would be gathering brooms, buckets, and sponges, ready to clean houses, workshops, temples, baths – and gymnasia.

Nobody barred our entry. Cornelius and I went through the palaestra porch into the colonnade. Anyone watching – as somebody must have been – would have seen my nephew bumbling after me, still with his eyes half-closed and clutching the back of my tunic like one of Augustus' anxious little grandchildren in that parade on Rome's Altar of Peace. Not that Cornelius would ever have been taken on an educational outing to see the Altar of Peace. All my sister Allia had ever taught her children was how to borrow from relatives. Verontius thought being a good father meant bringing home a fruit pie once a week; when he wanted to be a *very* good father, he bought two.

Cornelius needed wise adult attention or he would grow up like his parents. An onlooker would have seen me turn back to encourage the sleepy-head, tousling his hair affectionately. Someone may well have worked out that they could get to me through him.

A small band of workers in drab tunics was lazily raking down the dampened sand of the *skamma*. Wherever these slaves originated, they all had the same short build and swarthy features. A couple of torches flared in iron holders. Moths clung to the stonework nearby. Above the great courtyard, the sky was bleached but visible. It grew marginally brighter, as a hot Greek day began. People instinctively spoke in hushed voices, because the day was still too young for socialising.

At my signal, the slaves sauntered over and surrounded us.

I stretched, speaking slowly and hoarsely. 'Don't you just hate this time of the morning? It's all whispers and croaks, and finding out who died in the night . . . I need some help, please. Will you tell me about when you discovered the murdered Roman girl?'

As I had hoped, they were open to enquiry. Most slaves love a chance to stop and talk. No one in authority had thought it important to order them to keep quiet on the subject. If he had known I was coming, the superintendent would have done, if only to annoy me.

They had found Valeria in a corner, with the sand in chaos around her as though she had tried desperately to escape on hands and knees. She was curled up defensively, blood everywhere. Blood and sand were clogged together on her clothing; she was fully clad which, the slaves agreed, suggested things had gone wrong quite early in her encounter with the killer. They had noticed that there was also dust on her dress, the kind of dust athletes used to cover their oiled bodies. I had seen it being applied the other day, flicked on with the palm of the hand and open fingers, so it hung in the air of the application room in clouds. On Valeria the sand was yellow, always admired for giving the body a subtle golden glow; not that that helped me much. Yellow was the most popular colour.

When informed, the superintendent had ordered the slaves to throw out the body. They had lifted her up and taken her to the porch, where they placed her in a sitting position (so she looked more lifelike and took up less room). They were still standing around there when Tullius Statianus turned up.

He started screaming. He squatted on his heels, weeping

and staring. The superintendent heard the racket and came out from his office. He ordered Statianus to remove the corpse. After pleading for help, Statianus yelled abuse at the superintendent. Then he gathered up his battered young wife, and staggered off towards the campsite, with her in his arms.

'From what you say, Statianus was genuine. Not behaving like a man who had killed her?'

'No chance. He couldn't believe what had happened.'

That was interesting, though the unforced evidence of slaves would not count in a lawcourt. I tried to elicit names of any palaestra members who might have been suspect, but the slaves abruptly lost interest and started drifting back to their work.

We should have left. You never do. You always hope one last cunning question will produce a breakthrough. You never learn.

Then I heard a gasp. I turned around, and my heart lurched. An enormous man had arrived without me noticing and grabbed Cornelius. Now he was squeezing all the breath out of the boy.

XVII

The huge wrestler was waiting for me to turn and see it happening. Now the muscle-bound child-crusher lifted my nephew above his shaved head, intending to hurl him to the ground. On hard, damp sand, it could be fatal.

The brute paused, leering.

He was in his mid-twenties, his absolute prime. Solid waist, huge calves, astounding thighs, monumental shoulders. Apart from a leather skullcap and boxing thongs, he was stark naked. His fabulous body was covered with olive oil – there was so much I could smell it – over which he had applied a thick layer of grey dust.

There was a wrestler, once, who stepped into the high road and stopped a chariot going at full pelt. This man could do that. He could stop the traffic one-handed, while eating a bread roll. Milo of Croton used to stand on a discus, holding up a pomegranate and defying all comers to remove the fruit from him. Only his girlfriend could do it, but she must have known where he was ticklish. Oh for a willowy wench with sensual hands who could give a therapeutic massage!

'Put the child down and let's talk!' Greek wrestlers do not talk. They glare, circle, grasp opponents in rib-cracking clinches, then slog away without time limits, until one hulk has thrown the other three times to the floor. Or until one is so badly hurt he cannot continue. Or, even better, one is dead.

The wrestler shook Cornelius, to make me even more anxious.

'He's a boy. He's not in your age class. Obey the rules!' My pleas were desperate. Held up at arms' length, with one mighty fist around both his ankles and another gripping the

93

scruff of his neck, Cornelius was ashen, too terrified to whimper. 'Put him down. He's done nothing. I understand what's going on – someone does not like my investigation and you've been sent to dissuade me. So put down the boy and murder me instead.'

The giant let out a bloodcurdling cry, a part of his act. He bent his arms suddenly, elbows wide, as if about to hurl Cornelius across the *skamma*. The watching slaves stepped back nervously. From facing sky up to heading sand down, my nephew swung over like a rag, his chubby arms dangling. One free hand balled into a fist as if it was intentional and clocked the wrestler in the eye. The giant shook his head as if a wine-fly had flown at his lashes – but then, as you do, he just had to brush his eye with the back of his wrist, so he let go of Cornelius.

I leapt and captured the boy as he fell. To me, he was damned heavy. I managed to drop him to the ground fairly gently, though I wrenched my back. Then the wrestler knocked me flat. I sprawled on the sand; one-handed, I somehow shoved Cornelius out of danger. The wrestler kicked me away from him; I fell full length, eating sand.

Next the giant pulled me upright by one arm, looking disdainful. Neatly, he arranged the arm behind my back, paying attention to inflicting pain. I jumped around and struggled to position one leg behind his. To know the move was useless; he was six foot three and with my weight I could not budge his trunk-like calves. He held his stance, while I manoeuvred helplessly. He was playing with me. If he had been ready to finish me, I would be feeling his fists. Those fists were bound with hard rawhide, the heavy thongs extending up his forearms; bands of fleece allowed him to wipe away sweat, though he had shed none yet. Barely exerting himself, he bent me forwards like a girl folding up a blanket.

Then, with a sudden growl of annoyance, he tossed me on to the sand. Ideally I would have pulled him over with me. No chance. Arching my back in recovery, I saw that Cornelius had attached himself to the giant's left foot; the boy was bending the man's great toes backwards with all his might. The furious wrestler twisted, as he kicked out to shake Cornelius off. I threw myself into the fray again, this time attempting a headlock from behind. It was like wrapping an arm around a half-submerged pile on a waterfront and trying to strangle solid oak. I did my best to throttle him with one hand, while punching him in the ear. I doubt if he even felt it. The punch was legal in Greek boxing and pankration. He just shrugged me off his neck dismissively and brought me around within reach. Then he grabbed me in a ghastly hug and turned me upside down.

He rammed me to the floor, straight on my head. I managed to put an arm out, lessening the impact. I took the force on my neck and shoulder, but had no chance to re-engage. I was now at his mercy, yet the death blows never came.

'Falco!'

Assistance had arrived: Young Glaucus. He must have followed us down here – though he might be about to regret it. Despite our friend's mighty build, the giant wrestler was half as big again. When I struggled to a sitting position, they were squaring up. The giant bared his gums in a hideous grimace. He flared his nostrils. He produced a hideous gurning stare. His chest swelled. His biceps bulged. I had been a mere diversion; attacking Glaucus would be a real treat for him.

Our normally cautious Glaucus had to accept the challenge. Deliberately he drew off his tunic and threw it to me; he stood naked and proud, without oil and dust, but ready to fight. The giant gave him time to grasp a set of thongs from bunches hanging on the palaestra wall; Cornelius scrambled to help bind them on. All I could hear in my head was our friend's reply when Gaius had asked whether he could do this: *'Not really.'*

Oh Hades.

'Glaucus.' As he tightened the thongs, he introduced himself with a peremptory sneer.

'Milo.'

'Milo of *Croton*?' exclaimed Glaucus, betrayed into excitement.

'Milo of Dodona.' The giant enjoyed having fooled him. 'Oh!'

I was less surprised than Glaucus. It was not the first time I had met a modern hulk named after the six-times Olympic champion.

The fight began. Wrestling theorists will maintain that lighter, speedier men can use skill to outwit the heavies. A flyweight, they say, can nip in, kick away an ankle, and bring down a man-mountain . . . Sensible spectators do not bet on it. Glaucus knew that if this monster crushed him in a hug, it would be fatal. That must have been why Glaucus cheated.

They made a couple of feints matter-of-factly. They circled, scuffing sand like fighting bulls. The giant grunted, his slow brain deciding when he would let rip and smother Glaucus in a deadly embrace. Glaucus did not wait. He stooped, swiftly scooped up sand, and threw it in the giant's eyes. As his opponent roared and his eyes streamed, Glaucus then kicked him – with an admirable right-footed wrestling kick – full in his ostentatiously heavyweight testes.

Then Glaucus grabbed Cornelius and me and pulled us right across the *skamma* to the nearest exit.

'The sprint is my speciality. *Now let's run for our lives!*'

XVIII

We came out into the big gymnasium, where for a brief, foolish moment we caught our breath after the shock. Glaucus met my eye. For once he showed a sense of humour. 'Never be afraid of risk – but always know your limits!'

'Why can I hear your father's voice in that?'

We had a head start – but we had run the wrong way. Pain was Milo of Dodona's everyday stimulus; behind, we heard the monster bellow as he came after us. Glaucus pushed the boy and me ahead of him, as he stayed behind on diversion duty. I shepherded Cornelius, wishing we were out in the sanctuary where there might be some Greek city's treasury into which I could shove the puffing roly-poly child to be kept safe among the spoils of war. That's life; never a treasury when you want one . . .

We two ran across the end of the gym to a corner exit. Looking back, we saw Glaucus taunt the big man, then set off around the running track, trying to lure him that way. Milo of Dodona had his mind on one thing – and that was killing me.

'Cornelius – let's go!'

We hared out of the gymnasium, with the monster in hot pursuit. Glaucus failed to follow at once; I cursed his tactics. The boy and I came to the open-air swimming pool. A long expanse of serene water was warming up slowly in the morning sun on the bank of the River Kladeos. I pounded around the perimeter. Cornelius, too out of breath, had stopped, bent double and panting. Milo was almost on him. My nephew took a scared look; then he held his nose, jumped for it into the pool, and dogpaddled away like mad. The jump took him a yard or two, but his churning fists hardly moved him along. Milo hesitated, perhaps unable to swim. Well, that made two of us.

Glaucus had reappeared, holding something with one hand. I saw what he was up to. He stopped. In classic style, his body twisted back. He did a full three-quarter crouching turn, one leg bent, one shoulder dropped, then he spun back and unleashed his missile. Bronze glinted. A discus flew towards Milo. Once again, Young Glaucus was breaking rules; this time, the rule that says a discus thrower must ensure that no bystander is in his way.

The bronze plate caught Milo full on the base of his enormous skull. He never heard it coming. In the pool, Cornelius had turned on his back, mouth agape. Now he began a hasty backstroke, to avoid expected spume as the mighty man keeled forwards. In fact Milo landed on the edge of the pool. I covered my eyes as he smashed face down on the stone.

Cornelius reached the side; I hauled him out, dripping and shivering, and wrapped him in Glaucus' tunic. Glaucus himself had walked calmly up to the pool edge, considering whether the rules of combat required him to tender aid. He had a steelier mentality than I had thought; he decided against. In Greek athletics you win, by any means the judges will accept. The loser slinks off in shame – if he is still on his feet. 'Through the back alleys, home to mother', as they put it.

I took Cornelius to join Glaucus.

'He dead?'

'No.'

'Pity we can't just nip off – but I fear we have witnesses.'

Other people arrived, headed up by Lacheses, the damned priest who offended me yesterday. Affecting a superior air, he stood at the pool edge, ordering slaves to roll the wrestler over.

Today Lacheses wore full-length robes with a decorated hemline, and carried a spray of wild olive; this presumably signified he was attached to the Temple of Zeus. 'You nearly killed a pankration champion!'

'Him or us,' I answered curtly. 'Someone told him to attack me.' The priests of Zeus were my first choice for that. 'Glaucus my friend, I hope that your discus was of approved Olympic size.'

'Absolutely,' Young Glaucus responded, straight-faced. 'I took down an official standard from the gymnasium wall. Unfortunately for Milo, the ones used at Olympia are heavier than normal . . .' The priest drew a sharp breath at this disrespectful act. 'Mine was at home,' Glaucus apologised meekly.

I took a hand. 'Your champion wanted to kill us all. My friend had to act fast.'

'You abuse our hospitality!' snapped Lacheses. He had a quaint view of traditional guest-friendship. 'Your visit to our sanctuary must end. Leave Olympia before you cause more trouble.'

The crowd increased. A middle-aged woman pushed the priest aside. A satchel was slung diagonally over her travelling cloak; she wore a dress with brightly coloured borders, and a long matching veil, on which was pegged a high-pointed head-dress, an expensive gold *stephane*. A male attendant behind her was dressed in the long pleated robe of a charioteer. A younger woman held a pannier and looked on meekly. The female attendant was in a simple folded-over chiton, and had her hair rather attractively bound up in headscarves. She could have been a maiden on a vase, with a half-suggestive smile as she leaned on one elbow and poured perfume. Glaucus and I both flashed Roman smiles admiringly.

The matron in charge noticed and glared at us. A forceful presence. She shoved aside the slaves, then knelt beside the wrestler in a sprightly manner, checking him for vital signs. 'Well, gracious me, it's Milo of Dodona. Is he still hanging around Olympia? So devoted!'

'He can be taken to the doctors at the gymnasium –' Lacheses began.

'No, no; he will do better at the Temple of Hera, Lacheses. Let us look after him.'

Glaucus offered a hand, and the woman stood up, this time acknowledging that she had creaky knees. The priest bowed deferentially. She nodded, without wasting time on it, then told him she had brought him a pot of the preserved cherries he liked. That seemed to settle Lacheses.

Then she turned to me. 'I am Megiste. I am one of the Council of Sixteen.' It meant nothing. She explained briskly: 'In memory of the sixteen matrons of honour at the wedding of Hippodameia, the most respected women of Elis form a committee to organise the running races for maidens in the Games of Hera.' I bet they organised more than that.

The priest began to say something.

'I'll deal with this, Lacheses!' The wimp subsided. 'I have given some thought to the problem. It is all in hand. A wagon will take these people to the coast tomorrow; a ship will come from Kyllene to pick them up at Pheia.'

'Well, excuse me –' I should have known better.

'No, Falco!' How did she know my name? I came to the conclusion the Council of Sixteen knew pretty well everything. I hated interfering women of that type in public life. 'Strife is polluting the sanctuary. You must leave.'

'Oh, that's Elis for you.' I refused to be quashed. 'Always in there, brokering universal peace! You didn't need to set your champion to batter us,' I snarled bitterly to the priest. 'Just ask the matrons of Elis! This lady can fix up extradition for inconvenient visitors at the same time as she lays down a pantryful of salted olives, braids a four-colour floor rug, and cleans out her beehives.'

He gave me his priestly shrug. 'I hope you have enjoyed your time here, and found it uplifting.' He did let slip a trace of admiration. 'Let us hope Milo recovers.'

'Should do,' Glaucus assured him. 'The throw was at the end of its trajectory. He was unconscious, so he went limp as he fell. Anyway, he has plenty of padding!'

Milo in fact looked pathetic, but he was sitting up and starting to mumble. Megiste ordered the slaves to take him away to her temple. Lacheses ambled off as well.

*

Megiste watched the rest depart then tackled us.

'Now, let's see about you!' To our amazement she had switched straight from Greek to a polite version of our own language. When we looked startled, she giggled endearingly. 'Tatting and beekeeping don't keep me busy enough! I thought it might be fun to learn Latin.'

It was obvious that if the idea struck her, she would be just as enthusiastic about a practical course in glass-blowing or home druidry. I indicated her driver, the one in full charioteer's kit: 'And I suppose you fill in any tiny spare moments running racing chariots?'

'Yes, I am an owner. I'm very fortunate – ' She was very wealthy, then. She looked at me closely. 'Hmm. Clean teeth, haircut, and mended tunic – mended in *matching* thread, I see. There must be a woman somewhere. Is it too much to hope she has come with you to Greece?'

'You can deal with me.'

'I think not, Falco! We of the Council of Sixteen are chosen for our respectability.'

Wondering what else she had deduced about me in her scientific manner, I admitted that Helena Justina was at the Leonidaion. Megiste gathered her attendants. 'Tell your wife I have one or two errands at the Temple of Hera, then I shall trot along to see her. Ask her to make sure she is there; I am a very busy woman.'

Attempting to ingratiate myself, I said we had visited the Temple. To prove it, I commented on its fine painted terracotta acroterion, one of the largest and most handsome roof finials I had ever seen.

'I hope you noticed that the Doric columns are all different. They were dedicated by different cities, many years ago. The Temple of Hera is the oldest here,' said Megiste. 'That is why we stand no nonsense from the priests of Zeus.' She paused. 'There are things I have to tell your wife about Valeria Ventidia.'

'Valeria? That's good – but it's not enough, Megiste. If I am being kicked out of Olympia, I need some quick answers on Marcella Caesia too.'

101

'Ah, the little girl who was found on the Hill of Cronus . . . I am sorry. Nobody knows why she went up the hill, or what happened when she got there. Now, I must collect my thoughts and see your wife. We won't need you, Falco.'

I was not having that. 'My wife has a slight stomach indisposition –'

'Oh I can bring her something for that! In about an hour.' Megiste sensed my rebellion. 'As you are leaving tomorrow, young man, if you have not done it already, you had better take a brisk walk now up the Hill of Cronus.'

I loathed bossy women. And if commands were being handed out like free gifts at an amphitheatre, I had a girl of my own who could do it. Helena would refuse to take orders from this arrogant trout. I decided to lounge around the Leonidaion to watch Megiste and Helena facing up to each other like contenders at some female equivalent of pankration. Now that the townswomen's tyrant had instructed me to do it, there was no way I was going out on a hike.

XIX

Only the promise of information made Helena agree to the appointment. She was furious that the interfering Council of Sixteen had put a stop to our visit. The fact that they were women seemed to make her even more angry.

She took up a position in a colonnade, looking intellectual amidst a bunch of scrolls. I put a stool in the next bay and sat there deliberately idle, with my sandals tossed aside and my bare feet on a column pedestal. I was picking my teeth with a twig. On the Aventine that is understood to be an insult.

Somewhat later than she had promised, Megiste marched up, steaming ahead of her female attendant, and introduced herself to Helena, who – since she was receiving someone of such renowned respectability – had made Albia sit with her as a chaperon. I received a disapproving look from the new arrival, but was then ignored by all of them. The attendant in the colourful chiton had her back to me so I could not even flirt.

Helena intended to take charge. 'How pleasant to meet you, Megiste. I have been told how much you are involved in the community. Elis is to be congratulated. Few cities can summon up *sixteen* respectable women.'

'We are a tight little band,' Megiste confirmed.

'The same ones run the Council every year?'

'We try to attract new blood. It's never easy finding volunteers, and experience counts. It usually ends up with the same old group of us.'

'I had imagined all Greek women are still confined in their quarters at home, while their men go out and enjoy themselves.' This was meant to be offensive. Helena Justina hated the Greek system of penning up women in separate quarters in the house, unseen by visitors.

'My members are very traditional,' Megiste said. 'We believe in the old ways.'

I had never seen Helena smirk so much. 'Weaving and looking after the children – or booking the comely courtesan for your husband's next manly symposium?'

Megiste declined to take offence. 'Yes, I do like to hire the hetaera myself.'

Helena chose to take her literally. 'Marvellous. Do you pick them for big busts or intelligent conversation?'

'Decent flute-playing!' snapped Megiste.

'Of course; far better to keep their wandering hands occupied!' Having done her worst, Helena whipped back to business. 'Now – since we are being shipped out of Olympia so *very* unexpectedly, Megiste my dear, I do have urgent packing. Will you tell me what you came to say about Valeria Ventidia?' Megiste must have glanced over at me. 'Oh let him stay. I honour the Roman tradition,' boasted Helena. 'My husband and I have *no* secrets.'

'How very tiresome for you!' chipped in Megiste, evening the score.

Since she did want to obtain all possible information, Helena capitulated. She lowered her voice conspiratorially: 'Well, he tells me everything, like a good boy – while I just confide what I want him to know . . . Marcus, darling, you are hanging around like a dandelion seed. Why don't you take your dog out for a walk?'

I was a traditional Roman. As a man, I was king, chief priest, and all the gods in my own household. On the other hand, when my woman spoke, I took the hint. I whistled Nux to fetch my sandals, and we set off to explore the Hill of Cronus.

Helena Justina was indeed a traditional Roman wife. Later, she shared with me not just Megiste's information, but her own thoughts on it.

At the sanctuary, the death of a young woman had been

104

considered a matter for the Council of Sixteen. When Valeria Ventidia was killed, the stalwart ladies had investigated. They discovered the young bride had developed an unwise 'friendship' with a man. He was an athlete, a champion pankration exponent from a previous Olympiad, who was hanging around in the hope of attracting sponsorship. He had been given permission to erect a statue of himself among the hundreds which adorned the site, but he could not afford it. His home town failed to come up with the money, so he hoped to raise cash from admiring sports fans. The Seven Sights party – rich Roman travellers, all in love with the Greek ideal – had looked like possible patrons. He attracted Valeria's attention somehow and was working on her to persuade her husband, and possibly others, to sponsor him.

Curiously, the Fates had arranged that the champion in question was none other than Milo of Dodona. His attack on Cornelius, Megiste said, indicated his propensity for unprovoked violence.

The ladies were inclined to exonerate the athlete from sordid motives in befriending Valeria. They accepted, however, that the relationship could have turned nasty without him at first intending it. Valeria herself had been reckless and stupid. The ladies suspected it was the athlete who killed her – but they could not prove it.

This was a new turn of events. I was eager to interrogate Milo. Curiously again, another Greek quirk of fate had ruled it right out. Megiste regretfully told Helena that, although he had been in the best of hands, that afternoon while he was being tended at the Temple of Hera, Milo had died. He had been given a soothing sleeping draught – one of proven, traditional origin – which had seemed to help. But he never woke up.

This was doubly unfortunate for us. It *looked* as if Milo must have died from the injuries Young Glaucus caused with the discus. Concussion can work in peculiar ways. As Megiste pointed out to Helena, it was now even more in our interests to leave Olympia fast.

*

Spectators had been killed on occasion when hit with a flying discus; usually they died instantly. But Milo of Dodona was strong and healthy. When we saw him carried off from the swimming pool, he was groaning, but he had come round and should have had nothing worse than a headache. In my opinion all he had needed was a long drink of water and a few hours' rest.

'I am amazed, Helena, that in the expert care of a matron of Elis, Milo failed to make a recovery.'

'Never tangle with a townswomen's guild,' warned Helena darkly. 'Forget them pottering with their beehives, Marcus. We are in the land of Medea, the child-murdering mother; Clytemnestra, the husband-slayer; big strong girls like the fighting Amazons, who sliced off their own breasts to prevent them tangling in their bowstrings . . . Listen; after you left and Megiste removed her veil, I saw she had a black eye. I asked if she had been beaten by her husband. She said that it happened at the Temple of Hera.'

'I suppose she walked into a *cella* door?'

'Yes, and how appropriate. "Walking into a door" is a very traditional lie!'

'I get the impression, Helena, that the Council of Sixteen is called in to be the fixers when this sanctuary has some scandal. I'm none too certain that Milo of Dodona killed Valeria – Valeria was covered with yellow athletics dust; I noticed that Milo used the grey. Not proof, perhaps, but indicative.'

'So, Valeria was not killed by Milo?'

'And Milo was not killed by Young Glaucus. But it may be convenient for some people if it looks as if he was.'

Helena Justina said softly, 'Imagine Milo of Dodona, half pacified with a sleeping draught. It would be tricky to get the dosage correct for a man of his enormous size. Then he would be difficult to handle if he thrashed about – as he would do, if the dose was too low and he revived enough to realise he was being smothered with a pillow, say. Anybody holding down the pillow might well end up with bruises.'

'This is hypothetical.'

'It's right, Marcus!' Helena was rarely so prejudiced. She must have really loathed Megiste.

'So why would Milo need to be silenced?' I mused. 'Well, if he really had been involved with Valeria, then after she died, he must have become a frightened man. To anyone who found out that he had known her, he would look guilty. So he had a spectacular body but a small brain, a brain that had taken a few batterings in his career . . .'

Helena helped me work it out: 'The Council of Sixteen may originally have promised him protection. He was Greek; he was possibly innocent; and even if Valeria had behaved badly with him, respectable women with traditional values may have felt that a man is always in the right. To the Council, Valeria deserved her fate.'

'Cobnuts. "Respectable women with traditional values" are deadly!' I had made Helena smile. 'Then along comes Didius Falco. Even the Council of Sixteen had failed to make the scandal go away. The women, with or without the priests of Zeus, were forced to come up with new tactics. Someone persuaded Milo to attack me.'

'When that failed, thanks to Glaucus, maybe they feared it would rebound. I expect the priests set him on you,' Helena suggested, 'while the women thought that was a stupid idea. It meant you knew that Milo existed. You were about to discover his link with Valeria. Following the discus incident, you might have gone to talk to him –'

'Yes, when a gigantic bastard attacks me, I always have a few kind words with him afterwards!'

Helena had her own dark anger: 'It is possible that the priests or the Council of Sixteen or both decided Milo needed to be punished now, either for his stupid involvement with the girl, or for actually killing her, if he did so. Anyway, Marcus, Milo may have genuinely liked Valeria. If you had probed, perhaps he would have told you something he knew about her death.'

Utter frustration gripped me. 'And what was it? What could Milo have told me? Was he the real killer? If not, did he know who was?'

107

Helena and I were now certain of one thing: Milo of Dodona had been silenced. He had been put out of contention by the redoubtable dame from the Elian Council of Sixteen.

As for my trip up the Hill of Cronus, as I expected, that had been a waste of time. My turn for confiding: I described it to Helena. I had walked up, looked around at the scenery, found nothing, and walked back down again feeling very tired. Now we had to sail away from Olympia with no real new evidence, either in the murder of Valeria Ventidia or the mystery of Marcella Caesia three years before.

I warned my party to be packed and ready as soon as the tireless Olympia cockerel sounded his first note next day. They were all subdued, especially Young Glaucus. As if he wanted to atone for his part in the death of Milo, he came to me with an object that we would carry away with us, our one piece of tangible evidence: it was a jumping weight.

'I persuaded Myron, the flute-player, to steal this from the superintendent's office. It was kept in a cupboard, after Valeria was killed.'

As weights go, it was striking. Unlike the much plainer styles that Glaucus had shown me, this was made of bronze, in the form of a charging wild boar, full of character. A plain bar formed the handgrip. In use, the boar's curved body would extend over the knuckles. His sharp spinal crest would make the weight doubly dangerous if used to bludgeon someone.

'Is this the one they found covered with blood?'

'We think so, though it's been cleaned up. There were two on the wall. The other one has not been seen since the attack.'

'I wonder if the killer took that. Some of them want a trophy . . .' Running my finger along the wild boar's crest, I did not go on.

Glaucus shuddered. I wrapped the boar weight in a spare cloak and put it away with the rest of my luggage.

*

I refused to be hijacked. I would not meekly accept the ship Megiste had arranged and then go where she sent me – probably straight back to Rome. Instead, we would saddle up our own donkeys, and head for Pyrgos, thence overland to Patrae on the southern shore of the Gulf of Corinth, where we would take a ship of *my* choice up to see the provincial governor.

Stuff the respectable ladies. This was my brief from Claudius Laeta at the palace. Normally I ignored official instructions. For once I would stick to them.

Our independence presumably annoyed the sanctuary authorities. I hope so. It certainly upset almighty Zeus. That evening, we noticed flashes of light intermittently, as if there was a storm far out on the Ionian Sea. These gradually increased. As darkness fell, all the hills around us were lit by ever more intense bursts of sheet and forked lightning. The pine-scented air grew heavy. We ate a frugal evening meal, sweating and argumentative, amidst wild and eerie flickers of light. It became all too clear why this remote place had inspired the ancients to say Zeus ruled the area. Closer and closer came the storm, until a slight skirl of rain preceded sudden huge drops. A long, heavy rainfall then lasted all night while Olympia resounded with thunder for hours, until any among us who believed in divinities must have believed that our presence had angered the all-knowing gods.

PART THREE
CORINTH

Up on top of Acrocorinth is a shrine of Aphrodite. They say the spring behind the Temple is the bribe Asopos gave to Sisyphos. I have heard this was Peirene and the water in the city runs down from it . . .

Pausanias, *Guide to Greece*

XX

Corinthus.

Rome had governed Greece, our province of Achaea, for over two hundred years now, so we had stamped our own style on the capital. First, the Consul Mummius robustly subdued ancient Corinth after it failed to support him. Standing no nonsense, he burned it down, levelled the walls, and buried the foundations. Architects like to start a rebuild on a cleared site. For added cleansing, Mummius had killed all the men, sold the women and children into slavery, and auctioned the city's art treasure in the marketplace in Rome. To call him thorough was rhetorical understatement. Still, those were the bad old days. We, for our part, hoped the Greeks understood that point.

For a hundred years the once rich and famous city of Corinth remained a wasteland. Then Julius Caesar rebuilt it with heavy grandeur. Corinth, full of shops, temples, and administrative buildings, was settled anew with freedmen and foreigners. Nowadays it was a haunt of traders, sailors, and good time girls, its houses and markets peopled by Italians, Judaeans, Syrians, and immigrant Greeks from other locations.

The famous Isthmus was only about eight Roman miles across. There were two harbours, Lechaion looking west down the Gulf (where we landed) and Kenchreai facing east. Many people landed at one, then crossed on foot and took a new ship from the other harbour. Alternatively, a paved tow-road, the *diolkos*, allowed empty ships to be transported on wheeled carriers right across the land bridge, to save them having to sail all the way around the Peloponnese. At the narrowest point of the Isthmus we saw two partly dug immensely deep channels for a canal – one of Nero's spectacular ideas, ended by his death. I reckoned it would never happen now.

Corinth had a ground-level settlement and a steep, rocky acropolis, which was included in a great loop of the city walls. Corinth town was low by anybody's standards, because of its shifting commercial population; we heard the acropolis was not much better, though emptier because rioters and drunks hate climbing hills. Both the low and the high towns had temples to Apollo and Aphrodite, and both had fountain outlets for the famous Peirene Spring. Gaius and Cornelius had convinced themselves that one of the Temples of Aphrodite was famous for its thousand official slave prostitutes. Don't ask me who had told them that. I swear it was not me.

I had a mandate from Claudius Laeta to report progress to the governor. I would make that useful. I had in mind to insist that the governor provide me with a pass for a repeat visit to Olympia, backed up this time by an armed guard.

He might have done it, had he been there. But naturally, in a world where all Romans who could afford it were busying themselves sightseeing, the governor was away that month. When I turned up at his palace, I was told the bad news. He had disappeared on a long summer break – or as his official engagement diary put it, he was up country, 'inspecting milestones'.

Well, I never expected a governor to work. As in so many similar situations, I was stuck with the substitute. Even he was said to be locked in a meeting, but a few jokes with the petitions clerk got me in anyway. And just my luck. While the governor was swanning off on the milestone count, his deputy looking after Roman rule in Corinth was: Aquillius Macer. That's right. Still wet behind the stuck-out ears, he was the quaestor who had bungled the original investigation into the murder of Valeria Ventidia.

I had no hope that Aquillius would help me identify a killer he himself had failed to find.

'I say, Falco; I've never seen one of these things before.' A man of twenty-five or -six, he had a big Roman nose, heavy jowls, fleshy lips, and luxuriant floppy hair. He had, however, taken some trouble to supply me with refreshments. In a better mood, I might have found his unflappable attitude endearing. He was now looking at my letter of introduction from Laeta as if it was a poisoned arrow stuck in his foot. 'What am I supposed to do?'

'Treat it as top priority and give me every assistance.'

'Right! What do you need from us?'

I tried it on: 'Decent accommodation, a scribe who can write ciphers and a string of steady mules. Most urgently, a fast line of communication back to Rome.'

'Weekly reports to the Emperor?'

Weekly trinket-dispatch to my children. Best not worry a quaestor with these facts of life. He had enough impending anxiety: 'First, I need to sit down with you, Aquillius. You must give me a detailed debrief on this unholy balls-up on the Valeria Ventidia case.'

The quaestor went pale. I turned the screw: 'Can you put a stop on travel for the group involved, please? I want to grill these people. I can go to them, or they can be brought here, whichever is easier logistically.'

I had thought logistics would be a new concept. Aquillius surprised me: 'We've got them ready for you in Corinth,' he announced at once. 'I've dumped them in a lodging house; they don't like it; they are constantly complaining. They were due to bugger off to Rhodes and Troy, but I told them they are all suspects. I said a top-flight special investigator was coming out.'

Dealing with the Palace was normally a trial. But sometimes it could work in my favour. Claudius Laeta had made Aquillius believe I was Vespasian's best agent.

Having my suspects penned up was a luxury. The only thing that did cause me concern was that when I asked about Camillus Aelianus, Aquillius seemed never to have heard of him. Still, Aulus would not have wanted to be caught up in a house arrest. He must have seen the posse coming, so vanished smartly. I could hardly complain; it was the way I had taught him to act.

'Thanks for rounding them up. Can I take it that the governor positively wants the case sorted?'

'No,' replied Aquillius, unapologetically. 'He wants to ship them right back to Italy. Prove one of them did the murder, please, so we can be rid of the lot. We hate these culture tourists, Falco. Amateurs bumbling about, causing trouble abroad –'

'Causing you work?' I suggested mildly.

'You have no idea how much!'

It seemed best to pin Aquillius down. Otherwise, whenever I tried to discuss anything, he would be 'in an important meeting'. So I stuck him with an immediate case review.

'Just a few quick details,' I promised insincerely. 'No need to call for a note-taker . . . You were there at Olympia when Valeria Ventidia was killed?'

'Perils of the job!' He grinned. He was probably not on the take, yet eager to slack. The chance to visit the Olympic Games next year would be the best perk in his tour of duty. 'Working party. I had gone on an advance site visit. We like to show the standard. Let people know that Rome is in charge.' Have five days of sport and believe they were working . . .

'The governor will attend the Games?'

'Yes, he takes on a lot of official duties –' That would be: handing over bribes to the priests, munching cinnamon cakes with the respectable ladies of the Council of Sixteen, maybe exerting himself at the palaestra (where a free pass and a personal coach would materialise) or with his mistress, if he had one. They would stay at the Leonidaion; they would be provided with a prime suite, free of charge.

'It's a hard life, representing Rome abroad.'

'It is, Falco!'

'So you had gone on a recce, but you found yourself stuck with the trouble?'

116

'I think I handled it.'

I made no comment. 'What were your findings? I know the girl was discovered by slaves in the *skamma* very early in the morning, then carried to the party's tent by her hysterical husband.'

'They had marital problems. They were known to have quarrelled the previous day –'

'Was that a one-off, or routine?'

'It had happened throughout the trip. Their relationship was volatile; they often had heated exchanges.'

'Was the last quarrel special?'

'Who knows?'

'Subject?'

'People told me it was all about sex. Mind you,' said Aquillius, playing the man of the world, 'sex is what most tourists have on their minds most of the time.' I raised my eyebrows in gentle enquiry. 'They have all read up on the love lives of the gods. Then they start looking for personal experience. We have a terrible time at temples,' he informed me bitterly.

'Ah, the legendary Corinth temple prostitutes!'

'No, no; the pros are never any trouble. Well, they've been at it for centuries.'

'So what's the problem?' Informers have heard most things, but I felt wary.

'Travellers want thrills. We've caught them bribing priests to let them lurk in sanctuaries after dark, so they can breathlessly wait for a sensual experience with a "god" – it's usually the priest himself, of course. Priests will screw anything . . . We regularly have to peel masturbating male visitors off cult statues, especially if it's a beautiful sculpture.'

'Appalling!'

'You said it.' Aquillius looked genuinely disgusted. 'Maintaining good relations with the locals is bloody hard when Roman visitors have no sense of shame. Still, none of the drooling here is quite as bad as they get with the Aphrodite of Cnidus –' The Aphrodite of Cnidus, a

117

masterpiece by Praxiteles, had been the first fully nude statue of a goddess ever made and was still revered as sculptural perfection; I had seen Nero's copy in Rome and agreed with that. Aquillius was still ranting: 'Mind you, from what I've heard, the Cnidians ask for all they get, not least by charging extra to go through a special gate for a viewing of their Aphrodite's exquisite backside . . .'

The worldliness was a veneer. Aquillius seemed uncomfortable with his own salacious stories. He would not be the first virgin sent abroad for his country, who then grew up fast.

'So, quaestor – has Seven Sights Travel been accused of lewd midnight love trysts and temple desecration?'

'Not on this trip,' said Aquillius.

'Then let's get back to basics – What were your conclusions about the Valeria Ventidia murder?'

'I told you that: the husband did it.'

I gazed at him. 'Any proof?'

'Most likely candidate.'

I gazed at him some more.

'Falco, look – most of the others liked the girl. None of them stood to gain from bashing her head in with a discus –'

'A jumping weight.'

'What's the difference?' Not much if you were the victim, dead. But her friends and family, wanting answers, deserved accuracy. 'The husband denied it, naturally.'

'You interviewed the others?'

'A sample.' That would be a *small* sample. It would not surprise me if Aquillius just asked the tour leader, Phineus. Phineus would have passed him off with whatever story suited Seven Sights.

'When was she missed?'

'When people settled down for the night. Then the husband went out, ostensibly to look for her.' I saw no reason for 'ostensibly'; looking for her seemed a good reaction, quarrel or no quarrel. Aquillius took a harder line. 'I reckon he found her – maybe in the arms of her lover – and that was when he killed her.'

'What was his answer to that charge?'

'Oh he claimed he never saw her.'

'And you were unable to find anyone who saw them together at the palaestra the night Valeria died?'

'Right.'

'The first real witnesses were next morning, when he found her dead?'

'Yes, that was tough. We had to let him go. This is a Roman province, Falco. We do have standards!'

Not high enough standards for me, however.

'What was your take on Milo of Dodona?' I asked, giving nothing away.

'Who's he?'

'A friend of the girl, apparently.'

'Silly cow! Milo was never mentioned.'

'Maybe nobody knew. Maybe Milo was Valeria's special little secret.' I left Aquillius to work out any relevance. 'Now tell me about the other dead girl – Marcella Caesia.'

'The one with the bloody awful father?' The quaestor groaned. Caesius must have really made a nuisance of himself, though Aquillius had only heard about it: 'Before I came to Greece.'

'Can I see the file? The father was given a banning order. He presumably had a lot of contact with your office, if he managed to annoy the governor that much.'

'Oh, I can't show the file to you, Falco. Security.' This probably meant the governor had given vent to his feelings too rudely – or more likely Aquillius knew the scroll had been put in their dead archive and re-used for packaging souvenirs the governor was sending home. 'Our view is that the girl either went up the Hill of Cronus to meet with a lover, or –' He lowered his voice in hollow sympathy. 'Or she did away with herself.'

I gave him the silent treatment again. Aquillius took it with his normal good nature. 'No, we don't really go for the lover story. By all accounts she was a quiet little scrap. No looks and no personality.'

I told him her father had mentioned that before her trip

there had been 'trouble with a young man'. Aquillius blanked it and stuck with his own version: 'We think she got carried away by the mystique of Greece, and had a breakdown of some sort.'

'So officially it was suicide?'

'Yes, but the governor is a soft old cove. He just could not bring himself to say that to the father. When Caesius kept on agitating, the best solution was to expel him.'

I was tired. I had had a long sea journey; now I faced a week of irritation with bureaucracy. I gave up.

I asked for and was given the name of a reputable lodging house.

'Will Claudius Laeta foot your bill, Falco?'

'As the crime occurred out here, he'll suggest you fund me against your petty cash.'

Aquillius Macer accepted it. He was the province's finance officer but had no clue how to fiddle costings. He could have passed this expense straight back to Rome and saved the money for entertaining influential locals. He was a hopeless overseas ambassador – and I was keen to preserve my meagre funds from Laeta, so I let him subsidise me.

Aquillius then supplied the address where the Seven Sights group were staying, in some fleapit called the Helios. 'Well, all except the escort –'

A new surprise. 'Phineus! What's happened to him?'

'Oh nothing. But we all know Phineus, he's no problem. He has other groups to look after. He's been set loose on parole –' That almost sounded as if Phineus was given a governmental travel pass and free hay for his donkey.

'When Caesia died,' I butted in, sounding snappish, 'this Phineus fled straight back to Rome. It's suspicious to me! Any sign of similar in the Valeria case?'

'No, no. Phineus is all right,' Aquillius reassured me. 'Really knows his stuff. Understands this country better than anyone. If I was booking a culture tour, Falco, I'd travel with Seven Sights. Phineus gives people the best time.'

'So what if I want to interview this man?'

'Oh he'll be back.'

When I asked Aquillius if I could see his interview tablets from the Olympia investigation, he had to confess he had not taken any notes.

'Go and get your head down, Falco. Let me know if there is anything that we can do. Enjoy your stay. And don't forget – the governor's office only wants to help!'

XXI

To work.

After waking late and settling in next day, Helena and I took ourselves for a mid-morning brunch at the Helios, the rooming house where the Seven Sights group were penned up. Glaucus had gone to find himself a gymnasium. Our youngsters were out seeing the town. We knew that meant looking for the temple with the official prostitutes, but we were confident they would just stand around and stare. Helena had said if they got into *any* sort of trouble in the administrative capital of a province where I was working, we would abandon them.

'She's joking!' Gaius protested.

'Dear nephew, do not be too sure. If you commit a crime here, you take your chance with local justice.'

Gaius had no idea that one of his uncles had been eaten by an arena lion when he offended local sensibilities whilst accompanying me on a mission overseas. (To be truthful, we did not entirely abandon Famia. We cremated the few pieces of him that survived the gnawing, and took the ashes back to Rome.)

The Helios had a porch with a colourful terracotta architrave, but that was its only gesture to graciousness. We could see that the rooms were tiny and dark; the corridors managed to smell damp, even on a baking hot day. We wondered what favour Aquillius Macer had owed the proprietor, to make him place the suspects here. This time, he really was keeping down the demand on his contingency fund. They were crowded in a sour billet.

Still, there was a small courtyard, shaded by pergolas

from which dangled still-unripe bunches of grapes. Beneath, stood a selection of wobbly tables and benches. Helena and I ensconced ourselves side by side against a wall, so we could both survey the area. Food was available; they sent out to a nearby fish restaurant.

While we waited, Helena drew up a list of reasons why people went on leisure tours. 'Escape; culture – art and architecture; other kinds of education – curiosity about the world beyond Rome . . .'

'Sex.' I was thinking of my conversation with Aquillius yesterday.

'Religion!' she countered, unaware that that fitted my category. Helena, who had sharp sensitivities, then quizzed me with those great brown eyes. I told her what the quaestor had said about the Aphrodite of Cnidus. She giggled. As always, this reduced me to helplessness. 'Showing off!' Helena added, for some reason.

'Sport.'

'Collecting things.'

'Adventure.'

'Writing a book –'

'Oh lady, now you are being silly!'

Helena chuckled again, then steadied and advised that when I interviewed the group members, I should find out which of them were writing travel diaries.

I concentrated on trying to wedge bits of broken pot under a leg of our table to stabilise it.

The trapped travellers came to lunch early. We were barely into our stale rolls and pan-fried octopus when in strolled a man with a short body on extremely long legs; he was thin and balding and everything about him said he was a self-opinionated fool. Helena had unrolled our letter from Aulus on the table; assessing the man, she placed the clean, pointed end of her spoon against the name of Tiberius Sertorius Niger, the father of the family in the family of four. Sure enough, his wife joined him: a pale woman reading Herodotus (she read bits aloud, mainly to herself; no one else took any notice. Helena, who had whizzed through the histories on our way out from Italy, recognised the passage). Soon after, their two children came, gobbled a few mouthfuls, spilt a jug of water, then kept wandering off from the table and looking for mischief. The boy was about fourteen, the girl slightly younger. They were sullen and bored.

Next came a middle-aged woman, solo, rather stout, with wispy hair, struggling to manage her over-large lop-sided garments. She nodded to the mother, who must have previously discouraged the widow (as we had guessed this was) from sitting among the Sertorius family. Instead, Helvia plonked herself down at the table next to ours. Helena might have made conversation, but we needed to remain detached observers for a little longer; she became absorbed in the letter from Aulus, while I just scowled anti-socially. Although Aulus had called Helvia 'fairly stupid', she must have deduced that I was a dangerous dog who might froth at the mouth if spoken to. She avoided looking at us.

Suddenly she began a prolonged consultation of the chalked slate which served as a menu board (deciphered, the spidery Greek letters simply said there was octopus in sauce, or octopus without). Helvia's fixed preoccupation was a cover, so she could avoid a shabby, slouching man, wearing a large conical hat, who wandered in and looked around for someone to disturb: this had to be Volcasius.

Helena dug me in the ribs; I countered with a lecherous squeeze, to make it look as if we were lovers on a private tryst. No use.

'Is anybody sitting here?'

'We are waiting for friends!' Helena put him off coldly. Volcasius stared at her as if he needed an interpreter, but as he hovered on the brink of joining us anyway, my sweetheart waved him away like a bothersome wasp. No one meeting Helena for the first time was ready for her blistering glare. Volcasius wandered off, and was soon shifting from empty table to empty table. The waiter must have experienced his unsettled behaviour before and ignored him.

Two men came in together. Helena decided they were

Indus and Marinus, who as single men of mature years had palled up. They were oddly assorted, one short and one long, both in their fifties, both cheery and sociable. We could not work out which was the widower and which the man Aulus had defined for some reason as 'disgraced'. They glanced around for the least awful spot to sit, though without making it obvious; then they politely shared with Helvia. Volcasius looked as if he were thinking about squashing in with them too, but the taller of the men had adroitly moved the spare seat sideways, then stretched out his leg on it as if he had a painful knee. After perusing the menu board, he joked, 'Same as yesterday! Bootstraps with gravy, or bootstraps plain . . .'

At this point two couples arrived together, making lots of noise, all with very white garments and heavy jewellery. The foursome may not have been drinking yet, but with lunch on hand they were cheerfully expecting it. We guessed that the loudest pair must be Cleonyma and Cleonymus; he had a pristine short haircut, hers was piled high in elaborate turrets and swayed as she tottered about on problematic wooden heels. The 'fun folk' as Aulus had called them, Minucia and Amaranthus, were bitterly complaining. He had run out of money and been flagrantly cheated by a currency-changing Egyptian at the local port of Kenchreai (this seemed to have been several days ago, but still rankled). She had just been through a revolting experience in the public lavatory the group had to use (as they moaned loudly, the Helios let them sleep but not shit); the sit-down had flooded all over her cerise suede sandals (not for the first time, apparently, though nowhere near as badly as a legendary facility at Paphos . . .) Despite their fury, Minucia and Amaranthus were bearing up with engaging good nature, assisted by the willingness of Cleonyma and Cleonymus to ply them with red wine.

Copious jugs had appeared as soon as Cleonymus arrived. This must be a daily ritual; it looked as if he acted as a regular paymaster for the whole group. I saw Sertorius' wife shake her head rapidly in annoyance. She refused the waiter's proffered tray, then muttered darkly to her husband. Sertorius, though, looked as if he thought, why refuse a free drink? Plenty of scope for family tension there.

'Oh it's all experience, isn't it?' shrieked Minucia to Helena, as she lurched against our table. 'No point coming away unless you see the funny side of life!'

Helena smiled, but tried to remain unobtrusive. Unfortunately, I noticed the Sertorius parents with their heads close again, having another angry discussion. I hoped it was still about the big-hearted, wealthy Cleonymus always supplying wine. Not so. Sertorius Niger pushed back his seat noisily. He stood up, strode across the courtyard and came directly to our table.

'You!' he cried, in a voice that made everyone else look up. 'You are spying on our group, confess it!'

'That's right.' I put down my spoon calmly. 'My name is Didius Falco and I represent the Emperor. I am here to interview you all – so why don't you sit down right now? You can be first.'

126

XXII

Sertorius had sat down before he realised I had given him orders. He coloured in indignation. His wife scuttled up, protectively; she must expend a lot of effort in saving him from the effects of his rudeness. Then their children came over, looking inquisitive. The girl placed herself behind her mother, hanging over her with her thin arms around the woman's neck in a display of unnecessary affection; she had knocked her mother's beaded ear-rings awry. The boy swaggered up and helped himself to our remaining food. We had finished eating, so we ignored it until he began flicking a strip of octopus at the sauce in the serving dish to make it splash all over the place (yes, we had chosen the version with sauce, hoping for our favourite at home, pepper and fennel in red wine; we never learn).

Helena closed her hand around his wrist. 'You know, Tiberius Sertorius, son of Tiberius,' she informed him, with blistering sweetness, 'I would not allow bad behaviour like that from Julia, my three-year-old! Please, either listen quietly, or if you cannot stop fidgeting, go and wait for your parents in your room.' She released him, and let his shock register.

Helena had observed that the two teenagers tyrannised even their own family, mainly because no one ever pulled them up. Her public rebuke startled all of them. The parents were nonplussed and had the grace to look embarrassed. The boy subsided grumpily. Behind the father's back, I could see Indus and Marinus silently applauding. They were the group's subversives. I had hopes of juicy gossip from that pair, later.

'You have worked out all our names!' Sertorius senior accused us, still annoyed about spying.

'Nothing sinister.' My reply was mild. 'It is my job to be well briefed. May we talk about Valeria and Statianus? When did you first encounter them?'

'We all met up for the first time when we took ship at Ostia –' the wife began.

'Let me deal with this, dear!'

As the husband interrupted, Helena cut across him and spoke directly to the woman in a friendly voice: 'I am so sorry; your name is one we *don't* have specifically.'

'Sertoria Silene.' Her Greek second name, taken with the shared family name, explained some things. The rude bastard with the superior attitude had married his ex-slave. He never let her forget it. Now they had two children he could not control, while she was too diffident to try. The children had little respect for their mother, taking the lead from their father.

'Let your wife contribute,' I murmured to Sertorius, with mock-confidentiality. 'I find that women have the best memories.'

'Oh well, if you want trivia . . .' At his scathing sneer, I merely smiled, aiming to mend fences. Helena would give me all Hades for it afterwards, but my business was to humour these folk. 'As she says –' He referred to his wife without naming her; he must be ashamed of her origins. 'We met as a group on board ship; the *Calliope* – absolutely ghastly hulk. Bilges were so full of water, they could hardly steer the thing. *Not* what we were promised. That's going to be the first point in my letter of complaint. Before I get started on this place, of course. Putting us up here is an outrage. The manager is running a brothel on the side –'

'Tell Aquillius. It's up to him how he houses you. Stick to facts, please. First sighting of the wedded ones?'

I knew my rebuke would rile Sertorius; he believed he was ultra-efficient. He squinted at me angrily, then said in a tight voice: 'The newly-weds were pretty well invisible at first. Later they peered out of their shells a bit.'

'They had only been together a week at most, when we started,' put in Sertoria Silene.

'Were they happy?' asked Helena.

'You mean, were they having a lot of bedtime fun?' broke in Sertorius coarsely, as if he were accusing Helena of prudery.

'Actually, I meant both.' She met his eyes directly, chin up and challenging.

'No doubt both applied.' Sertorius answered as if he had not noticed Helena answering back, but his voice rasped – a sign of uncertainty.

'Did their relationship deteriorate?' Helena turned from the husband as if he did not exist, seeking details from Sertoria Silene.

'They did argue sometimes. But I thought if they stuck it out, they would settle down eventually. They were young. He had never had control of any money before, so he bungled it – and she was brighter than him.'

This was a sharp evaluation. I had underestimated Sertoria. While her fool of a mate seemed to dominate, I wondered if she had married him knowing she could run rings around him. It was citizenship at a price, but the price might have been worth it. She could read – poring over her Herodotus, clearly for her private pleasure; she would never have been a mere kitchen skivvy, but must have occupied a good household position. Helena told me later, she could imagine the woman as the educated secretary and companion of some previous, probably wealthy, wife. The wife died; Sertorius hated to live alone, so he picked up the nearest female who would accept him. That made sense. We did not envisage them having an illicit liaison while the first wife was still alive; mind you, anything is possible.

'And what do you know about the day Valeria died?'

'Oh nothing, really.' So Sertoria Silene had been told to prevaricate. I blamed the pompous husband for that.

I took up the questioning, addressing him. 'The men went to watch combat sports that day. Statianus came with you all?' He nodded. 'While the women took a tour of the Pelops relics?' Both looked surprised that I knew so much. People like this would never have met an informer before.

129

'Valeria too?' This time Sertoria nodded. Then she stared down at her lap. The daughter, still dangling around the mother's neck in a way that must have been painful, was suddenly still. I leaned back and stared at them, then asked softly, 'So what happened?'

'Nothing happened.'

Untrue, Sertoria.

I resumed my questions to Sertorius. 'And that night, you all ate together?'

'No. We men were dragged off to a so-called feast.' He sneered. 'It was supposed to simulate how winners in the Games celebrate at a banquet in the Prytaneion – if theirs is the awful standard that *we* had to endure, then I pity them. The women stayed at the tents, and all complained when we rolled home slightly merry!'

Helena pursed her lips in sympathy at Sertoria Silene, who rolled her eyes, to indicate how disgusting this had been.

'At what point that evening did Statianus and Valeria have their final quarrel? Was it when *he* reappeared drunk?' I wondered if it was Valeria's first experience of this. Given that she had been brought up only by a guardian and a remote grandfather in Sicily, the girl might never before have seen a close relative staggering and vomiting and behaving unreasonably. Maybe she was squeamish.

'Before we men went out.' Sertorius disappointed me.

'It was just a tiff,' his wife murmured, almost whispering the words.

I rounded on her. 'So you do know what it was about?'

She shook her head quickly. Helena shot me a warning not to harass Sertoria, then leaned forward to her. 'Please tell us. This is so important!'

But Sertoria Silene insisted, 'I don't know.'

Her husband then told us, just as decisively, that none of them knew anything of subsequent events. As a family, he said, they retired early to bed – because of the children, he charmingly explained. His wife had already told us he had

130

been drunk, so no doubt there had been angry words, followed by tortured silences.

As if scared that somebody would say too much, they all stood up and retreated to their room, ending our interview.

Helena let them go with the mild comment that it would do the Sertorius children good to have an enforced afternoon nap.

XXIII

The other two couples saw the family depart and noisily waved us to their table.

'Up for it?' I muttered to Helena.

'Don't get sozzled!' she hissed back.

'Don't get cheeky! I am total sobriety – but can *you* keep your hands off the winecup, fruit?'

'Stop me when I go purple.'

'Ah too late, too late!'

The foursome shrieked a welcome. They had watched us bantering snappily; they liked us for it. The men were already beaming like debauched cupid grape-treaders on a wine bar wall-panel. They were well glued to their stools by now, incapable of shifting until their bladders became quite desperate, but the women were probably never static; they leapt up at our approach and together hauled a bench nearer for us, straining in their flimsy frocks like navvies and then flailing into the wrong husbands' laps. Cleonymus and Amaranthus groped them, automatically, then shoved them on to the seats they had previously occupied, like men who had gone through this routine before.

All four were older than befitted their behaviour and bright outfits. I put the men at sixty, the women older if anything – yet it was the men who looked to be flagging at this lunch table. Cleonymus and Cleonyma, the two freed slaves with a huge inheritance, had hands which had quite clearly done much manual labour, though their fingers were now expensively be-ringed. The other couple were harder to place. Amaranthus, the suspected adulterer, had narrow, wary eyes, while Minucia seemed tired. Whether she was tired of life, of travel – or even tired of Amaranthus, we could not deduce.

They positively rushed to tell us all they knew, making the details lurid where they could. I tried saying I hoped they did not mind more questions, at which they bellowed with laughter then assured me, they had hardly been asked anything yet. So Aquillius was too snobbish to speak to freedmen. That was no surprise.

'It was me who heard him coming.' Cleonyma took centre stage. She was a thin, wiry woman who burned off her physical excesses with nervous energy. Good bones and lack of fat gave her a handsome face; had she laid off the eye paint she would have looked even better. She shuddered, her skinny shoulders lifting beneath the fine pleats of her gown; it was held together with vivid clasps and, as she moved, ovals of oiled, scrawny, suntanned flesh came and went between large gaps in the material.

'Statianus? Was he calling for help?' asked Helena.

'Yelling his head off. No one else bothered to notice; you know how people are. I was going outside. As I went through the tent door, he staggered up, weeping bitterly, with the bloody corpse held in his arms. Her dress was all filthy with sand from the exercise yard. Her head, though – her head was so horribly battered you could hardly tell that it was her . . . I nursed my master through ten years of a wasting illness; I saw enough there not to faint at mess, you know – but Valeria's body turned my stomach, and I only glimpsed her.'

Cleonyma now looked haggard beneath her glinting face powder. Minucia took her hand. An emerald ring flashed. She carried more weight than Cleonyma, and although she too almost certainly carted around a compendium of face creams, her skin was very coarse.

Overcome, Cleonyma leaned her head on Minucia's shoulder; about four pounds of Indian pearls lurched sideways on her flat chest. A fully rounded perfume of rose petals and jasmine on one lady clashed waft for waft with a headier essence of Arabian balsam. After a moment of comfort in a mingled aroma cloud, Cleonyma sat up again; her pearls strands clacked and tumbled straight once more. The women's two scents uncoiled and slid dangerously against each other like towering clouds moving one way while a second raft of weather moves in the opposite direction underneath. Just like a coming coastal storm, it left us restless and unsettled. Minucia even mopped her forehead, though that could have been the drink overheating her.

More subdued now, the party of four described subsequent events: how Statianus was persuaded to relinquish his ghastly burden; the few muddled attempts by locals to discover what had happened; the cursory investigation carried out by Aquillius. Nobody at the site took any real interest in Valeria's fate initially, beyond the usual lascivious nosiness about whether the young woman had been having affairs.

'Who called in the quaestor to take charge?' asked Helena, thinking it must have been Sertoria Silene, or perhaps the widow Helvia.

'I did!' Minucia surprised us. In outward style she resembled Cleonyma, especially since the two couples had shopped for their present outfits at the same market boutique. I found it hard to place her otherwise. She could have been a freed slave too, but equally I could see her as the hardworking wife of some freeborn craftsman or shopkeeper; maybe she had tired of arguing with a lazy husband and rebellious children, had run off with Amaranthus in desperation, and now knew she could not easily return to her home town.

'How come, Minucia?'

'Things were getting ridiculous. I had nothing against Valeria, poor soul. She did not deserve what happened to her. The priests were all trying to ignore the problem, some damned women from Elis were *extremely* obnoxious – what in Hades had it to do with them in any case? – and when I heard there was a Roman official at the VIPs' guesthouse, I just marched right up to him and made a fuss.'

'Aquillius seems convinced Statianus was the guilty party,' I said.

'*Never!*' We all looked at Cleonyma. True, she was

enjoying the drama. Even so, her verdict was that of a shrewd, quietly observant woman. 'I saw him straight after he found her. I'll never forget his face. The boy is innocent.'

'Aquillius Macer must be fairly inexperienced,' Helena brooded. Amaranthus scoffed, summing up the quaestor as a man who would abuse his mother. Cleonymus insulted that noblewoman even more lewdly, not only casting doubt on the quaestor's paternity, but suggesting that an animal had been involved. Not one of the cuddly ones. Helena smiled. 'You are saying Aquillius could not organise his way out of a bran sack?'

'Not even if he had a great big map,' agreed Amaranthus, glumly drinking wine.

Until now, Helena had barely touched her cup, but now she topped it up herself. 'Here's a question for you. Your tour is supposed to be escorted. So where was your organiser, Phineus?'

A silence fell.

'People think Phineus is wonderful,' Cleonyma remarked, to no one in particular. She left the statement hanging.

'One or two people think he's bloody terrible,' her husband disagreed, but they did not argue over it.

'Did Phineus help, after the murder?' Helena persisted. 'Aren't you all paying him to keep you out of trouble?'

'He did what he could,' snorted Cleonymus. 'That wasn't much – still, there wasn't much *anyone* could have done, given that Aquillius was determined to keep us trapped in that tent until he could arrest someone – and that he failed miserably to decide who it should be. Only the fact that Aquillius wanted to come back to Corinth made him say we could all go free. Even then – ' Cleonymus gave me a dark look. 'Our reprieve was temporary.'

'So what, to be precise, did Phineus really do for you?' I asked.

'Kept the food coming and ensured the wine improved,' Minucia told me, caustically. 'I thought he could have

135

moved us into decent accommodation, though that never happened. But he kept at it, talking to Aquillius. "Negotiating for us", he maintained.'

'Aquillius speaks well of him.'

'Mind you –' Amaranthus used a heavy, mannered delivery which combined making a point with making a joke: 'We have established to general satisfaction, haven't we, that Aquillius Macer is so bright he could lose himself in an empty sack.'

I smiled at his response. 'So, my friends – any idea where your wonderful escort is right now?'

Apparently, Phineus was earning himself a few drachmas, trotting off to Cythera with some other visiting Romans, while he waited for this group to be given their release. Cythera, an island at the extreme southern end of the Peloponnese, seemed a damned long way to let a suspect travel.

'I hope, for their sakes, he doesn't take them to that conniving murex-seller who cheated us last year,' said Cleonyma. Murex is the special shellfish dye used for purple cloth; its cost is phenomenal. Cleonyma and her husband apparently had an intimate knowledge of shopping for luxury goods.

Since we seemed to have exhausted their knowledge of the murder, Helena started asking Cleonyma about their past travels. Although this was their first trip with Seven Sights, the couple were old hands.

'We've been on the road for a couple of years. While we can last out, we'll keep going. The money came from our old master. He had a lot – mainly because for decades, he never would spend any. Life with him was bloody hard, especially after he got sick. But in the end, he seemed to change his attitude. He knew he was dying, and he started handing out presents.'

'Was he frightened that you might stop looking after him?'

'Bribery? No, Helena; he was scared of the pain, but he knew he could trust us.' Cleonyma was matter-of-fact. I could imagine her as a brisk but efficient nurse. Receiving a bed–bath at her hands might be a worry. Especially if she had been drinking. 'He never said beforehand, but when he went he left us everything.'

'So you know he valued your loyalty.'

'And no one else could put up with him! – We two had been together unofficially for years,' Cleonyma reminisced. Slaves are not allowed to marry, even other slaves. 'But as soon as we got our windfall, we made it proper. We had a huge bash, all the works, ceremony, contract, rings, veils, nuts, witnesses, and a *very* expensive priest to take the auguries.'

Helena was laughing. 'The auguries were good, I hope?'

'They certainly were – we paid the priest enough to guarantee that!' Cleonyma too was relishing the story. 'He was a clapped–out old pain in the buttocks – but he managed to see in the sheep's liver that we shall have long life and happiness, so I like to think he had good eyesight. If not, you and me are finished!' she warbled to her husband, who looked on, bleary but amiable. 'Now we just think, let's see the world. We earned it, so why shouldn't we?'

We all raised our drinks in a friendly toast to that.

'Somebody else took an interest in Valeria's fate.' Helena asked, trying not to look worried: 'Wasn't there a young man from Rome, called Camillus Aelianus?'

'Oh him!' The loud foursome all guffawed.

'He got up a lot of people's noses,' Minucia declared.

Helena said sadly, 'It means nothing. He doesn't know he's doing it.' She let the truth sink in. 'Aelianus is my brother, I'm afraid.'

They all stared.

'He said he was the son of a senator!' Cleonyma exclaimed. Helena nodded. Cleonyma looked her up and down. 'So what about you? You are with an informer, so we assumed –'

Helena shook her head gently. 'Make no mistake – Marcus is a very good informer. He has talent, connections, and scruples, Cleonyma.'

137

'Any good in bed, though?' Cleonyma giggled, giving Helena a poke in the ribs. She knew how to defuse an awkward situation by lowering the tone.

'Oh I wouldn't have looked at him otherwise!' Helena replied.

I drank my wine impassively. 'So where is Aelianus – does anybody know?'

They all shrugged and told us he had simply vanished.

XXIV

A lull allowed Volcasius to interrupt. With unabashed lack of social skill, the man nobody wanted to sit with suddenly accosted me: 'I've finished lunch. Better speak to me!' He was on his feet and about to leave the courtyard.

I gathered my note-tablets and went over to the table he had occupied alone. He sank back on a bench again, with an ungainly sideways motion. His clothes were unkempt and exuded a waft of body odour. Though his manner towards me was abrupt, I would treat him with courtesy. People like that do know how others regard them. He was probably intelligent – perhaps *too* intelligent; that may have been the problem. He could well provide useful information.

'You are called Volcasius?'

He glared. 'So some snitch gave you our biographies!'

'Just a list of names. Is there anything you can add to what the rest have told me?' He shrugged, so I asked him, 'Do you think Statianus killed his wife?'

'No idea. The pair were wrapped up in themselves, and frankly did not interest me. I never gained any impression of whether he was jealous or likely to snap.'

I surveyed the oddball thoughtfully, wondering whether he himself had ever had any tricky exchanges with the bride.

As I had thought, the man was bright: he read my thoughts. 'You are imagining that *I* killed her!' The way he put it was very self-centred. He seemed almost pleased to rank as a suspect.

'So did you?' I challenged.

'Certainly not.'

'Any idea who might have done?'

'No idea at all. Is that the best you can come up with?' His

139

tone was contemptuous. As an investigator, he thought I stank. I knew the kind; he believed he could do my job for me – though of course he lacked experience, persistence, skill, or sensitivity. And if he had had to park in a doorway to watch a suspect, the mark would have spotted him instantly.

I leaned back, looking relaxed. 'Tell me why you are on this trip, will you?'

Hooking himself into a crazy position, he peered at me, now deeply suspicious. 'Why do you want to know, Falco?'

'I want to establish who had a motive. Perhaps I wonder whether you attach yourself to travelling groups in order to prey on women.' He humphed. 'Not married, Volcasius?'

Volcasius grew hot and bothered. 'That applies to plenty of people!'

I gave him a conciliatory smile. 'Of course. You see the obvious way of thinking, however. But I never follow obvious lines of enquiry . . . Are you keen on culture? Is that the lure?'

'I've nothing at home to keep me. I like to visit foreign places.'

'Nothing wrong with that!' I soothed him, while also implying that there might be. I could see how it was. He would never fit in, wherever he was, so he kept moving. I guessed that he also had a genuine, even a pedantic interest in the provinces he toured. He was carrying a note-tablet set much like my own. His tablets lay folded open so I could see scrawled lines of madly minute handwriting, lines which made my eyes ache as I tried to decipher them at a distance. There were place-names underlined, then long inches of detail; he was creating an enormous travel guide. I could imagine that when he had been at Olympia he compiled not just descriptions of the temples and sports facilities, but lists of the hundreds of statues, probably each with its inscription copied down. 'You strike me, Volcasius, as the kind of observant man who may have seen something other people missed.'

I hated myself for flattering him, and since he was far from

140

grateful, I then hated myself more. 'I've been thinking about that,' he retorted. 'Unfortunately for you, I have not been able to remember anything significant.' I looked rueful; he was triumphant. 'If anything should come to mind, have no fear, I shall report forthwith!'

'Thank you.'

Volcasius had a way of leaning too close which, combined with his sour smell, made me desperate to be rid of him. 'So what is your solution for that other girl, Falco? The one who was found on the Hill of Cronus?'

I kept my voice low, to match his: 'Marcella Caesia?' Some of the group must have known her story, because the apparent connection was why Aulus had written to us back in Rome. 'It now appears that the two cases are not linked.'

Volcasius let out a short bark of derision, as if with that I had just proved myself incompetent. He said nothing to assist me, needless to say. I never had any patience with idiots who gave me that superior *'Little do you know!'* snot.

He stood up again. 'As for that young man you enquired about, Falco – the Aelianus fellow – nobody else seems to have spotted it, but when we were all put under house arrest here, he took off somewhere with the dead girl's husband.'

Volcasius strode away with the air of a man who had just given himself a big thrill by annoying me. I failed to point out that he had left his hat behind, lying on the table. It was the kind of greasy straw affair that looks as if it harbours wildlife. If there had been an oil lamp lit, I would have taken a spill and deliberately set fire to the hat in the cause of hygiene.

XXV

I rejoined Helena Justina, who had stayed with her new friends, the colourful foursome. I pulled a face, to express my feelings about Volcasius, but they were too polite to comment. I guessed that in private they said how dreadful he was; in public, since they had to endure him as a companion, these expert tourists appeared forbearing.

Helena looked amused by my plain loathing of the loner. She had more urgent things on her mind, though. 'Marcus, listen! Cleonyma and Minucia have been telling me about the day when Valeria went on the Pelops tour.'

The two women shuffled closer together like schoolgirls and looked reluctant. But eventually Minucia confessed in a near-whisper: 'It's nothing – but when we were going around the site, that big brute, Milo of Dodona, spoke to her.'

I leaned my chin on my hands. 'Milo? What did he say to Valeria, any idea?'

'She was embarrassed. There was a lot of whispering; she tried to get rid of him.'

'So what was his game?'

'Oh, he wants sponsors for a statue of himself.' Minucia did not yet know Milo was in the past tense. 'He had been around asking all of us. Valeria was a kind-hearted girl and he picked up on that. She had no idea how to get rid of him. She and Statianus had no real money. Milo was wasting his time there.'

'Was there anything sexual in his interest?' I asked frankly. 'Or in *her* interest in *him*?'

Cleonyma shook her head. 'No, no; he's an ugly bastard –'

'Marcus has seen him,' Helena interposed.

'Worse,' I said. 'I've been thrown on my head by him.' Cleonymus and Amaranthus winced at my heroics. 'Some women like the idea of being crushed in the strong arms of a well-developed lover,' I suggested. The women to whom I propounded this coy theory heard it in silence, implying *they* were all admirers of intellect and sensitivity. Cleonyma inspected her fingernails; even Helena straightened her bangle with a very refined motion. 'We suspect Milo invited Valeria to meet him. Was that in your hearing?'

Cleonyma and Minucia glanced at each other, neither wanting to tell me.

'Come on, ladies; this is important. I can't interrogate Milo, by the way, because he's died on me.'

Looking shocked, Cleonyma pressed a hand against her lips then muttered through her fingers, 'He was trying to lure Valeria to the palaestra to hear some poet reading his work.'

The palaestra would be used as an auditorium by authors of celebratory odes. During the Games, philosophers and panegyrists would hang around there like midges. We had even dodged a few during our own visit. 'Valeria was a literary type?'

'Valeria was just bloody bored!' Minucia muttered hoarsely. 'We all were, Falco. There is nothing for women at Olympia – well not unless you're a girl in the leisure industry; they make as much in the five nights of the Games as they can in a year!' I did wonder briefly if Minucia had special knowledge of this service industry.

'Had you been to Olympia before, Minucia?'

'Amaranthus gave me that awful pleasure once. He's athletics mad.' He looked proud of it. Minucia carried on bitterly. 'The Games were on – well, never again! The tent city was full of fire-eaters and floozies, drunks, acrobats, puppeteers doing lewd shows – and the bloody poets were the worst. You couldn't go out without stepping on some seedy hack, spewing hexameters!' We all looked sympathetic, to allow Minucia to settle down. She was still remembering. 'There was even a bloody man trying to sell off a goat with two heads.'

I sat up. 'I know that goat! I nearly bought him once.'

'No, you didn't.' Helena smiled dreamily. 'You wanted to buy one whose head was on backwards.'

'He was called Alexander, because he was great.'

'At Palmyra. But, darling, he only had one head.'

A silence fell. Nobody could decide whether we were being serious. I brooded to myself about the goat, and my lost chance to become a travelling sideshow at festivals.

'Valeria should have learned her lesson. She had been to one recital with us,' Cleonyma told me. For all her flamboyant outward style, she took a grave interest in the girl's fate. 'We all went, to fill in an hour, the afternoon before. Phineus laid it on; he told us the orator would be really good. We soon learned better! The horrible fellow called himself the New Pindar, but his odes were old tripe.'

'If Valeria went to the palaestra to hear Milo's poet, why has nothing ever been made of that?'

Again there was an awkward silence. This time it was Cleonymus who filled me in. 'What the girls don't want to tell you, is that this Milo of Dodona came to the tent the next morning. He appeared not to know that Valeria had died – and we thought that was genuine. He was complaining that he had waited outside the palaestra for her, but she never came.'

'You believed his story?'

Helena leaned forwards: 'If Milo killed Valeria, why draw attention to himself, Marcus?'

'We thought he was a big stupid mutt who just wanted a statue of himself as a champion,' Cleonyma said. 'We sent him packing. There was no reason Valeria's husband had to be upset any more than he already was.'

Cleonymus agreed: 'Statianus was in serious trouble, and we wanted to protect him. Bad enough him being accused by the quaestor, when we thought he was innocent. The locals were all prattling about Valeria's low morals – which again was unjust. She was a silly girl, and she should have sent the wrestler packing. But we did not think she'd slept with him, or ever intended to. So, why bring Milo into it?'

Helena asked them, 'Was the quarrel she had with Statianus on the last evening over Milo?'

'We think it may have been,' murmured Cleonyma. 'She told him she was going to listen to the poet, and at Milo's invitation. Statianus – understandably – refused her permission.'

'He should have tied her to a bloody tent pole to make sure!' Amaranthus scolded.

I said I disapproved of subjugating wives in most circumstances – but I agreed that this would have saved Valeria's life. To myself I was wondering whether, if Valeria *had* stayed at the tent that night, the killer would have found himself another woman to prey upon. Was it purely coincidence that he had killed one who was travelling with Seven Sights? 'Were there any other groups visiting Olympia off season, by the way?'

'You are joking!' scoffed Amaranthus. 'Anyone with sense is going next year.' His voice expressed longing and Minucia glared at him balefully.

'So people in this party were unhappy with your itinerary, at that point?'

'"Unhappy" as muck, Falco,' Cleonymus told me. 'Most of us had expected the Games, on Seven Sights' say-so – and we were livid.'

Amaranthus joined in: 'Phineus keeps muttering promises for next year, but he's a cheapskate. He took us to Olympia now, when it was quiet, to save on costs.'

'Exactly!' snapped Cleonymus. 'He could have put us up at the main guesthouse, or got us into that villa of Nero's – very nice! But dear Phineus chose to cramp us in tents, because he got them for nothing. All along, it's been the same. Our food has been appalling, the donkeys have been mangy, the drivers are shite – when he provides any – and now we've ended up stuck here, only one grade down from being thrown into jail on trumped-up charges.'

'And still some people think that Phineus is wonderful?' I asked drily.

'We're captives,' Amaranthus groaned. 'People are scared they will never get back to Italy if they complain.'

Both couples seemed to feel that they had said too much now. After a few more neutral comments, they became restless so I let them go. They departed, the men seeking out a good souvenir-seller Phineus had told them about; they joked that they hoped he was better than the awful orator their tour guide had recommended at Olympia. The women scuttled on a quest for a public convenience that would not flood.

This left Helena and me, with the trio who were patiently waiting: Helvia, and her two male companions. We went across to them, pulled up seats, and although we all laughed because by now it was unnecessary, we introduced ourselves.

XXVI

As we settled into our new positions, I noticed that the Sertorius boy was lurking about, hiding behind a pillar as if pretending to stalk us. Then I spotted the girl too, making a better job of being unobtrusive. On her own, she would have got away with it. Helvia took it upon herself to shoo them off. Indus, the shorter male, said the brats had been a menace from day one. He once caught the boy going through his things. Indus' expression as he recalled this incident seemed to confirm he was a fugitive, scared of discovery.

As an assembly of five, we fell naturally into two sub-groups. Helena attached herself to the widow and was soon discussing Helvia's travelling. To go overseas we knew she must possess funds, though not as lavish as those enjoyed by Cleonymus and Cleonyma. A decent friend used to accompany her, a woman her own age who spoke several languages, but after an unfortunate experience in the souk at Alexandria, that ended. Now Helvia brought instead a little slave girl, who was always the first in any party to be struck down by the foreign food, and who lost Helvia's luggage every time they hit a new port.

Helvia had chosen to travel with Seven Sights because she wanted to meet new men. She came right out with this. Helena wondered whether the married ones might be a problem – or those travelling alone, who were married but failed to mention it? Helvia seemed surprised by this suggestion. When she glanced in alarm at Indus and Marinus, they were much amused. I guessed that already on this trip each had made it plain to Helvia that he was not interested in her (or thought he had). With that cleared up, they had convinced themselves it was safe to

147

be friendly with the widow. I would not have felt so confident.

Marinus fancied his chances as a raconteur. This was a real nuisance. We were trying to elicit cold facts from people who were unused to being questioned and my patter was geared to stop them telling lies. I was less efficient at interrupting this stream of anecdotes about lost participants (got up late, missed the mule train, missed the boat, just lost their way), locals handing out wrong information, guides who were ignorant, abusive, too clingy, or who reneged and left hapless travellers on their own in the middle of deserts, earthquakes, civil wars, or simply in the middle of Arcadia, which, despite its reputation for temples and a pastoral ambience, apparently contains nothing of interest.

We had already taken in a great deal of information, and a seafood lunch; I was helpless. Soon Marinus was even sidetracking himself, with a long, shocking tale of an innocent family, who had never been abroad before, being abducted by a psychopath (on a dark night on a remote mountain pass, naturally). When he launched into an incident with a crocodile, even Indus joined in. He was a hunched man, with long, lank hair and dark skin lesions. He had kept quiet until that point, perhaps because of the aspersions that Aulus had cast. If he was on the run for some sort of fraud or political disgrace, he would not want to attract my attention. But now he too set off on reminiscences:

'The worst thing I've seen is feeding time at Crocodilopolis. The poor chief croc there is supposed to be a god. You bring him hampers of stuff – bread and cakes, and wine to wash it down. He waddles out all covered with perfumes and jewellery, though looking apprehensive, if you ask me. The keepers wrench his jaws apart and force in the goodies – and sometimes he has hardly gobbled up one load when a new crowd arrive and bring him more to gorge on. When I saw him, he was so fat, he could hardly move. Can't say the priests were exactly slender either!'

'Of course they have their teeth drawn –' declared Marinus.

'Do you mean the priests?' Looking over from where she sat with Helvia, Helena found her voice, stopping the flow of stories with this deadpan jest. 'Marcus, did Indus and Marinus have any intimate conversations with Statianus? Were they able to entice anything out of him?'

'Sadly, not much there to entice,' Marinus apologised, giving in and returning to our real subject. 'Nice boy – but when the brains and spirit were handed out in that family, they must have passed him by.'

'Sad for Valeria?' Helena asked Helvia.

'No, they were well matched, in my opinion. Valeria was a sweet little thing, but scatty.'

'A bit lacking in judgement?'

'Utterly. She was fresh from the nursery, Helena. I don't think her mother can ever have taken her on so much as a morning drive to meet a friend and drink mint tea.'

'Her parents were dead. She had a guardian, Helvia, but you know how that works – so often a formality. I suspect she was brought up solely by slaves and perhaps freed-women.'

Helvia sighed. 'With hindsight, I feel dreadful that I never took her under my wing.' More tartly, she added, 'Well, she would not have wanted me. In her eyes she was a married woman, travelling with her husband; she knew nothing, but thought she knew everything.'

'Was she rude to you? Not give you the respect due a widow?'

'A little dismissive –'

'She was rude to you, Helvia!' Indus spelled it out. 'She was rude, at one time or another, to most people.'

'But probably had no idea she was doing it,' Marinus defended Valeria. The scatty girl must have been his type, I reckoned. Was it significant? 'She was outspoken even to her husband. She had a sharp tongue. If her killer propositioned her, she would have straightaway let rip with a riposte.'

'Perhaps that helped madden him?' I suggested.

'She could be a superior little madam,' Indus agreed. 'What was she? Nineteen, with no background and no real money. Neither of them had any clout. As newly-weds, they attracted a lot of attention; we made a fuss of them. They could have sat back and enjoyed it, and had a really good time. Instead they rubbed people up the wrong way; they insulted the guides, irritated us, and were fractious with each other. It was nothing too much, but just what you don't want when you are on the road in uncomfortable conditions.'

'So,' I said, 'they had alienated people. When the girl first went missing, Statianus had to look for her himself; then when he was accused of her murder . . .?'

'Oh that was when we rallied. It was not his fault. That idiotic magistrate needed a kick up the posterior.'

'So do you people know where Statianus has gone now?' Helena asked them, still hoping for news of her brother too. But they all shook their heads.

We seemed to have extracted as much as they could tell us, so we enquired about the two men themselves. Marinus owned up immediately that he was a widower, on the lookout for a new wife. We joked that since Helvia was in the same position, many would think that a neat solution.

'Oh Marinus is out of the question. He talks far too much!' Despite her wispy hair and uncontrolled drapery, Helvia was absolutely blunt.

'I do,' Marinus admitted without rancour. 'And *I* am hoping for a ladyfriend who owns half of Campania!' Helvia cast her eyes down, as if defeated.

'What about you, Indus?' Helena slipped in. 'Are you on the lookout for a wealthy new wife, or looking over your shoulder for some over-officious auditor?' She made it humorous. Indus took it that way – apparently.

'Oh I like to be a man of mystery, dear lady.'

'We all think he is a runaway bigamist!' giggled Helvia. So the rumours about Indus were openly mentioned – and he liked to let those rumours hover.

'You know the old maxim: never confess – and you'll never regret.'

'Deny and you'll get a black eye!' I retaliated.

After a few moments' silence, Helena sat up slightly. 'Statianus and Aelianus are missing; so is someone else,' she said. 'We were told you had a third man travelling by himself – whom nobody has mentioned at all. Wasn't there a Turcianus Opimus in your group? Our information is that he says this is "his last chance to see the world".'

The silence lingered.

'Has nobody told you?' Helvia seemed wobbly.

The two men glanced at each other. It was rather ominous. Indus puffed out his cheeks, blew air awkwardly, then said nothing. Helvia by now was twisting her transparent stole between both hands, apparently distressed. We looked to Marinus, who always had too much to say, and screwed out of him the fatal words: 'Turcianus has died.'

XXVII

Helena drew herself up, then slowly let out a breath. 'I hope,' she said softly, 'you are not going to tell us there was anything unnatural about *his* death?'

'Oh no,' Helvia assured her, a little giddily. 'We just are – well, I can see that news would have been rather a shock, after you came here to investigate Valeria. It's just that for all of us – well, of course, we really hardly knew the man –'

'He was ill.' I made it a statement.

Helvia calmed down. 'Well, yes he was. Very seriously, it turned out. But none of us had realised.'

Helena was still wary, thinking that this might turn out to be yet another untoward death. 'Was it true then: when he said he was travelling while he could – he knew that he had very little time left?'

'Apparently so,' Marinus replied. 'Without being cynical –' Which we gathered he always was. 'I doubt whether Phineus would have accepted Opimus on the tour, had he been aware of the true situation.'

'So much trouble . . .' Helena responded. 'Having to repatriate the ashes. So bad for his reputation, sending clients home in funeral urns.'

'The rate this tour is going,' Marinus quipped, 'Phineus will end up taking more urns back than people!'

'Oh Marinus!' Helvia reproved him. She turned to Helena and confided the story. 'Opimus seemed such a nice man. But he was very ill, we discovered, and he badly wanted to go to Epidaurus – where the Temple of Aesculapius is, you know.'

'I didn't know Epidaurus was on your itinerary,' I said.

'No, it wasn't originally. But we are doing Tracks and

152

Temples, after all, and Epidaurus has a very famous temple with a fascinating history. In fact there is even a stadium.'

'And a good theatre?'

'An astonishing theatre. When we found out how Opimus was suffering, we all took a vote. Most of us were happy to go to the medical sanctuary and let him seize his chance for a cure.'

'How did Phineus take this vote for a detour?' I asked. Marinus and Indus laughed heartily. 'I see! Still, you are the clients, so you persuaded him.'

'It was no loss to bloody Phineus!' Marinus said crisply. 'We pay for it if we want a new itinerary.'

'And this was *after* Olympia?'

'Yes,' said Helvia. 'We were all feeling shaken by Valeria's death, and perhaps a little kinder towards our fellow humans. When Opimus revealed how ill he was, we all felt it very deeply. You know, I think the shock of what happened to Valeria contributed to *his* decline; while we were at Olympia he deteriorated rapidly.'

'You were on good terms with him?'

Helvia blushed demurely. I imagined her disappointment if she had lined up Opimus as a possible new husband, only to lose him after she had spent much effort making friends.

Helena drew on her usual fund of knowledge: 'Is Epidaurus where people sleep in a cell near the temple, and hope for a dream that night, which will produce a cure?'

'Yes. It is a wonderful site,' said Helvia. 'It is set in a marvellous grove, all very spacious, with many facilities, some medical and some where people obtain help for mind and body purely by rest and relaxation. For the sick, the centre contains the Temple of Aesculapius, and not far away a huge building called the dormitory. There you sleep for a night, among tame snakes and dogs who are sacred to Aesculapius. They wander around, and some people dream they are licked by the creatures, which leads to them being healed.'

The sacred dogs must be more fragrant than Nux, then. (Nux had been left with Albia that afternoon.) 'So what happened?' I asked.

'One or two of us had little ailments we wouldn't mind alleviating, so we went with Opimus and slept in the dormitory that night.' Helvia looked slightly disapproving – the classic face of a tourist who knows she has been cheated, but who paid good money for the experience and still wants to believe. 'It did not help my rheumatism. None of us seem very much better since then, I'm afraid to say . . .'

'Somebody must get well. There are tablets hung up everywhere, praising the dream cures,' Marinus told us, in his sceptical tone. '*Lepidus dreamed that a snake licked his arse and with the assistance of the god he woke up absolutely cured of his piles* . . . Of course they don't say Lepidus had actually gone there with a goitre on his neck! Then people make pottery offerings in the form of the limb or organ that Aesculapius mended – lots of little wombs and –'

'Feet?' asked Helena adroitly.

'Feet – and hands and ears,' Indus assured her, with a smile.

Marinus leaned forward. 'I have all the luck: I was singled out for a special honour: I got *bitten* by a sacred dog!' He pulled back a bandage on the leg he had previously put up on the seat to ease it. We inspected the bite.

'No doubt they told you he was just being friendly, and nothing like it had ever happened at the sanctuary before?' Marinus stared at me suspiciously, as if he thought I might be a dog-owner. 'Seems to be healing, Marinus.' I grinned.

'Yes, I tell myself a friendly snake must have come along afterwards and licked it better.'

'Did you dream?' asked Helena, mock serious.

'Not a thing. I never do. As for Turcianus Opimus, whatever he dreamed turned into his nightmare, poor fellow.'

'Well?' prompted Helena. Marinus shook his head, looking sombre, while Indus sighed and sank into himself.

The widow was made of stouter stuff. It was left to her to tell us: 'He passed away peacefully during the night. Oh don't worry!' Helvia assured us quickly. 'He had the best medical attention in the world. After all, the healers at Epidaurus go back in a direct line to the teachings of

Aesculapius, the very founder of medicine. The one thing you can be certain of is that Turcianus Opimus would have died wherever he was. It was unavoidable and absolutely natural.'

Oh really? Doing my job for twelve years had tainted my ability to trust. Simple statements about 'unavoidable' happenings now sounded unreliable. Any reference to a 'natural' death immediately aroused suspicions.

XXVIII

Helena looked good for more questions, but I was flagging. Since we had now tackled everyone who came to the courtyard for lunch, we packed up and returned to our own lodgings.

With a recommendation from a quaestor, you might suppose this travel lodge would rank with the best in Corinth. Any visitors of note arriving at a provincial capital go straight to the governor's palace, in the hope of being offered luxurious rooms there. Lesser mortals will more likely be told that a great train of ex-consuls has just arrived unexpectedly – though then they should be sent to hotels where at least the bedbugs have been to charm school and the landlord speaks Latin.

Well, that's the ideal. Sorting out accommodation falls to the young quaestor; he is quartered at the residence, so he has never slept at any of the run-down lodgings to which he sends people. He only knows of them because their fawning landlords have given him presents, probably something that comes in an amphora; he's so inexperienced he can't even tell if the free wine is any good. The quaestor is just twenty-five, in his first post, and has only ever been travelling before with his father, a bossy senator, who organised everything. He knows nothing about booking rooms.

Our guesthouse was called the Elephant. It could have been worse. It could have been much better. It had more rooms than the Camel up the street and, according to the manager, fewer mosquitoes than the Bay Mare. Nobody was leasing out cubicles to floozies on an hourly basis, but that was mainly because most of the rooms had desultory builders renovating them. Beds were stacked in the courtyard, so its fountain was turned off and breakfast had to be taken at the Bay Mare, where we interlopers from the Elephant were served last, after the honey had run out. At our rickety hostel, a pall of dust hung everywhere. Gaius had already fallen over a pile of tiles and gashed his leg. Luckily he liked looking scarred and bloodstained. A huge extension with premier grade rooms was being added at the back, but this was still unfinished. I could have accepted rooms that had no doors, but I felt that we needed a roof.

The afternoon sun was still pleasant. The builders had gone home, as builders do. We knew from experience they would return around midnight, to deliver heavy materials while the streets were quiet.

Helena and I brushed dust from a stone bench and sat down gingerly. Nux was asleep in a patch of sunlight, a relaxed bundle of mix-and-match fur colours, curled up so tightly I could not tell which end was her head. Albia had perched on a plasterer's trestle, to watch Glaucus doing weight training. Apart from one of the smallest loincloths I had ever seen, he was naked. Albia gestured to him and exclaimed, 'The beautiful boy!' This was a phrase she had picked up from the pederasts at Olympia, who had it painted on vases they gave to young lovers. How pleasing to see travel had had an educational effect. And how nerve-racking, the way Albia gazed at him . . .

Glaucus ignored the compliment. Soon he stopped training and sat hunched against a pile of dismantled shutters. When a big strong man becomes unhappy, it is disconcerting.

'What's up, champion?' I was afraid Albia's attentions were too much for him. Teenage girls always hassle shy young men (well, the girls I had known on the Aventine hassled me) and Albia had not forgotten she grew up in Britain, where determined red-haired warrior queens were apt to seduce handsome spear-carriers the minute their husbands glanced away. It was not that, however. (Well, not yet.)

'Falco, I am worried about what I did to Milo,' Glaucus confessed, frowning.

'Contact sports are always a risk; your father must have told you. Spectators are hoping for blood and death.' My reassurance overlooked the fact that throwing the discus is not supposed to be a contact sport.

'I had never hurt anyone before, Falco.'

Helena broke in: 'Glaucus, don't be concerned about this. We suspect Milo of Dodona was drugged and suffocated later – to silence him.'

'In case he said something unwelcome?'

'At this stage we don't know,' I said. 'But you merely chipped him with the disk. He should have been up and grumbling in a few hours. It's good to have a conscience, lad, but don't waste it.'

Glaucus evaluated what I said. 'Have *you* ever killed a man in this work of yours, Falco? My father gives the impression that you might have done.'

'What we are doing here isn't dangerous. Helena and I just met the people involved – and they seem as meek as lambs.'

Glaucus gave me a long look. 'Never mind the people involved! I was wondering about you,' he said.

I could not be offended; sometimes I wondered about myself.

Maybe it was late. Maybe we had indulged too much at lunchtime. I too felt introspective. Certainly Helena and I had just spent an afternoon talking to people I would normally avoid. I could never have endured long weeks or months of travel with a Seven Sights group. Perhaps one or more of them felt the same way. Perhaps they were murdering each other.

I reflected some more on what Helvia and the two men had said about Turcianus Opimus. The more they had assured me his dying had been inevitable, the more I wondered. Ostensibly, it was ridiculous to think that a man who had a severe illness had met an unnatural death.

158

Without going to Epidaurus there was no way I could check, however. Even if I did go, the medical staff who had pronounced him dead would cite his existing disease. Doctors have to look as if they know what they are doing – even though anyone who has ever been ill soon learns the value of that. At Epidaurus I would be dealing with one more hostile Greek temple, where the attendants only wanted to preserve their good name.

Suppose he was murdered. What would anyone gain by killing an invalid? Only if Opimus had possessed incriminating evidence would there be a motive. Nobody had suggested Opimus ever claimed to have such information. But if he had known something, I could never ask him now, so the killer was safe.

I thought about the others. Was anyone I had met so far a likely killer? The belligerent, foolish Sertorius, the misfit Volcasius, Marinus limping with his dog bite, Indus looking haunted? None of them had the air of a sexual predator – and they were all lean-bodied men, who lacked the brute strength of whoever had beaten Valeria with the jump weight.

Cleonymus and Amaranthus were both sturdy. Still, both had women with them – not that marriage or its equivalent ruled out becoming a frenetic killer. I had known murderers who battered female victims, yet who had devoted wives. Some of those wives endured a lifetime of domestic hell but even so, when an arrest was made, they refused to believe the facts and would not testify against their mad husbands. Surely neither Cleonyma nor Minucia fell into that category. They were social, intelligent women who would spot a guilty man if they shared their bed with him. However, I knew if it really had happened, even those hard women might provide cover-ups.

Well, maybe not Minucia, whose strong sense of justice had sent her marching to the quaestor. It was unlikely she would have risked incriminating her own lover – and I rather thought Cleonyma would have stopped Minucia if the culprit had been *her* husband.

I toyed with the idea that Turcianus Opimus was the killer, and that guilt made his health deteriorate. But he must have been far too unwell to make advances to Valeria, let alone overcome a fit young woman if she rejected him.

If Valeria's killer came from this travelling group, that left either Phineus the guide – who *had* behaved suspiciously before, flitting suddenly back to Rome when Marcella Caesia disappeared – or, as Aquillius had believed at the time, the husband, Statianus. Having failed to meet either so far, I reserved judgement.

An alternative was that Valeria had been killed by an outsider, a stranger. It made it more likely that she and Marcella Caesia had met similar fates, three years apart but at the hands of the same man. My chances of identifying him were nil. No records were ever kept of who came and went to Olympia. With no sightings of Caesia going up the Hill of Cronus or of Valeria with her brutal companion, I was stuck. The only possibility I knew was Milo of Dodona; yet his behaviour the day after Valeria died convinced hard-headed witnesses he had no idea the crime had occurred. Anyway, he used the wrong colour athletic dust. He could have changed his usual colour, but that argued premeditation. The kind of frenzied attack Valeria suffered tends to be unplanned.

Another thing worked in his favour: people *wanted* me to think it had been Milo. So my choice was to eliminate him straight away.

I don't shirk issues: I then wondered about the establishment at Olympia. If someone like that useless priest, Lacheses, preyed on women, it would explain why I was so promptly sent packing after I asked too many questions. I did not particularly suspect Lacheses, but he irritated me, so was an easy target for my suspicion. If it was Lacheses, or any other servant of that ancient sanctuary, then no Roman investigator would ever manage to make charges stick. My only hope was that by stirring up trouble I might have forced the locals to deal with their own mess.

There was no chance they would do anything about

Megiste and her sleeping-draughts. Milo of Dodona would be lucky even to have a funeral – though I did wonder whether he would now gain his statue after all. Sometimes corrupt authorities atone for their bad actions with a public gesture.

Helena roused me from my reverie. Evening had drawn in. She was anxious about Gaius and Cornelius. With my mind still churning over problems, I whistled to Nux, who opened a lazy eye then closed it again. Helena jumped up more obediently, as if responding to my call. Together we went out to look for the lads.

Central Corinth was no easy place to search. We were staying near the town gate on the road from Lechaion, the western port. A straight road almost thirty feet wide took us to the main piazza, where an absolutely massive arch led in beside the Peirene Fountain. As town fountains go, this ornate piece of drama was astounding. The forum beyond it was thoroughly well supplied with basilicas, shops, altars, and temples. It had at least three basilicas, by my count, so the populace must be grasping and litigious. An unusual central feature like the spine of a racing circus contained extra commercial buildings and a high spot for orators; this prevented us from seeing the opposite side of the forum as we searched.

Unlike many a provincial town, the main piazza was just the start of Corinth's public areas. Further ornate squares had extra temples, some of them distinguished monuments. There were other markets. There was a leisure area with a very large theatre, dramatically carved out from a bowl of a hillside, with stunning sea views. A second auditorium was in process of being added.

Every god and goddess on Olympus seemed to have a magnificent sanctuary. There were other, stranger gods in Corinth, as we soon found out. Just as we gave up hope, we finally spotted the boys, looking sheepish and weary as they tried to remember the way home to the Elephant. They were clinging together, because they had attracted the attentions

161

of a small bunch of street hustlers and were now surrounded, as if by beggars, against whose wiles we had given Gaius the usual training. Trust that vague boy to forget. Helena strode up, pushed through the bothering jostlers and repeated the advice: 'Don't look at them; don't stop; don't listen to their patter – it is designed to distract you, Gaius! And if they should try to grab you, push them away very forcefully.'

They were not beggars; well, not in the usual sense. They were Christians, who wanted not just my nephews' money but their souls.

'Shoo!' cried Helena Justina, just as fiercely as when she had rejected Volcasius from our lunch table. She clapped her hands loudly, and flapped her arms with the gestures she used to make pigeons scram from our garden fountain. At home, she made me whang off pebbles with a catapult, but it did not come to that. The Christians could see they were beaten, so they slunk away. 'There, there, Cornelius, don't cry; they wouldn't have hurt you. They just like to smile and tell you they have found the answer.'

'The answer to *what*?' Cornelius was easily baffled.

'To the question,' I told him obliquely. Helena and I gripped one of the lads each and began walking home to our lodgings. 'Now you two, where in Hades have you been for hours, worrying us crazy?'

They had been up the acropolis, looking for the Temple of Aphrodite. They had climbed for two hours up the massive granite spur – and taken another two hours back. They had found that the temple existed all right, on the highest crag of all, and that it did harbour prostitutes, who were businesslike, extremely plain, and not the least interested in two Roman boys, since they had hardly any money.

'We didn't want to do anything,' Gaius assured me. 'We were just curious.'

'So you had a healthy walk!' Helena had been anxious, but knew how to avoid showing it. She had had enough practice with me. 'I bet there is a wonderful view from up there.' Gaius and Cornelius confirmed this. 'So nice for the temple ladies to gaze upon glorious scenery, while they are waiting for new clients . . .'

We had found the boys. They were chastened. That would probably have been the end of it.

Then Cornelius stopped snivelling over being jostled by the Christians and got himself into more trouble by telling us about the sorceress.

XXIX

The sorceress story took a while to be let slip. By then, Cornelius was back among our group, devouring his dinner at a local eatery as if he had never been scared. I noticed that Gaius remained rather quiet, but he was old enough to know they were in disgrace, even though we were no longer carrying on at them. That was still a possibility, once the wine flowed some more. Gaius knew that all the Didius family would moan on for days, polishing up the argument with every sit-down meal until somebody snapped and threw pots at the wall. 'Shut up; it was nothing,' he ordered his younger cousin grumpily.

'No, I know she was a sorceress! She had a conical hat.'

'Well, that proves she was a witch,' mocked Albia. 'Was she casting spells behind a tomb?'

'No, she was beside the road,' muttered Gaius.

'Vials of toad's blood?' queried Helena. 'Purple fire? Dead men's toenails?'

'Jugs of water.'

'We went up the hill for a long, long time,' Cornelius complained. 'We were tired out. We were desperate for a drink –'

'Climbing a steep hill, on a hot day. You took nothing with you?' Glaucus asked laconically, laying his big palms flat on the table edge. He had been trying to teach them to look after their bodies. Both boys became shamefaced again.

'Anyway, it was all right,' Cornelius sounded virtuous. 'We got some. We came on this *strange* old woman –'

'Really old?' Helena checked with Gaius. He pulled a face, implying not necessarily. 'And how strange exactly?' Gaius saw that defining female strangeness might embarrass him, so he ripped up a loaf and stuffed it in his mouth. Helena and Albia exchanged a glance.

Cornelius rushed on with his tale: 'This old woman was sitting cross-legged on a big ledge. She had water containers and some cups, and she offered us a drink. I was scared of her but we were *so* hot, I thought we would die if we didn't have any.'

'How much did it cost?' I asked. They wriggled and managed to avoid telling me.

'The thing was –' Now Cornelius was indignant. 'When we got just a little way further on, we came to a spring, which people told us was the upper fountain of Peirene. So we could have had a nice cold drink there for free. She cheated us.'

'No doubt the upper fountain was where she filled her water pots . . . And that's sorcery?' Helena smiled at him. 'Sounds as if she's just a good businesswoman.'

Gaius cracked a clam shell, deliberately trying to break a tooth. He was mortified at being outwitted by some crone in a straw hat. I assured him the Corinthian drinks scam probably went back centuries. 'You won't be the first sweet-natured innocent who fell for it.'

'She wasn't local.' Gaius spoke in a doom-laden voice. 'Just an itinerant, passing through Corinth on her way to a new pitch. Uncle Marcus, we did talk to her; we tried to pick her brains like professionals. She goes to different places. She always sets up on hills. People flag, as they struggle with the climb, and are grateful she is there. She works at Olympia sometimes. She sits on the Hill of Cronus. So Cornelius and I think you should go up the acropolis here and talk to her.'

'Well that's it.' I banged my spoon down on the table. 'This is the last time you two are let out on your own. As a consequence of today's ridiculous jaunt, I too am supposed to tire myself out and get heatstroke, in order to have some batty conversation with a gnarled old Greek granny who cheats little boys of their pocket money and calls it a public service.'

Nobody spoke for a few moments.

'You could take a donkey,' Helena suggested sweetly. After a second she added, 'I'll give you some pocket money, darling, so the sorceress can cheat you out of it.'

XXX

I was all set to scale the acropolis like an obedient informer. I would have gone mountaineering first thing next day. I got as far as preparing a portable breakfast, my hiking cloak and a staff to lean on. Then we had a visitor.

It was Aquillius. He had plenty of good manners, though little common sense: 'How are you finding the Elephant?' At last he looked around the courtyard of our lodging, and deigned to notice the building work. 'So sorry, Falco; normally this is a very comfortable billet. Many people have recommended it. I don't know why nobody told me there was renovation going on. I could move you . . .' It was not a serious offer.

I brushed aside his platitudes. 'I'll move us myself, if the wife wants it.' No chance to ask her: Helena had spotted the quaestor's purple tunic bands as he wandered through the entrance arch; she had fled indoors. 'What can I do for you?'

Aquillius handed me a scroll, another letter from Aulus. 'This came for you!' He seemed impressed that we were receiving correspondence.

'Where from?'

'On a boat from Athens. Somebody knows you are here, Falco?'

'Lucky guess,' I bluffed. 'Wife's brother; nice lad. We'll have to try and get to see him; he's supposed to be studying – bound to be homesick.' Since we had been told yesterday by Volcasius that Aulus had made himself scarce with Statianus, I decided not to link Aulus with my enquiry unless I had to. Statianus might yet turn out to be his wife's killer. If Aulus had allied himself with the bridegroom misguidedly, it could cause problems.

I was eager to read the letter – and to reply to it. Aulus needed to be warned off Statianus.

'Couple of points, Falco. Do you mind if we talk about business?' Aquillius was so used to treating his Greek post as a holiday, he seemed embarrassed to mention work. I waved him to a bench. Unwinding myself from my cloak, which he had apparently not noticed, I dumped my hiking stave and sat down with him.

'I'm glad you're here, Aquillius. Something I need to ask you. One of the tour group –'

'How do you find them?' he interrupted.

'They look like fluff balls, but every one is as sharp as a butcher's hatchet. One is missing –' Plucking at the purple band on his tunic, Aquillius grew nervous that this lost parolee might be his fault. 'I'll rephrase that,' I said, in a kind voice. 'Make it two.' Now he was even more nervous. Part of his purple braid was done for. 'One is *merely* missing – Statianus, the dead woman's husband. I'm sure you've done a head count, so I am sure you realised.' Irony is a wonderful tool. 'Another of them is dead. I expect you know that too.' I expected he did *not* know. Aquillius just looked wide-eyed and eager to please as usual. 'Turcianus Opimus, travelling for his health, died at Epidaurus. That death needs to be checked carefully. Once people start dropping from unnatural causes, you have to scrutinise those who die from so-called natural ones –'

'And make sure?'

'My boy, you are getting the hang of this. Now look – I don't have time to go to Epidaurus; it may turn out to be a wasted errand anyway. Why don't you send a runner to the Temple of Aesculapius, and order that whoever attended this man at the sanctuary gives us a formal statement?'

'I could summon them here.' He had big ideas.

'Fine by me. I want to know: what was wrong with Opimus? Was his corpse examined thoroughly? Did the mode of death match his supposed illness? Were there any signs of interference . . . Well, you know the procedure.' He knew nothing. I thought it unlikely anyone would ever come from Epidaurus. If they did, I would interrogate them myself. 'Aquillius, are you visiting the group today? It would do no harm for you to let fall that I've asked you to arrange this. I'm not saying that anything bad happened to Opimus, but I would like them all to realise I intend to interview the priests.'

'They have asked for me.' Aquillius sounded gloomy. 'I've had a rude summons from that tyrant Sertorius. Falco, they keep complaining.'

'They are having a terrible time,' I pointed out.

'Who told them foreign travel was fun?'

'I think you'll find,' I explained drily, 'it was Seven Sights Travel: Polystratus, their lying dog of a facilitator in Rome, when he took their bookings – and Phineus.'

That was when the quaestor remembered to tell me his most important news: 'Phineus is back in Corinth. I have told him to contact you.'

Now he had ruined my day.

I knew the agent would delay his appearance until it suited him. No point sticking around at the Elephant until Phineus bothered to call. I made Aquillius rack his brain for places where the man might hang out; then to make sure, when I set off to scour the drinking houses and markets, I dragged Aquillius with me. I like to provide training for government officials. Someone has to do it.

It was the first time Aquillius had ever worn out boot leather on a long seek-and-find. At first he thought it fun. Corinth was a mighty city, full of commercial crannies. By the time we two bloodhounds came upon Phineus, the quaestor had gained more respect for my tradecraft. He was moaning about lung failure. I too was blistered and bad-tempered, but after years at this game, I knew how to contain it. Anyway, I had to conserve energy. Finding Phineus was just the start for me.

Phineus was too Greek to be pure Roman and too Roman to be truly Greek. This wide-bodied heavy character wore a medium-length red tunic with sleeves; a glossy belt with a fat money purse on it; and battered boots showing huge calves and ugly toes. He had grizzled hair (once dark) and a short curly beard. Some things were as I expected: he was leaning on a bar counter among people who obviously knew him. He made his living as a man with contacts; it showed. He treated Aquillius Macer as one of his contacts, which disgusted me; I dispatched the quaestor to other tasks, just in case their relationship had moved from one of basic diplomacy to one with too much give and take.

'Nice boy!' Phineus spoke Latin, but in a deep Eastern voice.

'Very helpful,' I agreed. If he had been bought by Phineus, Aquillius was an idiot. Phineus would be an idiot too, if he let me find out. He was too canny; that would never happen. But I reckoned that Aquillius was not bright enough to sell out. He would not even recognise a dirty offer. At least rogues like Phineus would not know what to make of him.

While I was eyeing up Phineus, he returned the favour openly. I refused to be put off and kept on looking. He was physically strong, a man who had put in hard effort of some sort. Impressive legs, and his right arm stronger than the other. Prosperity showed. He was better groomed and more smartly turned out than many who arrange mules and ships. Even so, there was a well-worn air about him. He had three missing front teeth, though that applied to many people.

His survey of me would be equally two-sided: I was a Roman, but unlike most men who journeyed abroad, looked neither wealthy nor a slave. I had arrived with Aquillius, yet there was distance between him and me; I had given the order that sent Aquillius ambling off, which he had accepted as from an equal, or near equal. It would be clear I felt differently. When the amiable quaestor waved goodbye, I did not return his gesture.

I was wearing a loose brown tunic, good Italian boots, a belt with a Celtic buckle, a slightly fancy dagger in a Spanish leather scabbard. These were surface adornments; I came with more subtle trappings: skills which no slippery businessman should take for granted. I looked my age, thirty-five that year, and as tough as I would ever be. I had been around; I hoped it showed. I sported an Aventine haircut and an Aventine stare. I was ready for anything and would take no nonsense.

'So you are the special investigator!' Phineus said, keeping it light, keeping it well-mannered. 'You are very welcome. I cannot tell you how glad I shall be when you solve what has happened and free us from its shadow.'

He had to be a conniving rogue, yet he lied to me with sonorous, deep-voiced sincerity.

XXXI

'I heard you had gone to Cythera.'

'Oh – some other man took that group!' Phineus spoke dismissively; I could not decide whether he was looking down on the man, the group, or both. Maybe the other escort had pinched the Cythera commission from under Phineus' nose – and with it, the tips.

We were walking. The bar had been too intimate; neither of us wanted this conversation to be overheard by its nosy keeper and residents. Corinth had plenty of squares and colonnades to stroll in. We made our way to the main forum. It was so grandiose I for one felt anonymous there. But those multiple shops, arranged in neat sets of six or so, bunched along every façade of the frieze-bedecked piazza, could be full of ears. Corinth must have its version of Roman informers – if nothing else there would be street spies put in place to report to the governor on the activities of cults like the Christians.

'I need you to give me some background,' I said.

'Background on my clients?' Phineus enquired meekly.

'On your operation first, please. How long have you been running these escorted trips?'

'Since Nero's Grand Tour. That was the first big year for visitors; I could see things could only get better.'

So he had been on the road with tourists for the past ten years. I put him at close to forty. 'What did you do before that, Phineus?'

'This and that. I come from the south.'

'Of Greece?'

'Of Italy!'

'I've been there.' I had been to Croton, home of the

original wrestling champion Milo. I found the south hostile to Romans, its towns full of staring eyes and resentful faces. Helena's first husband came from Tarentum and he was bad news. My tone automatically went sour. 'What part?'

'Brundisium.' A port. Always liable to produce men with low morals. A major embarking point for Greece, however, so a good home for a man who had ended up arranging travel.

I gave up on his past. 'Who decided to set up an overseas consultancy? Is the business yours, or do I need to know about higher management?'

'It's mine.' He sounded proud. Judging by the current tour, customer satisfaction was not his goal. That saved him feeling depressed when he reviewed his lack of praise from clients; it was enough for him to count up his bank balance.

'You call it Seven Sights. So I guess you go to all of them?' I tried showing off: 'The Statue of Zeus at Olympia, the Temple of Artemis at Ephesus, the Colossus of Rhodes, the Hanging Gardens of Babylon – you go to *Babylon*?' Phineus laughed contemptuously. 'So you *offer* to go, and hope nobody asks for it . . . the Mausoleum at Halicarnassus, the Pharos and Library at Alexandria, the Pyramids and Sphinx at Giza.'

'I try to avoid Halicarnassus too,' Phineus told me, confidentially. 'That's halfway to Hades.' When it came to remote exploration, he liked a soft life, it seemed.

'Still, you've had clients scribbling *Tiberius was here* on some of the best cultural hotspots.'

'And they do it! *Laminus saw this monument and was amazed . . . Septimus had a good shit at this inn, and enjoyed the barmaid.* All right for them, Falco, but I have to return to those places. Last thing I want is furious temple priests who know that my previous customers defaced five-hundred-year-old pillars. Come to that, last thing I want is bitter barmaids who remember my old customers as lousy tippers!'

'You hand out hints on etiquette, surely? "Be discreet; pay what the bill demands; don't brag about the Circus Maximus or the new Flavian amphitheatre" . . .'

'"Pee when you can; don't steal votive offerings; souvenir-sellers want you to barter; money-changers don't. Never forget, Athens was a world-wide power when Romulus was sucking milk from the wolfie" – oh yes. Doesn't stop the bastards standing before the monument at Thermopylae, when their hearts ought to be broken, and sneering, "But Leonidas and the Spartans *lost!*"'

'Doesn't stop them continuously moaning?' I threw in.

Phineus favoured me with a caustic glance. 'Now what have you heard, Falco?'

'No Games at Olympia?'

He sucked air through the hole between his front teeth. 'They have no idea!' he shook his head mournfully. 'Great gods, Falco! Don't these fools know about the old story? – one man used to threaten his slaves that if they misbehaved, their punishment was to be sent to the Olympic Games.'

'That bad?'

'Worse! Oh I have taken tours there during the contests. *Then* you get some moaning! It's a nightmare. Even if they think they know how it will be, they reel when they come up against the actual experience. They can't move, they don't see anything, they get bitten by flies and are laid low, they sweat like pigs in the heat, they collapse from dehydration, they are robbed by incense-sellers and street entertainers and prostitutes –' All this was now familiar. I was unimpressed by the blather. Phineus glanced at me to see how I was taking it, then carried on insistently: 'They are packed so tight, people faint away. Once I get the men into the stadium we are stuck there until closing time. The Games are violent events, long days of being squashed together under a baking sun, tumult all around –'

'And you cannot take women?'

'I wouldn't take women even if I could!'

We had stopped in front of the southern stoa, a long colonnade cut from the rock on two levels. Above us reared the Temple of Apollo, hundreds of years old, on its spectacular bluff. It had a long and serenely confident array of the

174

wide, slightly squat Greek columns with which I had become familiar at Olympia; to me, not so refined as our taller Roman temple pillars. Helena always said Apollo was handsome enough, but she wouldn't invite him home to dinner. He would be bound to bring his lyre with him and would want to start a music contest. Like Nero, Apollo was known to sulk and turn nasty if he was not allowed to win.

'So, Phineus, ' I said quietly. 'Does your prohibition against women date from the year you took Marcella Naevia and her missing niece?'

Phineus breathed out, puffing his cheeks. 'That again!'

'"Again" nothing. It never went away.'

'Look, Falco. I do not know what happened to that girl. I *really* do not know.' The way he said it almost implied there were other things he claimed not to know, where some different measure of truth applied. I wondered what they were.

'And Valeria Ventidia, the bludgeoned bride?'

'How could I know anything about her either?'

He and I cooled off below a statue of a prowling lion, taking shelter from the sun's glare in the shade of its enormous plinth. A tattered stall was selling drinks. Without comment on Phineus' last remark, I bought two cups of honeyed wine. Well, it passed for wine. We stood to sip them, so we could return the beakers afterwards.

'I was with the men,' Phineus reminded me. 'I had taken the men to a mock-feast of victory. When the bride died,' he insisted.

I sampled my drink again, longing for more familiar street fare. 'And when the girl went up the Hill of Cronus, where were you then, Phineus?'

'Gods, I can't remember!' His voice was low and full of irritation. I lifted my mouth from the sticky cup, and gazed at him. He must have had an answer at the time – and I wanted to hear it. 'It was the last day,' he remarked, in his dismissive way.

Young Glaucus had told me the programme. As Phineus and I moved on, towards the Forum's massive triple

175

entrance arch, beside the huge complex of the Peirene Fountain, I counted off the events: 'Day One: swearing in competitors, contests for heralds, sacrifices, orations. Day Two: Equestrian events (chariots and horse races), the pentathlon. Day Three: sacrifice of the hundred oxen to Zeus, foot races. Day Four: the contact sports – wrestling, boxing, pankration.'

'And race-in-armour,' Phineus added. Pedantic bastard.

'Day Four would be particularly trying for any women present, I imagine. Penned up, with nothing much to do, waiting for their male companions to come home, knowing the men would talk obsessively about blood and battery.'

'The way I see it,' Phineus said, pompously and without much sympathy, 'if these rich women agree to accompany their men on an athletics tour, they must know what they are letting themselves in for.'

'I think my wife might say, all women underestimate what men will impose on them!'

We were at the fountain now. We stood on the busy flight of steps, buffeted by people coming and going from the pools. It had six dramatic arches above gloomy cisterns, which lay some way below the level of the modern Forum. I wondered if that represented the old foundation level, before the brutal destruction wreaked in Rome's name by Corinth-conquering Mummius. 'Marcella Naevia is well travelled, I am told, but she and her young niece may have known little about the world of sport. Perhaps *they* were not prepared, Phineus. Was the aunt single, married, or widowed?'

'She was trouble,' said Phineus. 'Always raising protests. Always having a go.' A typical Seven Sights client, then.

'She took against you?' It was a guess, but accurate.

'She did.'

'Why?'

'Absolutely no idea.' I could have provided suggestions. Once more he closed off. Once more I waited. 'The woman was unreasonable.'

'The woman lost her niece, Phineus.'

'Nobody knew the girl was dead. She could have run off

with a one-legged sprinter, for all anybody knew.'

'Do virgins run off with athletes or otherwise frequently on your tours?'

Phineus laughed coarsely. 'No, they usually just end up pregnant. My job is to spot the bulge in time to ship them back to Rome before they actually have the child – then my company washes its hands of them!'

'That must save you a lot of trouble,' I said. He took it as a compliment.

After a while, we moved down the wide fountain stair ourselves, into its water-cooled open courtyard. The pools were still below our level, reached by a few further steps. We could hear the water cascading from six lion-headed spouts. Overshadowed by the enclosing walls, we trod carefully on the wet slabs. I glanced up to admire the elegantly painted architecture, then reminded Phineus of where we left off: 'So – Day Four, three years ago: what happened, Phineus?'

'The men had a really good day at the contact sports, then I had arranged to take them to a feast.'

'You can't get them in to the official winners' banquet, presumably? The Prytaneion is reserved for competitors. So you fixed up an alternative – like the one you arranged this year for the current group?' That would be a dreary night with execrable refreshments, according to the angry group member Sertorius. 'Any good?' I could not resist the chance to be satirical.

'Of course. Then next morning, the bloody girl went missing, her damned aunt raised an outcry, and just when we were due to leave, we spent a day fruitlessly searching for darling Caesia. I'll never forget. It was bloody pouring with rain. '

'She had vanished overnight?'

'The aunt reported it when we were ready to go. I think she waited until morning.' Phineus saw me looking sideways. 'In case darling Caesia had just found herself a boyfriend and wanted to stay with him.'

'Did you have any reason to think that she had?'

'Found a boyfriend? I wouldn't think so. She was a prim little mouse. Jumped, if anybody so much as looked at her. Didn't seem to like men.'

That was new. Inaccurate too. Her father had said there was an episode with a man at home in Rome. 'You thought she had no experience?'

'She hid behind the skirts of older women on the trip.' Hid from what, I wondered.

'Who was making advances?'

'Nobody.' Phineus looked annoyed. 'Don't twist my words. I never said that.'

I changed tack. 'Did you meet her father – afterwards?'

Now it was Phineus who jumped. 'Why? What's her father said, Falco?'

'Touchy! It was a straight question.'

'I met him,' stated Phineus. 'I was polite to him. He had lost his child and I sympathised. There simply wasn't anything that I could do to help the man. I know nothing about what happened to Marcella Caesia.' He paused then. I could not tell what he was thinking – but once again I felt there *were* things Phineus kept hidden. 'Except this, Falco – if Caesia really disappeared the night before we left, this is a certainty: none of the male clients on that tour harmed her. It would have been impossible. All of them were with me all Day Four, from when we left the women in the morning – with Caesia among them, perfectly all right.'

XXXII

It had taken Aquillius and me a long time to find Phineus, and it had been a hard walk. Talking to him had scrambled my brain too. I knew he was bamboozling me. After I left him, I felt unsettled. Looking up at the crag, with its distant temples dreamily far off, I was filled with inertia. I lost interest in climbing the acropolis today.

I went back to the Elephant, learned that Helena had gone shopping, and fell back on an informer's honest standby: writing up my notes. (There are other excuses, less useful, though often more fun.) The good work just happened to occur in the courtyard of the Bay Mare, where eventually I was offered lunch. Since I was occupying their table, it would have been discourteous to refuse.

When Helena came and found me looking guilty with a bowl and goblet, I escaped censure due to guilt of her own. She carefully arranged the folds of her light skirt and graceful stole – a delaying tactic that I recognised. Then she admitted she had been purchasing ancient vases. We could afford these antiquities, for which Corinth had once been famous, but her intention was to export most back to Rome for my father's business. I said what I thought of that. Helena thought I was unfair to Pa. We had a satisfying wrangle about the meaning of 'unfairness', after which, since none of our party was around, we slunk off to our room, threw off our clothes, and reminded ourselves of what life together was all about.

Nothing that is anybody else's business.

Some time later, I remembered to give Helena the letter that Aquillius had brought from her brother.

*

Our vagrant scholar was as trusting as ever that we would have rushed out to Greece when he whistled. How he guessed we might come through Corinth was not revealed. Aulus wrote a blunt epistle, void of frills; explanations were not his strength. It boded ill for his career as a lawyer, should he ever take it up.

He must have reasoned we would go to Olympia because that was where the deaths took place, then since Corinth was roughly in a line with Athens, we would rest here on our way to see him. He had convinced himself that if we were in Greece we were coming to find him. That he, Aulus Camillus Aelianus the layabout law student, might not be my priority during a murder hunt never struck him. There was a time when I disliked this fellow; now I just despaired.

After hoping we were well (a courtesy which meant he must be running short of funds already), he dropped into cipher for a résumé. Neither Helena nor I had brought code-books with us, but apparently Aulus always used the same system and Helena Justina could work it out from just one or two points she remembered. I relaxed on the bed, playing fondly with parts of Helena that strayed within reach, while she frowned over the scroll and buffed away my playful hands; she broke the code far too quickly for me. I told her I was glad I had never kept a diary with details of liaisons with buxom mistresses. Helena chortled that she knew I kept no diaries (had she looked for them?), and said how fortunate, too, that since she always used an extremely difficult code, I could not read hers. We got down to business eventually.

Aulus had decided Tullius Statianus was innocent. I wondered if that meant Statianus loved hunting and dinner parties, just like Aulus? Playboy or not, the bereaved husband now felt he must take responsibility for solving his wife's gruesome death. Statianus was addressing this not by using our process of logical investigation, but by travelling to Delphi to consult the oracle.

'Oh nuts!'

'Don't be sceptical,' Helena cautioned. 'Many people do believe in it.'

I restricted myself to the scathing remark that many people were idiots.

'Just to be doing something may calm him, Marcus.'

'Doing *this* will waste his money and drive him crazy.'

We were dealing with travellers who had come to Greece in search of its ancient mysteries, so Statianus' pilgrimage was in character. Even I conceded that he must be deeply shocked and devastated by the classic feelings of helplessness. Aulus had tried to promise our aid, but had to confess the possibility that his letters had never reached us. So the two men had gone across to Delphi together. There they had discovered what is rarely spelt out in the guidebooks: only one day each month is assigned for prophecies – and, worse, only nations, major cities, and rich persons of extreme importance tend to be winners in the inevitable lottery for questions.

'Apollo's oracle has a *queue*?'

'Truth is valuable, Marcus. They have to ration it.'

Given that by tradition no one can understand the prophecies, this seemed doubly harsh on the desperate.

Aulus had never been famous for sticking-power. Since the oracle seemed a waste of time, he gave up. With no sign of hypocrisy, he wrote to his sceptical sister that he now felt it proper to honour his parents' wishes and make his way to university. Helena guffawed. I amused myself imagining their parents' reaction. We assumed that once Aulus had seen the Statue of Zeus at Olympia and explored the Delphic sanctuary, it was time for him to add the glorious Parthenon to his wish-list of fancy sights.

Statianus, the distraught bridegroom, had been left behind, still looking for a chance to submit a lead tablet asking 'Who murdered my wife?' to the Pythia; she was the frantic priestess who, even in these modern times, sat on a tripod chewing bay leaves until the god (or the bay leaves) overwhelmed her with unintelligible wisdom and a bad headache afterwards.

If Statianus did not rejoin the travel group soon, someone would have to go to Delphi and gather him up. I bet I knew who that would be. It might be easier to extract him when I could answer his tragic question myself, so I filed the obsessive widower in my 'do later' pigeonhole.

'As an oracle, you are a lazy bastard, Falco!' Helena commented.

'O woman of disbelief! As an oracle, I am hot stuff. I prophesy this: seek for him who comes and goes amongst those who go and come.'

'You think Phineus is the murderer? But Phineus told you he was occupied with other people at the crucial times, so that's impossible.'

'Phineus is a blatant liar,' I prophesied.

XXXIII

Since no other delaying tactic struck me, next morning I did set out for the acropolis.

I crossed the Forum on its north side, in my hiking gear and with Nux at my heels. At one point I noticed Phineus outside a shop. He was deep in conversation with another man, one of his many contacts, no doubt; I put my head down and got by unseen. Then a voice hailed me. It was just Cleonymus, the freedman; he was sitting on the central rostrum on his own, waiting for the wine shops to open. His wife and their two companions were all asleep with hangovers, so he said he would come up the crag with me to see the views. Nux was wagging her tail at company, so I agreed. Cleonymus was wearing a massive belt buckle against his richly embroidered tunic, with such heavy gold bangles on his muscular forearms that I thought it a duty to remove him from the envious crowds.

We walked over to the east end, and climbed a short flight of steps which led to a row of about six individual temples to minor divinities. This town was certainly pious. Next we passed through some small shops, emerging opposite a much larger temple in the Roman style which had the standard air of an imperial family dedication. Its columns had elaborate acanthus-leaved Corinthian columns; belatedly it struck me that the florid Corinthian style of capital was actually named after this city. I had never liked it. Glancing back, I saw the more straightforward Doric Temple of Apollo, exquisitely outlined against the deep blue waters of the Saronic Gulf and a lustrous sky. Its Greek austerity tugged at my old-fashioned Roman core.

'That's handsome, but I don't take to Corinth, Cleonymus – too much religion and too much shopping.'

'Oh you can never have too much shopping, Falco!'

Over on our right where the land dropped away lay the theatre; to the left was a gymnasium where I knew Young Glaucus had already established his credentials. We passed a very old fountain, into which Jason's young wife was supposed to have thrown herself to quench the pain of Medea's poisoned robe; beyond that was another fountain, a sanctuary of Athena, and a sanctuary of Aesculapius.

'So Turcianus Opimus could have brought himself here! Then he could have died where the Roman governor might arrange to ship him home.'

'Epidaurus was even more beautiful – though not very peaceful when the sacred dogs all had a yap.' Cleonymus had spotted the stone money box for donations; he dropped a silver coin in the slot. 'Show willing.' It was like his generosity in buying wine for everyone. He thought he should share his own good fortune. Few owners of a vast inheritance retain so much benevolence.

We soon felt we ourselves might have to offer the god of medicine some votive statuettes of lungs. The road took us upwards, its steep incline challenging our stamina. Nux chased to and fro around us, heedless of the slope, a small excited bundle of fur with ears pressed back by her own momentum and eyes turned to slits in the wind she created. Eventually I put her on a lead, fearful the crazed animal would leap off the cliff. As the views became ever more spectacular, I was less and less minded to climb giddily down the rockface to rescue Nux from some tiny ledge. The mad dog would probably topple me over into oblivion in the act of welcoming me.

Initially Cleonymus proved a surprisingly good walker, considering his wine intake, though it was soon clear I had more long-term stamina. We puffed up in silence for a while then got talking as we settled into our stride. I let him guide the conversation. He told me a little of his travels, before I asked how he and Cleonyma came to be hooked up with Minucia and Amaranthus.

'Oh we just met them on this trip.'

We climbed on, then I prodded again: 'Helena Justina thinks Minucia seems a bit restless with Amaranthus.'

'Minucia doesn't say much, but she seems to miss her family.'

'She dumped a husband? Children too?'

'I believe so, Falco. Plus aunts, sisters – and a puddle full of ducks! She's a home-lover who made a run for it to prove she could,' Cleonymus told me. 'Now she's hankering to see dough rising in her own crock again.'

'Will she leave Amaranthus?'

'They've been together quite a while, I think. Cleonyma and I think the sad events on this trip are having an unsettling effect.'

'Sudden death makes you wonder about your own life expectancy . . . Was Amaranthus married too?'

'No, never. He's a loner at heart, if you ask me.'

'So what's his background, Cleonymus?'

'Salt-fish export. He's made a packet from shifting amphorae of sea bass. Looking for markets got him started on travel; now he combines work and pleasure. He's a real sports aficionado too. He was hopping mad when we got to Olympia and he realised there were no contests.'

'Was that mis-selling by Seven Sights?'

'According to them, no.'

'And according to you?'

'Guess! The fact that the dates have been muddled up since Nero is now twisted around to become our own fault. We all convinced ourselves this year was next year, while Phineus claims he and Polystratus – do you know that slime-ball, by the way? – would *never* have deluded us . . .'

'Yes, I met Polystratus back in Rome. He tried to sell me the Olympic Games for next year, funnily enough.'

'So now he does know the proper date,' scoffed Cleonymus. 'What was your verdict on him, Falco?'

'True salesman – idle, devious, full of sharp practice. He

upset Helena Justina by treating her as if she was a miserly hag, holding me back.'

'I'm not surprised.' Cleonymus tweaked up the corner of his mouth. 'Cleonyma nearly bashed him with her travel scroll box when we were booking – he would have really felt it; Cleonyma has a *lot* of travel narratives.' We saved our breath for the next few moments. 'Pity she didn't do it,' Cleonymus murmured, more obliquely than usual.

As the road wound upwards, the views improved but we sweated more. The crag was almost sheer; only this western side could be scaled at all, and it was hard going. High above, we could make out what must be the other Temple of Apollo, this one straddling the acropolis peak, together with scattered roofs and columns of several other temples. The effects of prolonged imbibing were slowing down my companion now. We paused, with the excuse of admiring the fabulous panorama. Nux lay on my foot, licking my insole through my bootstraps. She might be a street dog from the Seven Hills, but she preferred walking on the flat.

'Indus seems to enjoy a raffish reputation,' I suggested to the freedman.

'Enjoy is right; he loves being the centre of intrigue.'

'Has he confessed his history?' Cleonymus gave me the finger to the nose which is the universal sign of keeping mum. 'Oh go on! What's he running away from?' I begged.

'Sworn to secrecy, Falco.'

'Tell me this at least: does it have a bearing on the deaths I'm investigating?'

'Absolutely none at all!' Cleonymus assured me, laughing.

Doggedly, I pursued the issue. 'I'm having some trouble placing both of those caustic bachelors. Something about Marinus keeps you guessing too.'

'He's looking for a new partner,' Cleonymus said, rather firmly.

'Yes, he comes right out and says so. Helena thinks it's not quite normal.'

'Normal enough for a professional fraud.' I raised an eyebrow. After a moment, Cleonymus told me, 'My wife and

186

I have met him before. Marinus doesn't remember; his tracking system concentrates on single women, not married couples. It was a couple of years back; we ran into him on Rhodes. He was looking for a new partner then too – and he found one. Unfortunately for the lady.'

I caught on: 'Marinus is a professional leech? Emptied her coffers, then did a bunk?'

'Absolutely.'

'He seems such a decent fellow.'

'Secret of his success, Falco. Left her broken-hearted and bankrupt. She was too embarrassed to admit it, or to do anything about it. Between ourselves, Cleonyma and I had to lend her the fare home.' When he said 'lend', this good-natured man probably meant 'give'.

'Is the same true of Indus?' I asked, but Cleonymus only twinkled in reply.

'Well, if Marinus is defrauding rich victims, I'd be worried about Helvia – but it looks as if he has checked her out and finds her too poor.'

'Ah, Helvia!' Cleonymus was smiling again. 'A woman to watch, maybe. We suspect there could be more to dippy Helvia than most people think.'

I grinned in return. 'You're giving me a fine exposé – though tantalising! Any views on the tortured Sertorius family?' He shuddered. 'And I think I can guess what you feel about Volcasius?'

'Poison.'

'So what about the masterly Phineus, purveyor of dismal feasts and dirty donkeys?'

Cleonymus had stopped again, visibly out of breath. His only comment on Phineus was elusive: 'Interesting character!'

He was badly in need of a rest by now, whereas I had to continue with my errand to the so-called sorceress. We agreed Cleonymus would sit down here and wait for me, while I carried on in my search for the boys' water-seller, then I would pick him up on my way down. I left Nux to keep him company while he recovered.

I toiled on, leaning on my stave to help keep the legs going. The air, always clear, now seemed even thinner. Dazzling views lay below, over the city and on to the blue waters of the Gulf of Corinth, with a dark line of mountains behind, indicating mainland Greece to the north. Down on the Isthmus, I tried to convince myself I could make out the straight line of the *diolkos*, the ship-towing track. After a short breather, I slogged upwards again until finally I came upon what could only be the upper Peirene spring. That meant the old crone Gaius and Cornelius met was no longer on the acropolis, or I would have passed her.

I refilled my flagon at the spring. It was ice cold and crystalline, trickling over my hands in refreshing runnels as I tried to persuade the liquid to flow into the container's narrow neck.

I had met people coming down the hill, though not many. Knowing about the Temple of Aphrodite, it was no surprise to see a woman dallying by herself. She looked middle-aged and perfectly respectable – so I guessed she must be from the temple, and was one of its hard-working prostitutes. I was too old and far too wise to expect voluptuous fifteen-year-olds.

I gave her a polite smile and said good morning in Greek. She was not much to look at; well, not by my standards. That was usual in her calling. She wore a classic folded-over robe, in white, with her greying hair bound up in a bandeau. Give her a double flute and she could be on a vase – that would have been twenty years ago. She had a pot belly, flabby arms, and vacant eyes.

She was gazing out across the view to the Gulf, with a dreamy, don't-approach-me smile. I had no need for and no wish for her services. Still, it was fun to imagine what kind of tricks this worn-out minion of love would turn with the hard-bitten sailors and merchants who made the effort to come up here. Frankly, she looked far away with the nymphs.

'Excuse me, do you mind if I ask you a question?' No

answer; in fact, her stony silence implied she thought me a loser with a *very* old seduction line. 'The name is Falco, Didius Falco.' That was supposed to reassure any business-woman; clients do not provide personal details, not unless they are local town councillors visiting venerated half-retired prostitutes for a regular appointment they have kept for decades.

My friendly request was meeting resistance; I did feel a few doubts. I even wondered if this woman was herself the so-called old water-seller. She was minus a hat, and I could see no suitable equipment with her, though a little way off there was a mangy donkey, nibbling at the barren scree in search of sustenance. He looked up at me despondently.

'If this was a myth,' I suggested to the floozy, 'you would be a sphinx who would issue tortuous riddles – and frankly, I'd be stuck. I rely on my wife to unravel codes . . .' The charm was failing. 'Look, all I want is this: do you know anything about an elderly lady who sometimes sells water to travellers on their way up the crag? I just need to find out is she is still in the vicinity?'

The loopy-looking dame turned her head and surveyed me as if she had never seen a man before. In view of her supposed profession, this could not be true. Surprisingly, she answered the question. Her voice had a remote quality, but she made sense: 'Why do you want her?'

'Need to ask her about something that happened at Olympia three years ago.'

She gave me a wilder stare than ever. 'She has left here now.'

'Thank you.' I was tucking my flagon back into my belt, ready to descend the hill again.

'I am Philomela,' announced the woman suddenly.

'Nightingale! Good pseudonym for a working girl.' Must be a reference to her singing out convincingly as she faked orgasms.

She looked confused but made me the usual offer: 'Is there anything else I can do for you?'

'No thanks. The act of love is difficult when travelling, but my wife and I made up our losses yesterday. Sorry.'

Once again I was subjected to the weird gaze. 'I have no idea what you are talking about,' said the so-called Philomela. Then she realised what I had meant – and I too saw my error. Oops! She was *not* a prostitute.

I saluted her smartly, and turned on my heel. Before either of us had time to be embarrassed, I made off hastily back down the road to Corinth.

XXXIV

Going down that towering crag was even harder than coming up. Different, more awkward leg muscles were stretched, and there was a constant need to avoid gaining too much momentum and tumbling. Leaning back against the gravitational force, I skipped and slithered. Pebbles slipped away beneath my feet. My flagon banged against my waist. I used my stave to steady myself; I had to dig in its point hard, for the most part fixing my eyes on the treacherous road surface. The stave was bending against my weight, so uncontrolled was my descent.

As I came in sight of the spot where I had left Cleonymus, I heard Nux. An ear-splitting edge to my dog's barks alerted me. I could see a small crowd. Although it had seemed there was hardly anyone about on the acropolis road, people had emerged from nowhere. They had come to help in an emergency.

At first I could not tell what was going on. Nux spotted me; she ran up and danced around my feet, yelping in agitation. From time to time she put her muzzle to her side, giving a brave little whine, as if she had been hurt but would not make too much of it. I raced down the last stretch. With a grim feeling, I pushed through the small group of spectators to the road's edge. Satisfied, Nux followed me; she lay with her nose on the very edge of the precipice, whining again piteously.

'Good girl. Good girl . . .' Talking to the dog was supposed to soothe me. Instead, as I craned over the drop, panic surged.

I was too late to join in and help. Too late altogether.

A man had gone over the edge. A chain of courageous

locals were risking their lives as they struggled to reach over, using a short rope someone must have had with him. They had dropped the rope to the man below. He was clinging to a few dry bushes that had rooted in the sheer side of the hill. A line of broken foliage showed where he must have already slipped down, perhaps in stages.

Dear gods, it was Cleonymus. I recognised his rich blue tunic, then the top of his head as he pressed himself against the rockface. He was clinging on by his fingertips. One hand grasped a twiggy shrub above him, while the other reached out sideways, desperately clutching variations in the bare limestone. The rescuers had managed to lower the rope very close to him, but if he let go with either hand to grab it, he would fall.

I wanted to call out to him. That could be fatal. I grabbed the rescuers' rope, adding my weight to the human ballast. Then someone shouted a warning. I let go, looked over the edge, and was just in time to see the shrub give way, its shallow roots wrenched from their tenuous hold. Cleonymus went crashing down the cliff. He travelled many feet. Once I thought I heard him yell. Then there was silence. Far below, his body lay still. We all started down the road as fast as possible, but we knew that by the time we reached him wherever he had come to rest, there would be no help we could give.

'Did anyone see what happened?' As we stumbled along, I tried to make sense of the accident.

A passer-by, himself in shock now, had heard the dog barking and a man calling for help. At first Cleonymus had come to rest almost within reach, clinging to the rockface close to the road. Minutes later, he panicked as he tried to climb to safety, lost his grip and fell further. A ragged group of helpers assembled. One brave soul ventured over the edge, but it was too dangerous; others pulled him back.

Everyone assumed Cleonymus had stood too close to the edge. He either lost his balance as he looked down over the perilous drop, or perhaps part of the road gave way under him.

'Did he say anything?'

'Apart from screaming "Help me!"?'

'Sorry. Was anybody with him when he fell?'

One witness had seen Cleonymus talking to another fellow earlier. But the witness was elderly and vague; the other man could easily have been me when I was with Cleonymus. Then someone else claimed to have seen a man in expensive clothes walking briskly downhill just before the tragedy. Nobody like that had passed me on my way to the spring. If the sighting was true, this well-dressed man must have followed Cleonymus and me up, then turned back.

With great difficulty, we managed to retrieve the body. It took over an hour, and by the time we brought Cleonymus to a lower part of the road, he had been with his ancestors too long to be revived. For his sake, I hoped death had happened quickly. We laid him down with gentle hands. I removed his jewellery and purse for safe keeping, then covered him with my cloak. One of the helpers had transport; he promised to convey the body to the governor's residence. Aquillius could take responsibility.

I called Nux. She came over slowly, still walking as if she had been kicked in the ribs. She yowked in pain when I picked her up. As I carried her back to Corinth, she lay subdued in my arms, tail down and trembling.

The freedman had told me a few new facts today. He had known more, I felt sure of it. Now I was left frustrated, wondering whether somebody had thought his knowledge so bad for them that they silenced him. Did Cleonymus share something Turcianus Opimus had known? Were the two travellers killed by the same person, for the same reason?

I remembered how I left Cleonymus, sitting in a perfectly safe position, with Nux lying contentedly at his feet. He had wanted simply to rest quietly for a while. In the short time I took to reach the upper Peirene spring, fill a flagon, and insult a woman, it was unlikely that Cleonymus would have moved from his recovery spot.

Something had made him fall. My dog had seen it. It

sounded to me as if this 'expensively dressed man' had pushed Cleonymus and kicked Nux, maybe when she tried to defend the freedman. Nux was unable to explain to me, but I stroked her to bring us both comfort. Now it fell to me to break the news to Cleonyma. I always loathed that task. It was all the worse when the victim was someone whose generosity and intelligence I had come to like.

It was worst of all when I suspected the 'accident' that killed him had been no accident at all.

XXXV

The women were shrieking with laughter when Helena and I walked into the inn courtyard. Most of the group were there at the Helios. Everyone seemed tipsy. To me the day seemed to have been endless, yet it was just after lunch. Helena squeezed my hand in encouragement. Nux was now being cared for by Albia; the dog had not wanted us to leave her.

Within a few minutes my task was done and nobody was laughing.

The atmosphere changed to funereal. Cleonyma sat motionless, trying to take in what I had said. Helena and her friend Minucia waited to console her, but so far the new widow's reaction was straight disbelief. There were questions that I needed to ask her urgently, but not now. She could not speak. After a while she tilted her head back slightly. A short rush of involuntary tears ran down her tinted cheeks, but she ignored them. Soon she recovered her composure.

'We had a hard life, then a good one,' she pronounced, to nobody in particular. 'He and I were true friends and lovers. You cannot ask for more.'

She could have asked to enjoy it for longer.

She was flamboyant and loud yet, like her husband, underneath she had unusual modesty. The couple had been humane and decent. Helena and I respected them. We had decided that since there was so little evidence I would not mention my fears about what had happened – but to myself I made a vow that if those fears proved to be well founded, I would track down whoever had pushed Cleonymus down the crag.

*

Cleonyma had closed her eyes. Grief was starting to overcome her. Minucia moved closer and took her friend's hand. As she did so, Minucia shot me one quick, hard look, as if challenging me about the freedman's abrupt and unexpected extinction. I shook my head slightly, warning her off the subject. Then she devoted herself to Cleonyma, signalling for the rest of us to leave them alone in the courtyard while the long process of mourning began.

Most of us went out on the street side, emerging into bright sunlight like stunned sheep after a hillside scare with a wolf. Helena sat me on a sunny bench, one arm around my shoulders protectively.

'You look as if you need a drink,' Marinus offered, but I shook my head. He and Indus seemed to need to give someone hospitality to ameliorate their shock; they went off, leading Amaranthus instead. Helvia had been swallowed up by the Sertorius family. That left Volcasius. He came and plonked himself right in front of us.

'This is a new twist, Falco!' I just nodded. 'So was it an accident?'

'Apparently.' I did not want him upsetting Cleonyma with some blunt revelation that could not be proved.

'Doesn't sound like it!'

I forced myself to answer. 'Nobody saw anything, so we cannot be sure what happened.' I glared at Volcasius as he stood there, shambly and lop-sided in his irritating sunhat. 'Unless you have any particular reason to suppose someone was out to get the freedman?'

Volcasius made no reply, but continued to stand there. He was a man with fixations and seemed fascinated by disasters. He would hang around unwanted, where those of us who understood the etiquette of crisis would leave the bereaved alone.

Helena shared my thoughts. She too must be wondering if Volcasius had clung to the bridegroom in the aftermath of the earlier tragedy. 'Cleonyma will have a lot to go through now. You saw all this with Statianus at Olympia, Volcasius?'

'He was hysterical,' Volcasius said. 'Nobody he knew had ever died before. He had never seen a dead body, or had to arrange a funeral.'

'You talked to him? Did anything come out of it?' Helena spoke unexcitedly. She seemed to give her attention to me, stroking my hair. I let myself go limp, soothed by her long fingers.

'Did I think he was the killer?' Volcasius demanded. 'No. He didn't have the willpower, or the necessary strength.' Volcasius had previously denied any opinion on this.

'But he and Valeria argued all the time, didn't they?' Helena probed.

'That was just their way. They would have gone on arguing, even if they stayed married for the next thirty years.'

'Their domestic routine? – Yes, I have seen couples who are locked in endless disharmony,' said Helena. 'If one of them dies, the other is devastated. They miss the wrangling . . . Statianus has gone to consult the oracle at Delphi. My brother wrote and told me.'

'Is Aelianus with him?' Volcasius looked eager to be on that trip himself.

Helena avoided answering. 'Statianus has now shouldered responsibility for finding out who slaughtered his wife.'

'He should have stuck around here then!' scoffed the loner.

'Why – do you know something about it, Volcasius?'

'I know he won't find whoever did it from the *Sibylline Leaves* at Delphi.'

'The *Sibylline Leaves* are in Rome now.' Delighted to catch out the pedant in an error, I bestirred myself. 'The prophetess at Delphi mutters and growls her riddles orally.'

As I expected, being put in the wrong made Volcasius vicious. 'You think you're very clever, Falco!'

'No, I think I'm being treated like a fool,' I snapped.

'Not by me.' He was so self-righteous I could have leaned forward and chopped him off at the knees.

'By most of the people in your travel group. You are all

197

accepting what happens far too casually. If you know something, do your duty and report it!'

'Three of the tour group are dead. Valeria, Turcianus, Cleonymus . . .' Volcasius counted them off. 'Someone is picking us off like cornfield rats. Should the rest of us be scared, I wonder?'

'You should all be very careful.' It was Helena who growled that at him. Like me, she was churning with anger after the freedman's death. Volcasius tossed his head and without any farewell or warning, suddenly stomped off.

Typically, he threw back a confusing remark over his shoulder: 'Did you see our wonderful organiser, when you were with Cleonymus?' He did not wait for me to answer – nor, of course, did he explain. But it sounded as though he was aiming accusations against Phineus.

I sat on the bench for a while longer, sharing my deep melancholy with my wife.

In the end, curiosity got the better of me. I hated to feel manipulated by Volcasius, but his fingering of the tour escort fitted my suspicions and action was my style. I kissed Helena, rose, and said I was going in search of Phineus. Helena was on her feet as well. She kissed me again, holding me for an extra moment.

'You too be careful, Marcus.'

'Trust me.'

I found Phineus in a bar, near the one where I first saw him yesterday. He was alone, though there were two empty winecups in front of him; one of his many cronies had recently left. For some reason, I remembered the man I had seen talking with Phineus that morning, just before I met Cleonymus. He had seemed vaguely familiar. Still, Phineus would seek out a certain type. The one I saw earlier had been similar in dress and manner to Phineus himself, lighter built but also bearded.

'Have you heard the news?'

'What's up, Falco?' He seemed sincere. He was standing

at a counter, on the verge of paying his bill from a very fat purse. The size of the purse riled me.

A man in his position, always alert for some new problem with customers, habitually stays calm. He was already halfway to his 'nothing to worry about; let me handle it' expression and I had not told him anything. Being what he was, he was preparing to do nothing and hope the crisis would just go away.

'You have lost another of your clients.'

'What?' He groaned. If he was faking, he must be a good actor. As an informer I had met plenty of them, mostly not on a stage. 'What's happened now? Which one is it?'

'The freedman.'

'Cleonymus? He's a character!'

'Not any more. He fell off the acropolis.'

Phineus steadied. 'Is he dead?'

'Unfortunately.'

Now Phineus sighed deeply, standing still to take it in. He signalled the waiter to refill his wine beaker. I had a good look at his tunic, the same he wore yesterday: full nap, dyed to a gemstone hue of gorgeous dark ruby. Heavy belt, sharp boots, bulging pouch, hardstone signet ring with a thick laced strapwork setting: all his accessories were good. You could describe him as a well-dressed man. But was he the same well-dressed man who went up the acropolis? This prosperous city was crammed with businessmen who looked equally high-priced in style.

I put it to him straight out: 'Someone thought they saw you going up to Acrocorinth today.'

Phineus hardly registered that this was a dangerous question. 'Not me. I've been at the port all morning.' He quaffed the whole new cupful in one go. Now he came out with whatever had preoccupied him: 'Oh pig's piss. This is a blow.' He looked to me for consolation; I had none to give. 'Travel is never safe. I've had a mule fall on someone and crush them, and a man struck on the head by a full amphora of Cretan red. We try to take precautions, but you cannot cover everything. Accidents will happen.'

I gave him a bleak stare. 'That presupposes this was an accident.'

Without another word, I left him and went back to find Helena.

I had no evidence against Phineus. I was not yet ready to accuse him. I dared not even ask such pointed questions that he guessed what I was thinking. I could not risk frightening him off.

I would continue to watch the others. But he was in my sights now.

XXXVI

Back at the Elephant, I was relieved to find that the builders had taken an afternoon off. I could not have borne their dusty, noisy renovations. The landlord was hanging about. He had heard we had a connection with a fatal accident. This little excitement drew him to us, as if he thought a death gave us magical attributes. I asked what the public were saying; he said the rumour was that Cleonymus went over because he was drunk. I snarled that the public were idiots then, and sent the landlord packing.

In a clear space in the courtyard, Albia and my two nephews were crouching around Nux. She lay in a basket I had never seen before, putting on a brave little invalid act. When I appeared, she allowed the end third of her short tail to twitch; she lifted her nose to me. I knelt down and put my palm on her side; her eyes showed a look of panic through their matted fur fringe, though she managed not to yelp.

'That dog's had a real bashing!' Gaius exclaimed. He sounded more admiring of whoever had bashed her, than of Nux for enduring the agony. I lifted my hand from her ribs, where her small heart had been pounding; she settled down warily, allowing me to stroke her head. After a moment she even gave me a sad lick, to show there were no hard feelings.

'Good dog. You're safe now with us . . . Who hurt you, girlie?'

Nux put a hot black nose against my palm. Normally this was disgusting, but I let her snuffle.

Albia, whom Helena and I had first met saving the lives of some dogs in a building fire, stood up from bending over Nux. 'Are we sure it was not you, Marcus Didius?'

I was shocked. 'Don't even think that!' I stared at the girl.

Her early life had been brutal; we forgot that a little too readily. She still had a lot to learn about trust, and when to apply it. 'Nux is a mongrel with appalling habits – but she's mine.' I took her in from the streets just like you, Albia, I thought – but did not say it.

Gaius and Cornelius were watching us too closely for comfort. Albia said uncomfortably, 'Young Glaucus thinks you kill people.'

'I don't know what his father told him to make Glaucus believe that.'

'Uncle Marcus was in the army,' said Cornelius, trying to convince himself that excused anything. He was right too.

'Uncle Marcus looks like a comedy clown, but he's secretly dangerous!' Gaius chortled.

I had had a hard day. 'Stop it, all of you.'

'Who was there when the man fell?' demanded Albia sternly. She had at least learned from Helena and me how to address a puzzle. I rose to my feet awkwardly, and fell on a stone bench. At that moment I was hardly the heartless exterminator they wanted to believe. I must have looked as I felt: washed out, depressed, and fending off feelings of guilt.

Since I had not answered her, Albia repeated her question. I forced myself to say, 'All that's known for certain is that I left Nux with the freedman, who went over the edge.'

'So did Cleonymus like dogs or not?'

'No idea.'

'We can ask someone,' Albia decided. 'If he hated them, he could have kicked Nux.'

'Cleonymus was sitting with Nux perfectly peacefully when I left them.'

'And was *Nux* happy with *him*?' the girl asked me, intently.

'I would not have left her otherwise.'

The last thing I had expected this evening when I came home, was to find myself hemmed in by this bunch of suspicious interrogators. Gaius and Cornelius had gathered around, like Albia more concerned about Nux than the human fatality.

'Someone else came up the hill and attacked Nuxie,' Gaius declared.

Albia rounded on him. 'How do you know that?'

'It's obvious.' Cornelius backed his cousin up. 'Some horrible man hit Nux, then the freedman yelled out, "Leave our dog alone!" He was trying to defend her –'

'When this other man pushed him right off the cliff!' Gaius announced. 'Don't you think so, Uncle Marcus?'

'It is a possibility.'

'Or someone attacked Cleonymus, so Nux got hurt trying to guard him. Yes, that sounds like the answer,' Albia informed us. 'How are you going to find the man, Marcus Didius?'

'Well, I asked all the bystanders for details at the scene,' I admitted weakly. 'But we were all very busy trying to get to Cleonymus –'

'It's too late now!' Albia snapped with great impatience. 'If you go back tomorrow, you won't find the same people. You don't know their names –'

'I took names,' I protested weakly, waving my note-tablet.

'Probably false! Even if they live in Corinth, they won't want to get involved.'

'Human nature.'

'If you do find that man, I hope you kill him,' whispered Cornelius, sounding wistful. He was still sitting cross-legged by the basket, patting Nux.

I had to rouse myself. I told them that we were obliged to ascertain first what had really happened – then we could apprehend any killer. I said that Greece was a civilised province. That the Areopagus, the homicide court at Athens, was the oldest in the world and would deal with the man. I maintained I would follow the proper procedures.

Maybe it was true.

'Anyway, I am the head of this group and I am fed up with you three bossing me. I am very tired. Now please leave me alone.'

Nux knew that today she at least could take liberties. She climbed out of the basket, letting us see how much it hurt,

203

then limped over to me, begging to be picked up. I took her on to my lap, where she curled up, gave a queenly sigh, and went to sleep with her snout pressed under my elbow. Albia and the boys looked on approvingly.

Not long afterwards, Helena appeared through the inn gate. She too observed my position as dog-plinth with an affectionate smile for both Nux and me. Then she led in a companion who was playing shy. It was the Sertorius daughter. At the girl's approach, both Gaius and Cornelius behaved like Aventine lads. They assumed she was after their bodies, so they rushed from the scene. Albia looked hostile, but she wanted to hear what this was about, so she said nothing and stayed.

Tiberia was a pale thing who seemed nervous, though I suspected she was devious. We had seen her lurking about with her brother at the Bay Mare, taking too sly an interest in my investigation. Our own Albia was listening in here, but her presence was open, her curiosity frank.

Tiberia had mousy fair hair, pulled back tightly in a ribbon, which she continually untied and tied up again. Her skinny body and long legs had been dressed in a rather mean white tunic. One of her sandals had a broken strap. It made her look neglected by her mother, though perhaps she enjoyed rejecting improvements. (I was a father; I found myself increasingly prone to assume that parents meant well but their children were difficult.) Like many girls her age, she bit her nails. Her fingers were small and childish, her features younger than her age. I put her at thirteen. I bet she stared at boys and dreamed of them, but if anything male looked back at her, she had no idea how to react.

Albia had taken against her and was showing it. Helena pushed Tiberia forward, nudging her. 'Go on. Tell Marcus Didius what you came about.'

Tiberia had other ideas. She hung back, leaning against Helena, head down awkwardly. I heard Albia growl in her throat. I took a firm line. 'We are all feeling a bit sad here. Come on please, don't be girly. Let's hear it, Tiberia.'

Given another unsympathetic shove by Helena, the girl

spoke her piece. Her voice was almost too confident, though its tone was languid: 'It's just that, well, after you told us about Cleonymus, I heard you say you were going to see Phineus.'

'So?' It was probably too curt, but I had had enough that day.

'Why did you want to see him?'

'Never mind – what's the interest for you, Tiberia?'

'Oh . . . nothing.'

'That's soon dealt with then.' I showed I had lost interest in her. It worked.

'I don't like him,' she whispered.

'He's not my type either.' I tried softening my tone. 'What's he done to you?'

Tiberia squirmed. I gave her the sceptical gaze I reserve for when I am too tired to bother. Deep questioning was out. She could tell me if she wanted to, or go to Hades. 'I don't like the way he always helps you on to the donkey.'

Helena finally helped me out. 'Hands everywhere?' Tiberia nodded gratefully. 'Is that all he does?' Again a nod. It could have been much worse, though to a girl this young, the man's behaviour could assume monstrous significance. 'I suppose,' suggested Helena, 'you don't like what happens, but you feel there is nothing specific to complain about?'

Again Tiberia nodded hard. Phineus would deny there was any wrongdoing; he would suggest the girl had made it up, for all the wrong reasons – or that she was over-sensitive to perfectly normal behaviour.

Helena loathed gropers. She encouraged Tiberia to open up more. 'It happens, but I always hate it too. If you say anything, men like that have a habit of suggesting you are a prude. Nobody ever takes it seriously – but we do, Tiberia.'

'No sense of fun, he'll say,' I contributed, myself now sounding more friendly. 'Sarcastic references to the Vestal Virgins . . .' There was a risk the women present would suppose I shared the Phineus view. Maybe once I would have done.

205

Tiberia went pink. 'My father said I had imagined it.'
Bastard. If she had been one of my daughters, Phineus
would be for it. But Sertorius was more gauche than he
would admit, and people in general conspire to ignore such
a situation.

'I expect your mother knows the truth,' said Helena
gently.

'Mother hates him too. All the women do.'

'Did Valeria Ventidia hate him?' I asked. 'Had he
bothered Valeria?'

Tiberia nodded. That was an excuse to fiddle with her
hair again. By now I was ready to strangle her with the
damned ribbon.

'And is he just over-familiar? As far as you know, he never
takes it any further?' checked Helena. When the girl looked
puzzled, she specified, 'For instance, does he ever try to get
you to meet him secretly?' Tiberia looked really alarmed.
'Just a suggestion. Don't worry about it. He won't ask and
even if he did, you wouldn't go, would you? . . . Well, thank
you for telling us this.'

'What will you do?' demanded Tiberia. Her voice still had
that languorous note, but she was pleading with me, wanting
rescue.

'That's for me to decide, when the moment is right,' I
said. 'As for you, if any man annoys you in that way, try
shouting loudly, *"Don't do that!"* – especially when other
people are present. He won't like to be shown up in public.
And the other people may be shamed into taking your
part.'

Tiberia went off, looking as if she had wanted more
reaction. I did not expect her to be grateful for my good
advice, but I hoped she would follow it.

Helena joined me. I tweaked her nose. 'It's not like you to
make me handle that confrontation, fruit.'

'I could tell that she would slouch and pose and play with
her hair,' Helena admitted, unabashed.

'Hmm. What were you like when you were thirteen?' I
grinned, though I wished I had known her then.

206

'More direct! She irritates me so much, I knew I was going to bungle it.' After a moment Helena asked, 'Do you believe her?' I acknowledged that. 'So is it significant?'

'Probably,' I said.

XXXVII

The worst part of my job has always been attending funerals. If it's a victim, I feel angry and sour.

To my great surprise, Cleonyma asked me to officiate. I had been expecting her to involve Amaranthus. Still, we knew she and Cleonymus had only met him that season, and although we had seen them so much together, apparently she viewed the relationship as temporary.

Helena reckoned that I represented authority. She said it without irony, but I was not fooled. I suggested to Cleonyma that we ask Aquillius Macer to assist me. She agreed. Aquillius looked horrified but could hardly refuse. So Cleonymus, who had once been a slave, was dispatched to his ancestors by an imperial informer and a patrician diplomat.

Marinus and Indus organised a whip-round to cover a feast. The collection was fixed up with great efficiency; well, they had already done it twice before. Cleonyma provided her dead husband with a good send-off and a magnificent memorial stone; that would eventually be placed on a public building which she planned to donate to the city, thus recording and celebrating Cleonymus for all time.

The ceremony was held in the grounds of the governor's residence. The governor himself was still away on his milestone jaunt, but all the group turned out, together with Phineus. He had come up with an undertaker and musicians, though I know Cleonyma paid for them. Aquillius and I performed our duties without a hitch. He cut the throat of the sacrificial sheep; he did it with dispatch, looking perfectly cool. Afterwards he told me that a down-to-earth uncle had given him lessons in ritual when he first stood for the Senate. Knowing that he would be called upon to officiate at public sacrifices, a professional priest had been brought to the family's Campanian villa; Aquillius spent a whole day learning, until half a flock had been slaughtered and Aquillius could butcher anything with four legs.

He was, however, terrified of public speaking, so it seemed fair that I should compose and deliver the eulogy. I found enough words of praise, and I meant them. The widow wept gently. She thanked me for what I had said; although I still felt like a fraud to be taking the lead role, it was better than most of the alternatives. I still had not told her I suspected that Cleonymus had been murdered, though I wondered if she had guessed it for herself.

Cleonyma went through the day calmly. She supervised the start of the feast, though I noticed she ate and drank nothing. Once the meal was under way, she slipped outside. Feeling no joy in feasting, I followed her. The residence had the usual elaborate but slightly sterile garden, everything doubled, everything surrounded by miniature hedges, long pools lit by tiny lights to prevent people splashing into them, a subtle scent of jasmine wafting everywhere from unseen climbing plants.

'Well, I got through it, Falco!' To my amazement I could now tell Cleonyma was pretty drunk. All day, I had never seen her take a drop. 'Now you're going to tell me, aren't you?'

'Tell you what?'

'What really happened to my husband.'

So then I told her what I knew for sure and what I suspected. For a while she stood considering. 'Yes, I thought it must have been like that.'

'Any ideas about this "well-dressed man", Cleonyma?'

'You think it's Phineus.'

'I can't prove that. He denies it – Of course, he would do,' I said quickly.

'He fits,' she replied, with an air of resignation.

'Well, if it's possible to show he did it, or that he caused any of the previous deaths, I'll do my best for you.'

'I know you will. You're all right, Falco. Cleonymus and I both thought that from the start.'

'Thank you.' I waited a beat, then tackled her. 'Look, I don't want to distress you, especially today, but I think you're tough and you want real answers. Can I ask you some questions?' She made a gesture of acquiescence. 'When Cleonymus and I were walking up the crag, he started to talk to me, but our conversation was never finished.'

Cleonyma shrugged, as if she were expecting this.

First I asked about Marinus and Helvia. She confirmed that Marinus was a confidence trickster, preying on rich women. There was nothing more to say about that, except on this tour he had not yet found a mark. The richest single woman in the group was now Cleonyma herself, and she was wise to him. He would make a play, she thought – and she would tell him what she knew about his past, threatening to turn him over to Aquillius. She joked that maybe she could blackmail Marinus. At least, I thought it was a joke.

When I asked about Helvia, she gave a low chuckle. Although Helvia appeared a befuddled innocent, Cleonyma reckoned she was doing exactly the same as Marinus. The wobbly widow was an accomplished manipulator; men always underestimated her. Helvia moved from province to province, relieving unwise male protectors of thousands. The woman friend she had mentioned, who no longer travelled with her, had in fact been so taken with Helvia's success, she went into that line for herself, when a dimwit from Crete fell for her, while she was acting as Helvia's chaperon.

'How do you discover all these nuggets, Cleonyma?'

'They think I'm too boozy to notice what they're telling me.'

'Do you do anything with the information?' It seemed best to check up.

'I just enjoy it.' Cleonyma paused, with a sad little smile. 'I shall miss that.'

'Oh don't deprive yourself! Will you give up on travel?'

'Won't be the same without him. No, Falco; I'll go

210

home – when you and Aquillius let me. I'll settle down and be a menace. Miserable and sober.'

'Try not to be miserable. He would not want that for you.'

Cleonyma looked rueful. 'Being a party girl is hard on your own. And there will never be another for me.'

'Never say never.'

'Don't be foolish, Falco. You would be the same, if you lost Helena.'

'Right.'

We gazed at the stars for a time. The sky was very black. We avoided looking over our shoulders to where the acropolis towered. We walked around slowly, avoiding the ornamental fishponds. Then I asked about the rest of the group.

Cleonyma agreed that the Sertorii were an unhappy family, though she knew of no particular reason, other than the husband's unpleasantness. Things between Minucia and Amaranthus seemed rocky, but she thought they might stick it out.

'Volcasius?'

'Beyond help!'

'Think he's malicious?'

'Just peculiar. He won't change. He'll live for years, travelling until old age and arthritis get the better of him, then he'll go home and skulk.'

'What about Indus? Is he another Marinus? A predator?'

'No!' An almost kindly note came into Cleonyma's voice.

'Your man told me you know his story.'

'It's very simple.'

'And reprehensible? He's running away from *something*! Or do I mean somebody?'

'Yes.'

'Anyone special?'

'Ought to be!'

'I'm no good at riddles.'

'Leave him alone, poor man.'

*

I changed the subject obediently. When a witness is such good value, no informer causes upsets. So we moved on to the last member of the group: Phineus.

'I can't say he has ever upset me, but the young girl is right about his habits. He crawls around the women. Any chance to stand too close, put his damn arm around a waist, give a surreptitious squeeze. All the time, he speaks very respectfully. For me, that's the most annoying part! He backs off if anyone stands up to him – though the inexperienced girls don't understand that.'

'Valeria?'

'She was nineteen; she was a bride; she was fair game. Statianus was jealous, but useless, of course . . .'

Cleonyma paused. I listened too. She had heard Helena calling us.

Cleonyma and I turned back. I put out an arm to shepherd her – then in view of the strictures against Phineus, I thought better of it. Bright woman that she was, Cleonyma noticed and gave a short laugh.

Just before we reached the house, she took a small glass flask from a bag she was carrying, and discreetly supped liquor. Then, straightening up, she walked firmly indoors. Beneath the thick layer of face powder and the gold jewellery, she was showing her age but as we re-entered the house she looked serene, collected and, to a casual observer, quite sober.

XXXVIII

Helena was talking to Aquillius. I saw her frown slightly. There would be a good reason why she had interrupted my tête-à-tête. She knew that Cleonyma and I were not discussing tombstone design.

The widow tottered over to Minucia, leaving me free to investigate.

'Marcus, Phineus has asked Aquillius for leave to travel to Delphi; he says he ought to go and look for Statianus!'

'He has given me his parole.' Aquillius already knew I disapproved.

'So you are letting him go?' I was horrified.

'Actually no. I just want you to know that, Falco. I refused him permission.'

'Well, that's a start – How will you ensure he stays in Corinth?'

'He won't disobey my orders,' Aquillius claimed stiffly. I gazed at him, letting him read my doubts. He gazed back, visibly wavering. 'Oh dear . . . Well, he told me he would send one of his men.'

'One of the drivers he uses?' That pulled me up. This was an aspect I had been neglecting. 'Tell me, quaestor – does Phineus have workers who routinely accompany clients on these tours?'

To my surprise, Aquillius did know the answer. 'No. He hires local people at every site, as and when he needs them.'

That was a relief. He probably hired different ones each time, depending on who was available, so it was unlikely these temporary workers were suspects. 'Should have guessed! Piecework.'

Aquillius was puzzled, so Helena explained: 'Paid by the

job and then dismissed. Phineus doesn't keep a regular workforce because he is probably too mean. This will be cheaper.' At least it saved me having to spend days wearing myself out in aimless interviews with hostile muleteers and bloody-minded factotums.

I gazed around the banqueting room. We had been granted the full service of the governor's chamberlain, chefs, and table slaves. Most of them would be top-class household staff brought to Greece from the governor's house in Rome. Providing a huge, slick entourage would be part of establishing his personal status, as well as an essential tool of Roman diplomacy. Even on campaign, Julius Caesar used to impress shaggy Gallic princes with an enormous marquee which contained not just flunkeys and folding thrones, but a portable floor mosaic. Now that tragedy had brought the Tracks and Temples group at least temporarily within the embrace of their embassy, they were dining off gold plate for once. I would never have risked my best dinner service with this lot, but the governor was not here to object, and Aquillius must see it as his duty to supply the best tureens and salvers.

That did not stop Sertorius grumbling as he passed us that he would have thought Cleonyma would have bought in better wine.

As part of my funeral duties, *I* had chosen the wine. It was perfectly acceptable. The food had been good too, even though my annoying nephews had played their now-customary game of pointing to cauldrons of aromatic cooked meats, loudly screaming '*Pelops!*', then giggling hysterically. At most dinners it would not have mattered, but people on this tour had had myth laminated on to their fraught brains. The tasteless reference to cannibalism among the deities was lost on very few of them.

I looked around for the boys. With Albia and Young Glaucus, they were now amusing themselves fairly politely: Cornelius had brought his soldiers board game and Albia was teaching Glaucus to play, while the boys sprawled on the serving table as spectators. So long as she stopped with the black and white counters and did not start initiating my trainer's son into other moves, I could leave them to it.

Helena, Aquillius, and I surveyed the wake. People had been badly in need of a release; with plenty of nourishment and drink inside them, they were now letting go. The noise level had risen. Soon this would be like a celebration, with little reference to the dead.

First to go was the seating plan. Amaranthus had stayed put, staring into space alone. He looked saturnine and brooding. I wondered if he was considering who would next be picked off by the killer. If so, it definitely bothered him. If he was the killer himself, he should have tried to look more nonchalant.

His partner Minucia had turned her back on him. I could not tell if the couple had had a tiff today, but she was totally ignoring Amaranthus as she ministered to Cleonyma. Cleonyma was standing beside her; she now wore a little wavering smile, not saying much but looking blissful and swaying very, very slightly. It would not last; any minute now she would crumple and weep uncontrollably.

Sertoria Silene had left her family's table and was intently conversing with Indus. Their voices were low, as a sign of respect for the occasion. Still, they looked as if they had been chatting for some time; it was unforced and agreeable. Her children were not bothering them, for one thing. She was talking with an assurance she never dared show with her husband, while Indus responded happily. Tiberia and Tiberius were slinking around in a colonnade, stalking a kitten they had chosen to torment. A slave they had not noticed was standing in the shadows, keeping an eye on them. She was grasping a large metal ladle. Good.

With his friend Indus occupied, the slyer bachelor, Marinus, was deep in conversation with the widow Helvia. She was letting him enjoy himself as a raconteur while she rearranged her stoles and chuckled at his stories. Now that I knew I should distrust the air of muddled innocence, Helvia seemed a much more intriguing character. She wore a necklace of rather good gold chains. Was this unexpectedly

215

fine item her secret bait? Was Marinus, who thought himself such a smooth operator, about to be tickled into a subtle trap by Helvia's chubby fingers?

Marinus talked on. This was what he did so well. I could just overhear him. Most garrulous fellows with a reputation for an 'endless fund' of tales have a much smaller stock than they reckon, but Helvia fluttered admiringly even when his anecdote about the 'magic' temple doors that were operated by underground fires came around again. Yes, I could see it now; Helvia knew what she was doing. Marinus clearly underestimated her and his career as a sponger could be under threat.

Everyone had managed to avoid Volcasius; he was demanding secrets of life from the chamberlain, a thin, bald slave who replied with perfect manners, though his dark eyes had glazed over.

Phineus came back to the room with Sertorius, as if they had both been to relieve themselves. Aquillius dug me in the ribs. 'Should I tackle him again about his Delphi request?'

'Don't lose him, at any rate,' I warned. 'He is my best suspect.'

Aquillius perked up. He had quaffed a goblet or two. 'Then shall I fasten him in a neck-iron and throw him in a holding cell?'

'That's up to you. It depends how brutal your regime is in this province . . .'

Helena was looking troubled. 'Aquillius, can I ask something, please? You said Phineus doesn't use permanent staff – but you also said he wants to send a representative to Delphi. Have I missed something? Who can he dispatch on this errand?'

Aquillius shrugged. 'Phineus must feel more beleaguered than he shows. He has summoned assistance from head office, I understand.'

'From *Rome*?' asked Helena.

I put down my wine goblet on a side table. 'Who is it?'

'Some partner in his agency.'

We only knew of one Seven Sights staffer back in Rome –

216

one who, come to think of it, looked rather like the fellow I saw with Phineus the other day. Out of context, I had failed to make the connection. Suddenly it was all too clear. 'A pushy swine called Polystratus?'

Aquillius shrugged. 'I've not met him.'

I raised an eyebrow to Helena, wondering what this meant. All I could imagine was that, as Aquillius said, Phineus felt more need of support than he generally revealed. Well, that was good. I liked him being nervous.

'So shall I arrest him, Falco?' Full of drink, the quaestor was single-minded.

'Up to you. You could decide that since several of his clients have been murdered, you need to arrest the organiser, while we investigate.'

'At the very least Phineus has been careless in protecting clients,' Helena contributed.

Aquillius liked that. He liked it so much that he bolted from the room, in search of soldiers from the governor's armed guard. Next thing, Phineus was trying to look unconcerned as he was bundled out by several bemused looking legionaries in red tunics. This was so rapid, most of the group failed to notice.

'That was fun!' Aquillius slapped his hands together. It was probably the first time in his tour of duty he had managed to take the initiative. I was unsure he had done the right thing, but Phineus had had previous experience of arrest. That showed in the resigned way he marched off, with no protest and no resistance. Whatever happened about this, he would take the episode philosophically.

'When in doubt, clap some bugger in chains,' I said. 'Even if he did nothing, other people may get jumpy when they hear him rattling.'

I was less than keen on the quaestor's reply: 'So what's *your* next move, Falco?' He managed to sound as if he thought I had run out of options. There was no need for him to be so pleased with himself. In Corinth I had indeed explored all possible avenues. But I had one last idea.

'Phineus is right about Delphi. We do need to reunite

217

Statianus with the others – and I need to ask him some hard questions. So, if you'll give me the transport I asked for in the first place, Aquillius, *I* will go to find him.'

'See Delphi and die!' quipped Aquillius. Some old travel joke, apparently. Then his amiable face clouded guiltily. He blushed. 'Well, not literally, I hope!'

PART FOUR
DELPHI AND LEBADEIA

The city of Delphi is a steep slope from top to bottom, and the sacred precinct of Apollo is not different from the rest of it. This is huge in size and stands at the very top of the city, cut through by a network of alleyways. I shall record those of the dedications that seem to me most memorable. I do not think it is worth worrying about athletes or obscure musicians . . .

The entrails of most victims do not reveal Trophonius' mind very clearly, but on the night a man is going down they slaughter a ram at a pit . . . It makes no difference if all the earlier sacrifices have given good omens unless the entrails of this ram carry the same meaning. But if they agree, every man goes down with true hope . . .

Pausanias, *Guide to Greece*

XXXIX

Delphi. A mistake, perhaps.

Once I decided on action, my brain cleared. Back at our lodgings that evening I made rapid plans for a trip across the Gulf. Helena insisted on coming with me, wanting to see that ancient sanctuary. I opted to leave behind most of our luggage, plus Albia, my nephews, Glaucus, and the still convalescent Nux. Travelling light, Helena and I would make a flying visit, retrieve Tullius Statianus, and return to Corinth.

It sounded good. Aquillius Macer was finding us a reliable ship, a fast one if possible. I reckoned on three days at most.

There were two reasons why I left behind the youngsters and the dog. Apart from my wish for speed, I gave Glaucus instructions that when Nux seemed her lively self again, he was to put her on a lead and walk her past the various members of the tour group. 'See if she growls at anyone. But if she reacts, don't tackle the suspect. Tell Aquillius, the quaestor.'

Glaucus looked nervous, but Albia and the boys were keen enough to do it. I wanted the test carried out, even though I doubted they would identify the killer of Cleonymus this way. For one thing, the odds were on Phineus, and he was now out of reach, under arrest.

One thing had struck me: Statianus was supposed to be in Delphi. If true, he at least could not have killed Cleonymus. Unless he had returned to Corinth secretly (making our Delphi trip an utter waste of time) then either Statianus was innocent – or if he killed his wife in Olympia, some second killer dealt with the freedman here. Our witness at

Acrocorinth had described the mysterious 'expensively dressed man' as older than the bridegroom. So did that make Statianus innocent? Was the bride's brutal killer this new man, the middle-aged smart dresser – and if so, did he have any connection with Marcella Caesia three years earlier?

The situation got more complicated at every turn. And worse was to come. Helena and I were bidding our companions goodbye before our walk to the port at Lechaion, with our bundle of clothes, a money pouch, and my sword. As we stood outside our lodgings at the Elephant, we were accosted by Volcasius.

'I am very surprised to hear you are leaving Corinth, Falco!'

'Just a scenic trip.'

The bony fool stood right in the way of my hired donkey. That suited the donkey, whose reins I jerked to no avail. 'We have to make haste, Volcasius. Have you something to say?' asked Helena coldly.

'Hardly my place,' he sneered. 'Falco is the expert.'

'Say what you came for.' I encouraged my mount again, ready to shove Volcasius aside if I had to. The beast stretched out its nose to him, as if to a friend.

'There is an obvious clue you have overlooked.'

Knowing I was about to swear at him, Helena quickly answered for me. 'What is that, Volcasius?'

'Your dog was hurt during the events up on the acropolis. Either you don't know, or you have strangely discounted this: one of our party had a nasty dog bite previously.'

It was true, but I was none too pleased to find Volcasius making an issue of it. 'I know all about that. Marinus was bitten by a sacred dog at Epidaurus, the night Turcianus Opimus died. Marinus told me himself, so why don't you keep out of it?' I covered my frustration. 'Volcasius, stop being self-righteous. I always distrust the man who comes singing that one of his companions is the guilty party. I'll be looking at Marinus – but I'll be looking at you too.'

I kicked up the donkey and made it walk around him. Helena followed me on hers. We left Volcasius standing there, convinced of his own cleverness and our stupidity. Gaius, who was coming with us in order to return the donkeys to their stable after we took ship, leered at the man as he passed.

Not until we were aboard did Helena and I break our silence.

I kicked at a bulkhead. 'Cobnuts! I am completely slipshod: I missed that.'

'We both missed it.' Helena beat one fist against her palm, so hard I winced and gripped her wrists to stop her. I won't accuse women of talking themselves out of trouble – but Helena was quicker than me at rationalising this dog bite: 'Marcus, maybe Marinus was simply unlucky at Epidaurus. Nobody has suggested that the sacred dog bit him because he had lashed out at it. The way Marinus told the story, he was asleep in a cell when he was bitten.'

'Perhaps he *wanted* us to think that.'

'He didn't have to draw attention to it. The bite was on his thigh – under his tunic. He had no need at all to show us. Still . . .' Helena began to analyse the clue, if clue it was. 'Suppose Volcasius has a point. Say *Marinus* silenced Turcianus and Cleonymus – or even just Cleonymus. Let's consider his motive.'

'He preys on women.' I was terse. But I stopped blaming myself, and my next response was balanced: 'He does it for money, not sex. Killing the bride – or even arranging a tryst with her – would be out of character. Valeria wasn't his type of victim. She was married, for starters. She had little cash in her own right; even as a couple, she and Statianus were travelling on a budget. One of the women commented that they were bad at managing their money.'

'And someone said Milo of Dodona was fooling himself if he thought they were possible sponsors for his statue. So,' Helena mused, 'did Volcasius name Marinus to draw away attention from himself?'

I barked with laughter. 'Do you see *Volcasius* as a sexual predator?'

She thought about it, more carefully than me. 'He is

223

certainly odd. I don't suppose he has had normal experiences with women.'

I was still dismissive. 'Prostitutes, most likely. If he bothers.'

'In that case, he might have gone up the acropolis to find gratification at the Temple of Artemis. We can ask the women there when we return to Corinth.'

'They won't tell us. By then, they will never remember. Whores have short memories; given their life, who can blame them?'

'He smells,' replied Helena. 'I know you will say, prostitutes meet plenty of stinkers, but taken with his odd manner, I am sure Volcasius would attract notice. Oh but nobody would ever call him "well-dressed", Marcus!'

Possibly he cleaned up and dressed better when visiting professional women. But I thought Helena was right. I could not really imagine Volcasius getting spruced up for anybody. Even if he used prostitutes for sex, he would despise them.

'This is a false lead, Marcus.'

I let Helena reassure me – but I spent the rest of the sea journey brooding. At least that took my mind off feeling queasy.

Well, it did to some extent. I wanted to disembark at Kirra, but the helpful captain took us past it to a nearer beachhead. By the time we landed at Itea, I was wishing we had gone the long way round by land, where I had heard the roads were good enough to take the largest wagons, so even if it took forever, you could relax in family-size comfort, almost the entire way.

Note 'almost'. Even people who came coach-drawn all had to climb out and lug their goods on their backs the final mile or so. Despite the need to bring pilgrims and visitors to the oracle and the Pythian Games, the last stretch of the road was dire. It was a hard pull even for a man on foot. Helena tackled it bravely, but by the time we staggered to a halt in the village, she was weeping with desperation. I was little better, though I had reckoned I was generally in good shape.

Our bags fell from our hands. We turned back and looked

over the plain below. Covered with a thick forest of wild olives, the land fell away gracefully to the sea which twinkled in the distance. The sanctuary clung to a steep hillside on twin peaks of Mount Parnassus, with other mountains crowding around it. Above us towered enormous unclimbable crags. Huge birds of prey circled languidly on the updraughts, so far away that their long wings looked mere threads of black against the brilliant sky. The air was thin and chilly, even though the sun was shining. The beauty of the setting, the bright light, and the rarefied atmosphere gave pilgrims their first notion that they were approaching the gods.

We had made it. As our breath hurt our windpipes, we clung to each other and were proud of our exertion. We could not speak, but we were grinning with triumph to have made the climb.

Had we known what lay ahead of us, our mood might have been different.

XL

We wasted time next morning asking in the town for Statianus. Delphi was bigger than I had expected. If he was staying there, we could not find his inn.

Next task was to familiarise ourselves with the sanctuary. We knew it would be a dramatic experience. Even after Olympia, with its massed temples and treasuries and its hundreds of statues of athletes, we were awestruck by the plethora of monuments. Nothing prepares the traveller for Delphi. In its heyday it must have been staggering, and it remained spectacular. We were seeing the sanctum when it was sadly in decline. That was due to Rome. Not only had bullyboy Sulla stolen all the precious metal donations to finance his siege of Athens, but things had then deteriorated until the final indignity, ten years ago, when Nero attended the Pythian Games and carried off five hundred of the best statues. Nero loved Greece; he loved it so much, he stole as much as possible.

More importantly, Roman rule had meant the loss of Delphi's political power. Cities and states no longer came here to consult on matters of policy. Without their gratitude for good advice, no more treasure would be deposited.

As you would expect, the sanctuary of Pythian Apollo was surrounded by a wall. Parts were made from enormous polygonal blocks which seemed to be the handiwork of giants. There were several gates, the purpose of which in my opinion was to funnel visitors into the hands of money-grubbing souvenir-sellers and guides. We had decided not to use a site guide. The clamorous guides decided otherwise. We were mobbed as soon as we stepped through the main gate on to the Sacred Way. Despite us shaking our heads and striding ahead, one man attached himself to us. He was a round-faced wraith with receding hair, so short that as we walked beside him we felt like over-healthy demigods. He proceeded with his patter whether we wanted it or not. Around us were other groups of pilgrims and tourists, all looking bemused by the same torrent of stories, recitation of inscriptions, names of battles, and lists of donated weaponry and gold plate. In the past, every city in the Greek world had jostled for attention by making ostentatious gifts, seeking the favour of the gods and the envy of other cities with varying degrees of taste and extravagance.

The monuments nearest the gate score highest. Later, visitors are far too jaded to remember much. Our guide talked us past the bronze bull dedicated by Corcyra and the nine bronze statues of Arcadian gods, heroes, and heroines. I chortled at the outrageous belligerence of a Spartan commemoration of a naval victory over Athens, which boasted no fewer than thirty-seven statues of gods, generals, and admirals (each one meticulously named by our guide); Helena preferred a more dignified and austere Athenian monument, which commemorated the battle of Marathon. These were just tasters. We could see the great Temple of Apollo above us, fronting a dramatic open air theatre, but at this rate we would take three days to reach it.

'Can I pay you to skip?' I asked the heedless guide.

'Can we pay him to shut up?' muttered Helena. He was now dragging us to a replica of the Trojan Horse, prior to Argive statues of the Seven against Thebes – and then another set of Argive gifts: the seven *sons* of the Seven against Thebes. We looked at each other in horror. Luckily the seven sons had managed to destroy Thebes, which spared us further generations. Even so, the magnanimous Argives kept going and managed to install ten more statues, these set up to emphasise their kings' links with Hercules. Do not ask me what links; by then I was looking for a chance to wander off. Helena was gripping my hand tight, in case I abandoned her with the guide.

Soon we were in among treasuries. They were neat little

roofed buildings, rather like tiny temples; instead of colonnades all round, their porches were generally adorned with only a couple of columns or caryatids – although the spectacular (rather too well draped) caryatids on the Treasury of Siphnos (where the hell is Siphnos?) sparkled with gemstones on their diadems and in their hair. The guide trotted out mentions of winged-victory acrotiria, sphinxes, continuous friezes, and sculptured Herculean metopes. The only way to cope with his bombardment of information was to copy the caryatids and affect a slight archaic smile (while wondering how long it was until lunch).

By the time we reached the Council Chamber, my archaic smile was openly disfigured by bared teeth. Local government upsets me: old men making wrong decisions to protect their own trade interests. At least we were getting somewhere: the spring once guarded by the rampaging dragon called the Python, which had been slain by the infant Apollo. Apollo's mother Leto had stood on a rock and held him in her arms to shoot. This Leto must have been a liability. Helena and I had once been plagued by a neighbour who allowed her child to loose off toy arrows in the street; however, we hid our disapproval of feckless mothers and nodded wisely as the guide proclaimed Apollo's institution of a peaceable and spiritual regime.

Our guide droned on. 'Now we are standing before the most famous statue of antiquity – the Sphinx of Naxos, also called the Delphic Sphinx. It stands on an exquisite Ionian capital, in front of the polygonal wall. The column has forty-four flutings and six drums; it rises to a height of approximately forty feet, or forty-one and a half at the wing-tips. The Sphinx, who set very famous riddles, wears a dreamy, quizzical smile –' Helena had a quizzical expression too. She was inspecting its hairstyle. 'The most famous riddle was: what creature walks on four legs in the morning, two in the afternoon, and three at eventide?'

'Man! Crawls, walks, uses a stick –' I had had enough. Informers are notoriously gruff. Sometimes I try to overturn the stereotype; not today. I wished I had a stick myself, to beat the guide. 'Save it. Look here! I'll give you this –' The coin I offered was three times what he was worth. 'Now leave us alone, please.'

'You don't like my guiding?' The fellow pretended to be astonished.

Informers, who need to be unobtrusive, are followers of etiquette. When in shrines devoted to tolerance, I avoid getting into a fistfight. I stayed quiet and crisp. 'We want to commune with the gods in silence. So go back down the hill and kidnap someone else.'

'But you must have a guide!'

Cobnuts to etiquette: 'And you must have a kick up the backside if you don't go.'

He went.

Other tourists had overheard our rebellion with interest. Sub-groups began huddling together; we could see them muttering, then squaring up to take action. Soon arguments broke out all around the ancient cave of the Python. The gods of immemorial earth and the deities of subterranean waters must have gurgled with mirth, as normally timid tourists stood up to their guides and dismissed them. Apollo, the arbiter of moderation, tickled the strings of his lyre and rejoiced.

I had no conscience about causing a rebellion. The bastard guides would be back tomorrow, boring new victims.

Helena and I gazed up at the Sphinx, hand in hand, glad of the chance to enjoy one famous statue undisturbed.

'She reminds me of you, my darling, in some ways. Beautiful, seemingly remote and mysterious – and clever, of course.'

'Older, though!' returned Helena cattily.

The time-honoured Sphinx showed no reaction, but assuming she was a woman of the world, I winked at her.

In our own time now, we moved on along the Sacred Way.

The narrow route wound upwards, its worn stones sometimes dangerous underfoot. Delphi could have used a

229

Roman road-maintenance gang. Freed from our obligation to absorb every detail, we scurried past altars, columns, tripods, porticoes, pedestals, and victories, pausing only to admire the towering statue of Apollo himself beside the spring of Cassotis. At long last we reached the temple. We could hear guides listing the many previous versions of the building ('first woven laurel, then beeswax and bees-wings, then bronze, then porous stone in the Doric style . . .') They came up with more of these suspect details, but I stopped listening. (I'm all for myth – but you just try knocking up a garden gazebo from bees-wings when you have a free hour or two!) We took a quick circuit around, saw the east façade, with its scene of Apollo arriving in Delphi, and the west, with Dionysus and various maenads.

'Apollo goes to spend winters with the Hyperboreans,' Helena said.

'Hyper whats?'

'Boreans – peoples behind the north wind. Don't ask me why; what do you think I am, Marcus, some damned site guide?'

'I think you'll find,' I smirked, 'this myth symbolises the absence of the sun – or of light, as represented by Apollo himself – during winter.'

'Well, thank you, encyclopedist! Anyway, while Apollo is on holiday getting frostbite under his drapery, Dionysus takes over at Delphi. The oracles cease and the sanctuary is given over to feasting.'

'Sounds like fun.'

'Sounds like very bad news for Statianus,' Helena said, 'if he is still here in the question queue. Oracles are given on Apollo's birthday, which I think is February or March, and afterwards only on the seventh day of the month. So if they cease in winter, Statianus is about to miss his chance altogether.'

'The October oracle has passed; he's stuck until after Saturnalia. But does he have a chance at all?' I asked. 'What are the rules about applicants? Who exactly gets to put their questions?'

230

'Citizens of Delphi first, then people to whom Delphi has awarded rights of precedence –'

'Official queue-jumpers? How does anyone get to be one of them?'

'Money, no doubt,' Helena sniffed. 'And finally, the rest, in order drawn by lot.'

'With as much chance as cuckoo spit!'

We had already poked our noses into the temple interior and been shooed out from the inner *cella*. We had dutifully stared at the legendary mottoes: KNOW YOURSELF and NOTHING IN EXCESS. We had made the inevitable bitter joke about the Delphi guides not taking any notice of either. Now we found a spot on the steps, shaded by a column, where we sat down to rest, hugging our knees and drinking in the majestic views. I wished we had brought a picnic. To distract me from my hunger pangs, Helena told me what she knew about the rituals of the oracle.

'Prophecy has an ancient history here. There is a fissure in the earth which breathes vapours that make people clairvoyant. The priestess, the Pythia, was in ancient times a young virgin, but nowadays she has to be at least fifty.'

'Disappointment!'

'She's not your type. She has to live in the sanctuary, irreproachably –'

'I've met lots of so-called irreproachable girls. I won them over.'

'Really?'

'Well, you should know, Helena!'

Helena was used to ignoring my jests. 'Applicants – successful ones – are cleansed in the Kastalian Spring, then they pay a fee, which is variable, depending on their question.'

'Or depending on how badly the priests decide they want an answer,' I guessed cynically.

'I imagine they are all fairly desperate, Marcus. Anyway, they make a sacrifice, usually a kid. It has cold water poured over it; if it trembles, the god is at home and amenable to hearing questions. In that case, the Pythia purifies herself with Kastalian water and enters the temple. She burns laurel and barley flour on the hearth where the immortal fire burns. Then she descends into a space below the nave while the priests and applicant wait nearby. The applicant asks his question in a loud, clear voice. The priestess drinks more Kastalian spring water, chews bay leaves, mounts the sacred tripod beside the umbilicus – the navel of the world – then as the spirit emanates from the fissure, she falls into a deep trance. She speaks, though it is meaningless.'

'Typical woman!'

'Bastard. The priests write it down, then they translate the gibberish into words – though they leave you to interpret for yourself what is meant. Typical men,' retorted Helena neatly.

I knew an example: '"If Croesus crosses the River Aly, a great kingdom will be destroyed". Croesus eagerly decides that's the Persians so he rushes off with an army. Of course the Persians annihilate him and he destroys his own kingdom.'

'While the oracle chortles, "Told you so!" The let-out clause, Marcus, is that the oracle at Delphi "neither reveals nor conceals the truth". Whoever wants answers has to unravel the meaning.'

'Rather like asking my mother what she wants for a Saturnalia present . . . Though Ma never needs a bay-leaf snack to make her confusing.'

Abruptly we thought of home. We were silent for a while.

'So,' I said. 'Even if Tullius Statianus ever did win a place in the lottery, the Oracle would never tell him straight out "who killed Valeria". The Pythia would hedge her bets and disguise the name in subterfuge.'

'Well, how could she know?' scoffed Helena. Ever logical; never mystical. 'An elderly Greek lady, living on a mountainside, permanently sozzled with sulphur fumes and out of her mind on aromatic leaves!'

I loved that girl. 'I had assumed,' I returned mildly, 'the incomprehensible Pythia is a smokescreen. Her unearthly moans are just a sideshow. What happens is, as soon as applicants present themselves, the priests do a hasty background check on them, then *the priests* invent the prophecies, based on their research.'

'Sounds exactly like your work, Marcus.'

'They are better paid!' I was feeling morose. 'I once heard of a man who constructed a model of a talking snake, then let it answer people's questions in return for enormous fees. He made a fortune. I would earn more, and certainly gain more prestige, if I turned myself into an oracle at a thousand sesterces a go.'

Helena seemed thoughtful. For a moment I wondered if she took the suggestion too seriously and was planning to set me up in a booth on market days. Then she grabbed my arm.

'*I'll* make a prophecy, Marcus! See that young man over there having the argument with the temple assistant, who has heard it all before? I say it is Tullius Statianus.'

XLI

As arguments go, it was a one-sided contest. The young man was frantically making his case. Meanwhile the temple attendant was letting his eyes slide off in preparation for welcoming other people.

We knew Statianus was about twenty-four. That fitted. If this was him, then physically, he was unremarkable. He wore a white tunic and looked as if he had been in it for a week, and a circular travelling cape, into which he huddled like a man who would never feel warm again after serious illness or shock. Although not formally dishevelled, as litigants or people going to funerals are in Rome, his hair was too long and barely combed.

The acolyte tired of him and brushed him aside, moving with a practised sidestep towards someone else.

'There are other oracles!' we heard Statianus shout angrily. Helena and I had pulled each other upright from our seat on the steps and now skipped down to his level.

'Statianus? Excuse me –'

Something about us alarmed him. After one frightened glance towards us, Statianus took off.

If you have never tried chasing a fugitive through a very ancient religious site, my advice is: don't. In Rome, the merest hint of a skirmish with a pickpocket sends people diving behind columns in case they get their best boots scuffed or their togas torn in the scrum. Visitors to foreign shrines won't get out of the way.

I realised we knew little about this man. I had assumed he was spoiled: a leisured son of rich parents. His wedding trip to Greece was compensation for not being put into the

Senate. Avoiding politics could mean he lacked intellect (or that he had too much good sense). More we had never discovered. Now I learned that Statianus looked after himself. He must go to a gym – and he took it seriously. The bridegroom could run. We needed super-fit Glaucus. Otherwise, we were going to lose this suspect.

Immediately below the Temple of Apollo, people came snaking up the Sacred Way, sad bunches of visitors, some standing still in groups to listen to their dogged guides. The crowds made Statianus turn aside. He rushed away from the temple portico. High pillars bore statues of various Greek kings. They made excellent turning-points to skid around. Statianus must be familiar with the layout. He nipped among the monuments, buffing aside pilgrims who were dutifully staring skywards as their guides described the stone dignitaries. Seconds later, I crashed into these people just as they turned indignant after Statianus barged them.

We jumped down a level, to the astonishing Tripod of Plataea, its three towering intertwined bronze snakes supporting a mighty gold cauldron. Next was a huge plinth bearing a gold chariot of the sun. Statianus tried to hide behind it. When I kept coming, he bounded uphill again, dashed between two more columns with kings atop, and headed for what looked like a fancy portico. Its columns had been infilled with walls; thwarted by the solid barrier, he turned left. I nearly caught him at the Tomb of Neoptolemos. He was the son of Achilles. This was my nearest brush with the heroes of Homer, and I missed its significance. Never mind; Neoptolemos was dead, killed by a priest of Apollo (whose priests love music and art, but are tough bastards) – and I was gasping too much to care.

Three women huddling over a travel itinerary blocked the free space by a floral column which supported a trio of dancers; I slid around them all. Temple attendants swarmed in my path by the spring of Cassotis; I plunged into their midst and elbowed my way through. A dopy man asked me to point out the Column of King Prusias; he was right beside it. Statianus had pushed his way through all of these, but as he raced past the spring he was accosted by Helena. She had waited at the temple, saw us doubling back towards her, and now stepped out to remonstrate with our quarry. Statianus pushed her aside. She lost her footing. People rushed to assist her – getting in my way – and Statianus loped off along the back of the temple.

Helena was all right.

'Stay there –'

'No, I'm coming –'

I carried on after him. He was into his stride now. I was more than ten years older, but I had done my share of weight training. I had a sturdy build and had never lacked stamina. I hoped he might tire first.

The Temple of Apollo is a mighty edifice, and makes a dramatic running track. Above us we had the theatre, dramatically carved out of the crag. It was reached by a very steep flight of steps; to my relief Statianus ignored them. At the far end of the temple we passed yet more perfect art: a creation in bronze which showed Alexander the Great wrestling a spectacular lion among a striving pack of hunting hounds, while one of his generals rushed to assist. I could have used that general to assist me.

My quarry turned downhill. Opposite the west end of the temple was a gate through the steeply stepped sanctuary wall. The usual scrum of guides and statuette-purveyors milled around. Tiring, Statianus had become less sure-footed. He knocked into a hawker, spilled his tray of votive clay miniatures and was held up in a furious argument. Seeing me catch up, he shoved the hawker into me. I grabbed the man, spun him out of my path, and felt my ankle give as I turned it on one of the scattered statuettes. Cursing, I took my eyes off Statianus and lost him.

He must have gone through the gate. I followed, though doubt gnawed. The path outside led to the legendary Kastalian Spring. Its waters were used in the Delphic rituals, so pilgrims on the full guided tour were dragged here for a sample. Dazed by a mixture of exhaustion and mystic awe, they bumbled everywhere, completely oblivious to anybody

236

wanting to get past them. This really slowed me up. An elderly lady sitting on a rock at the roadside insisted on asking me how far the spring was, trying at least three broken languages when I failed to answer.

The spring rises in a wild ravine. It must once have been a peaceful, rocky haunt of lizards and wild thyme. Now crass voices resounded as visitors washed their feet in the sacred torrents, calling out to their friends how cold it was. Steps led down to a rectangular basin where seven bronze lions' heads set in clean-cut stone slabs spouted water which was collected by touts with little drinking cups, all eager to obtain a tip, assuming visitors had any money left after purchasing the stickman statues, tacky tat, and crumbling votive cakes. I bet when the pilgrims had gone on their way, the shrine parasites just collected the goodies from the handily positioned niches and sold them again.

I scanned the people, searching for Statianus. By now, I myself felt like a barley cake that had been left too long on a ledge in the sun. A cup-pedlar tugged my sleeve. I jerked away.

I stood on the roadway, thinking I had lost him. Breathing hard, I startled a few pilgrims as I gazed out at the mountains and swore at the scenery.

Then I saw there was a second fountain. Older and almost deserted, this one had a small paved courtyard with benches around it on three sides. Here, just four rather friendly looking old bronze lions spewed water in hiccupy trickles, while a solitary attendant lurked, without much hope. I bought a cupful, dashed it down, and tipped him.

'Seen a man out of breath?'

Amazingly, he waved an arm. I thanked him and set off once again, heading further down the path. Almost at once I heard Helena behind me, calling. I slowed. She caught up, and we continued together, jogging through shady olive groves until we passed the Delphi gymnasium. Beyond it lay a small enclosed sanctuary which had an air of immense age.

We slowed right down. We glanced at each other and walked into the sanctuary. Altars with inscriptions against the retaining wall told us we had come to the long-revered sanctuary of Athena Pronaia. Apart from the clutch of altars, it had just five or six main buildings, arranged in a line, including a large abandoned temple which had been destroyed by an earthquake. A newer, smaller temple had replaced it. There were a couple of treasuries, fronted by a large pedestal bearing a trophy. In the centre of the site stood a beautiful circular building, surrounded by Doric columns, with exquisite decoration on its upper features, of the type called a tholos. We had seen one at Olympia, where Philip of Macedon and Alexander the Great had collected statues of themselves and their ancestors. This stood on a circular base of several steps. Collapsed on these, struggling to recover his breath, was a young man in a white tunic.

We walked across to him.

'Tullius Statianus!' Helena's voice was hoarse but she sounded strict and determined to stand for no nonsense. 'I believe you know my brother, Aelianus.'

He looked up with dull eyes, unwilling or unable to run away from us any longer.

XLII

We took him to the gymnasium. It was close by, a familiar place where Statianus might relax; and it was bound to have food-sellers. Helena found a place in the shade outside (since as a woman she was barred), while I set us up with pastries, stuffed vine leaves, and olives. Statianus ate most of it. He seemed ravenous; I wondered if he had run right out of money.

Spending cash, I mean. He must possess funds, but out here he could be stranded. Men of his rank only need a banker abroad who knows *their* banker in Rome, but without such a contact they are as helpless as the rest of us. Delphi would have money-changers, but since the shrine's decline there would be few international financiers who took letters of credit. Statianus was said to be bad at managing and once he had used up what was in his pouch, he could find himself stuck.

Now we took a proper look at him. He was probably clean but he needed a shave. Under the stubble, his face was devoid of character. He had a limited range of expressions: he could look up, down, to the left and to the right. His mouth never moved and his eyes had no animation. A kind person would say grief had wiped him out. I was never that kindly.

Helena and I finished eating first. As Statianus ravenously continued, Helena began the softening up process, first asking about Aelianus. Between mouthfuls, Statianus told us how they had become friends at Olympia. Aulus seemed to have expertise in tragic situations and persuaded Statianus to trust him. He sympathised with the way Statianus had been hounded by the quaestor during the investigation into

239

Valeria's death. When the group were taken to Corinth and put under house arrest, Statianus could not bear to face Aquillius again; he despaired and decided to bunk off to Delphi as a last resort. Aulus tagged along.

'So where has he gone? Why did he leave you?'

'I don't blame him. He thinks this is a waste of time. There's nothing to do here except wait, month after month, while the organisers at the temple give out the questions, always to other people. Aulus said my connections aren't good enough ever to get a chance at the oracle. But I can wait. I do a bit here at the gym. Sometimes I run –'

'Yes, we know you can run!' I snarled wryly. 'You use the training tracks here at the gym?' The sports facilities were on two levels, with a washing area between them. The lower building appeared to be a palaestra, with the usual large courtyard and side rooms for boxing practice. When I bought the food I had seen that the upper building had an indoor covered running track for use in hot or otherwise inclement weather, with an open-air colonnade at the back; both tracks extended a whole stadium's length. 'Aulus is pretty athletic. Did he practise with you?'

'Yes, but being stuck here bored him. He tried to persuade me to abandon the oracle, but I am adamant. I need the gods' help to find out what happened to my wife.'

A raw note had entered his voice. We let him alone for a few minutes. Eventually Helena took him back to the beginning of his marriage, asking how Valeria had been chosen as his bride. Statianus confirmed that prior to the wedding the couple hardly knew each other. Valeria's mother had been a friend of his own mother's years before.

'She was respectable, but she came cheap?' My frankness grated. Statianus steadied, as if he recognised he was up against a fiercer interrogator than he had encountered so far. Aquillius Macer had stubbornly thought him guilty, but lacked push; even Aulus would go easy on a fellow aristocrat – he rarely used charm, but had a snobbish politeness with his own level of society.

Impatient with my rudeness, Helena leaned towards

240

Statianus. 'We met your mother in Rome. She is thinking about you, missing you. She wants you to come home and be taken care of.'

He let out a very small humph. I guessed he realised Tullia Longina thought he should get on with his life – which meant a speedy remarriage.

I let Helena continue the interview. More sympathetic than me, she drew from Statianus his version of what had happened to his wife at Olympia. It mostly matched what we had heard. Valeria wanted to meet Milo of Dodona, in order to hear a recitation. They had quarrelled about that; her husband admitted that they quarrelled frequently.

'Were you in love with your wife?'

'I was a good husband.'

'None of us can ask for more,' Helena assured him gravely.

She had more. She had much more, and she knew it. She pressed my hand briefly, as if she thought I was about to erupt indignantly.

They discussed the fatal evening. Statianus had dined out with the men; he came back and found Valeria missing, went out again to look for her. Nobody else took any interest; he searched alone. He could not find her. 'Did you go to the palaestra that night?' Helena asked.

'No. I have cursed myself for that a thousand times – but it was a private club. They had people on the doors to deny non-members admittance. If I had gone, I might have saved her.' If he had blundered in on the killing, he might have been bludgeoned to death too. 'When I did go there the next morning –'

He could not continue. Helena, who was tougher than she looked, calmly described for him how he had found the body; the hostile superintendent ordering him to remove it; carrying his dead wife back to the group's tent; screaming for assistance. He seemed surprised we knew it was Cleonyma who first came out to him. 'A good woman,' he said briefly. We sensed how stoically she must have responded to the ghastly scene.

241

'Tullius Statianus, did you kill your wife?' Helena asked.

'No.'

Helena held his gaze. He stared back with only a tired look of defiance. He had been asked the same question too many times: he would not rant in outrage at it. He knew he was the chief suspect. Presumably by now he also knew there was no direct evidence to arrest him.

'This must all be very hard for you,' Helena sympathised.

'At least I am alive,' he replied harshly.

I took up the questions, tackling him again about his relationship with Valeria. He knew I was probing for a motive. Like all relationships, theirs had been complicated, but it sounded as if they were realistic about their fate. Although they had scrapped all the time, they had one thing in common: both had been put into the marriage for other people's convenience.

'Would you have divorced? Was it that bad?'

'No. Anyway, my parents would have opposed a divorce. Her relatives, too, would have been disappointed.'

'So you reached an accommodation?' Helena suggested. He nodded. It seemed the couple were resigned. In their social circle, if they had given up on this marriage, both would only have been shunted into new ones – which could have turned out even worse.

Later, Helena and I discussed whether Statianus had hated the situation more than he now said. Did the prospect of nagging parents force him to decide that killing Valeria was his only way out? I thought sticking with her was the easiest option – and he liked the easy ones. Having met his mother, Helena felt that if he really wanted out, he could have got around the opposition eventually. So she believed the marriage would have lasted. 'At least until one of them found somebody who offered more love.'

'Or better lovemaking!'

'Ah, that would definitely count,' Helena agreed, smiling.

While we were with him at the gymnasium, I tested Statianus as hard as possible. 'So would you say you had learned to tolerate your wife – and she felt the same?'

'I never would have harmed her.' It did not answer my question, and when he saw I was dissatisfied, he snapped, 'It is nothing to do with you!' I could see how this attitude would have upset Aquillius.

'Statianus, when a young woman dies a brutal death, all her relationships become matters of public record. So answer me, please. Was Valeria more restless than you were?'

'No, she didn't like Olympia, but she was happy with me!' His frustration was showing. 'I don't know who you are, Falco – I trusted Aelianus and that's the only reason I'm talking to you.' Now self-pity took over. 'I shall never get through this.'

'That is why you should talk to me. By finding the truth, I help people contain their pain.'

'No. As soon as I saw my wife there dead, I knew every-thing was over. Everything has changed for ever. Whoever he was, the man who took her life – when she had enjoyed no life to speak of – also ruined mine. If I go home, I know my brothers and my parents will not understand. I have to carry this alone. That is why I stayed in Greece,' Statianus said, answering one question that I had not asked yet.

Helena and I were silent. We understood. We even understood his certainty that nobody he knew would ever truly share his devastation. His misery was genuine.

For the first time, Tullius Statianus had revealed his heart. We saw why Aelianus had been sure he was not the killer. We too believed him innocent.

Belief was not proof.

We had reached a natural break. Statianus complained he was tired; he had eaten so much he must be ready for a nap to sleep it off. I wanted to ask more questions, to gauge his thoughts about the others on the trip who must become suspects if we decided he was innocent, but I agreed to defer it. He told us where he was staying – a dismal inn, though he said it was no worse than the places to which Phineus took his clients. In fact, Phineus had told him where to stay. I noted that he spoke of Phineus with routine disparagement.

He promised to meet us tomorrow; I arranged to collect him from his inn. He seemed perfectly willing to talk to us now, and I wanted to extract everything I could from him while we had him in Delphi, separate from the group. Then I would take over from Aulus the task of persuading Statianus to give up on the oracle. But that could wait overnight. There was no rush.

XLIII

Next day, when we went to pick up Statianus I felt my first pangs of doubt. His lodging house was a dingy hole. I could see why he would not want to hang around there. Even so, when the landlord said the young man had gone out for some exercise, it worried me.

'He's gone running. Try the gymnasium.'

This could be the start of a long search. We had let Statianus fool us. We had failed to win him over; he was ignoring the arrangement to meet. Neither Helena nor I said it, but both of us reconsidered. Was Tullius Statianus *not* an innocent man, as he had convinced us, but guilty and a superb actor?

Never. He was not bright enough.

Still, he was jumpy enough to do something stupid.

I knew Helena wanted to see a building in the sanctuary they called the clubhouse. It contained fabulous ancient paintings of the destruction of Troy and the descent of Odysseus to Hades. Lovers of art had to see these famous pictures. I sent Helena off there, saying that when I found him I would extract Statianus from the gym and bring him along.

He was not at the gym. By the time I reached it, I had faced up to my anxiety. When I could not find him, I was not surprised. I feared that he had done a bunk. But where could he go?

Clearing my head, I stood in the central courtyard. I had searched both the gymnasium tracks, indoors and out, and the palaestra; I had even inspected clothes on hooks in the dressing room, in case I recognised his white tunic. Finally I stopped for a good curse, a lively event which took place in

245

the washing area. There was a big pool in the middle of the courtyard. Against the far wall were about ten individual basins, fed with water through lions' heads. After venting my rage there, I turned away towards the exit.

Somebody was watching me.

My spine tingled. I was suddenly aware of my surroundings. A couple of men were bathing in the pool after their endeavours on the track. Their splashes joined the melodious trickles from the waterspouts. From the palaestra came the low *thunking* sound of sand-filled punchbags being rapidly hit. I could hear music too. The gymnasium was haunted by flautists and lyre-players, as well as teachers, orators, and poets. One voice seemed to be delivering a scientific lecture, though the speaker sounded slow and the room he was using echoed hollowly as if he had only a small audience.

The man who was watching me stood nervously in a doorway. I stared him out. I knew from his stature that he was more likely to be one of the entertainers than a dedicated athlete, even an amateur. He was pale, thin, and nervous-looking. An unsatisfactory sky blue tunic hung awkwardly on his shoulders as if it was still on a pole at a market stall. Scrolls poked from a battered satchel slung across his pigeon chest.

When I glared at him, he dropped his gaze. I kept mine level.

'See something you like?' I challenged. I made it sound as if he had best answer me, damn fast, or something he certainly would *not* like would happen. 'I'm looking for Tullius Statianus. Do you know him?'

Words came out in a pathetic bleat. 'I try to avoid him.'

Now that was a surprise.

The men in the pool had stopped splashing about and were listening. So I led the stranger out of doors, where I could interrogate him in confidence.

'The name's Falco. Marcus Didius Falco. I am a Roman, representing the Emperor, but don't let it worry you.'

'Lampon.'

'You a Greek, Lampon?' He was. He was also a poet. I should have known from his weedy behaviour. I was a spare-time poet myself; it gave me no fellow-feeling for professional writers. They were unworldly parasites. 'So, my versifying friend, why are you hiding from Statianus – and what made you stare at me?'

He seemed glad to confide. So I soon found out Lampon was not just any old poet. He was a poet I had already heard about – and he was very, very scared.

Earlier this year he was at Olympia, where he was hired one night by Milo of Dodona. Milo set him up to give a recitation to Valeria Ventidia, hoping she would then nag her husband and fellow-travellers to sponsor Milo's statue. Lampon knew Valeria had been killed that night; recently he heard that Milo was dead too.

'You are right to be nervous,' I told him bluntly. 'But telling me is the best thing you can do.' Lampon, being a poet, inclined to both cowardice and doubt. 'I'm your man for this situation, Lampon. You tell me everything – then trust me to look after you.'

He was easily convinced. Eagerly, he told me all he knew.

Lampon and Milo had waited in vain for Valeria to show. Then they spent most of that night getting drunk. Milo was miserable over his failure to attract sponsors, and Lampon pretended the wine helped him to be creative; like most poets, he just liked it. Together, they gulped down many flagons. Since both athletes and authors have a lot of practice with wine, they nonetheless remained awake. So Lampon could now vouch for Milo of Dodona, who did not leave his presence until dawn; Milo could *not* have killed Valeria. Alive, the mighty Milo could have given the same alibi for Lampon. Despite Milo's death, I was prepared to exonerate the scribbler anyway. I knew about poetic recitals. I knew all about turning up with your scrolls but finding no audience. While drink would be a natural solace, killing a girl who failed to show was not worth the effort for a poet.

The next thing Lampon told me was even more important. 'The girl had a better offer!'

'You *saw* the better offer?'

Lampon looked shamefaced. 'I never told Milo.'

'Did you tell anybody else?'

'I went to the tents with Milo next day. He wanted to know why she hadn't come. He could never tell when people just weren't interested in him . . .' Clearly the poet was more experienced.

'What happened at the tent?'

'We were told she had been killed. Milo was shocked – and nervous, in case he got the blame. A couple of men talked to him, then they sent him away. While they were in conversation, I saw an elderly man on his own. He looked ill; he was taking medicine, sitting on a folding stool in the shade. I spoke to him.'

'Medicine?' Turcianus Opimus.

'Something strong,' said Lampon, with a faint note of envy. 'He was looking dreamy. Maybe he took a few too many swigs. I mentioned that I had seen the girl with someone; he smiled a lot and nodded. I never found out what he did about it.'

'Nothing, apparently. But it gave you a clear conscience . . . So tell me about Valeria and the man. What were they doing when you saw them? Were they up to no good?'

'Nothing like that. He was leading her into the building, as if he had just offered to show her the way.'

'Did she look worried?'

'Oh no. Milo and I were leaving the palaestra when I saw her, and I wanted a drink, not hours of reading. We were outside and it was fairly dark. I grabbed Milo and pulled him in another direction before he spotted her.' Leaving Valeria to her fate.

'You had no reason to think the girl was going into the palaestra against her will?'

'No. Well,' added Lampon, 'she thought she was going to find us.'

'If you had believed she was in trouble, you would have alerted Milo?'

'Yes,' said Lampon, with the unreliable air of a poet.

I took a deep breath. 'And who was this man with her? Do you know him?'

That was where the poet let me down, as poets do. His head was filled up with shepherds and mythical heroes; he was useless at noticing modern faces or names. When I begged him to provide a description, all he came up with was a man in his forties or fifties, solidly built, wearing a long-sleeved tunic. He could not remember if the man was hairy or bald or bearded, how tall he was, or the colour of the tunic.

'You've seen Statianus here, I take it?'

'Yes, I was in a complete funk when he turned up. I thought he was after me –'

'The poor bastard only wants the truth. Was it him at Olympia?'

'Definitely not.'

'Would you know the man again?'

'No. I don't take much notice of the old-timers.'

'Old-timers?'

'I assumed that was how he could get admittance to the palaestra – he looked like a retired boxer or pankration exponent, Falco. Didn't I say so?'

'You omitted that telling detail.' A detail which not only cleared Statianus, it exonerated all the other men touring in the same group. Well, all except one. 'Do you know the Seven Sights Travel operator, Phineus?'

'I think I've heard of him.'

'Would you know him by sight?'

'No.'

'Well, he's a heavily built man, who conceals his past, so he could have been an athlete – and he has missing teeth. Lampon, you're going to come with me to Corinth, when I leave here, and tell us if you've seen Phineus before.'

'Corinth?' Lampon was a true poet. 'Who is going to pay my fare?'

'The provincial quaestor. And if you vanish, or mess up your evidence, he'll be the man who throws you in a cell.'

Lampon looked at me with troubled eyes. 'I can't appear in court, Falco. The barristers would shatter me. I go to pieces if I'm shouted at.'

I sighed.

XLIV

Lampon looked queasy but he agreed to follow orders. He gave me one more suggestion. According to him, Statianus not only ran at the gym; he liked to climb up to the official stadium. The stadium lay about as high as could be, above the sanctuary of Apollo, where the air was even more refined and the views were breathtaking. Statianus had been heard to say that he went there to be alone and to think.

With directions from the poet (which, since he was a poet, I checked with passers-by at intervals), I made my way along the track, back to the Kastalian Spring, then into the sanctum and up past the theatre on a route I had never yet taken. A narrow path led upwards. The climb was steep, the situation remote. A man who had suffered a great calamity might well be drawn here. After the bustle of the sanctuary and the businesslike hum of the gym, this was a solitary walk where the sun and the scents of wild flowers would act on a tortured mind like a soothing drug. I suspected that when Statianus reached the stadium, he generally lay down on the grass and lost himself. You can think as you walk but, in my experience, not when you run.

I myself was thinking as I went, mainly about what Lampon had told me. Turcianus Opimus, the travel group's invalid, had learned more about Valeria's killer than the killer would have liked. From the poet's description, he may even have recognised who the killer was. Whom had he told about this? Was he ever sufficiently free of his pain-killing medicine to realise what information he held? Perhaps something he said or did about it led to his death at Epidaurus. Or perhaps he really died naturally – but someone believed he could have passed on the poet's story to Cleonymus.

251

I wondered if the poet himself was in danger. Damn. Still, as far as I knew, the killer was in Corinth.

I consoled myself with the thought that he was probably a bad poet anyway.

I took my time. If Statianus was up here, well and good. If not, I knew we had properly lost him. I held off blaming myself until I was sure. It would come. Every step I took convinced me he had run away from me. If he left Delphi altogether, I would have no idea where to look for him.

I was so certain that I was completely alone, I peed on the grey rocks, not even moving from the path. A gecko watched me, tolerantly.

I wished Helena was here. I wanted to share the glorious view with her. I wanted to hold and caress her, enjoying the silence and sunshine in this isolated spot. I wanted to stop thinking about deaths that seemed unsolvable, griefs we could never assuage, brutality, fear, and loss. I wanted to find Statianus at the stadium. I wanted to convince him to have faith. The misery he revealed to us yesterday had affected me. Standing alone with the gecko and the faraway wheeling buzzards made me aware how much.

As I slowly resumed walking, I transferred all my thoughts to Helena. I lost myself in memories of her warmth and sanity. I filled my head with dreams of making love to her. Yes, I wished she were here.

When I came upon the woman, I was so surprised I nearly jumped off the path, over the edge into oblivion. That was before I realised I had met her before at the top of a crag – in Corinth. It was the middle-aged dipsy nymph I had treated like a prostitute, who called herself Philomela.

XLV

She was standing on the narrow path, gazing out at the vista with extravagant enjoyment. She wore a many-pleated white Greek dress, folded over on the shoulders in the classical manner – a style which modern matrons had abandoned decades ago, instead copying Roman imperial fashion. Once again, her hair was bundled up in a scarf, which she had wrapped around her head in a couple of turns and tied in a small knot above her forehead. The classical look. This lady had gazed at a lot of old statues.

Now she was looking at me. Her wistful air was immediately familiar; that kind of wide-eyed wonderment seriously annoys me. She too was startled by our sudden confrontation. She stopped the blissful reverie, and became nervous.

'Well, fancy!' I made it avuncular. Not much choice but to gulp and be cheerful. Maybe she had forgotten how crassly I had insulted her. No. I could see she remembered me all too well. 'I'm Falco and you are Philomela, the Hellenophile nightingale.' She had dark eyes and had spent hours with hot tongs making herself a fringe of curly hair, but she was not Greek. I remembered she had spoken perfectly good Latin. I spoke in Latin automatically.

She continued staring.

I continued the jocularity. 'Your pseudonym comes from a savage myth! You know it? Tereus, King of Thrace or some other place with hideous habits, lusts for his sister-in-law, rapes her, and cuts her tongue out so she cannot tell on him. She alerts her sister Procne by weaving the tale into a tapestry – then the sisters plot against Tereus. They serve up his son in his dinner –' *That* charmless Greek cannibalism

253

yet again! Having dinner at home in classical times must have taken a lot of nerve. 'Then the gods turn everyone into birds. Philomela is the swallow, in the Greek poems. She's lost her tongue. Swallows don't cheep. Roman poets changed the birds around, for reasons which defy logic. If you think she's the nightingale, that shows that you're Roman.'

The woman heard me out, then said curtly, 'You don't look like a man who knows the myths.'

'Correct. I asked my wife.'

'You don't look like a man with a wife.'

'Incorrect! I mentioned her. Currently she is looking at art.'

'She's sensible. When her man travels, she goes too, to keep him chaste.'

'Depends on the man, lady. Or more to the point, it depends on the wife.' I was dealing with a man-hater, apparently. 'Knowing her virtues is what keeps me chaste. As for myths, I am an informer.' Time to get that straight. 'I deal with adultery, rape, and jealousy – but in the real world and with undeniably human killers . . . Where are you from, Philomela?'

'Tusculum,' she admitted reluctantly. Close to Rome. My mother's family, who grew vegetables on the Campagna, would sneer. This glassy-eyed mystic would not surprise them. My uncles thought people from Tusculum were all pod and no bean. (Though coming from my crazy Uncles Fabius and Junius, that was rich!)

'And what's your real name, your Roman name?' To that there came no answer. Perhaps it did not matter, I thought – mistakenly, as usual.

Philomela must already have been up to see the stadium. She was now looking past me, yearning to squeeze by and make her way downhill. The path was narrow; I was blocking it.

'You travel alone?' She nodded. For a woman of any status that was unusual, and I let my surprise show.

'I went with a group once!' Her tone was caustic.

'Oh, bad choice!' My own tone was sour too, yet we shared no sense of complicity.

Who was she? Her accent seemed aristocratic. Her neat hands had never done hard labour. I wondered if she had money; she must have. She should have been married once, given her age (she looked menopausal, which could explain her crazy air). Were there children? If so, they despaired of her, for sure. I bet she was divorced. Under the fey manner, I saw a stubborn trace of oddness. She knew people thought she was crazy – and she damn well did not care.

I knew her type. You could call her independent – or a social menace. Many would find her irritating – Helena for one. I bet Philomela blamed men for her misfortunes, and I bet the men she had known all said it was her own fault. One thing was sure: innkeepers, waiters, and muleteers would think she was fair game. Maybe she was, too. Maybe this woman stayed in Greece for free love with menials, thinking Greece was far enough from Rome not to cause a scandal.

She had watched my mental summing up; perhaps she saw it as disparaging. Now she chose to give more explanation, making it sound mundane. 'I live in Greece these days. I have a house in Athens, but I like to revisit sacred sites.'

'You enjoy fending off bad guides?'

'I ignore them. I commune with the gods.' I managed not to groan.

'You must be a woman without ties.' Relatives would lock her away.

'I like to be alone.' Dear gods, she really had gone native. No doubt she only ate honey if it came from Hymettus, and she harboured obsessive theories on the ingredients for home-made ambrosia . . .

'A convert to Achaea?' I gestured to the scenery. 'If it were all as beautiful as this, we would all emigrate . . .'

Abruptly she was through with me. 'I don't enjoy small talk, Falco.'

'Good.' I was bored with her anyway. 'Straight question: if you have just been right up to the stadium, did you see a

255

man running on the track? A bereaved man taking solace there, grappling with his grief?'

'I saw no one . . . May I pass, please?'

'Just a moment more. I met you before in Corinth; now you are here. Have your recent travels taken you to Olympia?'

'I dislike Olympia. I have not been there.' Never? She must have been, to decide she disliked the place.

Instinct made me persist. 'The man I want lost his young wife there – murdered in terrible circumstances. They were very recently married; she was just nineteen. The experience has destroyed him too.'

Philomela frowned. She lowered her voice and spoke less dreamily than usual. 'You must be worried for him.' Almost without pausing she added, 'I cannot help you with this.'

I made a gesture of regret then courteously stepped off the path, leaving her way free. She passed me in a rattle of cheap bead bangles and a haze of simple rosemary oil.

She looked back, chin up as if she intended to say something significant. Then she seemed to change her mind. She could see I was still going up to the stadium; she chided me: 'I told you I saw nobody. There is no one up there.'

I shrugged. 'Thank you. I have to check everything for myself.' I stepped back on to the path, then saluted quietly. 'Until we meet again.'

Her eyes hardened as she decided, *not if I can help it.* But I was sure it would happen. I don't believe in coincidence.

I carried on up to the stadium, which I found lay just ahead.

Anyone who liked running would enjoy running here. The stadium at Delphi seemed to lie on the doorstep of the gods. The bastards were up in the blue heavens, all lying on their elbows, smiling at the fraught actions of tiny mortal men . . . I could not help myself. I made a rude gesture skywards.

A standard track had been carved out of the hillside, with crude earth stands and one long stone bench for the judges. Stone starting-lines were at the end, like those Glaucus had demonstrated at Olympia. The place was crying out for a big Roman benefactor to install proper seating, but with Delphi so run-down nowadays that would need to be someone brave enough to love Greece and the Greek ideal very much indeed. Vespasian was a generous emperor, but he had been dragged along on Nero's embarrassing Greek tour and would have bad memories.

Nobody was visible. Up here on the tops, eagles or buzzards were languidly circling, but they made useless witnesses. There was nowhere to hide. Statianus was not here and I guessed he had probably not been here today. He had broken our appointment and become a fugitive. That was bad enough. But if he was really innocent, then somebody else was guilty. Phineus was locked up in Corinth, but maybe some other killer was still out on the loose. Tullius Statianus could be a target now. I had to find out where he had gone – and I had to reach him first.

XLVI

It took us three days to find any useful information. It was three days too long.

After I had checked out the stadium, I returned to the sanctuary fast. I found Helena in the building they called the clubhouse where she had gone to look at the art. Without a glance at the famous wall-paintings, I fetched her out of there. She saw from my face that something was amiss. I explained as we set off back to the town.

We made straight for the inn where Statianus had been staying. I tackled the landlord angrily; he still insisted Statianus was in residence. He even showed us the room. True enough, luggage remained. For the landlord that was enough; so long as he held property he could sell, he did not care if a lodger ran out on him. We tried to believe he was right. Stratranus would reappear.

With no other clue, we spent the next three days searching the town and the sanctuary. We asked questions of everyone; some even bothered to answer. Nobody had seen Statianus leaving Delphi – if he did so. He had certainly not hired a mule or donkey from any of the normal hire stables. I went down to the sea, but as far as I could tell, no boats had left with him. In those few days, he never went back to the gymnasium – and he never returned to his lodgings. He must have gone somewhere, travelling very light, on foot.

We lost those three days, and I knew at the time it could be a crucial error. Then a messenger came across the Gulf from Aquillius Macer: almost as soon as we left Corinth, Phineus had escaped from custody.

I toughened up. I marched back to that dismal inn where Statianus had spent weeks in misery. I let the landlord know he was in trouble, trouble which could affect his business and his health. I laid it on thick, mentioning the governor, the quaestor, and the Emperor; I described Vespasian as taking a personal interest. That was stretching it, but a Roman citizen in a foreign province ought to be able to hope his fate matters. Vespasian would sympathise with Statianus – in principle.

At last my urgency infected the landlord. Apart from gasping at my heavy-duty contacts, it turned out Statianus owed him rent. On inspection, the luggage he was holding hostage had a lower value than he thought. He knew what days without sighting a lodger normally meant. Suddenly he wanted to help me.

He let me in and I searched the room again. From the few things here, I reckoned Statianus must have left a load of stuff at Corinth. A man travelling on his wedding tour would have brought much more baggage than this. For Delphi he had packed only necessities, and now he had shed even those. There was no money, nor other valuables. I had hoped for a travel journal, but he kept none. Apart from the cloak I had seen him wearing, the landlord reckoned everything the young man brought with him in the first place was still here. That looked bad. If Statianus had skipped, he no longer cared about comfort or appearance. He was desperate. He was almost certainly doing something stupid.

He had abandoned even his mementoes: folded in cloth, I found a woman's finger-ring. Valeria's, no doubt. It was a decent piece, gold, probably bought in Greece, since it had a squared-off Greek meander pattern. Maybe he gave it to her.

Then I found something else. Flat against the bottom of his leather pack, where it would be safest from knocks, lay a modest square of parchment. At first I thought it was scrap; there was half an old inventory inked on one side. But I should have known better. When I was a struggling informer, in my grim rented apartment at Fountain Court, I used everything from old fish wrappers to my own poetry drafts as writing material. This inventory had been re-used on its good side by some ten-minute sketch artist.

For one wild moment I thought the bridegroom had left clues. This drawing was nothing so helpful – yet it wrenched my heart. The couple must have succumbed to one of those scribble-you-quick cartoonists who hang around on quaysides and embankments, trying to earn the fare back to their home village after their career fails. The youngsters had bought a drawing of themselves: leaning against one another but looking out at spectators, right hands intertwined to show their married status. It was not bad. I recognised him. Now I was seeing her. Valeria Ventidia was wearing the meander ring that I held in my hand: a fearless, impertinent kind of girl, with small, pretty features, a complex set of ringlets, and a direct stare that made my heart lurch. She was not my type now, but when I was much younger, her self-confidence might have made me call after her saucily.

I knew she was dead, and I knew how terribly she died. Meeting her fresh gaze, so sure of herself and so full of life, I could see why Statianus wanted to find the man who killed her.

I left the room and gave Helena the portrait. She groaned quietly. Then a tear dashed down her cheek.

I faced up to the landlord. I was certain he was holding something back. I did not touch him. I did not need to. My mood now was obvious. He realised he should be afraid.

'I want to know everything. Everything your lodger said, everyone he spoke to.'

'You want to know about his friend, then?'

'Another young man was with him when he first arrived,' Helena interrupted impatiently. Her thumb moved gently on the double portrait. 'He left Delphi for Athens. I can tell you everything about him – he's my brother!'

'I meant the other one,' the landlord quavered.

Ah!

'Statianus had *another* friend here?'

'He came three nights ago, Falco.'

*

The landlord gave us a rough description: a man in middle life, in business, ordinary-looking, used to inns. It could have been anyone. It could have been Phineus, but the landlord said not. It could simply have been someone Statianus met, with whom that lonely young man just fell into conversation, some stranger he would never see again. Irrelevant.

'Would you call this man expensively dressed?'

'No.' Not the killer from Corinth, therefore – unless he had dressed down for travelling.

'Did he look like an ex-boxer or ex-wrestler?'

'He was a lightweight. Run to seed a bit, big belly.' Not the killer from Olympia either – unless different witnesses saw him differently. As they so often do.

The landlord could be lying. The landlord could be unobservant (as Helena put it) or blind (as I said).

'Did he ask for Statianus?'

'Yes.'

Not a passing stranger, then.

At first, the landlord pretended he had not heard any conversation between the two men. He admitted they had eaten together at the inn. It was Helena who demanded swiftly, 'Do you use a waiter to serve food?'

There was a moment of bluster.

'*Get him!*' I roared.

It was the waiter who mentioned Lebadeia.

'I reckon he's gone to Lebadeia.'

'What's at Lebadeia?'

'Nothing much.'

Wrong. Something bad. Something very bad.

This waiter had heard Statianus say the name to his companion, who seemed to reply with encouragement. As the waiter told us at first, Lebadeia was a town on the way to other places.

'So why do you think Statianus would go there?'

This weary tray-carrier was a plump, acne-disfigured

fellow with slanty eyes, varicose veins, and a visible yearning to be paid for his information. His employer had lost him any hopes of a bribe; I was too angry. I screwed out of him that Statianus had talked excitedly to his visitor, and the name of Lebadeia had been overheard.

'Did you know the second man?'

'No, but Statianus did. I thought he had come from the travel firm.'

'What? Was it Phineus? Do you know Phineus?'

'No, it wasn't him. I know Phineus.' Everyone knew Phineus. He knew everyone – and everywhere too; if Ledabeia boasted any feature of interest, Phineus would have it on his list of visitable sites. 'I assumed,' whined the waiter beseeching us to agree with him, 'this one might be Polystratus.'

This was the second time recently his name had come up. Helena Justina raised her eyebrows. I straightened up and told her, 'That's right. The Seven Sights "facilitator". The man you didn't like in Rome. The man Phineus is supposed to have sent over here to persuade Statianus to return to the group.'

'So do we think Statianus has gone back to Corinth, Marcus?'

'No, we don't. Why has he abandoned his luggage, in that case?'

'He was very worked up,' murmured the waiter, now anxious that he might have got into trouble. 'People heard him pacing his room that night, and in the morning he was just gone.'

'There's nothing to say he went to Lebadeia, though.'

'Only,' admitted the waiter nervously, 'the fact that he had asked me the way.'

I gripped him by the shoulders of his greasy grey tunic. 'So what's he gone there for? He must have had a reason. I can tell by your shifty eyes that you know what it was!'

'I suppose,' said the waiter, squirming, 'he must have gone to try the oracle.'

XLVII

When we looked at the map Helena always brought with her, we saw why even the waiters of elegant Delphi disparaged Lebadeia: it lay on a major route from Athens to Delphi, the processional way taken every year by dancing maids who indulge in winter rites to Dionysus. But Lebadeia, a town close to the Copais Lake, was in Boeotia. I had read enough Greek comedies. I knew that for the xenophobic Greeks, Boeotia represented the world's unwashed armpit. The district was barbarian. Boeotians were always represented as brutes and buffoons.

'Well, my darling,' Helena murmured heartlessly, 'you'll fit in well there, won't you?'

I ignored that. I pointed out hotly that Lebadeia was miles away. Well, twenty as Apollo's crow flies – though much more, allowing for one or two damn great mountains. One of those was where the maddened maenads tore King Pentheus to shreds in Bacchic frenzy: just the kind of bloodsoaked spot where informers like to dally, terrifying themselves with history.

'I am not going.'

'Then I shall have to go instead, Marcus. The road passes between the hills, I think; it's not difficult. We can have no doubt where Statianus is. Look here at the map – ' Her road map depicted mansios and other useful features, shown as little buildings. It confirmed our fears: 'Lebadeia has an oracle.'

I was all set to head straight back to Corinth and tell Aquillius Macer to dispatch a posse to pick up the prophecy-besotted bridegroom. Only the mention of Polystratus worried me. Phineus had said he was sending one of his people to find Statianus, and it seemed that he had. I was very unhappy with the outcome. From the waiter's description, Polystratus appeared to have encouraged Statianus to head off on a new quest for divine truth – a crazy quest, I would say – instead of bringing him back to the fold.

It was interesting that the waiter, who had never met him, had nonetheless heard of Polystratus. I had assumed he did all his 'facilitating' from the Rome office, then had no connection with the travellers until they came back to Italy and he fielded their angry complaints about their trips. So how come a waiter in a back-alley doss-house – albeit a regular stopover Phineus used for his clients at Delphi – still knew of Polystratus? What kind of reputation did he have in Greece? I had no time to enquire.

I felt anxious about what his orders from Phineus had really involved. Hades, now that I knew Phineus himself had escaped from custody, I was worried where he had got to, and what he might be planning while on the run.

'What if you were the killer, and more conventional than us?' Helena asked me. 'We have a cynical view of oracles – but what if you believed in them and thought Statianus might one day hear the truth from a prophetess?'

'You would want to stop it.'

'You might think that Delphi was too public. You might like Statianus to go to a more remote oracle and deal with him there.'

Helena was right; we had no option. We had to go to Lebadeia and find Statianus again ourselves.

We took the poet. He was a witness, one I could not afford to lose or to have coerced behind my back. I was reluctant to leave him, in case his nerve failed and he vanished. Besides, the killer might know he was a witness. For Lampon, that could be dangerous.

Anyway, poets come in handy when you are riding through landscapes which are rich in myth and literary connections. Before we reached Lebadeia, Lampon had proved himself a good source of information on the shrine we were approaching. It was called the Oracle of Trophonius. The Boeotians had made a mint there, by offering prophecies to distraught pilgrims who failed in the question lottery at Delphi. But as oracles go (and for me you can stuff them) I hated the sound of this one.

According to Lampon, the Oracle of Trophonius worked in a different way from Delphi. There was no Pythia muttering gibberish. The applicant was allowed direct contact with whatever divine force lived there. He learned the future for himself, through what he saw and heard. The bad news was that to acquire it, he had to subject himself to an appalling physical ordeal, which left people terrified, traumatised, and often unconscious.

'They lose the power to laugh,' Lampon announced darkly. 'It can be permanent. When someone is particularly gloomy, with a dark mentality, we say they must have got that way at the Oracle of Trophonius.'

As we journeyed for a day across country, that was our first intimation of what was really bad at Lebadeia.

XLVIII

The River Hercyna dashed down noisily from Mount Helike in a steep gorge. In flood, it must be icy, deep, and full of clashing rocks carried down from the lonely, near-vertical crags. Plenty of water also rises from springs on the area.

Lebadeia lay mainly on the east bank of the river. For a town in the world's unwashed armpit, it seemed decent and prosperous. Maybe the Attic Greeks were wrong. Of the legendary Boeotian brutality there was little sign in the agora, while the shopkeepers seemed to run businesses on normal commercial lines. People grunted when we asked directions, but locals do that everywhere. It would have been more unnerving if they stopped in their tracks and were helpful. Even without local assistance we found a small rooming-house. Then I started asking around for news of Statianus, but got nowhere.

At dinner in a foodshop with few customers, we found a waitress who was willing to expound on the oracle. It involved much pursing of the lips and sucking in of breath. She wiped down her hands on her skirt and sombrely told us that there was a great deal of ritual, much of it taking place in darkness, and all designed to put the applicant into a state of dread.

First, he had to spend three days living in an appointed house, washing only in cold water, and making sacrifices. Then, at the dead of night, two young boys would lead him to the moonlit river, wash him in its freezing water, anoint him, take him through various acts of worship, dress him strangely in a beribboned outfit with heavy boots, then pass him on to the priests for his scary initiation. He would drink Waters of Forgetfulness, to wash his mind clear. Then he descended by a flimsy ladder into a purpose-built underground chamber, where he was left alone. In pitch darkness, while holding barley-cakes in either hand, he had to insert his body, legs first, into a narrow cleft, where – according to the waitress – supernatural forces would physically suck him in, reveal the truth in an awesome manner, then spit him back out, a shattered wreck. Priests would take him to drink the Waters of Memory, after which he would remember and record for posterity all he had learned – if and when he recovered consciousness. His friends and family had to gather him up and hope he would survive the experience. Not everyone did.

Unnervingly, we were told of one person who avoided the full ritual and was fatally punished. Perhaps he entered the oracle in search of treasure. He disappeared that night, failing to emerge from the sacred fissure. His dead body was found days later, some distance from the oracle.

That was one way to ensure no one rebelled against procedure. All the best magical sanctuaries have horrible stories to warn off blasphemers and looters. The details of what happened to genuine applicants at this shrine were nasty enough.

'You would have to be very desperate,' Helena commented. Our waitress, who had grown up with Trophonius, agreed – but her sympathy was fleeting and she then skipped off to fetch us a big dish of honey into which we could dip pastries. She had never been to the oracle, and knew nobody local who had taken part in its ritual. Clearly it was a tourist trap.

We sat silent for a while. We knew one man who was desperate enough for this. We were appalled at Tullius Statianus being subjected to rites that were intended to overwhelm a fragile mind in torment. To put himself through this terror all alone was dreadful. He had no devoted friends or family to wait outside the shrine for him. Even if we had believed that Trophonius really would reveal the truth, what Statianus then heard in the sacred chamber might be unbearable. But I for one thought oracles like this all worked by trickery.

*

Neither Helena nor I slept much that night.

Next morning we went straight across the river looking for the oracle. Since river water was needed during the ritual, we knew it would not be too far away. There were various shrines on the banks of the Hercyna. In a grove on a hillside stood a small temple to Trophonius, a local king and minor deity. Just beyond the grove, the oracle itself consisted of a sizeable man-made earth mound. This supported a round drum-shaped feature constructed from white marble, about the size of the average threshing floor and roughly three feet high. On top were bronze posts, linked by chains, and a double set of trapdoors. Through these, hapless enquirers must descend for their ordeal.

I was dreading this. In the course of my work, I had been forced to enter several ghastly pits and wells. The mere thought of another made me claustrophobic. I could do it if I knew I had to rescue someone, but I liked to have back-up from a group of strong men I trusted. Bad memories were lurking close. Helena slipped her long fingers around one of my clenched fists. Cold sweat trickled down my back; it had nothing to do with the weather. Now here was another pitch black hole down which, if I knew anything, sooner or later I would be sent.

Before it came to that, we asked a priest about Statianus. The priest tried the usual blank response, citing confidentiality. I cited the Emperor and threatened to close down the shrine. He saw reason. Faced with loss of revenue, they generally do.

'Such a young man as you describe came to seek the truth here,' he admitted.

'Who came here with him?'

'Nobody.'

'Are you sure of that?'

'He carried out the full ritual. We had him in our community for three days. We would have known if anyone was in Lebadeia with him.'

So no Phineus or Polystratus – apparently. Well, that was

something. But then whatever poor Statianus went through, he endured it alone. I would not have let that happen. Dear gods, if the young fool was fully determined to suffer this pantomime, I would have escorted him to Lebadeia myself. I would at least have been waiting to lift up his comatose body and wrap him in a blanket once it was all over.

The priest told us the story. Statianus had turned up, looking frantic. They were used to that. This oracle was not for the casually curious.

The temple attendants had calmed him, and carefully explained what he would have to do. According to them, they used every means to dissuade him from going through with it. If that was true, the bastards were now making sure they were morally covered. No chance here of a compensation claim afterwards for personal injury. I was only surprised they did not make all applicants sign a disclaimer.

'Do you suggest people make a will?'

'Unnecessary, Falco!'

Statianus chose to proceed. So they made him stay at an approved lodging to prepare himself – dwelling on it. On the third night, he was taken to the river by two teenaged acolytes, bathed, dressed in a special costume of tunic, ribbons, and very heavy boots, and anointed with oil. The priests transferred him to what they called the Fountain of Forgetfulness, from which he drank. After worshipping a secret image of Trophonius made by Daedalus, and praying (no doubt that it would all be over quickly), Statianus was led in procession to the oracle. He climbed the mound. Its trapdoors were opened, the ladder prepared, and he climbed down alone into the chamber. The ladder was removed; the heavy doors clanged shut above him.

He knew what he must do then. Between the walls and the floor he would find a crevice, into which he had to press himself, feet first. Presumably he got that far.

'Presumably?' My voice was harsh with foreboding.

'Something happens occasionally,' the priest said, coldly. He made it oblique, distancing himself.

I felt sick. 'He was harmed there?' I saw the priest's face

and guessed the worst. 'You can't mean this. You *lost* him?'

Appalled, Helena Justina begged, 'Tullius Statianus never emerged from the oracle chamber?' The priest finally confirmed it with a stiff nod. 'He *vanished*? Then you had better tell us,' Helena instructed fiercely, 'whether you have found that poor man's body yet – and if not, where you suggest we look for him.'

XLIX

We never found him.

I could tell the priests were nervous from the start. Whatever they planned to happen must have gone badly awry. Since they refused to admit what was normal procedure, we could only guess how.

Sure of a tragedy, I made it official straight away. I chivvied the priests and involved the elders of the town. We scoured Lebadeia itself. Then parties of men searched in all directions: along the main road to Chaironia, up a track that led over Mount Helike to Delphi by a wilder route, and also out along the famous road to Thebes. Riders and youths with dogs came out to look for him. We beat the rocks and dragged the river. He was nowhere.

When it grew dark, we had to abandon our efforts. The townspeople had done all I could expect. They had devoted a day to it. They wanted to exonerate their oracle, so they showed willing, even though we were foreigners and strangers. But when I gave up and returned to my room that night I sat wearily with my head in my hands, and knew they would do no more. We had all failed. By then I was sure we would never see Statianus alive again – and we might never even know if he was dead.

At that point, Helena was not with me. When I stumbled back to our hired room, I failed to find her and assumed she had gone to eat without me. I was surprised. Soon, anxiety took me in search of the poet. Lampon said she had gone back to the sanctuary; she had wanted to try to find out what really happened to questioners down in the chamber. She was sure the oracle worked by some trick.

That had been this afternoon.

I crossed the river and raced to the oracle. Lampon came with me, guilty that he had not told me earlier. I wished he had gone with Helena, but I knew her independence and could not blame him for it.

The grove was dimly lit with tiny lamps. The mound was more brightly illuminated, as if somebody might be consulting the oracle that night. But nobody much was there, just two boys in matching long white tunics, aged about thirteen. They were hanging about playing knucklebones and hoping for excitement. One saw me coming, took fright at my grim face, and decided he had to go home to his mother. The other either had a feckless mother who would never miss him, or else he just could not bear to miss anything. Lampon and I accosted him. I assured him he was not in any trouble, then slowly extracted news.

Helena Justina had come to the oracle, and had found these same boys. She sat down and made friends with them. She guessed they were the pair who took part in the ritual, leading questioners to the river for ceremonial washing. Winningly, she asked whether they knew more about the oracle than that. Of course they did. They knew how the priests worked it.

I gazed at the lad who was telling me. Helena and I had already discussed this. We had heard numerous tales of temple 'magic' from Marinus and Indus. Egypt was particularly good at trickery, but delusion happened everywhere. Statues that eerily nodded or talked, for instance. Temple doors that swung open mysteriously, after priests lit fires on altars, activating buckets of water or mercury, hidden beneath, so they operated pulleys; doors that then miraculously closed when the altar fires were doused. Compared to these manoeuvres, it would be simplicity to bamboozle a man you had locked up in the dark underground – especially in a contraption built specifically for that purpose.

'I bet I know what Helena suggested. When the initiate is down there in the chamber, somebody else goes inside?' The

272

boy seemed amazed I too had worked out this obvious ploy. 'Is there a secret passage?'

With an eagerness that suggested he had a guilty conscience, the boy admitted it. He knew of the passage for the simplest of reasons. 'When the doors shut and the questioners are in the dark, most of them shit themselves. I get paid a bonus to go in next day and clean up.'

Then to my horror, he confessed he and his friend had shown Helena where the secret passage was. She had gone in. She was a long time there. They called, but she never came out. They knew Statianus had vanished and were too scared to investigate. Frightened, the two boys had hung around outside, hoping somebody would come along and deal with the situation for them.

Like most boys in trouble, our informant had not confessed until he was asked. He was very relieved to be telling me at last. I myself was hysterical. I ordered him to show me the hidden entrance immediately. My urgency was a mistake. The lad leapt to his feet and fled.

There was still a way in. Lampon and I took lights. With the poet trembling behind me, I strode to the top of the mound. He made a limp effort to help me, as I heaved up one of the bronze doors and flung it over on its hinge so the hole was accessible. We clung to the edge and peered down. I thought I could see a white figure lying about twenty feet below.

Statianus had been put down there yesterday, using the shrine's famous narrow ladder. Ladders of that length are rarely stored far from their operation area. Lampon and I ran around the sanctuary like trapped rats until we found it.

'Don't fail me, Lampon. I need you, man. I'm going down, but you make sure you stay here holding the ladder steady. Then I may need you to fetch help.'

The dark shaft was horribly like a well-head I once had to be lowered into. Still, I scrambled over and I went down that ladder almost without touching its rungs. I was holding a lamp; scalding oil splashed my hand. I found myself entering a conical cave, fashioned like a kiln or bread oven. The walls were about ten feet apart, the depth twice that. Foul, musty air chilled me.

When my feet hit the rough earthen floor, I looked up. A pallid semicircle showed where the entrance door was open. Lampon's head was outlined dimly against a far-off starlit sky. I yelled up to him not to shut down the trapdoor whatever happened.

Now there was no time for panic. I dropped to my knees beside the motionless figure. It was Helena – thankfully warm and still breathing. As soon as I touched her, sliding my hands along her arms to rub life back into her, she groaned and struggled.

'I'm here. I've got you –' Relief and joy swamped me as I held her in my arms. On principle, I found a few words of admonishment: 'Now I know why the Greeks lock up their women indoors . . .' But I also knew why she had done it. She remembered how many fearsome wells, tombs, and underground shrines I had had to endure; she had wanted to spare me yet another dose of terror in a dark confined space. In the end I just clasped her tightly, forgetting her folly and thanking that wonderful idiot for her bravery and love.

Then we heard angry voices above us. Sanctuary guards were accosting Lampon. He protested with vigour, but we heard him being dragged away. Somebody pulled up the ladder and, despite my shouts, they banged the door shut. My lamp went out.

'Oh thank you, gods!'

'No, Marcus; that was men – men protecting their mysteries.'

'We must stop getting ourselves entombed in dank places. Don't panic.'

'I am perfectly calm, darling – Marcus, Marcus, I have to tell you. I know how they do it. Someone hits them on the head!'

'Someone hit *you*?'

'Not hard –'

My palm went to her scalp, feeling for damage. She

squeaked. I pulled in a long, ferocious breath. Any man who attacked Helena Justina was as good as dead. But I had to get us out of here and find him first.

To keep her still as she thrashed about trying to talk to me, I went along with the revelations: 'Right! The poor fools with questions are brought here, weak from fasting. They have been drenched with cold water, inside and out, so their brains are frozen. Disorientated by fear, they fail to notice when somebody slides *out* of the cleft they themselves have to wriggle into.' Where was it, incidentally?

'No, I don't think anyone waits in here, or crawls in either. They would be noticed. My theory is, they lie in wait outside in the secret passage. They pull the victim feet first through the cleft – then bop them and push them back in here. The questioners have been told to hold barley cakes soaked in honey in both hands – so they can't defend themselves,' Helena burbled. 'And they have been told they will experience being dragged helplessly into the cleft as if pulled by the force of a river –' She was shaking with cold, after lying here all afternoon. I had to take her out of this filthy cave, and quickly.

'Tell me later, sweetheart. You came through this secret passageway – now where is it?'

Then Helena helped me feel at floor level for the hole where the questioners inserted themselves. Through this crack 'supernatural forces' sucked them and then – if they were lucky – the so-called gods later spat them out back into the chamber. The cleft was about two feet long and one foot high; a chubby gourmet would get stuck.

Oh pig's piss. It was too small. Hot waves of primeval fear swept over me. This was my worst nightmare. Before I came down here, I had told myself there must be a nicely hewn corridor. Even if the secret tunnel had been made for boys and dwarves, I had imagined it as walkable – perhaps with a decent door into this chamber . . .

No chance. Bad luck had caught me out again. We had to lie down and squeeze out feet first through the sacred pothole.

275

L

No force of nature or divinity seized us.

We lay down, used our own strength to push our feet through the gap, then wriggled our bodies after them. Helena went first, before I could stop her – but she had come in this way, so she was more confident. I felt her slip away from me, then heard muffled shouts of encouragement. I followed Helena and squeezed through into another dark cavity where it was possible only to crouch half upright. Feeling the wall on our left hand, she then pulled me for some distance along a back-breaking tunnel, to a door which led outside. With huge relief we emerged into the moonlit grove.

We straightened up and breathed the cool night air.

'Well, that's drastic – but effective! A sanctuary attendant creeps inside with a mallet. Some questioners are so badly concussed they never get over it. Dear gods, love, that could have been you.'

Helena hugged me to comfort me. 'It may not have been the priests. In fact, that is rather unlikely. Someone may have overheard me talking to the boys and followed me in there. When I had scrambled into the main chamber I could see nothing in the dark, so I started wriggling back to the tunnel. I heard someone there. I backed into the main chamber again but he followed. I gave his hair a good pull and poked him in the eye, I think. His blow glanced off, but I groaned very loudly and pretended to be done for.'

'You passed right out. Don't pretend otherwise.'

'Just play-acting, Marcus.'

'Cobnuts. I found you, remember. Helena Justina, you will promise me now – you will never, ever do anything that ridiculous again.'

'I promise,' she said quickly. It had all the weight of a market-trader telling me her eggs were fresh. 'They will never admit how they cheat, Marcus.'

'No, not even with your evidence.'

'The boys who showed me the way told me everyone at the shrine thinks a stranger got in yesterday and stole away Statianus. Whatever happened to him was quite unplanned by the authorities.'

'So the priests don't believe the gods took him?' I asked drily.

'They had seen someone, lurking in the grove.'

'Description?'

'Just "a shadowy figure", I'm afraid.'

'Oh the old "shadowy figure" is at it again? I wonder if he's now called Phineus or Polystratus – or did somebody else trail our man here?'

'It must be someone who knows how the oracle really works,' said Helena.

'Someone who works in the travel industry would probably have a good idea!'

We tackled the priests. They released Lampon into my custody, claiming their security guards had mistaken the poet for a thief. He bravely made a joke agreeing that he had a furtive manner and communicated badly. This had my style. A few more weeks with me, and Lampon would give up scribbling, marry for love, and learn how to earn hard money boot-mending . . .

I accused the priests of fiddling the oracle. They accused me of blasphemy. We settled on calling what was per-petrated on questioners: 'divine manipulation in the cause of truth' – where my definitions of 'divine' and 'truth' differed from theirs.

To protect the good name of their oracle, they were eager to prove that some evildoer had taken Statianus from the chamber, and that the same man then attacked Helena. They could not risk other pilgrims hearing that descent into the cavern was genuinely dangerous. The official story was that only one man had ever died at the hands of Trophonius, and that he – known to be the lowlife bodyguard of a man called Demetrius – had deliberately gone into the cavern to steal gold and silver. His fate was divine vengeance, according to the priests. I told them I had a healthy respect for revenge.

After a stupid feint when the priests suggested to us that Trophonius had claimed our man for the underworld, they stopped messing with the mystic tosh and confessed themselves baffled. They absolutely denied sending in a man with a mallet to strike people on the head; I never decided whether that had happened to Statianus or if the mystery man got to him first.

Nervous about future takings, the priests now told me all they knew. Tullius Statianus came to them about a day after Helena and I met him in Delphi. Somebody had told him of a rocky short cut, so he had made good time.

At the shrine, Statianus had claimed he was in danger. The priests simply assumed that like many of their customers he was haunted by demons – figments of a tormented imagination. Thinking no more of it, they prepared him with the rituals and sent him into the chamber. According to them, when the bronze trapdoor was opened again after the regulation period, instead of finding him in shock on the floor, he was simply gone.

I believed them. There would have been no benefit to them in lying. They needed to pull questioners out after their ordeal, alive. Dead men would only deter future trade.

Only after they found that Statianus had vanished, had attendants talked among themselves and recalled sightings of the unknown man in the grove. By then it was too late. Nobody had spoken to him at the time. Nobody had seen him since.

'Has a travel company from Rome, called Seven Sights and led by a man called Phineus, ever brought clients to this oracle?' Occasionally. The priests discouraged it. Tourists in general took one scared look, then declined to carry out the ritual. There was no money in their visit and it wasted time. 'Still, you do know Phineus. Could he be your skulking

278

man?' Too far away to tell. 'Anyone ever met his sidekick, Polystratus?' Not that they were aware of.

Exhausted and frustrated, we had to give up. We had searched; we had asked the right questions. If anything new was discovered, messages would be sent to the governor. Our business at the oracle was over.

It was hard to leave, beset by guilt that we were abandoning Statianus. We had no choice. There was nothing more we could do in Lebadeia. Next day the priests supplied transport and we travelled to the coast. At a fishing village, we picked up a boat and sailed back across the Gulf of Corinth. Our mood was bleak.

We landed at Lechaion, feeling that the past few days had been a disaster. The first person we saw was a soldier in uniform. He told me he had been ordered to the port by Aquillius, watching for Phineus.

He was not much use as a lookout. Helena clutched my arm. Disembarking from another vessel was another suspect. This was a man we had not seen for weeks. We watched as he oversaw the unloading of several large amphorae, wine or seafood containers, presumably. He was joking with the sailors and looked completely unconcerned.

I sent Helena ahead into Corinth with Lampon, to find our young folk at the Elephant. Without bothering to alert the lookout soldier, I walked across and hailed the new arrival, as he shouldered an unwieldy round amphora on to an already laden donkey-cart.

'Remember me? I am Didius Falco. We met in Rome. I need an urgent talk with you, Polystratus.'

Polystratus, the facilitator, remembered to look amazed at meeting me out here in Greece – though I had a feeling it was no surprise at all.

LI

Polystratus was wearing the long, vomit-yellow tunic I remembered from when I first met him, at Seven Sights Travel's crude booth in the Alta Semita. I noticed that he was less tall than me, and must once have had a spare frame, though he looked as if he could handle himself in a ruck. Misguided eating and drinking had put weight around his midriff. He was still the pot-bellied, dark-chinned smooth operator, full of bluff and braggery. He seemed brighter than I recalled. I would need to watch how I treated him.

I led him to a nearby seafood caupona. It had two tables outside. A couple of locals were playing dice at one, squabbling mildly; we took the other. People could sit there to watch boats landing and fishermen messing with nets on the quayside. There was a pergola shading the area and a scent of frying squid. A water jug appeared instantly on the table, but then nobody hurried us.

Now that I had met Phineus, I could see similarities in this man. Polystratus sat down with the same cheerful, easygoing manner, as if he too spent a lot of time talking to contacts in wine bars and eateries. This was his natural environment. When he grinned at me, he had missing teeth too, though more than the couple Phineus lacked. Amazingly, I had forgotten just what a wide front gap disfigured Polystratus' mouth.

'Just landed?' I asked.

He betrayed not a flicker. 'Been across the Gulf.'

'Delphi?'

'That's it.' There was no pretence. He must know that I knew that Phineus had sent somebody to Delphi. Now I was wondering if Phineus had gone there too.

'Go on your own?'

'Oh I'm a big boy! Someone said *you* were seeing Delphi, Falco.'

'Who told you that?' No answer. Polystratus had been struck by salesman's deafness. 'You knew I was in Greece?'

'Word spreads.' He appeared to forgive me for any deception: 'I gather our meeting in Rome was not a complete coincidence?'

'Business.' He did not ask me to explain. 'So why did you go to Delphi, Polystratus?'

'Looking for poor Statianus.'

'Did you find him?' I asked quickly.

'Oh yes.' So it was Polystratus who went to the inn at Delphi and ate with Statianus. 'That man has had his troubles. We don't like to think of a client of ours struggling to cope on his own.'

'Oh? Would you be able to swing it so your client wins the Delphi lottery and gets a question at the oracle?'

'Sometimes we can,' Polystratus boasted. And sometimes not, I thought. But you never know. In a province like this, where the ancient sites were losing ground politically and where commerce mattered, even the most aristocratic establishments might cosy up to a firm that was brash enough, one that could bring plenty of visitors. Bribes would help. Seven Sights Travel must achieve most of its business success from knowing when to give backhanders, who needed them, and how much. Even at Delphi, they might know how to swing it.

'Did you offer to obtain question rights for Statianus?'

'No.' Polystratus shook his head, so I leaned away in case the overdone gleaming hair oil shed drops on me. 'Delphi is shutting down for the winter now. The oracle goes into hibernation. He's lost his chance there.'

'So you made him depressed by telling him that – and you left him?'

'Yes, I left him.' It was said matter-of-factly. In some people such a casual tone would confirm their honesty.

'You didn't encourage him to try his luck elsewhere – at Lebadeia, for instance?'

'Where?' asked Polystratus. He was lying. The waiter had said he and Statianus talked about Lebadeia.

I was losing my grip on this slippery sea-slug, so I changed the subject: 'Let's talk about you. Do you hail from Greece, Polystratus?'

'Italy.'

'Brundisium?'

'Aye; that's how I know Phineus.'

'Are you two in full partnership?'

'Known him for years, Falco.'

'Well, he's done a bunk now.'

'Good heavens,' said Polystratus, with knowing blandness.

'He was in jail. He slipped his chains.'

'I wonder what made him do that, Falco?'

I was not wasting time on why, I just wondered where he had disappeared to.

'He knows what he's doing,' said Polystratus. 'He's done nothing wrong. The authorities can't hold him.'

'So did he come across with you to Delphi?'

'Why would he? He gave me that job. So he stayed here.'

'When did you first get here from Rome then?'

'About a week ago. Is it relevant?'

'Could be,' I said, hoping to rattle him. Thinking back, it could have been Polystratus I had glimpsed with Phineus in the Forum, the day I ducked my head and walked away, *en route* to the Corinth acropolis with Cleonymus.

Wine was brought to us. I could not remember ordering. Maybe Polystratus was the type who, wherever he went, had a drinks flagon placed on his table automatically. It was not bad wine either. I wondered whether that surprised me.

I foresaw that I would be paying the bill. That's the way with men who have multiple business contacts. Unless they want to put you under an obligation – which can only be bad news – they tend to jump up and leave, a moment before the bill comes.

My father would actually ask for the bill with a lordly gesture – then slip away with perfect timing just as the waiter wrote his equals sign in the addition.

I drank in silence for a while. Thinking of Pa always dampened my mood.

Then I asked Polystratus, in a noncommittal voice, to recount what had happened on his visit to Delphi.

'Not a lot.' He shrugged, narrow shoulders rising within the slightly overlarge hollows of the yellow tunic. He passed a hand over his darkly stubbled chin. 'I wanted to bring the client back here with me to rejoin the others, but he refused. As a rescue mission, it was pointless. I saw him one evening at his lodging – he mentioned you, Falco. And your lady is here, I gather?'

I stuck to my point. 'So Statianus proved stubborn – but did he tell you what he was intending to do next?'

'No, he didn't.'

'And you yourself then left Delphi?'

Polystratus looked surprised. 'I had to get back. I'm needed. We have people stranded here, as you must know. Phineus called me out to Greece to help him deal with the quaestor's office. The bright boy in purple won't let our group leave.' He pretended to look sideways at me. 'Anything to do with you, Falco?'

'Aquillius decided to hold them under house arrest all on his little own.'

Polystratus nodded, though of course he and Phineus blamed me. Aquillius may even have said it was my fault. 'We are trying to get hold of the governor. He should sort this problem out for us.'

'Do you and Phineus know the governor, Polystratus?' Nothing would surprise me.

'Oh, you are supposed to be the man with heavy contacts, Falco! Do *you* know the governor?'

'No,' I said sadly. I left it for a beat. 'I only know the Emperor.'

*

We were getting on superbly. We were the best of friends now. Sharing a drink; gazing at the sparkling waters of the Gulf of Corinth; considering whether to indulge in a plate of crispy whitebait; each wondering just how much the other knew.

'You must have spent several days across the Gulf,' I said. 'When Statianus refused to accompany you back,' I asked, 'what were your movements?'

'I went to a local village,' replied Polystratus. 'Things to organise on my own account. Things to buy. Sidelines, you know.'

'In the big jars?'

'Salted tuna. Want a taste? I've kept one open in case anyone asks for a sample. I'd rather sell on out here and save the shipping costs, if I can manage it.'

I agreed to taste. It was an easy way to check his story. He borrowed a spoon from the men at the other table, who looked bemused but surrendered the implement as if they thought he was somebody important. Like Phineus he had that air; he expected to get his own way.

I stayed where I was. Whistling, Polystratus walked over to his cart, where he fiddled with one of the globular amphorae. He brought me a spoonful of fish, not too salty. I doubted it would travel well, but I had tasted worse.

'Not bad.' I challenged him about the containers. Most you see in Greece are the tall slender type. 'Last time I saw those fat, round-bellied amphorae, they were in Baetica, used for olive oil. I didn't know that shape ever came east for other commodities.'

Polystratus immediately nodded. 'Recycled. The miser I buy from doesn't even supply new jars . . . Can't interest you? I'll keep trying. Someone may like the stuff. I'll have to lug the whole consignment around with me, when we move –'

'You are planning to restart the tour?'

'Oh haven't you been told?' Polystratus enjoyed being ahead of me. 'Aquillius can't hold up our clients indefinitely. We threatened him with an injunction and he's released

284

them. We'll be shifting them to Athens – sniff at the Pnyx, give the Spartan girls the eye on the Erechtheion – are you a caryatids man? – scuttle up the Parthenon to pay respects to Pallas Athena, then sail off from Piraeus across the wine-dark sea.'

I hid my disappointment – knowing he could see it. I noticed he said 'we'; did that mean he and Phineus were in contact, even though Phineus was an escapee?

'Apart from Delphi, did you only go to the salt-fish village?'

'You're fixated, Falco!' Polystratus gave me the street scoundrel's look of surprise. 'Here and there. This and that. What's the big issue? You'd be surprised how long it takes to persuade some lousy Greek fish-bottler to sell you a few amphorae. A day to roust him out of his hut and wake him up. Another day arguing about the price. A day while you buy him drinks to celebrate him ripping you off . . .' Without appearing to challenge me, he asked, 'What were *you* up to over there, Falco?'

'Same as you. Trying to lure Tullius Statianus back to civilisation.'

'No more luck than me?'

'No, after you met him, he left. He went straight off to Lebadeia.' Polystratus again feigned not to have heard of the place. 'Trophonius,' I prompted. 'Statianus knew it had another oracle.'

'Oh it's one of those Boeotian shrines! . . . Phineus takes trippers. We include Trophonius in our Oracle Odyssey route – something a bit different – but there's not much take-up.'

'I can understand that.' If Phineus and Polystratus knew Trophonius was 'a bit different', presumably they knew all about the ritual. Maybe they even knew how the oracle was really worked. 'I'd avoid that place in future. Statianus, for one, seems to have discovered that your "infinite journey plan" stopped being infinite in the underground chasm. He vanished, complete with two barley cakes. At least it saves you having to repatriate him in yet another funeral urn.'

'What are you saying, Falco?'

'He's probably dead.'

'Not another one!' Polystratus groaned dramatically – then tackled it head on: 'Are you suggesting Seven Sights Travel may be at the back of this?'

'It looks bad.'

'You have just made a very serious accusation against us.'

'Have I?'

'Prove it!' cried Polystratus, with the forthright indignation of a businessman who was no stranger to serious accusations. 'Produce the body – or otherwise, leave us alone!'

LII

'I don't like releasing them any more than you do,' blustered Aquillius. Furious, I had accosted him that same evening at the governor's residence. He flared up in response: 'Falco, we can't show that any of these travellers had a hand in what happened to the bride at Olympia. They are menacing me with a lawyer. Your brother-in-law has put them in touch with his damned tutor in Athens, apparently.'

'*Aelianus?*' That seemed unlikely. I had taught him not to intervene in unsolved cases, lest he muddy the clues. Once I thought him positively unhelpful; now I would call him more of a dry observer. But not a meddler.

'He is studying with Minas of Karystos!' snorted Aquillius, impressed.

'Clearly a cretin.'

'Steady on, Falco. Minas has a stupendous reputation.'

'You mean he charges astronomical fees!'

Aquillius blinked nervously. 'I just think you may have overstated the case, Falco. Valeria Ventidia may have been killed by a passing stranger, whom we will never trace –'

'Lampon, the poet, saw who she was with.'

Aquillius kept going: 'You raised that query about the sick man – well, I've had a medical orderly here from the Temple of Aesculapius, and he swears blind Turcianus was already at death's door when he arrived at Epidaurus. The doctors knew he would be lucky to last out the night, and in fact he was *not* left alone in a dream cell but was nursed at their hospital through his dying ordeal. Somebody sat with him the whole time; he was not harmed by any third party.'

'Did he say anything?'

'He was beyond speech, Falco.' Aquillius was sounding

more and more harassed and annoyed. 'I never managed to trace anyone who fits the description you gave me of the "expensively dressed man" who allegedly attacked Cleonymus. Maybe he just fell down the hill accidentally. Face up to it: the travellers are in the clear. To tell the truth, I am relieved Phineus managed to escape; we had no real reason to charge him, either. The governor does not want a reputation as a harsh disciplinarian.'

'Why not? Most of them think that's a compliment.' Roman rulers came to steal antiques and tax provincials to Hades; the provincials expected nothing else. 'When Vespasian was praised for his just rule as governor in Africa, that was said with bewilderment. If you ask me, the townsmen of Hadrumetum, who pelted him with turnips, hated him for being too soft.'

'Don't joke, Falco. Our role in a province is to prevent local discontent. As for your claim that Statianus has met a bad fate, you simply cannot prove it. Without a corpse, this story is going nowhere. For all we know, he is perfectly safe. He could just have got bored with oracles, given up on everything, and sailed off home.'

'I don't think so, and neither do you. You are abandoning him.' Aquillius, who had always been good-natured, looked regretful. Still, we were back where we started. After a brief flirtation with honest enquiry, the authorities were once again trying to bury the problem. The fact that more people had died in the intervening period made no difference. 'Time will tell, quaestor.'

'No; time is what we don't have, Falco.'

The quaestor's new sense of purpose astonished me. That was until Helena worked out its cause. The governor must be coming back from counting milestones. His residence was stiffening up for an onslaught of aggravation. The governor was bound to think his staff had slacked in his absence. That is what governors do. Unwanted questions would be bouncing down the official corridors like boulders off a mountain in a storm. Aquillius Macer had been warned by a clerk in his office that his work output had better start showing improved cost/benefit ratios. No-hopers like this murder investigation were being put out to graze.

'Can I see the governor?'

'No you bloody can't. He has noticed how much I've charged the kitty on your account – and he's livid, Falco.'

So I was paying my own way in future.

It was all going wrong. I could feel the whole investigation closing down on me. Even with Statianus missing, there was no new impetus. The enquiry scrolls were being filed in library canisters. My hopes of reaching a solution were being dashed.

I wondered if the disappearance of Statianus would one day be chased up like that of the young girl, Marcella Caesia. Had I lost hope too easily? I had believed the search we carried out with the assistance of the people of Lebadeia was thorough – but was I wrong? Would someone more persistent have discovered more? If Statianus came from a family as determined as Caesius Secundus, Caesia's father, maybe in a year's time some angry relative would arrive in Greece and find a corpse lying on a hillside, even though I had failed . . .

No. No other search would ever happen. I had seen his mother, and deduced what kind of man his father was. His parents wanted to duck away from tragedy, not to lose their wits seeking answers. That young man's one hope of justice now, for himself and for his bride, lay in me.

But I was proving useless.

Wearied by our sea journey and by dealing with men who would not see my point of view, I accepted the inevitable. The travel group would be released from custody; no further enquiries would be possible.

Helena bore the brunt of my frustration. As usual, she came up with a plan that would keep me quiet when she was trying to read in bed: 'If the travellers are moving on to Athens, let us go there as well. At least we can see Aulus – which is what we came out here to do, remember. We can ask

289

him about this interfering tutor. Perhaps while we are there, Marcus, something new will come out.'

I doubted that. The mood I was in, I reckoned the killer had succeeded. It had taken several extra deaths, but he had covered his tracks and left my investigation stranded.

'Aquillius made me promise *not* to report to the Tullius family that we think their son is dead.'

'That's right, Marcus. You can't upset them needlessly. We don't for certain know his fate.'

'How many years will go by, do you think, before those trouble-shy bastards notice that their cherub has not written home? Will they just assume he went abroad and liked it so much he stayed?'

'It can happen.'

'It would never happen in your family. Julia Justa was looking for a letter from Aulus when we could still see his ship sailing away. Dear gods, even *my* father would one day start wondering why I wasn't there to be pushed around! . . . Helena, this is how killers get away with it.'

Helena put a marker in her scroll and let the ends roll together. 'It does make you wonder just how many clients Seven Sights Travel have shed over the past ten years, with nobody noticing . . . Settle down and rest. You often reach a low point like this in an enquiry, Marcus.'

Hearing Helena trying to comfort me, Nux climbed up on the bed between us, licking my hand. I looked down at her dark eyes peering at me anxiously from among her lugged fur. She had seen whoever killed Cleonymus. That took us nowhere: one of the disappointments that had awaited my return was hearing that when Young Glaucus and Albia took her on a lead past members of the group, Nux had wagged her tail happily at all of them.

Bitterly, I put the dog on the floor. Even she was useless.

Helena set aside the scroll she had been reading and lay down to sleep. She held herself a little apart from me. I knew why that was. My own brow was furrowed. Coming back to Corinth and meeting up with my nephews, Albia, and Glaucus, had reminded us of home.

Helena and I lay in darkness, each keeping our thoughts private. We were both badly wanting to see our daughters. Finding Aulus in Athens would be no substitute. Winter was approaching; the seas would soon be too dangerous to sail. We had come to Greece to solve a puzzle that now seemed impossible, and we would very soon be trapped here.

Suddenly the personal cost of this mission seemed too high. We would have quarrelled if we had discussed it, so we both lay in silence, grieving privately.

Next day the Seven Sights group left. We went along to see them off from the Helios, where they had been staying. Its landlord came out and stood around conveniently; despite their previous wrath at his low standards and brothel-keeping, several gave in and slipped him money. He thanked them with slimy ingratitude. He probably got much bigger tips from the working girls who used his rooms.

The group were taking a ship direct from the eastern port at Kenchreai. You could walk to the jetty from here. Even for that short trip the Sertorius family rode in a covered wagon. That enabled them to pretend nobody could hear the squeals of the their two squabbling teenagers pinching and punching each other, and the continual row between the idiot husband and his former slave wife; she seemed at last to be standing up to his obnoxiousness, but it had created a verbal battlefield. Tall Marinus had dreamed of quails last night, which apparently was an omen that he would be tricked by someone he met *en route*; Helvia heard this with a round-mouthed 'Ooh, Marinus!' while Cleonyma winked at me.

I was amazed to see they were being organised quite openly by Phineus. Clearly he had no fear of re-arrest. Had he bribed Aquillius, or was he just brazen?

He and Polystratus were busy counting and loading up the group's paraphernalia. It was the first time we had seen them in full procession for a journey. Their luggage included far more than just clothing for all weathers, though there seemed plenty of that. They carried with them blankets, pillows, and mattress overlays to improve on the poor bedding that inns provided; they had chamberpots; they had medicine chests, no doubt including flea powders and insect-bite ointments as well as bandages, stomach and eye remedies, foot creams, suppositories, and metallic wax treatments for sexual disease; they had cooking equipment – pots, dishes, goblets, griddles, sawn logs and charcoal, wine, oil, water, spices, salt, vinegar, cabbages, loaves, olives, cheeses, cold meats, and Polystratus' amphorae of salted fish; they had their own lamps, lamp oil and tinderboxes; they had ropes and a stretcher-board in case of accidents; they had bath oils, wooden-soled slippers, strigils, towels, bathrobes, and tooth powders; they had animal fodder and money chests.

It seemed cruel to interrupt when Phineus was loading up this mass of stuff, but I accosted him. 'Couldn't hold me. Nothing on me,' he asserted with a bold gap-toothed grin.

'So where have you been since you escaped – or should I say, you were "let out"?'

'Looking for my partner. We found each other – isn't that nice?'

'Did you go across to Delphi?'

'Now why would I do that?' asked Phineus.

Polystratus gave me a matching grin. 'Give up, Falco!'

'I never gave up on a case yet.' No case before this one had ever gone so cold on me.

It was a bright, sunny day, but the travellers had assembled like a cohort of soldiers setting off for an endurance camp in the far snows of Pannonia. Apart from the Sertorii behind their sealed leather curtains, some were on donkeys and some on foot. They all wrapped themselves in heavy woollen cloaks and several women had added rugs around their shoulders too. Amaranthus wore knee-length riding trousers – although he was walking. At the signal to go, the women shrieked excitedly and everyone donned flat-brimmed Hermes hats. Under their cloaks, they checked the money-bags they were carrying on strings around their necks. There was a last-minute delay while Sertorius Niger scrambled out of his coach to search through bags for his travelling backgammon board. Tutting, Indus looked up the time pointedly on a portable sundial. Volcasius was already making detailed notes on his waxed tablet.

We waved them off. Nobody had asked us about Statianus. They did not yet know we would eventually see them all again in Athens, though perhaps the wiser ones assumed it. They just wanted to leave at last. Relief at being allowed to continue their journey had made all of them light-headed. Maybe someone was even happier, thinking he had escaped detection for the murders.

Helena and I watched them go with a mixture of frustration and melancholy.

The quaestor had also come to see them off. I announced that we too were leaving.

'I'm going to keep Lampon here, this witness you found,' insisted Aquillius. Maybe he thought we wanted a household poet. He was wrong.

'You're welcome to him. Let him give recitals, though. He needs the money.'

'You're all heart, Falco.'

'I believe in looking after witnesses. In my job, I find so few of them!'

'Give me anything connected with Statianus.' The quaestor wanted to help. He was pleading with me. 'Any part of him. Anything we can say is directly associated with the man – I'll make arrests immediately, I promise you.'

I knew he meant it. He was no worse, and in some ways much better, than most young men in official posts. He had an amiable personality and had resisted corruption. I never saw him again after we left Corinth. They had a devastating earthquake there the following year; Aquillius was a casualty.

As for us, without his financial backing, we took far too long to reach Athens. We started out by road, not knowing that the overland route from the Isthmus was one of the worst tracks in the Empire. It wound in and out, high up among precipitous mountain tops, above the Megaronic Gulf. The track was often so narrow and corroded that only sure-footed donkeys in single file could manage to edge along it. Sometimes pack animals failed to keep their footing, and fell over the sheer drop into the sea. This road had been notorious for centuries. Helena said it was where heartless robbers used to lurk, including legendary Sciron, who made travellers wash his feet, then gave them a great kick right off the crag.

I groaned and said I always liked a good legend. Then I led us down a path to water level at Megara. Helena sold some jewellery, and we took a ship the rest of the way into Piraeus.

PART FIVE
ATHENS

At first sight visitors would doubt that this was the renowned city of the Athenians, but they would not take long to believe it. For the most beautiful things in the world are there . . . They have festivals of all kinds, and temptations and stimulation of the mind from many different philosophers; there are many ways of amusing oneself, and non-stop spectacles . . . the presence of foreigners, which all of them are used to and which suits their temperaments, makes them turn their thoughts to agreeable things . . .

Herakleides of Crete

LIII

Athenae.
Do *not* expect a description of the monuments and sights. This is a case report, not some Achilles-to-Zeus travel guide.

LIV

Of course we saw the Acropolis. There it was, spectacular on its domineering bluff, crammed with monumental gatehouses and gaily painted temples, just as it was supposed to be. Our hearts stopped – mine only for a moment. The others went on squinting into the distance to make out the light which shone off the bronze helmet on the great statue of Athena. I was too busy keeping an eye out for inebriated philosophers, fly-by-night old courtesans, inefficient pick-pockets, and loose sheep.

Yes, I said sheep.

As usual, we had landed too late in the evening. By the time we had negotiated for a hire cart at a less than extortionate price, dusk had fallen. We were running out of money. Helena could tap into her father's banker tomorrow and I knew Pa had a financial contact here, whom I would try to bluff into parting with coinage, but that evening we had only just enough cash left to get our bags hauled into town, with none over for a deposit at an inn. Helena had picked out a four-tower mansio on her trusty map, where we yearned to stay in luxury and recover from the privations of the Elephant at Corinth – but not tonight, my friends.

We knew where Aelianus lived. Although senators and their families by custom lodge with aristocratic cronies, no one expects a student to lumber himself with being endlessly polite to some old buffer his father knew vaguely, thirty years ago. Our boy had a hired room. Unluckily for him, he had told us where it was. The six of us headed straight there, and since Aulus was out and we were exhausted, we took possession of the place and turned in.

'This is a tip! How can a nicely brought up boy stay here? Mother would be horrified.'

'I bet your father likes the price, though . . . This bed has no mattress cords. No wonder he stays out all night.'

In fact Aulus came home about four hours after darkness fell. We knew about it when Nux barked at him. She may not have recognised Aulus, but he knew who she was even in the dark and he growled my name irritably. Like most students, he was not at all surprised to find six people, some of whom he had never met before, fast asleep in his room. He fitted himself into a space between Gaius and Cornelius, chucked his heavier items of clothing into a corner, and fell silent again.

'Who is this man?' I heard Cornelius whisper to Gaius.

'Total stranger to me. Give him a knee in the bollocks if he tries to bother you.'

'Keep your knees to yourselves – or I'll have you!' remarked Aulus, in the crystalline accents of a senator's son.

After the briefest of pauses, Gaius feigned an apology: 'Any friend of Uncle Marcus is . . . an idiot.'

With a large sigh, Helena commanded, 'Please be quiet, all of you!'

I found myself unable to drift off again once they had disturbed me. When Aulus stumbled in, it had seemed polite to wake up enough to mutter, 'Hello; it's us!' As leader of the party, I had accepted that matters of etiquette were my job; I could not leave it to Nux to greet our host. Now I lay awake, holding Helena gently against my shoulder and occasionally shifting as she kicked out in some bad dream. In her head she was probably still travelling from Corinth. Beyond a shutter, the little owls of Athena took over the city. The level of snoring within the room rose gently, led by the dog; the level of brawling in the streets outside gradually fell. That allowed me to hear the squeaks and scuffles of the Athens rats.

As we came from Piraeus, I had barely taken in the sights, but my tired brain must have recorded them. Now my first impressions all crowded back. In any city, the street from the port looks dusty and impoverished; it tends to be lined with workshops for peculiar trades and restaurants where not even the locals eat. Now I smiled to myself over the sordid scenes that greeted visitors. Athens was in decline. In fact, Athens must have been declining for three or four centuries. Its golden age had been replaced by the drabbest kind of village life in daytime, and nights of riotous debauchery. I was now in the heart of Greece, the Greece that had sent Rome art, literature, mathematics, medicine, military engineering, myth, law, and political thought. And in Athens, the golden city of Pericles, the famous public spaces might be filled with vibrant life, but the shantytown houses were derelict, rubbish stank out the crystal air, rats scampered underfoot, and the Panathenaic Way was full of wandering sheep.

An owl shrieked, very close at hand. Since the room now contained seven people, it became perilously hot. Just as I was preparing to do something about it before somebody collapsed and crossed the Styx, I fell back asleep.

They all survived. Next morning I felt as if I had eaten rabbit shit, but the rest were cheerful. Helena and Albia had gone out to buy breakfast. I could hear the lads playing ball energetically outdoors in the street. On what passed for a balcony, Young Glaucus was discussing short-distance sprint techniques with Aulus.

I cleaned my teeth with an old meat skewer and a piece of sponge, splashed my face, combed my hair, and turned yesterday's tunic inside out. Travelling was much like my early years as a run-down informer. Young Glaucus kept himself immaculate but, from his uncombed hair and limp tunic, it looked as though Aulus had taken to the life of a lazy loner. I joined them, saluting my brother-in-law with affection. 'Greetings, exemplary associate! Well, this is a fine problem you have landed me with.'

'I thought you would be intrigued,' chortled Aulus. Then the hangover caught up with him; he went pale and clutched his head. Glaucus and I rearranged him in a prone position, then as the balcony was cramped Glaucus went out to exercise. I sat quietly reflective until Aulus felt up to hearing all our news.

Of Helena's two brothers, Aulus made me most wary. I never felt sure which way he would jump. Still, it was good to see him again. We had worked together; I had grown fond of him. He was about my height, sturdy, though with a young man's body – not so hard as me, and bearing fewer scars. He had the family looks, dark eyes and hair, plus the family humour and intelligence. Even in Greece, the land of beards, he had remained clean-shaven like a good Roman. He had always been conservative. Originally he had hated the thought of his sister living with an informer; later, I think he saw my good points. Anyway, he accepted that our marriage was a fact, especially after we had children. He was a cautious uncle to Julia and Favonia, still too raw to be comfortable with very young children.

There had been problems finding a career for him. He should have gone into the Senate; still could, if he wanted to. The Camilli had had a relative who disgraced himself, which by extension disgraced them. That did not help; then Aulus and his brother Quintus quarrelled over who would marry an heiress. Quintus won her. Aulus lost more than the rich wife, for bachelors don't win elections, so he sulkily gave up on the Senate. He was rootless temporarily, then surprised me by becoming my assistant. During a case where we acted as prosecutors in the Basilica Julia, he decided to become a lawyer. I joked that for a man who complained that *my* career was seedy, he had chosen one even more polluted. But a legal career would be better than none (and much better than mine). The senator sent him off to Athens before Aulus had a chance to dither. But his reaction when he heard of the murders at Olympia showed that his time working with me had stuck him with a love of mysteries.

'Let's not talk about the murders until Helena returns. So, how is the academic life in Athens, Aulus?' He sat up slowly. 'This will be disgusting, I see.'

301

'Athens,' declared Aulus, working his brain into use, 'is absolutely full of pedagogues, all specialists. You can choose any branch of philosophy: Pythagorean, Peripatetic, Cynic, Stoic, or Orphic.'

'Avoid all of them. We are Romans. We despise thought.'

'I certainly avoid the dirty ones who dress in rags and live in barrels!' Aulus had always been fastidious. 'Men with big beards and big brains teach absolutely everything – law, literature, geometry – but what they are best at . . .' He slowed down again, lost for words temporarily.

I helped out: 'Is drinking?'

'I knew how to party already.' He closed his eyes. 'But not all night and every night!'

I let him rest for a moment. Then I asked, 'Want to tell me about your tutor? I gather he's called Minas, and has a *stupendous* reputation.'

'Stupendous stamina anyway,' Aulus admitted.

'Was that why you latched on to him?'

'He found me. Tutors lurk in the agora, looking for newly arrived Roman innocents whose fathers will pay fees. Minas chose me; next thing I knew he had persuaded Father's banker to pay him directly: *leave it to me, dear Aelianus; I will arrange everything; you will be troubled by nothing!*'

'For heavens' sake!'

'I am just a lump of dough, thumped breathless daily.'

'Fight back before the pace kills you! He recognised your senatorial stripes; you should have travelled incognito.' I saw it all. 'He assumes your loving papa is a multi-millionaire. Now Minas can have a really good time – which Decimus is paying for.'

'I haven't worn purple stripes since I left Ostia. He can just spot a young Roman.'

'It's all in the haircut,' I informed him sagely.

'He earns his money, Marcus.' Aulus grinned. 'He takes me to the very best dinner parties, sometimes several in an evening. He introduces fabulous women and exotic boys. He shows me drinking games, dancing girls, flautists and lyre-players – and then we talk. We talk at length, and about all moral issues – though in the morning I remember not a word.'

'I must point out, Aulus, your *mother* has paid for me to come here and see what you are up to.'

'Then I retract!' he chortled. 'I deny mentioning dancing girls.'

He subsided into a weak heap. I gazed at him, impressed. 'So, Aulus Camillus Aelianus, son of Decimus, tell me: have you learned any law yet?'

Then Aulus Camillus Aelianus, prospective top–class barrister, looked at me without guile. Before he put his throbbing head back into his trembling hands, he just smiled regretfully.

LV

Helena's foray into the markets produced an excellent Athenian breakfast of steaming hot honey-and-sesame pancakes. Those of us who were without a hangover tucked in, afterwards filling up any crannies with barley bread and olive paste, all topped off with pears.

'What's for lunch?'

'Anything you like, apparently – so long as it's fish.' That would explain why the Panathenian Way was so full of fish-heads, fish guts, crab claws, prawn shells, and cuttlefish.

Aulus asked us to stop talking about food.

We propped him up, made belated introductions where necessary, and shared our various discoveries about the murders. Aulus had nothing to tell us about Marcella Caesia and little to add to the details we had learned for ourselves about Valeria Ventidia. But he could tell us more of Turcianus Opimus, the invalid; he had met the man.

'He was desperately ill. It was horrible. He was being eaten up inside.'

'So you think his death was entirely natural?' Helena asked.

'I know it was.'

'You were with the group when they went to Epidaurus,' I chipped in.

Aulus looked embarrassed. 'The others were all twittering on about their aches and pains,' he complained. 'They were booking themselves into dream cells – and when they came out next morning there was a big fuss because Marinus had been bitten by a dog. None of them seemed to realise that their little rheumatics – and even a few septic teethmarks – were nothing to what Turcianus was going through.'

304

'So?' Helena, who knew her brother well, was watching him closely.

'Well, I just felt so sorry for Turcianus. He was struggling to keep up a façade of jollity. He tried not to be a nuisance. But he must have been regretting that he ever came on that last journey, he was in so much pain. Keeping it all to himself, he must have been lonely, for one thing.'

'*So?*'

'When the medics had assessed him, they tipped me the wink he was on his way out. Nobody else volunteered, so I sat by his bedside all that night. No one did anything to harm him. I was with him when he died.'

Aulus fell silent. He was about twenty-seven. As a senator's son, he had led a sheltered life in some respects. He would have lost grandparents and family slaves, maybe one or two men in his command while he was a tribune in the army. In Rome, he had once found a bloody corpse at a religious site. But nobody had ever died right in front of him before.

Helena put her arms around him. 'Turcianus was dying, alone and far from home. I am sure he knew you were there; you must have reassured the poor man. Aulus, you are good and kind.'

Gaius and Cornelius were shifting about awkwardly at this sentimental moment. I saw even Albia raise her eyebrows in that sceptical way she had. She had a tomboyish relationship with Aulus, which certainly had not involved seeing him as a philanthropist. We all tended to think of him as a cold fish. I for one was shocked to imagine him sitting with a virtual stranger, murmuring supportive words through the small hours, as the man slipped away.

'Did he happen to say anything?'

'No, Falco.'

'Marcus!' Helena rebuked me. I bent my head and looked humble. I had known it was useless. Deathbed revelations do not happen in real life. For one thing, anyone with money makes sure his doctors provide oblivion by giving him a good tincture of poppyseeds.

Still, I was an informer. So I had to ask.

'It was all sad, but perfectly natural,' Aulus assured me. 'I'll vouch for it; there was nothing untoward.'

'I'm glad. I don't *want* to find unnatural deaths at every turn.'

'From what you say, you have quite enough with Cleonymus and Statianus.'

'Reckon so.' Mention of Cleonymus made me think of our last venue. 'Aulus, something bothers me. Before we left Corinth, that quaestor, Aquillius, said he wanted to free the Seven Sights group from house arrest because they had threatened him with a lawyer. Your tutor, apparently!'

'Minas?' Aulus detected my note of disapproval; he was quick to dissociate himself. He shook his head in disbelief. 'I cannot imagine Minas has ever even heard of the group. I've never told him about them. I can't face him making me translate it all into some ghastly legal exercise.'

'You sure of that?'

'He wouldn't thank me for discussing a real situation. He may be a master of jurisprudence, but he tries to avoid legal practice nowadays. I am astonished if he has intervened. They just got hold of his name somehow,' concluded Aulus.

'Phineus used it to back up a threat. How could Phineus get the name Minas of Karystos from you?' asked Helena.

'He didn't.'

'Aquillius was specifically told that Minas was your tutor.'

Aulus considered that carefully. 'There is only one way. I wrote to Statianus after I left him at Delphi. For something to fill the scroll, I mentioned that Minas would be teaching me. But I only met Minas after I came to Athens, so nobody else could know. I never wrote to any of the others – Hades, they are a terrible lot! Statianus must have told them.'

As far as we knew, Statianus lost contact with his travel companions after he went across to Delphi. I had found no letters when I searched his luggage in that dismal hired room. I would definitely have noticed one from Aulus.

'The news of Minas must have got passed from Statianus to Polystratus. They spent an evening together. We'll have to assume your name came up in conversation.' I did not want to think Polystratus also searched the baggage, after Statianus left, and removed the letter naming Minas.

'It was just a friendly letter.' Aulus shrugged his shoulders. 'Why does this worry you, Marcus?'

'Phineus and Polystratus are my suspects. Suspects talking about you – that's not healthy.' He and I exchanged a glance. In front of his sister, I played down my concern. Alert now, he saw why I felt uneasy. 'Don't visit any oracles,' I warned, trying to make a jest of it.

Young Glaucus, who as usual had said nothing at all, caught my eye, looking professional. I nodded, keeping it discreet. But Helena Justina came right out and asked Glaucus to stick at her brother's side wherever he went. Our big young friend gave a sombre nod. This was why I had brought him, after all.

It would cause friction tonight when Aulus joined in yet another procession of party-going scholars, trailing around after Minas. Young Glaucus was so clean-living, he would loathe the debauchery. And Aulus became fractious if he was nannied.

I suggested we could ask the tutor whether anybody from the travel group had ever contacted him. Aulus, now recovering from his hangover, warned me to time it right: 'It's no use trying to see Minas in the morning, Falco. Even if you manage to wake him up, you'll get nothing. You have to wait until he comes alive at party time. Don't worry. I'll ask him this myself tonight.'

'Still up for another banquet? Well, you enjoy yourself so I can tell your mother you have thrown yourself into the academic life: the star of the symposium. Forget the case. *I'll* try to find the travel group.'

'Athens is too big to search for them haphazardly. If they are still here, Phineus and Polystratus will be showing them the sights. Marcus, I suggest you go sightseeing too;

you may run into them viewing a temple. Even if you don't,' Aulus urged, 'you are in Athens, man – make the most of it. Take my sister to the Acropolis. Go and be tourists!'

LVI

Helena Justina was not one to hanker for leisure pursuits when we had an investigation. She had shared my work ever since I met her, five or six years ago. She was as stubborn as me, hating to be thwarted when the evidence ran out, or when new clues seemed to prove our theories wrong. She claimed she was happy to spend all day searching for the Seven Sights party.

But I was not stupid. A man who has chosen to live with a woman he considers both beautiful and talented does not take that woman to Athens, the birthplace of civilisation, and fail to entrance her with a day on the Acropolis. Helena had been brought up within grasp of the world's literature in Rome's public libraries; her father owned his own collection, so many of the best works had existed in copies in her own home. Given that her brothers had both inclined to be slackers in the intellectual arena, it was Helena who had drawn out every last scrap of knowledge from the home tutors the senator provided for the two boys. I read for pleasure, intermittently; Helena Justina devoured the written word like a heron downing fish. Put her in a pond of information, and she would stand there until she had cleared it. We could have screaming children torturing the dog while a skillet boiled over, but if Helena was stuck in a scroll she was enjoying, she missed everything else. This was not wilful. She went into a space of her own, where she heard nothing of her real surroundings.

I took her to explore. I was a romantic lover; I did not take the others. I gave time and pretty well my full attention to this duty. For Helena it would be a lasting great experience. We looked at the ancient city, saw the agora, theatres, and odeons, then we climbed up the Acropolis slowly together, taking the main processional route past the Temple of Athena Nike and by way of the steep steps under the Propylaia, the towering ceremonial gate. There we had a fracas when we cold-shouldered the buzzing site guides.

'We guides can give you much useful information!'

'Guides give us a headache! Too late; we've already been punished at Olympia and Delphi – so just shove off.'

The day had begun overcast, but the sun had now burned away the clouds and was beating down. Up here, however, a breeze blew pleasantly, so in the wonderful Athenian light we could admire the sights and the views without discomfort. Once free of the guides, I let Helena wander at will around the Parthenon and all the other temples, statues, and altars, while I carried her parasol, water gourd, and stole. I listened attentively when she described the monuments. We marvelled at the Phidias Athena and the work of legendary Greek architects. We cringed at the Roman monuments imposed by Augustus' henchman Marcus Agrippa – a crudely positioned statue of himself and a Temple of Rome and Augustus. These were insulting and embarrassing. Greece might be conquered, but what other empire would despoil the Athens Acropolis?

I kissed Helena beside the caryatid porch of the Erechtheion. Informers are not complete worms. I enjoyed the day too.

I, however, was keeping my eye out all the time in case we ran into the Seven Sights group. They never appeared.

Late that afternoon, Helena and I returned to the others, happy but somewhat weary, then we braced ourselves to transfer our luggage to an inn. We did this by hand, that is, on foot. Since we had brought ample gear with us in the first place, and had added the Corinthian pots Helena had bought for Pa's business, it was a long, heavy job. At one point, I nearly broke my arm lifting a kitbag that belonged to Gaius.

'What the –' The boys were hopeless at looking after their

luggage, so the pack was familiar. I had had to rescue it several times. I knew it had not been this heavy originally. Normally I preferred not to investigate the nephews' personal possessions. I was sixteen once. The thought of the unwashed laundry was deterrent enough. This time, Gaius' guilty face made me tip out his collected treasures.

His bag was full of tiny bronze and pottery figures: miniature gods and animals. According to Gaius, he 'found' these.

'Don't lie to me. I'm not your dopey father. Found them *where*, Gaius?'

'Oh . . . just at Olympia.'

Thundering Zeus! These trophies of my nephew's were centuries-old votive gifts. Gaius admitted he had dug them all out of the twenty-foot-high mound of ash that formed the great, cumulative Altar of Zeus at Olympia. How he did it unseen was a mystery. I took a deep breath. Then I shovelled the offerings back into his luggage, and told Gaius that when he was arrested for defiling a religious site, I would deny knowing him.

He looked scared. Cornelius squirmed nervously. I warned them both that when I had more time I would conduct a full scrutiny of their luggage. A look that passed between them suggested there was more loot.

We carried on settling into our inn, which Helena Justina had rightly identified on her pictograph map as a four-tower effort: spacious enough to be an imperial post station, well equipped with stabling, baths, gardens, and eating facilities. While we were in the agora that morning, Helena had taken me to see her father's Greek banker. Julia Justa was now paying for our accommodation. Believing that a senator's wife would herself only stay in a really good lodging house, we were letting her provide us with a similar standard of comfort.

After dinner, Aulus joined us there, much earlier than we expected, which was good. His mother would like me to protect him from the night-life.

'All getting too strenuous, lad?'

'I told Minas I had to leave the party early because of my purse-lipped brother-in-law and my spoilsport sister.'

'Thanks, you dog! So, between mighty quaffs, what does Minas have to say?'

Minas of Karystos had never been approached by the Seven Sights group – though now he had heard of their many trials, he said he would be delighted to help them with compensation claims against the travel company.

'Students' fees must not be paying enough,' I muttered.

'He's bored,' said Aulus.

'Well this is not some party game!'

'Settle down, Falco.'

'You sister can tell me that. Don't you try it!'

Minas had thrown himself into trying to find the group. Aulus was confident that, provided they were still in the Athens area, it would happen. Minas knew everyone, having cadged dinners and so-called symposia out of most people who had a dining room or a courtyard that lay close to a good wine cellar. From tonight's perfumed banquet couch, Minas would put the word out; some acquaintance would have seen our people.

Helena sat down beside her brother, taking his hand. 'I am glad you are having such a good time here, Aulus.'

Aulus, a true brother, freed his hand as soon as possible. 'Are you teasing?'

Helena assumed her worried big sister face. 'You have been sent to this fantastic finishing-school to acquire two years' intellectual polish. But you don't have to stay here, if you don't like it.'

'Rome has its own jurisprudence teachers,' I agreed. If we ever suggested that Aulus was a shy flower who found the pace too hot in Athens, I reckoned he would feel obliged to stick it out. I was right too.

'This is a great environment,' replied Aulus rather stiffly. 'I feel completely at home and I am learning a lot.'

Well, we tried.

*

Gaius and his treasure trove of stolen religious offerings had unnerved me. I decided to supervise our younger companions more closely. I left Helena and Aulus munching hazelnut cakes he had brought back from tonight's party, while I tiptoed off to spy on the troublemakers.

In this way, I overheard a touching scene.

Young Glaucus had returned with Aulus. Freed from his duties as minder, he was now secreted in one of the cool, vine-scented courtyards with which this high-class inn abounded. I noticed him seated on a stone bench, talking to Albia. Normally he did no talking, so that pulled me up.

Albia was merely listening. That was another shock. She was by nature an interventionist.

I could see her sitting rather upright in her favourite blue dress, with her hands folded around a late rose one of them must have plucked. I guessed who had presented her with the flower. In his position, I would have tackled Albia with a packet of raisin pastry half-moons, but Glaucus was just a big lump of bone and muscle; he knew nothing about women and their weaknesses. I had been Cupid's personal representative on the Aventine once; years later it was still my job to understand women, especially the tricky ones. He should have spoken to me first.

Glaucus made his oration: a résumé of his long-term plans to remain in Greece and travel to the whole series of the Panathenaic Games. One day, he hoped to return to Rome triumphantly as an Olympic champion. According to him, with the right support package and personal dedication, this was feasible. His father, my trainer, would put up the money and perhaps even come out to supervise his son's programme. Young Glaucus was now asking Albia to stay here too, as his soulmate. Share his life, rub him with oil, encourage him.

Albia would make her own choice. I would have groaned in private and slunk off – but I could see Gaius and Cornelius hiding together behind an old cracked amphora containing a young fig tree. So far, Gaius had mastered the art of the silent guffaw, but that could not be relied upon. I stayed, ready to intervene.

Glaucus talked for far too long. He had clearly never done this before. I was amazed he could sustain such a long monologue. It remained one-sided, for Albia merely tucked her chin in, and listened with her dark head on one side. Planning his life was the young man's passion. Once he was cantering through the details, he couldn't bear to stop. If you liked sport, it was not too boring. If you hated sport, it was dire.

Finally Glaucus produced his masterstroke. From a fold in his tunic he drew a small moving object. In the light of an oil lamp which hung from a pillar close by them, he showed Albia an owl he had captured in the courtyard. Beautifully feathered – but extremely annoyed – this was his solemn love-gift. Albia, a sensible girl, refused to take it and be pecked.

Glaucus then summed up his curriculum vitae again. The owl struggled between his enormous dark hands. Albia must be wanting to escape too. Gaius and Cornelius were wetting themselves with mirth, the rascals. I was preparing myself to stride across the courtyard and grab the boys by the necks of their tunics if their mockery exploded.

No need for that. Albia jumped to her feet briskly.

'That was very interesting. I will consider when I have time!' I winced. Young women are so brutal. Helena must have been giving her advice on how to keep men guessing. Albia pointed at the little owl. 'Now Glaucus, your owl is very sweet but you had better let him go quickly. This is the symbol of Pallas Athena. But I have been told the Greeks are superstitious if an owl comes indoors. They nail it to the front door by the wings – alive!'

Albia skipped off. After a moment, the disconsolate Glaucus opened his palms and released the owl, which flew up to a roof furiously, feathers dishevelled. The boys scarpered. I slid unobtrusively towards an exit.

Only then did I see Aulus outlined in a dark doorway. If he saw me, he gave no sign of it, but quietly vanished.

LVII

Next day Helena and I made attempts to find the Seven Sights group in the agora. I was starting to think they must be sailing around the nearby islands, buying overpriced sponges at Aegina or fake vases with Trojan heroes from desultory potters on Hydria. Maybe Phineus and Polystratus had already whisked them off to Rhodes and all cultural points east.

That afternoon, once more we left the others and spent time together. This time we went a little way out of Athens, where the noisy crowds were bothering us. We hired a frisky two-wheel trap and saw the countryside. Eventually we came to Mount Hymettus, which despite clouds of dust from a marble quarry was famous for its honey. Inevitably it was girdled with honey-selling stalls. Helena did her duty and equipped us with many souvenirs: pots that looked like beehives and contained Hymettus honeycombs. Both our mothers would be delighted with these, or so we convinced ourselves in our desperation to find them presents.

We had brought Nux. Usually Albia was happy to take care of her, but Albia had seemed sulky today. I thought I had better explain that to Helena. 'We may be about to lose Albia.'

'To Young Glaucus? I don't think so,' said Helena. 'She says he will wear out his body with sport and die at twenty-seven.'

'That's rather precise! So is she yearning for somebody else?'

'She is not ready.' Helena was holding back. She shared her thoughts on most subjects with me, but could be secretive on matters of the heart.

'Not ready to yearn in general, or not ready to jump on someone in particular?'

'I am sure she has nobody in mind.'

'You mean, she hasn't finalised her scheme to get him yet?'

'Falco, you are so devious!'

Me?

Not devious enough to fix up what I wanted, anyway. This afternoon idyll might have led to romance for Helena and me, but Nux put a stop to it. Ever tried even kissing your wife with a jealous dog watching? Don't bother. This was one foreign trip from which we would not be returning home expecting our next child after a hilltop conception. If we were ever to be respectable parents of three and win our extra social privileges, we would need to make better arrangements.

There were more hills whose scenery, since we had no option, we doggedly admired. On our way back to town, we reached Mount Lykabettus, a steep little crag which dominates the north-east of the city. We had seen it from the Parthenon; it must have excellent views right across to the sea.

'The Lyceum.' Helena's sightseeing notes were becoming terse. 'Aristotle.'

Even she was growing jaded now; this time she stayed with the cart, while I took Nux for a constitutional. The dog walked to heel rather quietly as we went uphill, as if whatever happened on the Corinth acropolis with Cleonymus had permanently subdued her.

It was another fine day, though I had sensibly brought my hat. Even so, I was glad when Nux and I turned a bend in the road and came upon a small thatched hut. A local was sitting cross-legged outside, perched on a small platform; it looked like a low seat that had lost its back. She too wore a hat, a high-pointed straw thing of quaint design, as if she had woven it inexpertly herself. Beside her stood a large water jar; passing travellers could stop here to buy a cold drink.

My heart took a leap. Unexpectedly I had found a witness.

I must have finally caught up with the crone Gaius and Cornelius had met selling Peirene spring water on the way to Acrocorinth.

I approached quietly. Nux sat down and scratched herself. She always knew how to impose a casual tone on gatherings. A drink was poured for me in a decent sized beaker; I dropped coppers into the outstretched hand. Only then did the crone – as I assumed she would be – look up from under her eccentric hat to thank me. Now I had a second shock. No crone this; she was merely middle-aged and vague. It was Philomela.

'We meet again!'

'You do love clichés, Falco.'

I drank my water, savouring it thoughtfully. Nux was licking at the spout on the big water jar, so I poured more for her. The dog decided that if a drink was permitted, she did not want it.

'Silly girl, Nux! For some reason, I am now thinking longingly of my children; they are terrors too . . . Time to travel home, I think.'

'Then there is something I should say,' announced Philomela. 'I want to entrust a message to you, Falco. I want you to explain something to somebody in Rome.'

'Who? What? Something that happened where?'

'Olympia.'

Gaius and Cornelius had said their water-seller told them she had worked on the Hill of Cronus. Whatever Philomela was finally going to tell me, I knew it would be important.

I squatted on my haunches and surveyed her. Philomela remained silent as if she wanted to extract maximum suspense. She only achieved aggravation. I tried to spur her on: 'I hope this is about what befell either Valeria Ventidia or Marcella Caesia. I suppose your trade makes you likely to have seen Caesia?'

'My trade!' She laughed briefly. 'I live humbly, as you see –' she gestured behind her, to the hut, which was tiny and no doubt extremely crude inside. I preferred not to know. I

317

hate country cabins; they smell of smoke and chicken-shit. 'I sell water to earn a pittance, simply to survive.'

'No family to assist you?'

'Relatives by marriage. They are unaware that I have returned to Greece. They believe I am travelling in another province. That suits me. I wanted to lose myself.'

I could not bring myself to indulge her romantic attitude. 'People who "lose" themselves are either failures or frauds with guilty secrets.'

'You are a sad man.'

'I am an informer. I was a merry gadfly once, but informing makes you brutal. Philomela, tell me the truth. Were you in Olympia when Marcella Caesia went up the Hill of Cronus and then disappeared?'

'I was.'

'Were you actually on the Hill of Cronus that day?'

'Yes; I was there.'

'You saw her go up? Was anybody with her?'

'Two people went up the hill together.'

'One was a man?'

'No. One was Marcella Caesia; the other was a woman, Falco.'

That gave me pause.

'Do you know what happened to Caesia?'

'I do.'

At this dramatic moment we were interrupted. A familiar voice hailed me. Helena must have tethered the pony and followed me up the hill after all. Nux ran to greet her. 'So you do have a wife!' commented the so-called Philomela.

'I said so.' I made introductions. 'Helena Justina, daughter of the noble Decimus Camillus Verus, gracious wife to me; Helena, this is a lady from Tusculum who now calls herself Philomela.'

Helena regarded the wide-eyed wonder. I had warned her previously that I thought Philomela was not all there. 'I believe I know who you are,' Helena asserted cheerfully.

Philomela lifted off the peculiar straw hat as if unveiling her true personality. Helena herself tidied her fine hair back

318

behind her ears, pulling out a bone pin which she replaced with an unconscious gesture. They were like two friends settling down to mint tea at an all-women afternoon gathering.

'Tell me: are you Marcella Naevia?'

'Your wife is extraordinary, Falco!' warbled Marcella Caesia's aunt.

Caesius Secundus had assured us this woman was travelling in Egypt. All the time, she was loitering in Greece, under an assumed name.

I never supposed that the death of her niece at Olympia was what turned her into a moonstruck nymph. Marcella Naevia must always have had a tendency to be wide-eyed and wistful in the face of real life. It put a dark gloss on the tragedy. Entrusting a young girl to her sole care on a long-distance journey had been very unwise. Not that we would ever say that to Caesius Secundus. He would have enough to bear, without blaming himself for trusting the unsatisfactory aunt.

She was worse than unsatisfactory, as we were about to find out. I was glad that Helena had joined us. I needed a witness. Helena would back me up when I had to report the story. Now at last Caesius Secundus could stop wondering, although when he knew what had really happened to his daughter, it would increase his agitation. At least he could finally reconcile himself, bury those bones that I had seen in the lead coffin, apportion blame if he wanted to.

'My niece and I wanted to experience peace and solitude.' That fitted all I had seen in Marcella Naevia. And already I was viewing her apprehensively. I wondered if the girl had been another dreamer; maybe not.

The aunt's vague manner had hidden steel. I could imagine her being insidiously persuasive with her much younger companion, luring Caesia into her weird attitudes. Isolated with her aunt for weeks, a perfectly normal teenager might have lost her sense of reality. 'We walked up the Hill of Cronus to communicate with the gods. While we were

319

there, there was a dramatic lightning storm. We felt close to Zeus, the All-Thunderer.'

'That's hardly peaceful!' I muttered. We had seen for ourselves how storms raged around Olympia.

'We were in another dimension of the world. We had taken ourselves far away from other people,' Marcella Naevia rhapsodised. 'We had escaped . . .' She paused.

'Escaped from whom?' snapped Helena. 'Your niece was young, a lively character,' she supplied. 'Her father described her to us as curious about the world – but she was – how old? – eighteen, I think. Was she immature for her age? I mean socially?'

Marcella Naevia nodded.

'Let us suppose,' Helena pressed on, 'there was a man among the group you travelled with, a man who took advantage of women, a man who groped and harassed them. Marcella Caesia would have hated it.'

'I see you understand!' The aunt gushed with gratitude.

'Well, I would feel the same as she did. I can imagine your role too. You tried to protect the girl. You and she kept to yourselves. Eventually you went up the Hill of Cronus to get away from him.'

'Did he follow you?' I interrupted.

'He did not.'

'So he did not kill her?' So much for theories.

'No!' The aunt looked almost shocked that I'd suggested it.

Slowly I spelled out the situation to this ridiculous woman: 'Her father thinks that Marcella Caesia fell victim to a sexual predator. Caesius Secundus is tormented by that thought. If you know otherwise –'

'It rained heavily.' Marcella Naevia abruptly resumed her story. She took on the trance-like demeanour which I found so annoying. 'I knew that sheltering was dangerous, but my niece would not heed my warnings. She hated being wet; she squealed and tried to take cover under a tree. The tree was struck by lightning. She was killed instantly.'

'For heavens' sake!' I could not believe what I was

320

hearing. 'If you knew this, why not tell people?'

Helena too was outraged. 'You went back to the group; you said nothing that evening – but in the morning you raised a huge outcry. You held up the planned journey and made them all search – yet you never once said that you *knew* what had happened to Caesia? Then you let Caesius Secundus fret his heart out for a year before he himself came to Greece and found the body! Even then, he told us, you pretended to be devastated . . . One word from you could have saved all that. Whatever can you have been thinking about?'

The woman's voice was cold. 'I decided that Zeus had taken her. That was why,' stressed Caesia's aunt, as if anybody rational would see this, 'I left her there.'

I was used to unnatural deaths, deaths that had to be hidden because of the cruel ways they were brought about. Simply abandoning a body after an accident shocked me much more. 'You just left Marcella Caesia lying on the Hill of Cronus, under the burnt-out tree?'

Marcella Naevia sounded dreamy again. 'I laid her straight. I folded her hands gently upon her breast. I covered her with pine cones and needles. I kissed her and prayed over her. Then I let the gods, who so obviously loved her, keep her with them at that holy place.'

321

LVIII

There had been no crime.

Since Camillus Aelianus was associated with a juris-prudence expert, we would check that point, but I felt sure of the outcome. Minas of Karystos would confirm that in law Caesia's death was natural. We could not prosecute Zeus.

Of course, in life, what happened afterwards was reprehensible. In life, no one sane, no one humane would refuse a father proper knowledge of his child's fate. Prevent him giving her a funeral and monument. Condemn him to years of obsession and unending mental torture.

Even in Athens, the community which had founded democratic legal principles, there was a wide gap between law and life.

Helena and I returned to the city, deeply disturbed yet helpless.

We left Marcella Naevia to her hillside existence. If anybody wanted to pursue her for her actions, they would find her. She was going nowhere. Greece had claimed her. She would most likely live out her semi-reclusive existence without interference. Poor diet and lack of care would deny her a long life. Dreams and spiritual fantasies would sustain her for a few more years, until she wasted into a slow decline, perhaps tended by bemused locals.

People would believe she had money (maybe she did have; she must have been wealthy once). That would guarantee her some notice from the community.

We could not even tell if she realised her niece's corpse had now been removed from Olympia by her distraught father. Talking to the woman, it was hard to tell which of our words made contact and which she chose to blot out.

I never thought her mad. She was rational, in her own way. She had made herself different, out of perversity. For me, if Marcella Naevia was culpable, she should be blamed for that deliberate withdrawal from normal society. Good Romans respect the community. She had indulged herself, at the expense of destroying Caesius Secundus. He could be told the truth when Helena and I returned to Rome, but he would never fully recover from his long search. Once, he might have learned to live with the accident of nature that killed his daughter, but too much distress had intervened. He had lost his balance permanently. For him, peace of mind was now irretrievable.

Helena said, every family has a crazy aunt. But they do not all cause such anguish or inflict such damage.

LIX

Helena and I arrived back at our inn, appalled and subdued. We then dampened the atmosphere for our young companions, telling them what we had learned from Marcella Naevia, and what we thought of her behaviour. All of us retired early to bed.

The evening was sultry and had made us short-tempered. It seemed appropriate that we were woken some hours later when the weather broke. Flashes of light through my eyelids disturbed me first, closely followed by brief cracks of thunder. As the storm came nearer, Helena also awoke. She and I lay in bed together, listening to the rain's onset. The thunder passed over but steady rain continued. It matched our melancholy mood. I fell asleep again, lulled by the incessant wash of water on the shutters of our room.

Later I woke a second time, suddenly aware of my mistake. Shocked by Marcella Naevia's story, I had left a big question unasked. I should have pressed her for the name of the man who bothered women. I needed to make her identify him formally: Phineus, presumably. He may not have killed Caesia – yet the aunt blamed him, and her father would always regard Phineus as implicated. Even Phineus himself had fled back to Rome, as if nervous of the consequences of his bad behaviour. It made him now my prime suspect in the murder three years later of Valeria Ventidia. But to accuse him, I must have evidence that he was a menace and a danger to the women on his tours. I needed Marcella Naevia to make a statement naming him.

I would have to go back again to Mount Lykabettus. I would have to speak to the crazy lady again. Now even more depressed, I sank towards miserable slumber.

Helena grabbed my arm. She had heard something I had missed above the storm. Groaning, I forced myself back awake yet again. We listened. We became aware of voices in the inn courtyard, a storey below us. Men were shouting. One of the things they were shouting was my name.

I had been called out at night for many things – all bad. The old panic gripped immediately. If we had been in Rome, I would have thought at once that this commotion was caused by the vigiles – my crony Petronius Longus, the enquiry chief of the Fourth Cohort, summoning me once again to some grim scene of blood and mayhem in which he thought I had an interest. Here, who knew how the streets were policed? And why would anyone seek me to attend on trouble?

'Didius Falco – where are you?'

I grabbed a blanket and stumbled out on to the balcony which ran around the inn's dark courtyard. The night was pitch black and the rain currently pouring harder than ever. Only someone with an emergency would be out in this – or idiots. Angry shouts from other bedrooms told us most guests reckoned it was idiots calling out. I soon agreed.

Dim torches struggled to stay alight, showing us our visitors. They were too drunk to care about the weather. Hair plastered their foreheads. Tunics clung to their backs and legs, running with rivulets of rain. One or two still had wreaths of flowers, now dripping water into their reddened eyes. Some leaned against one another for balance, others teetered, solo. I spotted Young Glaucus, recognisable by his size, his sobriety, and the fact that he alone was trying to impose sense on the procession. Helena came up behind me; she had dragged on a long tunic and held another round her shoulders.

'What's happened? Is it Aulus?' Alarmed, she thought her brother must be in some desperate situation.

'Oh it's Aulus all right!'

Aulus looked up at me, with a hint of apology. Then bowed his head and slumped helplessly against Young

325

Glaucus. Glaucus held him up with one arm and with his free hand tapped his own forehead, signalling madness.

'You are Falco!' a man called out triumphantly, his Latin so heavily accented it was nearly Greek. Heedless of the weather and the late hour, heedless of good manners and good taste, he bawled to us at the top of his voice. It was a good voice. Baritone. Used to addressing the public. Used to silencing academic critics and opponents in turbulent lawcourts. It would be pointless to berate him. He would enjoy the challenge.

'Hail to you, Falco! I am Minas of Karystos! These are my friends –' He waved to a group of almost twenty men, all in advanced states of serious good cheer. I could see one fellow urinating at great length against a pillar; the sound of his monumental pissing was lost in the rain. Some were young, many older, old enough to know better. All had had a brilliant evening up until now. They were game for more.

'May we come in?' demanded their atrocious leader. He had the formal politeness of the very drunk, thank goodness. Whether we could fend him off remained debatable.

Quick thinking gave me a riposte. 'Sadly no – we have children with us, sleeping.'

Helena and I had squared up like the Few at Thermopylae, prepared to hold the field until death took us. We refused to yield to this colourful invading horde, although they seemed bound to overwhelm us. Under the balcony roof, rain was gusting in; we were soaked through. My feet were in standing water too.

Minas of Karystos made a curious figure. He was small, elderly, and keen, like a grandfather taking his grandsons to a stadium. He wore a long tunic in a gaudy hue, with a six-inch embroidered border in which precious metal glinted. Beneath a neatly placed wreath of flowers, grey hair hung in wet straggles.

'Minas of Karystos, I have heard much of your eminence and reputation. I am delighted to make your acquaintance –'

'Come down, Falco!'

'*You go and it's divorce!*' muttered Helena. Wimpishly, I chose to stay.

'*You get rid of him then!*'

'*How can I? Don't let them come up, Marcus.*'

'*If they do, here's the plan – we abandon the boys and dump the luggage. We'll just leave, make a run for it. Head for the harbour and take the first ship that's sailing . . .* Minas, it is very late and my wife needs to rest –'

'*That's right; blame the woman!*'

'She is pregnant –'

'*No chance of that on this trip!*'

'Falco, you are a hero; you make many babies!' *Oh gods!* I could see Aulus hiding his face in horror. I jabbed a finger at him, letting him know who would be blamed for this.

'You Romans are all too austere! Let go! Be free! You should learn to live, Falco!' Why are drunks so unpleasantly self-righteous? And foreign ones hideously worse? If we insulted a bunch of Greeks who were trying to get a good night's sleep, it would cause an international incident. The governor would send Aquillius Macer to ship us home, for endangering provincial stability. But Minas could be as rude as he liked and was unstoppable. 'Learn to enjoy yourself like a liberated Greek! Come down to us; we have wine; we have excellent wine here –'

Suddenly he gave up. Sensing that there would be no entertainment here, he was eager to move on to the next venue. 'Ah we shall show you pleasure tomorrow then, Falco! I have a plan; I have a thrilling plan – I have news!' he exclaimed, belatedly remembering the reason for this late-night call. 'Come down and hear –'

I shook my head. I gestured to the rain, and made as if to go indoors. For once it worked.

'I have found your people!' Minas roared, anxious to keep me. 'I have seen them. I have talked to them. We shall make the wrongdoer show himself. I have a plan; I will show you how, Falco. We shall bring them all together, you and I. Then they will interact and he will be revealed!'

'*Fabulous. Minas has invented putting all the suspects in a single room and waiting for the killer to confess . . . Tell him, Helena. That old ruse stopped working back before the Persians built their bridge across the Hellespont.'*

'*You're the hero. You tell him.*'

'I am going to throw a great big party for this group!' warbled Minas. 'We shall have wonderful food and wonderful wine – dancers, musicians, talk, and I will teach you to play *kottabos*! Everyone always wants to play *kottabos*. You will come, and bring my dear young friend Aelianus. Watch and see. I will find the truth for you!'

The rain continued falling, as the party-goers wandered off again into the night.

LX

I like a good party. Who doesn't?
  Believe me, I did not like this one.

I tried to pretend the event was not happening. The
following day, I went back to Mount Lykabettus, looking for
dreamy-eyed Philomela. She was not at her hut. I gazed out
across the plain to the ocean, and wished I was on board one
of the triremes and merchant ships that I could just make
out, moored on the distant blue water. I wanted to go home.

On my return to our inn, disgruntled, I found Helena
reading Plato's *Symposium* as research for the evening.
  'Lucky for some! Intriguing stuff?'
  'Pages of debate about the nature of love. Otherwise, little
has changed among the greybeards of Athens. Listen to this
passage, Marcus –'
  'I'm not in the mood for Plato, fruit.'
  'You will like it.'
  'Will I have any choice?'
  While I pulled off my dusty boots and cleaned them
grimly, she read to me: '*Suddenly there came a great knocking
at the door of the house, like revellers, and the sound of a flute-
girl. Agathon told the attendants to go and see who the intruders
were. "If they are friends of ours, invite them in, but if not, say
that the drinking is over." A little while afterwards they heard
the voice of Alcibiades resounding in the court; he was extremely
drunk and kept roaring and shouting, "Where is Agathon? Lead
me to Agathon," and at length, supported by the flute-girl and
some of his attendants, he found his way to them. "Hail,
friends," he said, appearing at the threshold, with a massive*

329

garland of ivy and violets, his head flowing with ribbons. "Will you have a very drunken man as a companion of your revels?" . . . I told you philosophy was fun.'

I laughed; as ever, Helena had mellowed me. 'I admit that's a horribly familiar portrait of a very drunk man. I think Minas of Karystos is a Platonist.'

Helena winced. 'And my brother is going to become his Alcibiades?'

'Don't worry,' I said kindly. 'Alcibiades may have been a lush, but he was a hugely charismatic character!'

'Drunks tend to think that of themselves,' Helena sighed.

The party was held at an inn, luckily not ours. Phineus and Polystratus had placed the Seven Sights group at a run-down establishment closer to Piraeus than Athens.

The travellers had changed little since we saw them at Corinth. Their current moans were that every time they wanted to visit the sights, they had to walk several miles there and back, or hire expensive transport. Phineus had taken them on one formal sightseeing trip into Athens, after which he left them on their own. On his trip the guide had been inaudible and only interested in taking them to his uncle's souvenir shop. Volcasius had stayed too long at the Temple of Athena Nike, was left behind unnoticed, and got lost. By the time he found his own way back to their inn, the others had left for a dinner, which he missed. Three days later he was still arguing with Phineus about that, because he had paid for his meal in advance. The others were arguing because promised dancers never showed and the drink ran out.

'Everything as usual!' Marinus told us, grinning.

In fact, we sensed differences. There was plenty of observation time, since Minas of Karystos did not turn up with his catering corps for two hours after the appointed start. Organising a party might be his forte, but he achieved it *very* slowly. I hoped that meant he was spending time on planning. But I feared he had gone to someone else's party and forgotten his pledge to us.

The group, or at least their current survivors, had assembled spot on time. We already knew they turned up promptly for any meals they did not have to pay for. If something is free, seasoned travellers form a queue.

The Sertorius family came first; we could see what was happening there all right. The tall husband looked grim; the once-dowdy wife was wearing a rather tasteful Greek head-dress, a pointed *stephane*. She gazed around her more openly instead of seeming haunted; the two adolescents kicked their heels more peevishly than ever, as if they had had their noses put out of joint. Amaranthus joined us next, alone and at a loose end. Marinus and Indus arrived together, tall and short, Marinus grey-haired and still limping from his dog bite, Indus hook-shouldered and saturnine, though he had had his lank hair trimmed recently. Indus greeted Sertoria Silene with an almost imperceptible nod; she responded at once, giving him a pleasant smile. Her husband glowered. His downtrodden wife was enjoying herself, and he clearly hated it.

'Oh wonderful!' murmured Helena, nudging me.

Cleonyma and Minucia bundled in through the street entrance, hot from a bath-house manicure and pedicure session, which had been carried out by some girl whose ineptitude was sending them both into hoots of laughter (until they remembered how much they had tipped her). They shrieked hello to everyone, then although they were already more brightly clad than any of us, rushed off to their rooms to get dressed up. The awkward curiosity, Volcasius, sloped in, still wearing his dreadful greasy straw hat and what appeared to be the same tunic we last saw him in. Then came the widow Helvia, neatly dressed in white with her impressive necklace (which we had seen before) and a new bangle; she angled this on her plump arm so that we would all notice it, giving a small smile to Marinus as if it were a gift from him that pleased her. So that little liaison must be going well.

Attendants finally arrived from Minas. They carried in couches, cushions, flowers, and garlands, with which they began to dress the courtyard. They took their time; no one planned to do in his back lifting furniture. The innkeeper sent out slaves with lamps, which they positioned very sluggishly and forgot to light. A flautist looked in, summed up the lack of preparation, and disappeared again.

Helena and I had found ourselves a centrally placed table, where we stationed Albia, my nephews, and my dog, all so far on their best behaviour. Young Glaucus had gone to fetch Aulus. We struggled to keep spaces for them. The attendants had no idea that a party was for people, and that people might want to be with their friends. They were designers. To them, placing equipment artistically took precedence over the happiness of mere guests. Gradually they created a theatrical setting – in which our presence seemed a messy inconvenience.

There was still no sign of any food or drink.

The travellers became tense about whether and when they would be fed. Helvia had gone fluttery and Sertorius Niger kept striding about in search of somebody to complain to. In his absence from their couch, his wife went over to talk to Indus. She remained there for the rest of the evening.

Cleonyma and Minucia returned. Wafts of hugely expensive perfume preceded their entrance. Drama was their natural element. In they tottered, in gold sandals with dangerously high cork soles. Both wore floaty purple dinner outfits, so transparent all the men were compelled to look three times. The ladies had piled their hair up in layered ramparts and cascades of ringlets, through which were threaded enormous gemstones. The jewels were real. Cleonyma told us that, mentioning just how much they had cost.

As soon as she joined the party, Cleonyma chivvied the landlord into bringing drinks all round. Even Sertorius Niger looked grateful. Since she was paying, she helped out the lackadaisical waiters, herself carrying brimful cups to our table, six at a time, and placing them deftly.

'Not a drop spilled. You've done that before, Cleonyma!'

'Gods, you could die waiting in some of these places.' She sat down with us. 'How do you like the dinner dress?'

'Erm . . . it's certainly an eye-catcher!'

'That stinker Volcasius told me it was too revealing. Spoilsport. You look lovely, Helena.' Cleonyma seemed unaware of the contrast between her own vibrant gauze costume, and Helena's elegant simplicity. Helena was wearing aqua silk, with discreet silver embroidery; she looked like a nymph, one who knew where the good groves were to be found. I would have followed her through any prickly thickets in the hope of a romp by moonlight.

I was in ochre, mildewed by frequent bad laundering. I had on the boots I cleaned earlier and a newish belt, the effect topped off by casual curls, a straight Roman nose and a bad Greek shave. I was clean; even my nephews were clean, though their party gear was basic. Albia was in blue, as usual, with a necklace Helena had loaned her. Nux had been combed and defleaed. She had tried to roll in muck straight afterwards, but Cornelius caught her in time. As a party we were presentable, though not modish.

Helena asked Cleonyma how she was bearing up. 'This is my last night in Greece. I've booked a passage home, leaving tomorrow; Minucia will come with me, to stop me brooding on the ship. Amaranthus has convinced himself she will come back and catch up with the group at Troy afterwards; between ourselves, there's no chance. I'm giving her an excuse to go home. It's what she wants.'

'Couldn't Amaranthus go with her, if they are a couple?' asked Helena.

'He could!' agreed Cleonyma. 'Not suggested – not by either of them. Let the man stay alone with his sport. It's all he asks of life. He's attending the Olympic Games next year. I see him dragging endlessly on for ever, from stadium to stadium.'

'Minucia has children?'

'They must be grown up now, but yes, she has children. She used to keep animals. She has a useless husband too – I think she even misses him. Funny what you can get used to!'

Still conscious that I had been Cleonyma's chosen male representative at her husband's funeral, I asked tentatively about arrangements for taking home his ashes. She was not at all offended that I had mentioned it, and burst out laughing. 'Oh that's dealt with, Falco! At first I put him in a valuable urn. Parian marble, with gold fittings – beautiful. But then I thought they'll get me to pay port duty on the dear lad's ashes. They can stuff that! It's twenty-five per cent for luxury goods. He used to get annoyed at that every time we went home and customs homed in on us; for some reason they always used to decide we were people worth stopping and searching . . . I wasn't prepared to transfer him to a nasty box to smuggle him in – though Juno knows, I've had enough practice. So I scattered him around a bit when we went to Marathon.'

'He would approve!' we assured her. I hid a grin as I imagined my brother-in-law Gaius Baebius, the tax official, spotting Cleonyma tottering up a quayside among her collection of souvenirs: a gift, who would fill up his duty targets for the next month in one swoop.

Cleonyma went quiet. 'I shed a little tear when I left him there. He would have enjoyed Marathon; he always liked places with a history.'

We were quiet too. Remembering Cleonymus' unforced generosity, we honoured him and raised our cups to his memory.

As she stood up to leave, Cleonyma leaned down to Helena and pointed to Sertoria Silene. 'She's leaving her husband, can you believe it? She's taking on Indus; well, he needs sorting out. She can be quite bossy, if she's given her head, and Indus seems to enjoy it. The best bit is, she's told Sertorius Niger he can keep those two dreadful children; there is no chance of her taking them!'

Helena smiled, in a way which I knew meant she was suddenly thinking about our children. 'Now, don't hold back, Cleonyma – tell us the truth, please do: *who* is Indus running away from?'

Cleonyma smiled. 'Oh surely it's obvious – he's fleeing from his mother!'

We roared with laughter.

'I'm going to get really drunk tonight,' confided Cleonyma. She was halfway there already.

Something must be due to happen soon. A solitary man with a bent taper started going around, lighting up the oil lamps. One table cheered him. He looked embarrassed.

Cleonyma went off to order more drinks; she asked for nibbles with them. The nibbles never came, though I had a feeling she paid for them.

The flautist returned. This time he was accompanied by a lame harpist and an extremely short drummer. They helped themselves to drinks, then stood around. An unhealthy-looking girl in a short tunic brought cut roses to every table, encouraging us to wind them into some wreaths of leaves which had already appeared unnoticed. Gaius and Cornelius both took to her; they set about avid flower arrangement. Close up, she was ten years too old even for Gaius, and probably married to a slobbish matelot who beat her.

At long last, caterers arrived. As they took over a corner of the yard, we gathered we had a long wait ahead of us. Raw ingredients were being carried in. Shellfish and mullet were still alive, and I swear I heard a chicken cluck. Simply lighting the fire for their cooking-bench took ages.

'There is Aelianus!' exclaimed Albia, spotting him first.

In the entrance to the courtyard we saw Aulus, shepherded discreetly by Young Glaucus. They were greeted enthusiastically on all sides. Smart in a tunic with purple stripes of rank, Aulus made a slow progress past the other tables, shaking hands with everyone. 'Your brother looks like a candidate courting election votes!'

'He's playing Alcibiades.'

'No; he's sober – so far!'

It was weeks since Camillus Aelianus had seen the travellers at Corinth, when the quaestor first arrested them and he bunked off. He was clearly well regarded and had to repeat for every group details of what he had been doing since. Someone gave him a wreath, though I noticed he resisted being crowned. He was trying to extract himself as speedily as possible.

When he reached us and dropped the wreath on our table, we found out why. He handed a scroll to Helena, a letter from their mother, then while she was distracted, he murmured, 'Marcus, you need to come with me. By the look of things here, there is time for a quick detour, and you have had a summons.'

Glaucus had apprehended a messenger at the inn where we were staying. He copied Aulus' low voice: 'Marcus Didius, that woman Philomela sent to tell you she has further information. Can you meet her tonight at the House of Kyrrhestian, by the Roman marketplace?'

'I've brought transport,' mouthed Aulus.

'I'm not deaf, you know,' said his sister.

As I stood up, apologising to Helena and the others, I realised that all of the Seven Sights group were here tonight – with the exception of Phineus and Polystratus.

LXI

I felt stricken with apprehension. Other messages in the past, received too late, had sent me chasing to find women, either too young or too naïve, who were waiting alone in places of danger. Sometimes I had failed to reach them in time.

Aulus had brought a fast trap. As a senator's son he had no notion of economising with donkey-carts. This was a light, high-wheeled affair that could have doubled for Athena's war chariot. All we needed was an owl on the footboard.

Aulus drove. It was a privilege of his rank to seize the reins and cause havoc. He scattered the other traffic as if he was in a race in the circus. I used the journey to bring him up to date. When I said what Helena and I had learned from Marcella Naevia yesterday, he snorted, astounded by her attitude. In the dim light of a torch I saw him biting his lip, wondering what nonsense she was about to impose on us now.

The Roman agora lay due north of the Acropolis, slightly to the east of the original Greek one. Ours had been instituted by Caesar and Augustus and, as Helena had said of the Roman infiltrations on the Acropolis, 'You have to pretend the new Roman buildings are a sign of Roman esteem for Athens.' She was a mistress of irony.

She and I had omitted the new agora from our self-devised itinerary, but Aulus found it easily. He parked beside an ostentatious public lavatory, which we both used – marvelling wryly that Roman esteem for Greece was expressed so well by this sixty-eight-seater shit-house with full running water. Now we were ready for anything.

The House of Kyrrhestian stood just outside the agora. It was an antique octagonal building, an exquisite marble creation, decorated with representations of the winds. This weather station and timepiece had been built by a famous Macedonian astronomer. A water-driven clock occupied the interior, showing the hours on a dial; there were sundials on each outer face; a rotating disk showed the movement of the stars and the course of the sun through the constellations; on top, a bronze Triton wielded a rod to act as a weathervane. You could not ask for more – unless it were for the automata, bells, and singing birds on a clock I had heard of from Marinus, which he said he had seen in Alexandria.

Aulus and I had a lot of time to view this scientific wonder. Philomela was late.

'You can tell she's a Roman woman.'

'If she was Greek, she wouldn't be allowed out of the house.'

'Maybe the Greeks have got something!'

'I'll tell Helena you said so.'

'Not even you would do that, Falco.'

Eventually the woman turned up, looking surprised that we seemed impatient. I saw Aulus surveying her sceptically; it was the first time he had met her. Always uneasy with female witnesses, Philomela – or Marcella Naevia – with her scarves and scatty expression, made him swallow nervously.

She plunged straight in. She was keyed up and agitated. 'Falco, I have to tell you about the man.'

'Yes, you need to name him formally –'

'Well, you know who I mean!' She grabbed me by the tunic sleeve. 'It is very important that you listen to me. This man may have caused that terrible murder.'

'Valeria Ventidia?'

'Of course. I should have realised before. I was at Olympia –'

'I thought you didn't go because you disliked the place? That was what you told me.' I was determined to test everything she said. To me, Marcella Naevia was an unreliable witness, too ethereal to be trusted. If she knew, she would say I was prejudiced.

Did I doubt her simply because her standards were not mine? Yes. Well, was I wrong?

'I had a reason.'

'I need to know it.'

'You just have to believe me.'

'No. It is time to stop messing. Marcella Naevia, I want to know precisely: why did you go to Olympia this summer? For all I know, *you* are the killer.'

'That's a mad thing to say!' I heard Aulus cough with laughter at her angry retort. 'I went,' Marcella Naevia informed us stiffly, 'because I always watch what happens when they bring people to Greece.'

'You hang around the Seven Sights Travel groups?'

'Somebody has to observe what goes on. There may be something I can do to help someone.'

I understood why we kept finding her everywhere we went. 'Were you at Delphi when I travelled there? Were you at Lebadeia?'

Now Marcella Naevia frowned and looked confused. 'Should I have been?'

'Statianus, Valeria's husband, was there. He had a misadventure.'

'I only look after the women,' she said. 'Only the women are at risk, you see.'

'Not true any longer,' I informed her curtly.

'I don't know about this.' She looked troubled. 'I have heard things about other tours . . . people die too often. Nobody seems to know or to do anything about it.'

With growing impatience, Aulus interrupted. '*We* are doing something about it. You are holding us up here, Marcella Naevia. Tell us why you asked us to come tonight.'

'Well, Falco –' She ignored Aulus. Middle-aged women generally did. 'I do not know if you realise this: they were *both* there.'

'Both? You mean Phineus and Polystratus?'

'At Olympia.'

'Which time?'

'Both times!'

Now that was new.

Marcella Naevia kept maundering; her manner was officious, though her subject matter was still muddled. 'The problem is, I was never certain *which* man was such a bother to my niece. Caesia just muttered how much she hated "that man". I always assumed she meant Phineus. It could have been either, I see that now.'

I had hoped Marcella Naevia would clarify the issue. A typical witness, she was making it worse. While I tried to think, she burbled on: 'Phineus was in charge. He was the most in evidence, whenever we moved on. He fixed up events, dinners, shopping excursions. Of course, whoever it was, it made no difference. Caesia and I went up the Hill of Cronus on our own account. He drove us to it, but you cannot bring him to justice for that.'

'Let's get it clear.' I addressed her firmly. 'Both men accompanied your tour? Nobody has told me that before. In fact, Caesia's father gave me a list of travellers which did *not* name Polystratus.'

'He came out after we started. It was supposed to be just for the Olympic Games. That was an excuse, we all thought, so he could watch the sports events at our expense.'

'Oh wonderful! Now – when Phineus fled back to Rome after your niece died, what did Polystratus do?'

'He had already left.'

I glanced at Aulus. That could mean it was Polystratus who had the guilty conscience. Maybe Phineus went after him, thinking that Polystratus really had killed Marcella Caesia. Maybe Phineus had a reason to think Polystratus attacked women. Maybe he knew Polystratus had done it on previous trips.

'And what about this year? You saw both men with the group again?'

'I suppose nobody told you that either?' demanded Caesia's aunt.

340

'When I first met the group at Olympus,' Aulus interrupted, 'only Phineus was there.'

'Polystratus was in Rome by then,' I said. 'I saw him there myself. Unless he got back to Italy on winged horses –'

Aulus shook his head. 'If he really shifted, there was time.'

'True. He could have been on the same boat as your letter! If he *had* brutally killed Valeria, he *would* really shift.'

Marcella Naevia looked relieved. 'Well, you must be glad I told you this.'

In my terms, she had told us nothing.

'Valeria died very brutally. Polystratus does not look strong enough to have carried out that killing,' I mused fretfully. Then Marcella Naevia at last told me something useful:

'Of course he is strong, Falco. He is a past pankration fighter, surely you know that? They both are!'

There had been no reason for this meeting to be held at the weather station. It was pure drama; Marcella Naevia was staying nearby at a respectable house with a woman who had befriended her. We escorted her back there safely. Although we probed, it was evident she knew nothing else material.

Still, we knew now that both Phineus and Polystratus had been present when Caesia took against being manhandled and when Valeria was killed. Both had athletics connections. Their missing teeth confirmed the violence in their past. Both would be at home in the palaestra. Both would be familiar with jumping weights.

We were about to see proof of their sporting careers. When we drove back to the party inn, the Sertorius children were larking about outside the main gate, with Gaius and Cornelius. The three boys had a ball, which they were kicking at the legs of anyone who came and went, pretending it was accidental. I was not in the mood for a discipline session. I helped Aulus deliver the cart to an ostler, hoping the trouble would have ended by the time we ran into the playfellows.

The boys saw us coming. Sertorius junior, Tiberius, gave

the ball a great kick into the courtyard. They all ran inside.
Tiberia was slower. As she turned to enter the building, two
men arrived for the party. They were kitted out in very
smart tunics, with luxurious braid at hem and neck; you
could describe either as expensively dressed. One was
Phineus, who held back, dealing with their donkey-cart.
Polystratus, the other, had noticed the girl.

Tiberia was aware of him too. She jumped like a hare. She
scuttled for the courtyard entrance. Polystratus swept a low
bow as she passed him. Tiberia pressed herself against the
far wall of the gatehouse, then ran faster as if she knew just
what was coming. Polystratus straightened up abruptly, and
patted her behind, grinning.

Tiberia stopped in her tracks and turned right around.
'Don't do that again, ever!' With set shoulders, she stalked
off, no longer running.

Phineus had seen what happened. He said something that
we could not hear. Polystratus must have retorted with an
obscenity. Next moment, Phineus was yelling at him.
Polystratus shrugged and turned away. Phineus flew at him
and jumped him.

'Whey-hey!' Aulus and I set off towards the fight.

Marcella Naevia was right, we saw that now: they were both
pankration contestants. It was ugly. Once they set to, any
move was permissible. You cannot bite in pankration, but
neither possessed front teeth and sucking is not disallowed.
Otherwise, they wrestled, punched, stamped, kicked,
squeezed, heaved each other upside down, threw each other,
elbowed, kneed, and chopped. Phineus had both weight and
bulk; Polystratus must have been one of the lighter, speedier
fighters. Despite his paunch, he danced and shifted his feet
nimbly, angling for a quick jerk off balance. Each took the
punishment as if he felt no pain.

Whatever was going on, the partners had now seriously
fallen out.

*

A crowd gathered quickly. Chefs, flowergirls, musicians, travellers all emerged from the inn, pushing and shoving for a viewpoint. Young Glaucus had found himself a long wand from somewhere; he tried to intervene like a judge. It was useless. Helena wriggled through the press to my side.

'When someone said there was a fight, I assumed it was you!'

'Such faith.'

We let them have their head for a time, hoping that would tire them. Eventually Aulus, Glaucus, and I moved in. 'Come on now. Break it up, you two!'

We jumped back. It was too dangerous.

Then, suddenly, the antagonists became aware of the spectators. Phineus broke first. He growled, a short irritated noise like an obstreperous lion. Polystratus was thoroughly worked up, but took the point reluctantly. Still tense, they stopped fighting. They made a few feints, all pretence but with an undercurrent. Then they shook hands, smiled at the crowd slyly and toothlessly, and strode off into the inn with their arms around each other's shoulders.

'Old sparring partners!' Phineus called back at us.

Polystratus gripped him, rather too hard, it seemed to me. 'Still testing each other, after all the years!'

'I don't think so,' murmured Young Glaucus to me. 'I don't think that was a bout for best of three throws, Falco. I have never seen such dirty tricks.'

'No. They both meant to kill if they could.'

Then as we all prepared to enter the inn for the party, Glaucus exclaimed with a little too much excitement: 'Let the Games begin!'

LXII

During our absence, the scene in the courtyard had changed for the better.

As the company flowed back indoors, we could see everyone was several drinks further along. The atmosphere had warmed up. Wreaths and garlands had been applied to curls and bald heads, then had listed, or slipped well down over one eye. Skirts had gaped open and the gaps had stayed unnoticed. Tight shoes had been tossed off.

A welcome blast of cooking smells greeted us. Spices sizzled in hot oil; steaming pots of broth wafted hints of delights to come. Overseeing the kitchen was Minas, who boomed encouragement to all. Red-faced from the cooking fires, he winked at me as I passed him, and whispered, 'I have guards standing ready. Once the villain is identified, he goes straight to the Areopagus.' For an instant I glimpsed the true lawyer in him. 'It is a long while since I conducted a murder trial.' He was planning to enjoy it.

A whirl of guests swept between us. Next moment Minas was extolling the wine he had brought. From the numbers of amphorae now lined up against a wall, it seemed drink was available to us in naval quantities.

Helena grabbed her brother by the hand and pulled him temporarily from the mêlée. 'Now you take care, for once. Here is what I found for you in Plato's *Symposium: It was agreed that drinking was not to be the order of the day, but that they were all to drink only so much as they pleased!*'

Aulus eyed her askance. 'Is my sister tipsy?'

'Hardly got going yet,' I said, shaking my head sadly.

My mind was on other things. Slipping away from them, I followed Phineus. He had been accosted by Cleonyma. I

344

missed the start of their exchange, but overheard her saying, 'So *he* will keep doing what he does, and *you* will keep on after him!'

'Your husband was a sad loss,' Phineus told her, in a patronising tone. He had noticed me and was desperate to shut her up.

'Oh he was!' hissed Cleonyma. 'He was a fine man, who should not have died before his time.' Her voice acquired real venom: 'You stink, Phineus!'

She turned away, disgusted. Then Phineus fixed his main attention on Polystratus nearby, who had been watching. Phineus walked right up to him and once more muttered angrily. He seemed to be warning Polystratus about me. This time they were acting up, to look good. Phineus pointedly slapped his partner on both cheeks. It looked playful. It sounded painful. Phineus then let go, and jokingly straightened the ornamented neck of his partner's party tunic. It was the long dark red garment Polystratus had worn when he came to our house on the Aventine, the one that looked as if a theatrical king should wear it. Close to, there were worn threads, but from a distance it would impress strangers.

Polystratus laughed and walked off. I moved in and stopped Phineus, grabbing him by the upper arm. He had more muscles than I would have expected, had I not known about the pankration. I kept my voice low. 'Let me tell you what this looks like, Phineus.'

'Don't bother, Falco.'

'Cleonymus and Cleonyma suspected the truth, didn't they?' I remembered my conversation with Cleonymus on our walk up to Acrocorinth. 'He gave me a strong hint, if only I had recognised it earlier: he told me he wished that Cleonyma had bashed Polystratus. Other people have spoken out too. The picture builds slowly – but it begins to appear. I think your old crony has been threatening your business by unacceptable behaviour. I think you waste a lot of effort trying to deter him, Phineus. In short, I think Polystratus is a killer – and you know it!'

'You're seeing things that don't exist, Falco. Go to an eye doctor.'

'Your partner killed Valeria. He is the so-called expensively dressed man who killed Cleonymus. You sent him to Delphi, then you had second thoughts. You feared he might harm Statianus, so you escaped from custody and ran off after him. Perhaps you went to Delphi, but you arrived too late. By then they were in Lebadeia, Phineus – where Polystratus committed yet another murder.'

'Such a good story,' Phineus crooned offensively. 'But not a hint of proof, is there?'

'I won't give up.'

'You don't even have a corpse, Falco.'

'The gods only know what Polystratus did with Statianus. But if we ever find any trace of that poor man – anything at all – your days of covering up will be over.'

I did not wait for Phineus to turn away from me; I left him. His contemptuous laugh behind me seemed to have a hollow ring. I hoped so.

My companions were gesturing me back to our table. We squashed up together on two couches. At a more refined dinner, each of these would serve for a solo male guest, but this party broke the rules in many ways. We had women and girls among us, for one thing. Minas kept making a point of this, carolling that he had invited all, as a gesture to Roman custom. His own womenfolk were trapped at home, presumably. Minas made a ghastly joke about our women possessing all the social skills of natural hetaerae; he gushingly praised them as dancers, singers, and conversationalists. To us it was embarrassing and, being frank Roman women, they derided him fairly openly.

Low tables had been set before the couches. Now waiters laid these with tempting starters. They brought baskets of bread to us, both brown barley rolls with a nutty taste, and soft white wheat loaves, luxurious but blander. The first course dishes of dainties followed in procession: savoury prawns, tiny roast birds, snails, crispy battered squid, mixed

346

olive relish to eat on the bread with its oil dripping down our chins, almonds and walnuts, sweetbreads, herbed cabbage in honey vinegar. Unidentifiable things in hot pastry sat on the dish longest, but as the service was leisurely, even they went in time.

More wine flowed. It had improved in quality and quantity. Minas had treated us to a Nemean red, rich without being too heavy, clove-scented and appealing. We approached it suspiciously, but were quickly won over. The waiters were counting out eight measures of water to one, swirling them in a huge mixing bowl. At first the result seemed curious, soon it seemed just fine.

Travelling entertainers poked their heads in at the gatehouse. As they scampered in and began acrobatics, our existing musicians were fired up to jealousy. Soon every table was assailed by one or another set of persistent pluckers, tootlers, or bellydancers. We paid the newcomers to go away, then we had to pay the official players to stop sulking. They lined up cheerfully and threw themselves into what they thought Romans liked best: an endless selection of the bland numbers Nero composed for his 'winning' performances on his Greek Grand Tour. This would only happen in the provinces; no one in Rome ever plays Nero's tunes any more. Out here the ghastly ditties seemed firm favourites. Meandering measures bored on interminably; the musicians smiled like fanatics and kept going, even when we had all obviously stopped listening.

The tuneless imperial riffs formed a surreal backdrop, mingled with smoke from the now large bonfire on which cooks were about to roast a mighty shark. This had been donated by Phineus, a present to his clients at their farewell banquet in Greece. Hanging lamps and the firelight provided a warm glow. Polystratus, too, had contributed a main course dish. His donation came in a huge bronze cauldron, within which dark gravy gurgled round a salt pork stew. Alongside this, whole kids were on spits. Characteristic scents of Mediterranean herbs hit us: oregano, rosemary, sage, and celery seed.

347

While we waited for the next course to be brought, Helena leaned towards me. She indicated the letter Aulus had brought when he arrived. 'Mother!'

I feigned delight. 'What does dear Julia Justa have to say?' Helena was silent. Fear struck me. 'The children?'

Helena patted my hand. 'No, no. They are tearing the house apart and don't miss us.'

'Never?'

'Not much.'

'Well, I miss them.' Aulus wriggled closer, taking note of our conversation. He and his sister exchanged a glance. Aulus must know what the letter contained. I thought the worst. 'There is something you aren't telling me!'

Helena scowled. She seemed annoyed with me about something. 'This is just a letter about Forum news, of course. For instance, Marcus, Mother says the esteemed Rutilius Gallicus is returning to Rome after his stint as governor of Germany – ' I was acquainted with Gallicus – consul, law-giver, and fellow mediocre poet – and I certainly knew Germany. 'Everyone keeps secrets, don't they?' Helena's tone implied ominous significance. 'Tell me, Marcus darling – what exactly happened in the forest that time, when you and my brother Quintus crossed over the river into Germania Libera? When you shared an adventure that to this day, neither of you ever talks about?'

I had told her most of it. Not enough, perhaps. What happened was extremely dangerous. It had included a rebel prophetess called Veleda, whose effect on the then-young Camillus Justinus explained why neither of us had ever broken our silence back at home.

Helena reached out and poured herself more wine. She knew more about our escapade in Germany than she had ever acknowledged. 'Rutilius Gallicus has captured Veleda. He is bringing her in triumph to Rome.'

With a pang, I realised what that would mean to Justinus. He had never forgotten Veleda. First love had struck him hard. The prophetess had been foreign, exotic, powerful, and beautiful. The best thing about her was that none of us had ever expected to see her again . . .

I nodded to her brother. 'Aulus, let me guess: your mother is changing her instructions. She wants us to go home.'

LXIII

I had a feeling of failure which was hard to dispel. I set aside my wine; it was not helping. Minas was wrong about this evening achieving solutions. Any minute now we would be given the main course dishes. Then the serving tables would be cleared for fruit and cheeses. After that, everything would be over. There would be no drama. There would be no court case, come to that. The evening would drag on pointlessly until we were all half asleep, then I would assemble my own small group to ride back into Athens. Helena and I, perhaps with Aulus, would arrange to sail west as soon as possible. The Seven Sights party would travel east tomorrow, crimes unsolved, murderer at large, justice denied for ever.

I had come so close. Knowing the truth was not enough. I had to prove it. For once, vital evidence had never surfaced. For once, I could take the case no further.

Polystratus and Phineus were cooking their gifts themselves; Seven Sights always liked to save money. Phineus had his long sleeves rolled up, and was slicing the shark into belly steaks, using a great knife in a way that I found worrying. He doused the steaks in olive oil and herbs, then panfried them individually, as and when people wanted a cut. Restless as ever, Volcasius, the loner, had wandered up with his notebook and was studiously writing down the recipe. Then he badgered Polystratus for details of the salt pork stew, forcing him to list every roasted herb: 'Aniseed, cumin, fennel, thyme, coriander . . . The liquor is white wine, grape juice, and white wine vinegar. Honey is optional. Bread to thicken everything . . .' Volcasius peered into the cauldron curiously; Polystratus pushed him away.

At this stage, the waiters were serving barbecued kid and a couple of bream stuffed with soft cheese. In a province full of dozy waiters, these were the slowest ever. Half the time they just chatted to the musicians.

Indus came up. 'Well, we're all off tomorrow, Falco. Just wanted to thank you for your efforts. You're back to Rome, I hear?' Word flies around.

'Some of you are finding happy endings,' Helena told him, smiling as she thought about him running away from his mother.

As it was their farewell evening in Athens, he felt the need for pompous summing up. 'There have been a few tragedies, but most of us will feel ourselves the richer for our experiences.'

Sertorius Niger, passing, humphed. 'Waste of time and money!'

I had noticed that my nephews had sneaked off; I excused myself. Gaius and Cornelius were crouched under a serving table, heads together with young Tiberius. He saw me coming; ever the coward, once again he made himself scarce. Cornelius nudged Gaius. 'Show him, then!'

'Show me what?'

'I've got something for you,' Gaius announced. 'I had to trade with Tiberius. It took my hoplite helmet –'

'However did you get a hoplite helmet?' We had seen them on souvenir stalls, but they were bronze and cost a purseful.

Gaius winked. Always unhealthy, he had a sty. His mother would say I mistreated him. Well, she could have him back now and neglect him herself.

He stood up and surreptitiously slipped folded material into my hand; it looked disturbingly like one of his grubby loincloths. I felt something heavy and metallic. Cautiously, I investigated the bundle. The boys watched, hoping for praise.

Wrapped in the cloth was a jump weight, in the form of a wild boar. Made of bronze, with a worn old handgrip and a narrow top crest. 'Without the pair it has less value, I told Tiberius,' Gaius bantered professionally.

'You sound just like your grandfather.' Pa must have taught him. Sensing a revelation, my voice was faint. 'You know what we are looking at?'

'Yes, we saw the one Glaucus got for you at Olympia.'

'Gaius, I've had this weight ever since then. Have you been poking through my luggage?'

'Oh no, Uncle Marcus! Tiberius had this one. The killer must have kept it as a trophy, like you said.'

'This is the second one?'

'Tiberius doesn't realise what he'd got.'

'There was no need to do a swap. If you told me he had it, I could have dealt with Tiberius . . .' No member of the Didius family could miss bargaining, however. 'So, Gaius, where did Tiberius get it?'

'Oh it comes with complete provenance, Uncle Marcus,' Gaius assured me, still sounding as brazen as Pa. I raised an eyebrow. Gaius was a ghastly tyke, but good-natured under the weeping tattoos. 'I only parted with the helmet on condition he told me where he got this. Tiberius pinches things from the other travellers.' He would. 'He took it from some luggage that belongs to the odd man, Volcasius.'

I refolded the napkin. I thanked the boys and sent them to Helena.

Volcasius was now talking to Minas. Well, that was convenient. I walked around the courtyard to reach them. Other guests shouted greetings, as I went by. I smiled faintly. On my way I passed Polystratus, with his cauldron on his hip and a ladle. He was moving from table to table, sharing out his salt pork stew. Everyone was tucking into the roast kid and shark steaks, so he failed to arouse much interest. He filled their foodbowls anyway.

I took my time, moving surreptitiously. I glanced over to our table, meaning to signal to Helena, who had just been served by Polystratus. After several bad bouts of stomach upset, she avoided hotpots nowadays. I noticed that she quietly bent down and placed the bowl on the floor for Nux.

Minas had seen me coming, and had read my expression.

352

I turned my back to the crowd and unfolded the napkin, showing Volcasius the jump weight. He gave an exaggerated start. 'How did you get that, Falco?'

'No – how did *you* get it, Volcasius?'

'It's the weapon that was used to kill Valeria.'

'I know.'

'I didn't kill her.' I knew that too. 'I was just doing your job for you,' Volcasius sneered.

He still believed he was better at my job than me. I remained calm. He was a witness. Minas needed him. Besides, although I would have got around to it, eventually, Volcasius had carried out the necessary search and I gave him credit. 'Where was this, Volcasius?'

'In his luggage pack.'

'Whose luggage pack?' Minas asked magisterially. 'Name him!'

'Polystratus.'

I turned back to the crowd. I thought Helena might be watching me, aware from the boys that I was on to something. Her attention was on something else. I saw a horrified expression seize her. Her stole slipped off, as she raised her arm and pointed, looking alarmed. She was calling to Nux.

I was too far away but I started to run. I was shouting in panic for Aulus and Glaucus. Then I was yelling at the dog.

Nux had her nose down in Helena's foodbowl. The dog was carefully cleaning up a piece of bone against the side of the bowl. The bone was of crunchable size, but she lifted it out delicately and placed it on the ground for special treatment. As I reached her, a final fast lick revealed a gleam of metal. It was a man's ring. I had seen a smaller one just like it: *a decent piece, gold, probably bought in Greece, since it had a squared-off Greek meander pattern* . . . We had found Statianus.

I had a momentary flashback to the globular amphorae Polystratus unloaded at Corinth. My gorge rose as I remembered tasting tuna. I could hardly bear to think about what must have been hidden in the other containers. I dared not imagine the butchery involved in filling them.

I bent to retrieve the finger-bone and the ring. Nux straightened her short legs in guard mode. A low grumble emerged from the back of her throat in defence of her bone. At the same time, because I was her master, her short tail wagged madly.

Aghast, Helena slid from her dining couch. She banged a goblet hard on the table. Those closest had noticed; they stopped talking.

'Everyone!' Helena called out. 'Please stop eating.' The party noise subsided. People were already raising goblets. They thought it was a toast.

Polystratus abandoned his cauldron and moved towards Helena. Glaucus and Aulus went for him. Glaucus kicked out. I saw a couple of jabs and a lightning move, then Polystratus was lying on the ground, with Young Glaucus astride him, one arm pressed to his throat. His father must have taught him that; I must ask him to show me.

Nux noticed Polystratus too. The growl changed from mere warning to frantic barks. Gaius rushed to restrain her before she attacked.

Helena spoke again. For the rest of my life I would remember her there, standing tall and erect in her silvery blue gown, clear-voiced and desperate. Nobody who heard her would forget it lightly.

'Please, everybody, place your foodbowls back on the serving tables. We will collect them up. If you want to avoid nightmares, I beg of you all – *Do not eat the stew!*'

THE END

Two for the Lions

Lindsey Davis

Lumbered with working alongside reptilian Chief Spy Anacrites, Marcus Didius Falco has the perfect plan to make money – he will assist Vespasian in the Emperor's 'Great Census' of AD73. His potential fee could finally allow him to join the middle ranks and be worthy of long-suffering Helena Justina.

Unexpectedly confronted with the murder of a man-eating lion, Falco is distracted from his original task, uncovering a bitter rivalry between the gladiators' trainers. With one star gladiator dead, Falco is forced to investigate and the trail leads from Rome to the blood-soaked sand of the arena in North Africa.

'Surely the best historical detective in the business'
Mike Ripley, *Daily Telegraph*

'For more laughter visit Ancient Rome in Lindsey Davis'
tenth novel'
Mail on Sunday

'If only all bestsellers were this satisfying'
Time Out

arrow books

Three Hands in the Fountain

Lindsey Davis

Marcus Didius Falco and his laddish friend Petronius find their local fountain has been blocked – by a gruesomely severed human hand.

Soon other body parts are being found in the aqueducts and sewers. Public panic overcomes official indifference, and the Aventine partners are commissioned to investigate. Women are being abducted during festivals, with the next Games only days away. As the heat rises in the Circus Maximum, they face a race against time and a strong test of their friendship. They know the sadistic killer lurks somewhere on the festive streets of Rome – preparing to strike again.

'Uniquely entertaining''
Time Out

'Bizarre, funny and satisfying'
Irish Times

'As always, Davis wears her research lightly, bringing Ancient Rome to avid life in a series of delicious vignettes'
Val McDermid, *Manchester Evening News*

arrow books